THE MEN OF AMISH FICTION

PRESENT

ENDORSEMENTS

The Men of Amish Fiction write completely differently than women do, and I appreciate their style. Their characters have depth. They struggle with life, as we do. The men write with emotion and aren't afraid to handle some tough subjects. And you may even chuckle while reading.
—**Vicki Sluiter**

The Men of Amish Fiction have done a fine job with this smorgasbord of Amish tales. Their attitudes [characters in "The Silo"] provide a great example to follow, and we can learn wholesome lessons from the rest of the tales too. This book contains diverse stories to entertain and provoke contemplation.
—**Mary Ann Hake**

THE MEN OF AMISH FICTION

PRESENT

A CHRISTMAS COLLECTION

Willard Carpenter † Patrick E. Craig † Jerry Eicher † Thomas Nye † Murray Pura † Amos Wyse

Thomas Nye

PUBLISHING THE POSITIVE
ELK LAKE PUBLISHING INC
Plymouth, Massachusetts

Cover and Interior Design: Derinda Babcock

Editor: Deb Haggerty

PUBLISHED BY: Elk Lake Publishing, Inc., 35 Dogwood Drive, Plymouth, MA 02360, 2020

Library Cataloging Data

Names: Carpenter, Willard (Willard Carpenter), Craig, Patrick E. (Patrick E. Craig), Eicher, Jerry (Jerry Eicher), Nye, Thomas (Thomas Nye), Pura, Murray (Murray Pura), and Wyse, Amos (Amos Wyse)

The Men of Amish Fiction Present a Christmas Collection / Willard Carpenter, Patrick E. Smith, Jerry Eicher, Thomas Nye, Murray Pura, and Amos Wyse

p. 23cm × 15cm (9in × 6 in.)

Identifiers: ISBN-13: 978-1-64949-098-8 (paperback) | 978-1-64949-099-5 (trade paperback) | 978-1-64949-100-8 (e-book)

Key Words: Amish, Mennonite, alternate life style, short stories, anthology, family, relationships, values & virtues

LCCN: 2020xxxxxx Fiction

DEDICATION

A Christmas Collection is dedicated to the Ladies of Amish Fiction. We want to thank you all for breaking the trail in a genre that has led the way in Christian publishing for over twenty-five years. We wouldn't be here without you. May this Christmas continue to find you all blessed and super-productive in your writing endeavors.

The Men of Amish Fiction
Willard Carpenter
Patrick E. Craig
Jerry Eicher
Thomas Nye
Murray Pura
Amos Wyse

TABLE OF CONTENTS

FOREWORD VII

BITTERSWEET CHOCOLATE—AMOS WYSE 1

A CHRISTMAS DAY WITH MARY—JERRY EICHER 77

A CHRISTMAS ROSE—WILLARD CARPENTER 117

HOLIDAY HARNESS SHOP—THOMAS NYE 187

THE LIGHT AT ST. SILVAN'S—MURRAY PURA 273

A LIGHT IN THE WINDOW—PATRICK E. CRAIG 339

FOREWORD

The Men of Amish Fiction are grateful they can bring this collection to you after the success of *The Amish Menorah*. The year behind has not been easy for any of us. But Christmas still celebrates the birth of a Redeemer, and a Redeemer brings redemption and restoration. A Redeemer brings forgiveness and mercy. A Redeemer brings salvation. Jesus Christ is that Redeemer. Christmas is about the life He brings to the world, regardless of what that world is going through.

May you have a Happy Christmas and a Blessed New Year!
—The Men of Amish Fiction

BITTERSWEET CHOCOLATE

Amos Wyse

CHAPTER 1

"Dad, why do we celebrate Christmas different from the English?" fifteen-year-old Jacob asked.

"Jacob, we do many things different from them, what has you asking?"

"But they have Santa Claus and elves and ..."

"And more presents than you?"

"Well ..."

"Christ himself got but three gifts, do you deserve more?" Jacob sighed. "No, Dad."

"Good, now help me with this last batch of fudge, and then we can clean up and go home," Nathan Wyse said to his youngest son.

"Do you need a sampler for this batch?"

"You know we need to sample every batch. Are you volunteering again?" Nathan barely held back his laughter as his son repeated the actions of childhood with his own dad probably making up the job of taster for him.

Nathan checked on the thermometer as he stirred. "There we go, two-hundred-thirty-six degrees, perfect." The fudge was poured out into small pans to cool and be cut up for sale. The two made fast work of washing the pots and sanitizing the working surfaces.

"I suppose the fudge is cool enough for sampling now. Which one did you want to try?"

"Chocolate with walnuts, please."

"How did I know that?"

"I sometimes like the plain chocolate too."

"Well, you were extra helpful today—you can have a piece of both. Tomorrow, we will make chocolate caramels. We are almost out and that would not do this close to Christmas." There were but a few weeks left before Christmas, and Wyse Chocolates was a must for many of the local Amish and English. They would make three or four more batches of nearly everything they sold before New Year's and take a short break before Valentine's Day.

Tomorrow never came for Nathan Wyse. On the buggy ride home, they were hit by a driver with too much eggnog and too little attention to the road around him. Jacob was thrown clear and only suffered with a broken leg and bruised ribs.

CHAPTER 2

Jacob awoke from his recurring dream. Four years ago, and it still haunted him, the last time he and his father made candy together. At the tender age of nineteen, Jacob was now *the* Wyse at Wyse Chocolates. He looked over at his wind-up clock—four a.m. Close enough to time for him to get up, get breakfast and get to work. His mother had breakfast for him at four-thirty, and he was unlocking his front door at five a.m. November had come and brought cold winds. He shivered and made his way three blocks to downtown Barnsville. Another four hours would go by before he opened to the public, but the candies did not make themselves.

Today, he was making chocolate caramels. He wondered if that was why he had the dream again last night. He gathered up the ingredients, then looked at his father's old recipe card, grateful the recipes were written down.

The recipes all were written as if making them for home, the way the business started three generations ago. Today, they made the batches twenty times as large to hold up to the demand.

Jacob looked at the card:

> 1 Cup Sugar
> 1 Cup Light Corn Syrup
> 3 Squares Baker's Chocolate
> 1/4 tsp Salt
> 1 1/2 Cups Heavy Cream

Jacob quickly did the math and combined the sugar, chocolate, salt, and, 2/3 of the cream over a low flame. He stirred constantly as the temperature on the candy thermometer slowly rose and the shop began to smell of warm sugar. The mix came to a controlled boil, and he watched over it until the temperature got up to 238 degrees, then he added the remainder of the cream to the mix, just as his father and grandfather had done before him. The mix came back to a boil, and Jacob watched closely until the temperature read 246. It was time to pour the caramels out into the buttered sheet pans to cool, stirring the pot until the last drop of caramel was poured out then smoothing the pans.

Some of these would get wrapped as is and others would get dipped in chocolate and put into sampler boxes. Jacob did a quick check and saw he had made five half-sheet pans of caramels—that would last him for at least a couple weeks. It was nearly time to open the doors and let his sister in. She would run the cash register while he continued to make candies. This was the time of year they stocked up on the usual favorites.

Jacob went to the door and looked. There was his sister, Emma, but with her was Twyla, a heavy-set girl he knew from church and had seen recently at singings.

"Emma, what is going on?"

"I found someone to work for us this holiday, and I wanted to give her some practice before it gets too crazy."

Jacob quickly ran the numbers in his head. He could afford to train Twyla for the few extra weeks, and to have someone up to speed on the second register they opened during the Christmas rush would be nice. "Sure," he finally said—long after the two girls had walked past him into the store.

"I remember coming here as a child. Your dad would hand out samples to the little kids. It was such a treat to get to come here."

"Well, if you can figure out how to run the register, you will be the one handing out samples this year."

"I will certainly try my best."

Emma joked, "You don't have to kiss up to him. He may run the place, but I hire the sales help. Feel free to kiss up to me as much as you wish."

The two girls laughed.

Emma did a quick how to on running the scales and using the charts to turn weight into cost. Twyla seemed to catch on quickly. At the end of the day, she had earned a "good job today" from Jacob—no small praise coming from him.

Within two weeks, Twyla was nearly as quick as Emma on the register and was substantially more friendly. She seemed to go out of her way to greet people as they entered the shop and to help them make their choices.

Emma found a keeper this year. Jacob watched from the glassed-off room where the candies were made. "Twyla, are you willing to get up early and earn some overtime? We are making peanut brittle tomorrow. I will need extra hands to help draw it out."

"Sure, I can always use a little more money coming into the holidays."

"Great, come in for seven a.m. We should be about ready to pull the brittle by then."

The next morning, Twyla got there an extra fifteen minutes early and watched as Jacob brought the sugar-filled mixture up to a hard crack stage, added the peanuts, then the soda to make it airy. He quickly poured the mix out onto the table and looked up.

"OK, now comes the fun part. It is hot, but we have to pull it quickly. Here, like this," he said, demonstrating the way to lightly touch the mix with rubber gloved hands to thin and flatten the mix.

Emma joined in like the seasoned pro she was. Twyla was a bit hesitant, so Jacob went over behind her and showed her how to reach into the mass and pull the brittle out, "It is similar to a taffy pull, just warmer," he said, taking his arms from around her. "Your turn."

7

Twyla reached in, dug a bit too deep and quickly withdrew her hands. "Ooh that is hot! How can your fingers stand that?"

"Don't dig so deep. Just pull the surface," Emma explained. "Watch me for a minute, then do what I do." Emma quickly spread out pull after pull of the mix creating a thin layer at the center as she pulled the mass toward the edges.

"When it is all that thin, we are done."

Twyla tentatively reached in and then began pulling in earnest. Like most of the things at the candy shop, the task came easy to her once she had seen it done. In another fast fifteen minutes, they were done with the stretching and waiting for the brittle to harden. Emma made a pot of coffee while they waited.

By the time they finished their coffees, Emma said, "Twyla gets the hammer."

Twyla spun around to Emma, then to Jacob. "The hammer?"

"Yes, I suppose she has earned it," Jacob agreed.

Jacob reached into a drawer and pulled out a rubber mallet. "Do I need to explain how this works?"

"I think I can figure out I hit something with it. Is this how the brittle is made into pieces?"

"You got it in one guess. Hit it a few times—you will know to stop when the pieces are all around three inches by three inches or slightly smaller."

Twyla looked at the table of brittle reflecting the light off its shiny surface. She got a gleam in her eye and yelled, "Aaaahhh!" as she hit the brittle for the first time and watched it break up. True to its name, the brittle split apart and cracked easily. A few more hits were all it took to get the brittle to the desired size.

"That may have been too a bit too fun," Twyla said, setting the hammer down.

"I get the next batch," Emma said.

Jacob teased his sister. "I don't know. Twyla did it in fewer hits than you and seemed to enjoy it more."

"I wouldn't turn down another chance to do that," Twyla agreed quickly.

"Well, before we start worrying about next batch, let's get this sorted into eight-ounce and one-pound baggies and ready for sale."

The three of them did just that, then wiped down and cleaned up as the first customers lined up outside. Brittle was a town favorite, and folks seemed to know when it was being made.

Despite the very early start, Twyla was as pleasant and professional as always throughout the day serving what seemed to be a never-ending line of customers who wanted brittle and ... well, maybe a bit of chocolate to go with it.

For his part, Jacob spent the day making batches of white, green, and red hard candy he rolled into ropes, braided, then rolled the braided mix into a new rope, spun it making six-inch-wide circles, and then stuck a lollipop stick into them while they were still warm. He would be making hundreds of these white, red, and green colored suckers between now and Christmas—the sweets another town favorite.

At the end of the day, Twyla was given a pound of brittle, a lollipop, and the now customary "Great work today, Twyla." from Jacob.

Tearing open the bag, she said, "Ooh, I have wanted to try this all day." She put a piece of the brittle in her mouth and closed her eyes, savoring the flavor as it melted. "It tastes like it smelled—delicious!" she exclaimed.

"You sound like you have never tried it before," Jacob said, surprise evident in his voice.

"We only moved to town last year. Before that, we would come into Barnsville just before Christmas, and Dad would buy us a candy or two. I never even saw peanut brittle."

"It has been known to run out before Christmas week arrives," Jacob said.

"This is just wonderful," Twyla said, feeling her face warm. She hated that she blushed when talking to young men—she hated being the big girl with the red face. "I need to get home—my cat will wonder what became of me," she said looking for an exit. *Great, now I am the big crazy cat girl with the red face.* She walked away from the shop.

CHAPTER 3

Jacob sat at the head of the table and said the dinner prayer. To his left sat his mother, Connie, and then his sister. Tonight was macaroni and cheese night, his favorite.

As they ate, Emma asked "How do you like Twyla?"

"She seems to be working out well."

"Yes, but how do you *like her*?"

"She seems nice enough."

"But do you like her?

"You mean *like* her? I haven't really thought of her that way. Why do you ask?"

"She gets all flustered when she has to speak with you. I think she has a crush on you."

Jacob shook his head. "I think you are seeing things that aren't there."

"Maybe so, but maybe not."

Connie shook her finger at Emma, "Don't be starting gossip, girl."

"Yes, ma'am."

The next morning brought snow, not the kind that buries you, just the kind that makes you start thinking of hot chocolate and the coming holidays. Jacob stood inside the candy shop and stomped his boots to clean the dry snow off himself. He thought back to what his sister had said the night before and smiled. Would it be so bad if a nice girl liked him? Twyla was so full of happiness and energy he wondered if he could keep up with her. He decided he would look for any sign she was interested, then maybe if she was, he could ask to walk her home.

Snow did not slow the townsfolk from making it into the shop. Jacob sold hot chocolate mix with shaved chocolate in it that was the "go to" drink for snowy days. Tins of it flew off the shelves, and a pot was made to give samples to people as they came in from the cold.

Twyla was pouring out sample cups when a customer about her own age came into the shop and bumped into her.

"You oaf, watch what you are doing!" Rachel McAdams said angrily. "You've spilled chocolate on my new sweater!"

"I am so sorry. I was just filling up some hot chocolate cups when you bumped into me ..."

"So now you are saying it is my fault? Where is your manager?"

Twyla felt her face warming and knew she was turning crimson and looking guilty. "Jacob Wyse is the owner. I will get him for you." *Great there goes this job, and I really liked working here.* Twyla walked over to get Jacob. "Jacob, the woman in the sweater wants to speak with you. She bumped into me, I spilled hot chocolate on her, and she demanded a manager."

Jacob looked at Twyla oddly then left the glassed-in area and came out onto the sales floor.

Rachel McAdams stood with her arms crossed tightly. "So, you are the owner? What are you going to do about this? Your bumbling cow spilled all over my new sweater."

A small crowd had formed, much like sharks in bloodied waters, waiting to see what would happen next.

"I'm sorry," started Jacob. "But from where I was standing, it was pretty clear she was doing exactly what I had asked her to do, and you plowed into her, knocking the hot chocolate everywhere."

"Your father wouldn't have spoken to me that way." Rachel said.

"Well, I guess I knew him a bit better than you. Yes, yes, he would have spoken to you exactly that way if you wrongfully blamed one of his employees and then called them a cow."

"There are plenty of other places to get candy from."

Jacob pointed to the door. "I am glad you realize that—perhaps you should leave now and go to one of them."

"Whatever happened to the customer is always right?" Rachel fumed.

"No one is always right_you are surely old enough to realize at least that much."

The crowd went back to shopping for candy and gossiping among themselves. Twyla went to the candy-making area to speak to Jacob.

"Why did you lose a customer over me? Wouldn't it have been easier to have fired me and kept the customer? I am just a temporary worker here."

"She was wrong—she should have apologized."

"I am so glad you saw what happened."

"About that, I may have overstated what I saw."

"How much did you see?"

"None of it."

"But you said that you saw her bump me."

"That is what you told me. I have not known you to be a liar or to spin tales."

"But this store is your livelihood, you can't just believe people who say something."

"I had to believe her or believe you. I chose to believe you. Was I wrong?"

"No, but ..."

"She spoke rudely to you. I apologize that you had to go through that."

"I have heard worse than that about my weight. I am just built this way—I can't help it."

"There is nothing to 'help.' You look fine."

Twyla soared inside—that was the closest to a compliment she had ever received from anyone about her looks. She did something impulsive and hugged Jacob quickly. "Thank you for believing me!" As quick as it started, the hug was over, and Twyla went back to work.

Jacob for his part stood there, apparently shocked but pleased.

CHAPTER 4

Jacob looked out at the pans he had prepped, crushed walnuts a layer deep in each of them, the chocolate caramel ready to pour so it would lock the walnuts in place. Next was to cover the mix in fondant. While the caramel cooled, Jacob would make the fondant mixture.

Jacob scaled up the recipe, set all the ingredients except the vanilla into his pan and began warming it over a low flame. He stirred until the sugar had all melted then stopped, covered the pan, and waited for the temp to rise to 240 degrees. Once he had the 240 degrees, he removed the cover, added the vanilla, stirred, then spread the fondant over the caramel nut sheets and rolled the pans up jelly-roll style, wrapped them in wax paper, and left them to harden. Once hardened, the rolls would be cut on an angle creating Caramel Nut Rolls.

Jacob had just finished wrapping the last of the rolls when the bell for the door rang. Looking up, he saw that it was too early for his sister, who was always on time but never early. Making his way to the door, he was pleasantly surprised to see Twyla on the other side.

"Come on in. You are early, nearly a half hour."

"I wanted to thank you again for yesterday. People in my life generally don't stand up for me."

"You need better people in your life then."

"Yes, I probably do."

"Since you are here early, you can help me cut the caramel nut rolls—they should be just about hardened. Well, after you sign in and make us some coffee. We can't sample the candy without a good cup of coffee to wash it down."

Twyla smiled. "I will get right on that."

The two sipped coffee while slicing the nut rolls, and when finished, they ate the uneven end pieces as a reward for their efforts.

Putting a finger to his lips, Jacob said, "Don't tell Emma. I do this with all the candies I have to cut. She will start showing up and that means less for me."

"Don't you mean less for *us*? Now that I know your secret, I am sure to arrive early every day."

"I'd actually enjoy that. Why don't you start a half hour earlier, and I can show you how some of the candies are made."

Before she could answer, a ring at the door announced Emma's arrival. "I'll get it," Twyla volunteered.

"Good morning, Emma," Twyla gushed.

With a questioning turn of her head, Emma answered, "Good morning to you too. What has you so extra cheerful?"

"Jacob asked me to start a half hour earlier each day."

"You are celebrating losing more sleep?"

"No, that he is going to show me how some of the candy is made. I find the process fascinating."

Emma quirked her eyebrows. "Do you like Jacob?"

"Of course I do. He is a good person."

"No, I mean *like* him."

"Oh, I am not sure I ever thought of him that way."

"I think he likes you. He never has said good job to anyone else, and he goes out of his way to spend time with you."

"I am sure you are seeing something that isn't there. Jacob is a handsome enough guy—he wouldn't be interested in fat old me."

From the other side of the shop, Jacob asked, "What are the two of you talking about?"

Both girls looked up with faces that spoke of possible guilt. "Nothing," they said in unison.

Thanksgiving came and went. Jacob noticed the crowds growing nearly every day from that point on. Some folks wanted to keep candy in the house for visitors, and others got an early jump on their Christmas shopping. He looked over at Twyla, working her charm on a customer who was trying to decide if they should get the nut clusters or the caramel nut roll. He was not in the least surprised, with Twyla's helpful advice, that they bought both.

Waving her over to him, Jacob asked, "Twyla, can you take a minute and call our supplier for gummy bears and gummy worms? We need to order extra. Ask them to add 30% to our last month's order—that should get us past Christmas."

"Is their phone number on the Rolodex?"

"Yes, under gummy." Jacob laughed, and Twyla joined in.

"Well, you two seem awfully chummy," Emma said with an odd look in her eyes after Twyla had gone into the office to make the call.

Jacob shrugged his shoulders. "I enjoy working with her, that is all."

Emma giggled. "Sure it is. Sure it is."

Jacob stopped and thought. Nothing in Twyla's words nor actions led him to believe she was romantically interested in him, nothing. He shrugged and went on with his day.

Emma nudged Twyla when it got slow. "Jacob sure does rely on you more than anyone I have ever seen. Are you sure he isn't sweet on you?"

Twyla shook her head back and forth. "He hasn't said or done anything to make me think so. I just think he likes working with me, and that is fine. I enjoy working with him too."

"You just can't see how different he is with you than with any of our former employees."

"No, I can't see into the past, if that is what you are suggesting."

Emma laughed. "You can't see what is going on today?"

"Why are you so eager to get Jacob and me together?"

Emma twirled a loose strand of hair. "Well, if you two were together, you could work here year-round, and I wouldn't have to. I don't really like doing this every day and besides, I am of an age when a suitable man may come calling."

"Has any particular boy grabbed your eye?"

"Never-you-mind that," Emma said.

A new wave of customers cut that conversation short.

During the next week, Twyla learned to cut and wrap caramels, to stir fudge while it cooked, to order the items they did not make themselves, and she got to use the brittle hammer again.

Monday morning before the store opened, Jacob gathered Twyla and Emma. "Christmas is only three weeks away—things are going to get hectic in here. I usually call Mom in to help in the kitchen. I am thinking of having Twyla help me this year. Do you know if Elsa has a job? She wasn't terrible last year—it shouldn't take too long for her to get back up to speed on the register."

Emma looked at Twyla, then at Jacob. "I can ask her, or we could have Mom come in midday to take the register and cover the later hours so the days are not so long."

"Check with Elsa first. I'd like to let Mom stay home—she has plenty to do there without helping here all day and evening."

The next day, Emma showed up with Elsa, a thin, incredibly attractive young girl ready to go to work.

Elsa looked over at Jacob with a big smile. "I was so hoping you would ask me to come back this year."

Jacob bobbed his head from across the store. "We certainly can use the help—looks like a banner year so far. Sorry to start you so late."

Elsa looked at Twyla, and a quick look of scorn went across her face. "Oh, you have some help already."

"Elsa, this is Twyla. She is going to help me in the back area making candy this year."

That makes sense, I wouldn't want her to be greeting customers either. She reached out her hand to shake with Twyla. "Pleased to meet you, Twyla," she said with a smile that was just fake enough to be noticed.

Twyla shook her hand. "You as well. So you worked here last year?"

Elsa quietly replied, "Yes, Jacob trusted me with the register in the busiest time of the year."

Excusing herself from the catty conversation, Twyla said, "Speaking of Jacob, I guess I had best go find out what he and I are making today."

Elsa turned to Emma. "So, your mom isn't helping this year? It isn't like Jacob to let the hired help in the kitchen."

Emma shrugged. "Jacob runs the place; it is his call who he hires."

Elsa asked quietly "So ... is he seeing anyone?"

"No, I thought he was sweet on Twyla, but he hasn't made any kind of move."

With a look approaching horror on her face, Elsa gasped. "Twyla? Why on earth would he settle for her?"

"She is a nice enough person. Why wouldn't Jacob like her?"

"She is the size of both of us combined."

"She has a great personality and is good with customers."

"Whatever ..."

The week went by, and as expected, the shop was exceedingly busy. Elsa came back up to speed slowly on the scales and register while Twyla was an immediate help in the kitchen. With the extra set of hands, they were able to more than double the output and keep ahead of demand.

Friday evening at the end of the day, Jacob walked Twyla to the door. "Twyla, I just want to say what a huge help you have been this week. I was a bit worried you might not be able to get up to speed quickly enough, but you have exceeded my goals for you this week. I think we are so far enough ahead that we can make another batch of brittle. We usually have to run out to keep up with the rest of the chocolates."

"I am sure your mother would be more help back there than I am, but thank you."

"Well, yes and no. She knows most of the recipes already, but she doesn't always do things the way I like to do them. I try to run as efficiently as I can. Mom likes to do things the way she did with Dad. It can make for some minor clashes in the kitchen. We haven't had any of those this year."

"Well, I will try to keep doing things the way you show me. Was there anything else?"

Jacob was gathering his courage to ask Twyla to dinner when Elsa interrupted. "Oh, Jacob, what a day, huh? We should go and grab some dinner at Mario's. I know how you love Italian food."

"That's a great idea—we should *all* go for a celebratory dinner. Can you come, Twyla?"

Twyla looked and saw Elsa slowly shaking her head no. "I have some shopping I have to do, maybe some other night."

Elsa looked across the room. "Emma, we are going to Mario's—come with?"

"I can't, I have a previous engagement."

Jacob's spun his head around to look at his sister. "Really? Do I know him? Is it serious?"

Emma laughed. "And that is why I never tell you anything, dear brother of mine."

Jacob and Elsa left for Mario's, leaving Twyla and Emma to lock up. Twyla turned to Emma. "OK, your brother is gone—do I know him?"

"I don't have a date. I just know that Elsa has her sights set hard on Jacob. I figured to give them a bit of time together." Then Emma noticed the look on Twyla's face. "Wait, you do like him, don't you? Why didn't you go to dinner with them? I would have gone if it was the four of us."

"She was shaking her head no at me. She didn't want me there."

"What about Jacob? Was he shaking his head?"

"No, but ..."

"Twyla, let me explain about Jacob. I love him like the brother he is, but I think he is incapable of asking a girl out. If you want to see him and have him see you, you are going to have to do what Emma just did—make it your idea."

"Well, it is too late to worry about it. I am sure that wisp of a girl is working her way into his heart already."

"Could be, but I know he resisted her all last year or maybe didn't notice her throwing herself at him. I just figured that was why he didn't bring her back this year and instead asked me to find someone new."

Listen to me, fretting about a boy that hasn't shown me an ounce of attention as if I could compete with a thin girl. Twyla made her way out the door.

The next day was chaos in the kitchen. Twyla and Jacob were not much talking with each other and kept bumping into each other. By the time the day was over, they were both glad for the end of it. Twyla said a quick goodnight and left without waiting for the "Good work today" she knew wasn't coming. *Why am I so worked up about him dating the twig? He had plenty of chances to ask me out. He clearly isn't interested in the fat girl.*

After Twyla and Elsa had left, Jacob walked towards the door only to find his sister smiling at him.

"What?"

"Please tell me you didn't notice?"

"Notice what?"

'Twyla was a mess today after you and Elsa went out last night. She thinks you two are dating."

"Why would she think that? I mean we just had dinner on a Friday night ... OK, I can see why she would think that except she was invited too. I was about to ask her to go to dinner when Elsa did it for me, then Twyla said no."

"Elsa was shaking her head no at Twyla."

"Great. You two left me to sit with that girl all evening and listen to her talk about herself."

"If you were going to ask Twyla out, you should do it. I don't know what you are waiting for."

"Sure, it is easy for girls. You just wait for a guy to ask, then you can say yes or no or maybe some other time."

"Yes, we wait, and wait and wait for the boy to man up with the courage to ask. That can be just as exasperating as well."

Jacob thought for a bit. "Yes, I guess it could be."

CHAPTER 5

On most Mondays, Jacob and Emma ran the registers, giving the hired help the day off. Today, they had Twyla there on a third register just to keep the orders flowing out of the store. Jacob could not recall a busier day in the shop's history. The volume of customers was constant throughout the day, leaving little time for much conversation at all other than the occasional "We are running low on Almond Butter Crunch" or the echo of "next in line."

As Jacob finally closed the door, an hour after the scheduled closing time, he looked over at Emma and Twyla, and after a moment, he started laughing. "Do I look as tired as you two do?"

Emma rolled her head on her shoulders to stretch her tired muscles. "I can't believe how busy it was—did you run an advertisement or something?"

Jacob shook his head "No, we never run ads this time of year. Foot traffic is heavy enough without. Can you imagine if I had?"

Twyla chimed in, "I just feel bad I was barely able to to restock the sample trays. They were always empty every time I made it out there. Same with the Hot Chocolate."

Jacob replied, "I never had a chance to leave the register to check on them."

Twyla looked at Emma and Jacob. "I was trying to make sure anyone who came in had the same experience I had years ago. This shop was magical to me."

Emma nodded her head. "You were great. I can't believe how you flew around the store helping people while still ringing up probably more than I did."

Jacob went to his small office to count the drawers and get the deposit ready—something he did each night to keep the money away from the shop when they were closed. He took about a half an hour to get the deposit ready while the girls cleaned up the shop and restocked the candies they had more of in stock.

"Wow, we are out of peanut brittle again," Twyla said to Emma

"That never stays on the shelves—we could probably just make that and still keep busy all day."

"Why don't we make more of it then?"

Emma yelled across the shop, "Jacob, Twyla wants to know why we don't make more peanut brittle?"

"I am only one man. I cannot keep up with the demand"

Twyla nodded. "With the two of us making it, I bet we could get another couple batches in."

Tuesday morning came early as Twyla and Jacob agreed to work an extra hour in the mornings to try to make room for more brittle. This morning was a similar product, Almond Butter Crunch

They melted the butter, added the sugar, syrup, and water while slowly raising the temperature of the mix. They took turns occasionally stirring the mix, watching for it to reach three hundred degrees. Once the candy hit three hundred, they quickly stirred in the coarse chopped nuts and spread the mix into ungreased pans. While still warm, the mix was covered with chocolate and sprinkled evenly with fine ground nuts. Once cooled, they turned the candy out of pans and broke it into pieces similar to Peanut Brittle.

They fell back into their rhythm and knocked out four pans of the almond crunch in harmony. They cleaned up and moved on to dipping some fondant, some caramels, and some creams into chocolate.

Wednesday came, and they made peanut brittle. Jacob walked Twyla through all the steps, and they were ready with a batch twice the size of normal when Emma and Elsa showed up to help pull it. Jacob never considered Elsa for the hammer job, instead he simply handed the mallet to Twyla and let her break the candy down.

Jacob looked at the broken candies "OK, let's get this bagged and ready for sale."

Twyla asked, "May I take a couple pounds and send it to our candy distributor as a Christmas gift?"

Nodding his head, he said, "Sure, I usually don't have any and send them a sampler box."

Hours later while she was ordering from the supplier, Twyla said, "Mr. James, I am sending you some of the Wyse peanut brittle. Let me know if this is something you might want to distribute to other candy shops."

"I have heard the rumors about that brittle. I will be glad to get a sample and let you know," Mr. James replied.

The two finished placing the order for the shop and arranged to have the delivery driver return the brittle to the distributor.

CHAPTER 6

The next two weeks flew by with chocolates being made, and chocolates being sold nearly as fast. The only drag on the operation was Elsa and her near nonstop flirting with Jacob. As the shop closed on Dec 22nd, Jacob found himself looking at the books after making the deposit ticket for the bank. This was already the best Christmas season the shop had ever known. and there were two more days to add to the total. Jacob normally gave the temporary employees a box of chocolates and a check for $50. This year he would be giving them a little extra.

The phone rang, a rarity for this hour of the evening. "Hello?"

Paul James replied, "Jacob, you have been holding out on me. That peanut brittle is amazing. How soon can you get me five hundred pounds of it? I have buyers waiting for your answer."

Quirking his brow, he said, "I hadn't thought about having you distribute it."

"Your new office girl, Twyla, seemed to think you were ready to go."

Smiling widely, Jacob replied, "I see, that sounds like Twyla all right. I will have to check the production schedule, but I am sure I can get that made and ready within a week to ten days."

"Perfect. Not everyone wants chocolate for Valentine's day. Merry Christmas, Jacob, to you and yours."

"Thank you, Paul, the same to you and your family."

Jacob sat for a minute and wondered how much to sell the brittle for in quantity and how much that meant they would be making for each shipment. They would need to order more bags with the shop name on them—it was Wyse peanut brittle after all. *How do I reward Twyla for finding a way to keep the shop busy during the slower seasons?* That thought would have to wait for the morning.

December 23rd started with Elsa being late by forty-five minutes. The shop had a line at the door when they opened, so Twyla went out onto the sales floor instead of helping Jacob make candies. That was more candy cooking than Jacob would have been willing to try alone. When Elsa did arrive, she had no real excuse for her tardiness. Instead, she just batted her eyes at Jacob, obviously assuming that would fix everything.

Jacob grabbed Emma and brought her to a quiet spot on the floor. "Do you have any other friends you can get to work New Years to Valentine's day?"

Emma's mouth dropped. "Jacob, you have never fired anyone. Why now?"

"It is one of our busiest day,s and she just floats in when she wants? That cannot be allowed, even for a friend of yours."

"I can ask around, but I don't know anyone off the top of my head who is looking for work. Are you really going to fire her at Christmas?"

"I did not choose the timing, she did."

Calling across the store, he said, "Elsa, please come see me in my office"

The office barely had room for two chairs and was the one place in the candy store that smelled like business instead of candy. "Sit down."

"If it is about the Christmas bonus, can't that wait for later? The floor is full of people."

The blood vessels on Jacob's temples throbbed hearing this. "Bonus? No, this is not about any bonus. This is about you not showing up on time to serve those people that are filling our store right now."

"I said I was sorry."

"Well, so am I. This was your last day. I would rather know I am a person down than have to find out and ruin another batch of candy because I had to let Twyla go out to help Emma."

"So, that pig ruins a batch of candy and you decide to fire me?"

Twyla was coming back to the office to let Jacob know she was headed back into the kitchen and overheard Elsa's comment. *Pig, Cow? Why am I always livestock? Can't they come up with anything original?* "Excuse me, Jacob," she called out from outside the closed door.

Jacob sighed, wondering how much Twyla had heard. "Yes, Twyla?"

"I just wanted to let you know we got that first big wave of people set, so I am going back into the kitchen."

"Twyla, I'm sorry to ask this, but can you stay out on the floor today? I will explain it later."

"You're the boss."

Turning his attention back to Elsa, he said, "You mentioned a Christmas bonus. I will pay you the $50 bonus the same as last year, but that is from my generosity, not something that you have earned."

Twirling a strand of hair, Elsa simpered, "Well now that we aren't working together, perhaps you could take a girl out to dinner?"

"Elsa, I keep telling you I am not interested in you that way. How completely inappropriate to bring that up now even as I am having to fire you."

"You are serious, aren't you? You need a pretty girl to keep the people coming in. They won't come in to see *her*."

Jacob folded his arms. "They were coming in record numbers before you graced us with your presence, and they will keep coming in for the best candy for miles, not for some self-proclaimed beauty queen. Go get me your timecard. I will write your last check now.

With the appropriate tear in her eye, Elsa said goodbye to Emma and promised they could still be friends regardless. Elsa had no words of goodbye for Twyla.

Jacob caught Twyla's eye and waved her over. "Twyla, my office, please."

Turning to Emma, she asked, "Are you OK out front alone?"

"I will be fine. Just try to rush him and for goodness sakes don't get fired too. I don't want to finish this year alone."

"Twyla, what on earth made you think to distribute Peanut Brittle?"

"I am sorry, I heard Emma say the shop could make just that and stay in business. It made me wonder if that was a way to take some of the cycling out of your business. Right now, you go crazy from before Thanksgiving to just after Valentine's day, then get slow for the rest of the year. Well, Mother's Day and Easter excluded.

"I am not angry with you. It is exactly the kind of thing that we need. I am extremely happy with everything you have done this year."

"But?"

"No 'but'."

"You called me off a busy floor to say that? Good thing you don't have a boss, he would eat you up for that. You could have said that at closing this evening."

"I did not want to forget it if the day got crazy."

"Well, thank you. Maybe you can keep me on till Easter to help with the extra work?"

"That is not the worst idea I have heard today." Jacob laughed. "Now, get back to the sales floor—I hear it is busy out there. Good thing I don't have a boss watching over me."

CHAPTER 7

"Are you sure you don't need me today?" Connie Wyse asked her son.

Jacob turned and smiled, "No, I decided not to make candy today, which puts three of us on the registers. I may need you if Emma doesn't find us a replacement soon, though. Twyla has talked Mr. James into distributing our peanut brittle so the kitchen will be busier than normal for a while."

"Wow, your father once talked about doing that—he would be so proud of you."

"He'd be proud of Emma for finding Twyla, I think. Speaking of which, I am keeping her on until at least after Valentine's day, maybe Easter. If the shop stays busy, I mean."

"You don't need to check with me on that. You run that business and run it well, I might add."

"Thanks, Mom. See you this evening."

Jacob put on his coat, hat, and gloves then stepped out into a light snow. This storm was expected to put two to five inches on the ground before it was done. There was already an inch or more on the ground as Jacob rounded the corner onto the street where the candy shop was. It was a short ten-minute walk most days, a bit longer today with the lack of traction in places. He was met at the door by Twyla, who always seemed to be early.

"Hello, Twyla, good morning to you."

"Good morning, Jacob. Looking forward to a busy day?"

Opening the door, Jacob replied, "We will be ready for whatever day finds us."

Twyla walked towards the kitchen. "I will start a big batch of hot chocolate."

"Careful not to spill it on anyone ..."

Looking over her shoulder, she said, "Still not funny, Mr. Wyse."

"I have become Mr. Wyse. Here I thought I was growing on you."

"And here I thought you had a decent sense of humor."

"Before anyone else gets here, can I speak with you?"

Twyla laughed quietly. "UH-OH. He got a taste for firing—looks like I am next."

"Well, that is part of what I wanted to talk to you about."

Twyla stopped what she was doing and walked over to Jacob. "What's the matter? Did I do something?"

Pointing to a nearby stool, he answered, "To be truthful, yes, yes, you did. Since you are here, grab a seat."

Twyla was silent, and the color seemed to have left her face.

"We usually tell the Christmas help they will be let go on New Year's Day."

"Oh, is that all? Yes, Emma explained that to me when I agreed to come here to work."

"Well, that is just it. I would like it very much if you could stay working here until Valentine's Day."

Twyla let out the breath she was holding. "Yes, I'd be glad to work an extra month or so. That is much better than the "You are fired on Christmas Eve" that you had me expecting."

"What? How could you think that? You have been a big part of our success this season."

"I joked about getting fired—you said that was a part of what you wanted to talk about."

"Oh, I meant keeping you on."

Twyla smiled. "You really need to work on your communication skills, Jacob Wyse."

Twyla got up and made a double pot of Hot Chocolate, went out onto the sales floor, stocked up the tins and canisters of hot chocolate mix around the display, and started a second batch of chocolate to keep the pot full past the early morning rush.

At eight-thirty, Emma arrived uncharacteristically early.

"Good morning, Emma."

"Good morning, Jacob."

"Hey, Emma"

"Good morning. Twyla, how has the morning gone so far?"

"Well, your brother told me he was firing me then changed his mind and asked me to stay on until Valentine's Day."

"Fire you? What did you do?"

"She didn't do anything, and I already apologized. I told her I needed to speak with her, and she joked about getting fired. I was so eager to ask her to stay that I wasn't thinking right and agreed that was what it was about.

Emma smiled. "You really need to work on your communications and people skills there, brother."

Jacob shrugged, "So I have heard."

The day flew by. People would come in, shake off the snow and the cold, grab a cup of hot chocolate and wish everyone a Merry Christmas as they walked out with bags of candy that was probably not on their list of things to buy today. Before anyone knew it, it was four-thirty.

Jacob stood back from the register, then said loud enough for all to hear, "Folks, as is our custom, Wyse Candies will be closing in a half hour for Christmas Eve. Please enjoy the hot chocolate and samples but remember to get your purchases to the register by then."

Emma walked over to where Jacob was ringing up the last customer in his line. "You sound so much like dad when you say that."

Jacob hugged his sister. "I wish he were here too, Emma."

"So did you ask her out yet?"

Jacob turned to look her in the eye. "Who?"

Emma shrugged and rolled her eyes. "Twyla. I can tell you like her, and I happen to know she likes you."

"I admire her as a person, but it is not the same, and I doubt she cares about me as anything other than a boss. A boss who needs to work on his communication skills."

Emma laughed quietly. "She told you that too, huh? Well, it sounds like she is comfortable speaking to you plainly without worrying you will get angry with her."

Jacob nodded. "Yes, I think she understands she is a big part of what worked this Christmas season."

"Why do you think that?"

"Well, I told her so when I asked her to stay on."

"You can say that, and you can't find a way to ask her to a simple dinner?"

"I will think about it. Not today though, the timing is all wrong."

"Really? Because who wants a New Year's Eve date anyway?"

Jacob shrugged and walked away from Emma

At five-twenty, the last purchase had been rung up, and the shop was closed. Jacob took the three register drawers to his office and began to do the daily cash out. They would be closed the next two days as they celebrated Christmas with immediate family and then the following day visiting extended family and friends. Emma and Twyla made short work of cleaning the store, washing the plates from the samples, and the hot chocolate pots and pans. They swept the floor and restocked the candies while Jacob was making out the bank deposit.

Jacob shouted out, "Emma, come into the office, please."

Turning the corner and stepping into the small space "Yes, brother dear."

"Here is your Christmas bonus."

Emma scrunched her eyebrows together. "We don't usually give ourselves Christmas bonus. Do we?"

"We haven't before, but this year has been extremely profitable, especially Christmas season. I am going to give Twyla the same amount."

Emma opened the envelope handed to her. "A thousand dollars?" she shrieked then hugged her brother.

"It has been a great year."

"Twyla!" Jacob yelled next.

Twyla came around the corner and joked, "Yes, Boss."

Handing Twyla an envelope, he said, "Emma and I want you to have this as an expression of our thanks for the work you have done and continue to do for us."

Twyla's shriek was louder than Emma's as she opened the envelope. "Thank you, thank you!" she said as she hugged first Emma then Jacob. Jacob's hug lasted a moment or two longer than Emma's as it seemed neither Jacob nor Twyla were eager to end it.

CHAPTER 8

Saturday, December 27th, came with another light snow and much chatter about the people visited and friends that came calling. For Jacob, it was another Christmas without his father and he was left feeling melancholy.

Seeing Jacob frowning, Twyla asked, "Is everything all right, Jacob?"

"I miss my father this time of year. His absence has taken much of the joy out of Christmas for me."

"I am sorry for that loss—I cannot begin to imagine it."

"Nothing to be done about it. I hear that time heals all wounds—I just wonder how much time that really takes."

Twyla shrugged. "Try doing something different—take a chance on something you wouldn't normally do."

"Maybe I will just try that, but for today, it is Pralines."

The two took out the brown sugar, regular sugar, cream, butter, and a huge bag of pecans.

"Now, we are going to raise this to the soft-ball stage."

"Why is it called soft-ball?"

"When you get between 235 and 245 degrees and spoon some of the sugar mix into a glass of water, the ball of candy will slowly flatten in your hand when you remove it from the water. We do that for soft candies and chewy candies instead of hard ball or hard crack like we do for brittle"

Twyla listened intently. "You sure know a lot about making candies. I guess that comes with owning a shop."

Jacob shook his head. "More like the fact I have made candy or helped make candy for as long as I can remember."

Twyla gave a genuine laugh. "That would help too."

They got the mixture up to temperature then spooned it out over an enameled table allowing the pieces to firm up. Jacob even took the extra time to show Twyla the process of how to check for soft-ball stage with water, as if he didn't have a candy thermometer available.

As they finished making the pralines, he asked, "Twyla, can you make us a pot of coffee? I am near certain we can find a couple of imperfect pralines in this batch that will need to be culled before we make them available to the public."

Twyla smiled and nodded. "It is a fine thing you are so willing to suffer for your customers, Jacob. So very noble of you."

Jacob shared the smile. "As my assistant, I expect no less from you."

Twyla flirted back. "The horrors of this job—no one understands the sacrifices made."

Emma came through the door and heard the tail end of the conversation. "'Sacrifices?' Ooh, what are you two sampling this morning?"

Jacob chuckled. "You know me too well, sister. We made pralines. I am guessing we can find an imperfect one for you as well."

"Imperfect? You pick them at random and call them that just so you can sample. You take after Dad that way. He always used to declare candy unsellable so that we could have some when he made it."

Twyla looked over at Emma. "I don't care who started the tradition, I am just glad to share in it."

Emma nodded. "I am glad both for the tradition and a happy reminder of Dad this time of year. Speaking of traditions, what are the two of you doing for New Year's Eve? Any plans?"

Twyla shook her head. "I am going to curl up with a good book and a warm cat and read—that is my New Year's Eve tradition."

"That is still better than mine," Jacob said. "I will be going to bed early. My internal clock is set. I will wake up at four a.m. even though we will be closed."

Emma shrugged. "You two are old fogies; I am going to the church singing they are having as a celebration of the New Year."

Twyla looked toward Jacob and seeing him looking her way immediately turned away. "Well, that sounds like fun, but I have already picked out my book."

Jacob's face flashed disappointment. "Well, these pralines are not going to eat themselves, let's get the bad ones eaten and the good ones ready for sale."

Wednesday, during work, Emma was all excited about the singing and who might be there. Twyla and Jacob were both silent on the matter.

"But, why don't you want to come, Twyla? Maybe some good-looking guy will want to drive you home."

Twyla shrugged. *No one wants a cow to ride in their cart.*

"Your loss." Emma sighed.

"What about you, Jacob?"

"I don't want a good-looking young man to offer me a ride home, thanks."

Twyla burst into laughter despite her friend Emma showing clear frustration.

The shop was quieter than before Christmas but still busy enough they couldn't talk about it much more.

At the singing, Emma saw Benjamin Lapp from across the lawn. More importantly to Emma, he saw her.

With a tip of his hat, he asked, "Did you want to play some volleyball?" barely able to meet her eyes.

"Why, thank you, I'd love to," Emma said and took Benjamin's arm, walking to the net.

They played for fifteen minutes and won. Benjamin proved himself an asset on the court, and Emma played well also.

"Let's cool off and get a drink," Emma suggested.

"That sounds like a great idea. I will go get them—wait for me?"

With a bit of dreaminess in her voice, she answered, "I will," but her mind was saying *I have been.*

They drank the punch, talked and talked. It turned out they had much in common, they both liked the idea of farming, they both preferred coffee to tea, and they both loved ice cream—vanilla fresh out of the churn best of all. When the singing had nearly ended, Benjamin slipped away from the other gentlemen and found his way to Emma's side.

"If it would not be considered too forward of me, I would love to drive you home tonight."

"I'd be delighted," came the swift reply, and the two made their way out of the home where the singing was held.

"Emma, I am not sure how I never really noticed you before, but would you consider letting me make you some ice cream this Saturday? I will bring the churn and the ingredients to your house."

"It is the middle of winter," Emma started, then continued, "And I would love to have some fresh churned ice cream." as she quickly caught herself.

Friday, January 2nd, there was a noticeable change in Emma—she was smiling and singing from the time she arrived for work. Both Jacob and Twyla teased her and tried to get her to tell, but she kept her news to herself until lunchtime.

"If you two must know, Benjamin Lapp drove me home from the singing ... and he is coming to the house tomorrow to make me some ice cream—vanilla just like I like it."

Twyla's face beamed. "Well, you should bring home some of the pralines to put on top—everyone loves pralines."

Jacob frowned. "Benjamin Lapp. Isn't he the youngest son on the Lapp farm? Won't he be a farmer?"

Emma couldn't look her brother in the face. "I suspect that he will be getting the farm ..."

"How could you work here and be a farmer's wife?"

Emma rolled her eyes. "I think it is a bit early to worry about that. He is making me ice cream, not asking me to marry him." *For now.*

CHAPTER 9

The first week of January brought cold temperatures and plenty of snow. The shop was less hectic than before Christmas but stayed busy enough to justify keeping Twyla working.

Twyla answered the phone, "Wyse Chocolates, Twyla speaking. Oh, hello, Paul. How did the peanut brittle go over so far? Really? Another five hundred pounds already? I will talk to Jacob and get it on the schedule. How soon did you want that? Next week should be fine."

Jacob overheard the conversation and was elated. The brittle was a success. He ran across the floor towards Twyla.

"That was Paul James?"

Twyla smiled. "Yes, it was."

"And he is already ordering more brittle?"

"Yes, he is. He said he hasn't seen a response like this in years for a product. He wants another five hundred pounds next week, then probably again two weeks later, but he will confirm that with you after this next batch is delivered."

Jacob was elated. He went over to Twyla and threw his arms around her, giving her a big hug. "Thank you. Twyla, this is all on you. You are the reason for this success.

Twyla, for her part, was also ecstatic. She was a vital part of a team for the first time in her life. And if Jacob chose to show his thanks with hugs, she was not of a mind to object.

"Let me go, so I can order the materials. I don't think we have enough glucose nor peanuts on hand to make that much. Should I order for five hundred pounds or the thousand?"

"Ask if there is any discount for the higher bulk. If we get at least five percent off, go ahead and have them ship a thousand pounds. We will need some for the store soon too."

Twyla was both relieved and saddened by him letting go. She found herself drawn to Jacob but did not want to get her hopes up. Fat girls don't get guys like Jacob, she told herself over and over.

"Jacob, do you keep track of what you sell by weight each month? How much of each item that is?"

"We haven't been. Why, do you think we should? What would the benefit be?"

"Well, since you are now also a wholesale kitchen, it would make it easier to make a schedule for production. Instead of waiting for things to go low, you can schedule to make them when they will just start to get low. Mainly the big items to begin with, then as time goes on and you have more information collected, you could schedule out a week or two and know that you won't run out of anything in the store."

"Is that something you would be comfortable doing, Twyla?"

"I can set it up for you. I think once you see it, it will explain itself so you can keep it going when I am gone."

"Gone? Where are you going?"

"It is only a few more weeks until Valentine's Day."

"That reminds me, can you stay on until Easter?"

"I would love to stay on another couple months—we can get the schedule working by then I think. Have I mentioned that you really need to work on your communications skills?"

As Valentine's Day approached, they made heart-shaped chocolates, made extra chocolate covered caramels, creams, and fondants for sampler boxes. Each evening, Twyla went into the office with Jacob, and while he cashed out the register and made the bank deposit, she totaled the amount of each candy sold and kept a daily log. Her idea soon started paying dividends as there were days on the schedule that were able to be filled with making fudge that wasn't quite out yet but according to the sheets, would be in a few days. The more of this that happened, the more interested in the whole process Jacob became.

"So, it will eventually tell us when to schedule everything? I won't have to go around the store looking for what is low to know what I am making the next day or run out of items before I make them?"

"There will still be a need to mind your store, Jacob. This will, however, reduce the number of times you run out of anything that people come in to buy. Let's say we have to make brittle for two days next week, and the books show that by then, we will be out of Nut Rolls—we can schedule the nut rolls before the brittle and never run out."

"Twyla, you are a genius! How did I run this shop without you?" Jacob gushed.

"Quite well as I recall,"

"Not as well as now, you have to admit that. You have brought Wyse candies forward and helped us to grow."

CHAPTER 10

Valentine's Day brought news to the shop. Benjamin Lapp had asked Emma for permission to court her, and she had accepted. This normally would have been private, but as it affected her future in the shop, she felt obliged to tell her brother.

"What am I to do? Bring Mother back to the shop? She has finally been able to get back to her quilting—you know how she loves it."

"I think you are missing the obvious answer."

"I can't make all the candy and ring it up too."

"Brother, you are dense sometimes. You have Twyla. I bet she would love to work here year-round and be your helper. I bet if you ever got around to asking her, she would want to be more than that."

"I tell you, sister, that I have been watching, and she hasn't shown any signs of interest. I would hate to ruin such a great work relationship, especially now that you are in the process of wanting to leave."

"I will be around until summer's end anyway, maybe a bit longer. Just ask the girl to dinner already. I can't believe you let Valentine's Day get past you on this. What an easy ask that is."

"We were busy getting a production schedule together. It was Twyla's idea. She really has been a great help at the shop."

"Do you like her?"

"Well, sort of, but not enough to ruin the working relationship we have if she does not feel the same."

"I keep telling you, the girl is pining away for you."

"I highly doubt that. With her personality and cheerfulness, I bet she has many young men interested."

"Ach, brother, you are not like most men. Most see her size and stop looking. They don't want a personality or a brain or a great helper. They want a pretty girl."

"Like your Benjamin likes you?"

"Did my brother just call me pretty?"

"No, you must be hearing things."

"Jacob, you need to work on your people skills and communication. You can't even tell when a girl wants you to walk her home."

"Jacob, the production schedule shows we will be out of chocolate caramels in a couple days. Do you want to do a batch of those as well today?"

Jacob's narrowed his brows in disbelief. "Caramels? Already? Let me go check the stock on those."

Jacob went over to the chocolate caramels and saw a few pounds of them waiting for sale. "I think we are good, there are a few pounds of them still."

Twyla explained, "Well, the schedule is full for the next six days with peanut brittle and then taffy. According to the way the caramels have been selling, we will go out of stock on them before the week ends."

"I guess it won't hurt to run a batch of them just to be certain."

"Trust in the process, Jacob. The schedule is your friend."

With a smile, Jacob replied, "It is starting to feel like the schedule is my boss and by the schedule, I mean it is beginning to feel like you are my boss."

"You have an odd way of saying, 'Thank you for getting a production schedule running, Twyla.'"

"I know, I need to work on my communication skills."

"Yes, yes, you do, oh boss of mine."

By week's end, they had made the now one thousand pounds of brittle that Paul James had ordered for the month and, sure enough, would have run out of chocolate caramels without Twyla's intervention.

"Trust in the process," Twyla reminded Jacob when he was checking the inventory of the caramels.

"We definitely would have run out a couple of days ago. I understand the English use computers for inventory."

"You don't need a computer, you have me. Well, until Easter."

"About that ..."

"Do you not need me till then?"

"Actually, the opposite. How would you feel about working here through the summer months?"

Twyla nodded her head and teased, "You are getting better at this—you didn't wait till the week before I was scheduled to leave before asking me. There may be hope for you yet, boss."

Summer came and went—the orders for brittle got larger and larger. Mr. James was up to ordering a ton of brittle a month now trying to stock it up for the fall and winter seasons. Emma was still running the register out front while Twyla and Jacob worked in harmony in the kitchen.

Early in August, Connie Wyse stopped by the store to get some chocolates for friends she was going to be visiting.

Connie finished her order, "... and some pralines."

Emma put all the selections in a big bag and brought her mother to the register. "Still no charge, but I have to list what we sell so Twyla can schedule when to remake things."

"She can do that already?"

"She can do anything, except to get Jacob to ask her out."

"Does Jacob know?"

"I keep telling him, but he refuses to see it. So does she for that matter."

"I can see it from here—they are a match. Look at them smiling and working together."

"I am going to have them both as side sitters at my wedding, maybe that will wake them up."

"Wedding, you say?"

"Well, I wasn't going to mention it this early, but Benjamin and I are planning to wed this fall. Nothing big or fancy."

"Does your brother know?"

"I am not sure how to tell him. He is not going to be happy."

"I am sure he will be happy for you."

"Yes, just not for himself nor the shop. I think he thought I would be here forever."

"I can come back to work here."

"I am not sure Jacob wants you to. He likes being the boss of the shop."

"He can be my boss as easy as yours."

"I am not his mother."

Across the dinner table, Jacob got the news of the impending wedding. "Do you have anyone who could come to work for us? With the brittle selling so well, I need Twyla in the kitchen with me. To keep up."

"I can still run a register," Connie responded.

Shaking his head no, he said, "You should be able to make your quilts and spend your time as you see fit, Mom."

"What if I see fit to check in on my son?"

"I just don't want to tie you down to the shop."

Emma muttered, "You were more than willing to tie me there."

"That was clearly a mistake on my part. I shouldn't have counted on you."

"I never missed a day nor was I ever late. You take that back, Jacob Wyse!"

"I mean I should have realized your long-term goals were not inside the shop."

"You really need to work on your communication skills, brother of mine."

CHAPTER 11

The chocolate shop was a flurry of activity as Jacob worked off the stress of losing Emma. Twyla, for her part, kept up with him step for step but only with much effort.

"Jacob, we have never tried to make so much brittle in a day. Can we really do two thousand pounds of it? That is usually two days on the schedule."

"After we break the brittle, I will start the next batch, you can clean the workstations, then wash the pots and pans. By the time you are done with those, I will need you again in the kitchen to help pour and stretch the next batch. I think we can do it."

Twyla asked the question he seemed to miss. "Who will bag the brittle?"

"Emma can. The register is not so busy right now, so she can keep an eye open for it as she wraps. It is not ideal, but it will be huge if we can run a ton of brittle in a day."

The three of them worked harder that day than any other in the history of the shop. When the day was done, the ton of brittle was bagged and ready for shipment.

Jacob turned to Twyla. "I knew we could do it."

"Let's never do that again ..."

Jacob teased, "You sound like Emma."

"That is because Emma is smart enough to know we need a fourth person in the shop to try that again."

Emma added, "My feet ache from running back and forth all day. Are you trying to punish me for leaving?"

"Leaving?" Twyla asked.

"Benjamin and I are to be wed this fall."

Twyla jumped up and down then hugged Emma. "That is wonderful! I am so excited for you."

"You and Jacob will be side sitters for me," Emma declared rather than asked.

Jacob turned to Twyla and she to him. "I would be honored, sister," followed by, "I've never been a side sitter before," from Twyla.

Later, when alone with Emma, she asked, "Isn't it more usual to have couples as side sitters?"

"You two are a couple, you just can't see it."

"I hope this doesn't make it awkward in the shop after."

Emma smiled. *For my brother's sake, I hope it does.*

CHAPTER 12

With the wedding now looming in the near distance, the shop was in full gear. There would be vanilla ice cream and pralines for everyone at the wedding to commemorate Emma and Benjamin's first date as well as sampler trays of chocolates at each table.

Jacob turned from his work. "Twyla, how is that batch of fondant coming? I have the nut rolls waiting for it."

Using her frock to wipe the sweat from her brow, she replied, "Should be ready to go in about five minutes."

"How are we going to account for all the chocolate we are taking from the shop?"

"I assume you are giving it to your sister and her new husband. Did you want to charge her for it?"

"No, no, no. I mean in your schedule. Won't this make a demand that doesn't reflect in the daily numbers?"

"You had me wondering there for a second. I am not going to count any of the chocolate leaving into the equation. We will just have to make a wide mix to restock. I think that is the best way. Otherwise, each year around now we will be flooded with pralines."

"What about the days we are closed for the wedding? How will you figure those?"

"I won't. I think the best way for that is to have the two days as no sales. It will all balance out in the long run."

"I trust you."

Twyla's face warmed, and she knew she was blushing. Such a simple phrase, but the three words made Twyla feel like she was where she belonged, where she wanted to be. "You are getting better at that whole communication thing, boss."

The wedding was now a scant week away. Jacob let Emma have the time off, not that an Amish wedding was as ornate and planned out an affair as an English one, but rather because the poor girl was giddy to the point of not being able to concentrate on what it was she was doing. Twyla stepped up and covered the sales floor while Jacob took care of production during business hours. Twyla was still coming in a couple hours early to keep production on schedule, and with the continued success of the peanut brittle sales, her wages were more than covered. Her staying on through fall was never in question.

"Twyla, what is on our must make schedule for this week?"

"We really should do a single batch of brittle, so that we are not behind when we return from the wedding. There are also a few of the regulars that are running low or will be by then. I will write them down for you—you can make them in whatever order you want."

Jacob went back into the kitchen and began a batch of chocolate caramels. He realized it was easier with Twyla in the kitchen to make enough for both loose caramels and for the nut rolls. *Everything is easier with Twyla.* He sighed and continued to stir the caramels.

With the wedding just a day away, the shop closed early, and Twyla put the 'closed for two days' sign up in the door. Most folks around here knew of the closing and the reason already, but it was good business to keep the clients informed.

"So, I will see you at the church tomorrow," Jacob said as they locked up the door.

"I will see you there. Oh, can I get a ride with you from the church to the reception? I don't know how long it will go, and I don't want to have my English driver wait too long."

"I could just pick you up at your house and drive you to the church and back," Jacob offered.

"If that wouldn't be too much trouble, I'd like that."

If Jacob saw the spark in her eyes, he never placed it.

CHAPTER 13

Jacob stopped the open carriage outside Twyla's home, and she came out before he could go and knock properly. "I am so excited," she said quickly, and her tone left no doubt to her honesty.

"Why, Jacob Wyse, picking me up in an open carriage. What will people say?" she teased.

"Mom and Emma wanted the closed buggy to keep their hair in place. Is the truth. I don't much care what people think is the rest of the truth."

He doesn't care what people think in general or doesn't mind what they think about us? He really does need to communicate better.

The wedding ceremony went perfectly, and the young couple left for the reception followed by a trail of buggies. Jacob and Twyla were near the head of the line as they had the honored responsibility of being side sitters—sitting with the newly married couple and enjoying their first meal together with them.

Twyla knew those spots were usually given to either newly married or couples that were at least dating. What Jacob knew, he kept to himself. Everyone enjoyed the meal and the conversation—the big hit was the dessert of vanilla ice cream with Wyse pralines.

Jacob was quick to praise Twyla for her part in making sure the pralines were available for the wedding, making her blush more than once when folks asked if there would be any more pralines left in the shop come Monday. Twyla's heart fluttered when she heard Jacob praise her work. No one had ever done that for her. She had always been OK or enough, never praiseworthy. She excused herself to wipe her eyes.

"What did you do to make Twyla cry?"

"I don't think I did anything. I was just telling Hershel how great it is to have her around the shop and how much easier she makes everything for me."

Emma gave a knowing look then a nod.

"Are you OK, Twyla? I am sorry if something I said made you sad."

"You really are bad at communication, Jacob. Those were tears of happiness. I have never had anyone brag about me to another."

"I find that hard to believe."

"Stop it, or you will get me started again."

Jacob scrunched his shoulders. "Uh ... OK, I guess."

As the reception wound down, aunts and cousins stepped in, stepped up and got the cleanup going. Jacob was politely told he was not needed for this part of the day, so he returned to Twyla.

"So, did you enjoy yourself, Twyla?"

"I cannot remember a better day in ages."

"Ready to head back home?"

"No, but it is that time."

The two walked over to the carriage, and Jacob held her hand as she climbed in. He went to his side and jumped aboard. A slow pull on the reins got the horse to step backward far enough to clear the nearby carts, and a quick flick of the wrist got the mare to slowly begin the ride home.

"I am happy for Emma," Jacob said, breaking the silence. "It must be something to find the person you are matched with."

Twyla looked at the distance between them in the carriage and said in a whisper, "It must be."

The rest of the ride home was quiet, broken up by Jacob talking shop and Twyla's short responses.

CHAPTER 14

Monday morning, back at work, Jacob handed Twyla a cup of coffee and asked her to sit a minute.

"I did not expect this when we met, but you have become invaluable here. I hope your plans include Wyse Chocolates for the next couple years anyway. I guess what I am trying to say is can you stay and work year-round from now on?"

"I'd love to. I really do enjoy working here with you, Jacob."

"We will probably have to get Mom to come in on busy days to help with the registers, or maybe you know some people looking for work for this fall through Christmas and New Year's?"

"I will ask around ..."

Thanksgiving came and went, and the business was even greater than the year before. Jacob hired two young girls to work out front and had Twyla train them. His mother worked the kitchen with him while Twyla was out teaching the new girls how to keep the samples stocked and still ring up orders and be friendly. Twyla was all smiles but all business when it came to the new hires.

During one of the training weeks, Twyla's parents came into the shop.

"Hello, Mom. Hi, Dad. Welcome to Wyse Chocolates"

"Hello, Twyla. We were in the neighborhood and decided to stop by and get a few chocolates. Do you know anything about them so you could help us, or should we get someone else?"

"I can tell you that with the exception of anyone with the last name Wyse, I know more about these than any person in the shop." Twyla tried to impress her parents.

Her mom whispered to her, "It is not proper to be boastful." Twyla shrank her shoulders. "Yes, Mum."

Seeing this, Jacob came over. "You must be Twyla's parents. I am Jacob Wyse. I cannot begin to tell you how happy we are to have had Twyla here with us this past year. She has been instrumental in making us more successful and a friendlier place to visit. Pick out what you want—it is on me. I can't have my best employee's family paying for their chocolate, not when their daughter helped to make most of it."

Twyla's parents looked at Jacob, waiting for the punchline that never came. They then looked at Twyla, seeing her perhaps for the first time through the eyes of someone who appreciated her for who she was, instead of who she might someday become. Twyla just blushed and smiled.

At the end of the day, after cleaning the shop and restocking and tidying the inventory, Twyla walked back to where Jacob was finishing the deposit ticket for the day.

"Thank you."

Jacob looked up, confused. "Huh?"

"Thank you for today. My parents were impressed with you."

"They should be impressed with you. You certainly have earned my admiration."

"That is why I am thanking you. They were impressed with you, and you went out of your way to let them know that you are impressed with my work here."

"I hope that isn't what you think."

Twyla spun to face him. "You aren't impressed with my work here?"

"Well, yes, but more than that, I am impressed by you. You are ... well, sturdy."

"Jacob, you really do need to work on your people skills. When you say sturdy, a fat girl hears fat, not dependable."

"Fat girl? You? I mean you are no twig like Elsa, but you are not fat."

"Jacob, I know me better than you do. I am fat, large, big-boned to those trying to be nice."

"I guess I just don't see you that way. You are just ... well, you."

Twyla swooned inside and went out on a limb. "Jacob Wyse, would you walk me home tonight?"

"Sure, why?"

"Never mind."

"Wait, do you mean walk you home like ... *walk you home?* I'm sorry ..." Jacob hesitated. "... I have been trying to get up the nerve to ask you to dinner since you started here. I just didn't think you were interested at all."

"Perhaps you have heard this before, you really need to work on your people and communication skills."

"Well, instead of just walking you home, would you like to go to Mario's with me for a pizza or maybe an eggplant parmesan and spaghetti unless you'd like something else?"

"No, I love Italian, and I hear Mario's is great. I have never been there yet."

"We will have to fix that. We can walk to Mario's, then to my house to get the horse and buggy for the ride to your house."

"I don't live that far away—we can walk it."

"I don't want people to get the wrong idea."

"What do you mean?"

"I mean when a young man courts a woman, he drives her around—he doesn't walk her around."

"Do you mean ...?"

"Unless you think you see too much of me around the shop already, I would like to get to know you outside the shop as well."

"I would love to drive around with you, Jacob Wyse."

The two were inseparable from that point on.

Just before closing the shop for Christmas Eve, Jacob walked up behind Twyla and whispered into her ear, "Would you be willing to be a spring bride? I am not sure I want to wait longer than that to have you as my wife."

Twyla nodded her head yes. "Jacob Wyse, you certainly have been working on those communication skills."

CHOCOLATE CARAMELS

1 Cup Sugar
1 Cup Light Corn Syrup (Karo's)
3 Squares Baker's Chocolate
1/4 Teaspoon Salt
1 1/2 Cups Heavy Cream

Combine sugar, syrup, chocolate salt and 1 cup of cream. Place over a low flame and stir until sugar is dissolved and mixture boils. Continue to boil mixture until 238 degrees. Stirring constantly, add the remaining 1/2 cup of cream and boil slowly until the mix reaches 246 degrees. Keep stirring and pour into 8" x 4" pan. DO NOT SCRAPE the pan. Let stand until cool. Cut into squares. Wrap in wax paper.

CREAM FONDANT

2 Cups Sugar
Dash of Salt
1/4 Cup Milk
1 Tablespoon Light Corn Syrup (Karo's)
1/2 Cup Heavy Cream
1/2 Teaspoon Vanilla

Combine ingredients (except vanilla) in a pan over low flame. Stir until sugar dissolves and mixture boils. Cover and cook without stirring to 240 degrees. Pour fondant at once on a cool to lukewarm wet plate.

Work until white and creamy then knead in wax paper. "Ripen in Refrigerator" 24 hours. Makes one pound.

CARAMEL NUT ROLL

1 Cup Chopped Walnut Meats
1 Recipe of Chocolate Caramels
1 Recipe of Fondant

Sprinkle nuts into two slightly greased eight by eight pans. Prepare chocolate caramels mix and pour carefully over nuts in pans. When cool, remove from pan and spread fondant evenly on the plain surface of the caramel. Use half batch of fondant for each sheet. Roll and wrap in wax paper. Let stand for several hours to harden. Cut crosswise into quarter inch slices. Makes about 64 pieces.

ALMOND BUTTER CRUNCH

1 Cup Butter
1 1/3 Cups Sugar
1 Tablespoon Light Corn Syrup
3 Tablespoons Water
1 Cup Coarsely Chopped Nuts
4 1/2 Ounces or Large Bar of Milk Chocolate Melted
1 Cup Finely Chopped Nuts

Melt butter in a large saucepan. Add sugar, syrup, and water. Cook, stirring occasionally to hard crack stage (300 degrees) At 300, quickly stir in coarse nuts and then spread out in ungreased 13 x 9 1/2 x 2 inch pan. Cover while hot with the melted milk chocolate, then sprinkle with the fine nuts. Cool thoroughly then turn out of the pan and break into pieces.

PRALINES

1 Cup Light Brown Sugar.
1 Cup White Sugar
1/2 Cup Cream
2 Tablespoons of Butter
1 Cup Pecans

Cook sugar and liquid until boiling, add nuts and butter. Cook to a soft ball stage 235 degrees. Take off fire (stove). Stir but do not beat. Drop onto aluminum foil then let cool.

ABOUT THE AUTHOR

Amos Wyse was born in the Midwest. Spending a great deal of his youth around good, hard-working farmers, those who lived near them and worked with them. When writing, he keeps those people and the life lessons they taught close by.

A CHRISTMAS DAY WITH MARY

JERRY EICHER

CHAPTER 1

Mary Wagler sat behind her schoolteacher's desk, late on Christmas Eve, with her hands clasped in front of her. Dusk had long fallen, but a single gas lantern still hung from the hook on the schoolhouse ceiling. The pulsating light fell around her desk and halfway across the empty schoolhouse, where the student's desks had been brought back to their usual tidy order. Quiet had returned. Beyond the reach of the lantern's illumination, the faint glow of the moon glimmered in the windows.

"Thank you, dear God, for this *wunderbah* evening," Mary whispered heavenward.

She should be exhausted after the evening's events, which had followed the last-minute rush of practice earlier in the day for the much-anticipated school Christmas program. Mary wasn't. Exuberance and joy filled her instead. The parents of the students, along with most of the community, had gathered for the performance tonight. There had been nothing but praise offered afterward. The chairman of the schoolboard had taken the occasion to remind her their offer of another year of school teaching was waiting for an answer. The Lord had indeed chosen to bless. The children had articulated their poems and recitals almost to perfection. Little Johnny Weaver had moved several people to tears, including Mary herself, with his dramatic dictation of the Isaiah prophesy, "For unto us a child, unto us a son is given. The government shall be on his shoulders, and his name shall be called Wonderful, Counselor, The Mighty God, The Everlasting Father, The Prince of Peace."

Behind the young boy's voice, trying to reach the deep tones of an yet unarrived manhood, had been the echoes of the aged Prophet lifting his staff and declared the coming of the Lord, proclaiming the birth of the Christ Child who would save the world.

"Thank you! Thank you, dear Lord." Mary breathed another quick prayer.

She jumped to her feet. Tomorrow was coming. She must hurry home, calm down, and get a few hours of sleep. The whole family would be gathered for Christmas breakfast, where they would experience another *wunderbah* day of the Lord's blessings at Mam's house. Esther, Lois, and Phoebe, her three sisters, would be arriving. They had been schoolteachers before her. Even with their combined experience, they had been profuse with praise after the program tonight.

"Couldn't have done better myself." Phoebe had pronounced.

"You're so talented," Lois had gushed, "but this is your second year, and there still isn't—"

"Don't bring up the subject tonight." Esther had leaped to Mary's rescue. "Not after such an accomplishment."

Mary's smile faded. Her sisters wouldn't feel restricted tomorrow, not once they were out of earshot of the community's ears. Her continued single status was a sore spot for the entire family. Mam seemed to understand at least—or kind of understand. Dat frowned but didn't say much when the subject came up. She should be dating a man, and perhaps getting married this fall. Why wasn't she? The question seemed to hang on her family's lips.

"We have so many handsome young men in the community." Phoebe reminded her often.

"Don't you have offers?" Lois would drop sideways, when everyone knew she did.

Esther was not beyond waging her finger. "Whatever dream man you are waiting for doesn't exist."

"How do you know?" Mary had dared challenge Esther once.

"Haven't all three of us found wunderbah husbands." Esther retorted as if the statement constituted proof.

She didn't have objections to dating. The right man hadn't come along.

"I agree." Mary replied. "I'm just waiting until ..." Well, of late, she wasn't sure anymore. Maybe the right man didn't exist?

"See." Esther wagged her finger, appearing to read her doubts.

Mary made a face. Why did she have to date a man? Why couldn't she teach school for the rest of her life and be perfectly happy. She was self-sufficient. She took care of the schoolhouse. She came up each morning during the winter months to light the fire before the break of dawn, plus helped Dat with the chores at home. This, on top of planning the next day's lessons and checking the student's papers. Her wages weren't high, but high enough for a single woman to exist. Happily, too. So there!

Mary calmed herself. She had no hard feelings towards her family. In a way, she understood them. There was the custom of the community, and by the customs she should be dating. What she needed was a reset—a new start somewhere far, far away from here. A place where she could teach for another two years before the questions started again. Perhaps even an Amish community where they didn't mind a schoolteacher willing to dedicate her life to her students. If a good man couldn't be found, a good place might be discovered. By some miracle, there might be a man living there, a single guy who would impress her—Mary doubted severely. Like Esther declared so often, there were plenty of handsome men right here in the community. Her heart hadn't been captured yet. If she was destined to walk this world alone, the Lord would bless her as he had blessed tonight. Mary was convinced.

"Thank you, Lord," Mary said again, locking the schoolhouse door behind her. "Thank you for coming to this world as a baby and saving us from our sins. Thank you for loving us and giving the school a good program tonight."

CHAPTER 2

The partial moon hung over Mary's shoulder as she came down the schoolhouse steps and turned to gaze toward the horizon. The moon would be full in a few days when night would be turned into a miniature version of day. Already the world was flooded with a glorious light. There had been snow earlier in the year, but a warm spell this week had removed the beauty of a white snow cover for Christmas. The Lord knew what he was doing. Brown fields didn't remove the fact the Christ child had come to bless the world with his truth and grace.

Mary checked the eastern horizon where a bank of clouds rose high into the sky. She hadn't paid much attention to the weather with the rush of the school program on her mind. Maybe there would be snow by the morning? What a glorious thought. A white Christmas! Either way, she was happy, and would be happy tomorrow, if her sisters didn't torment her too much. Maybe by another miracle, the subject wouldn't be brought up.

Mary laughed at the thought of her sisters forgetting her unmarried status for even one day. She walked briskly across the schoolyard, headed towards home, swinging her arms, and soon broke into song. "Silent night, holy night, all is calm, all is bright." The words seemed more magnificent and grander, more befitting the great gift heaven had given the earth, when sung in German. "*Stille Nacht, heilige Nacht, Alles schlaff; einsam wacht.*"

The eight graders, Lily, Martha, and Gerald had sung the song tonight in German. They had done so well, and everyone had joined in for the last stanza. Mary's voice choked at the memory of the sacred hymn filling the entire schoolhouse with such a haunting and blessed melody.

"Oh, God be the glory!" Mary almost shouted into the night. There was no one to hear her, and if they did, they might shout back for joy.

Mary turned into her footsteps into the driveway and took the shortcut across the lawn. A light still shone in the living room window, so Mam and Dat had not gone to bed. They were working on last minute preparations for tomorrow, no doubt. Mary took the final two porch steps in a single bound and burst into the front door. As she expected, Dat was standing at the end of the two long tables which had replaced their regular dining room furniture before she left for school this morning. Mam was directing his moves, waving her arms about. "A little this way. Just a little more."

"Everything looks perfect." Mary called to them.

"I thought so." Dat grumbled.

Mam sighed and sat down. "Sorry. I guess I'm a little tense and can't see straight."

"Can I help with something?" Mary offered.

"There's still the ingredients for tomorrow morning's breakfast, which should be gathered together, so we can get an early start," Mam said.

"I'll get things ready." Mary told them. ""Both you and Dat rest on your rockers."

Dat chuckled. "Thanks, but I think I'll head to bed. By the way, what a great program tonight."

"You're very kind." Mary gave Dat a warm smile.

"You had the children at their best." Mam agreed, and got up to follow Mary into the kitchen.

"Sit." Mary ordered once they arrived. "No more work for you tonight."

"What would we do without you." Mam sighed again but took the kitchen chair. "Of course, I know you will be leaving home soon. I wouldn't want to keep you—"

Mary ignored the comment. "What time are you expecting the first people tomorrow morning."

"Neither of the girls said," Mam smiled through her tiredness, "but early I'm sure."

"I'll be up to help you." Mary assured her. "What do you want out for tonight."

"The bowls at least, for the flour and sugar we need for the bread. I don't want us making unnecessary noise which might wake Dat."

Mary worked silently, opening the pantry door and lining up the items on the counter.

"You're such a *goot* schoolteacher," Mamm continued, "just like your three sisters—"

"Look, Mam, it's late. We should get to bed." Mary gave Mam her best smile. "I love school teaching. Why should I stop?"

"I know how you feel." Mam's smile was weak. "There just is no reason why—I don't understand sometimes, though I do trust the Lord."

"I haven't found a man who has impressed me—shall we say, sufficiently. Can you trust me?"

Mam seemed not to hear. "I looked across the room tonight. So many young couples with small children. They will be sending them to the schoolhouse in a few years. You should be sending your own, not teaching their children. Others can fill your shoes in the schoolhouse, but only you can be a *wunderbah frau*, for some worthy man."

"Mam." Mary chided. "We really should go to bed."

Mam frowned. "There is something I should tell you. Your sisters said not to, but I don't feel right—"

"What is this?" Mary showed her alarm.

"Nothing, really." Mam tried to smile. "Esther has in-laws visiting. Cousins of her husband. They're coming tomorrow for breakfast."

"Looking for a *frau*, I suppose." Mary couldn't keep the bitterness out of her voice. "I love my sisters, but why can't they stop interfering."

"They mean well," Mam said. "I wouldn't have invited them, but your sisters thought—"

"I know." Mary pushed one of the bowls further from the edge of the counter. "I'm going to bed."

"You're not too upset?" Mam appeared worried.

"They won't eat me." Mary forced a laugh.

Mam's worried look didn't leave. "Maybe the Lord will move on your heart. Albert and Joseph were both in attendance tonight. I'm sure they were greatly pleased."

"I didn't see them." Mary helped Mam stand. "Go to bed, and everyone should stop worrying about my life."

Mary heard Mam muttering on the way to her bedroom door. "When my last girl says the wedding vows, I will get down on my knees and thank the Lord for a whole week."

Mary retreated upstairs. She closed the bedroom door and leaned against the dresser. Was there something wrong with her? The truth was she hadn't noticed Albert and Joseph tonight—or any other young men, because she hadn't been looking. The program had been too exciting, too engrossing, too consuming, to leave room for thoughts of some young man who wanted her attention. Maybe she should try to leave a place in her heart for men? Mam had seemed more worried than usual tonight.

Mary walked over to the bedroom window to gaze out into the night. She didn't normally indulge in dark introspection about life. Tomorrow was Christmas Day, and happy thoughts lay just around the corner, even with the low clouds gathering on the horizon. Dark weather could be the harbinger of snow over night? A blessing in disguise. A white Christmas indeed! Maybe Albert and Joseph were low hanging clouds who would bring a blessing for her tomorrow—or one of them at least. Fancy being impressed with two men at once and having to choose between them. Her sisters would never let her live down the experience. The Lord's vengeance, they doubtlessly would conclude.

She would keep her mind open—if not her heart. Nothing would happen, though, Mary was convinced. Best to concentrate on the upcoming *wunderbah* celebration of the Lord's birth. If snow fell overnight—well, she expected those kinds of things from the Lord. A husband? The Lord seemed perfectly content to allow her to enjoy life, teaching school, blessing her in ways she could understand. Her sisters would have to live with the Lord's ways, even when the road didn't follow expected paths. So, there!

Exhaustion from the long day swept over Mary, and she prepared for the night, climbing under the warm quilt to think once more of those words little Johnny Weaver had proclaimed so boldly at the school program earlier in the evening, "For unto us a child is born—"

Mary drifted off to sleep with visions of angels singing and cattle gathering around a manger gazing devoutly down at the young baby who would be the Savior of the world.

CHAPTER 3

The old windup alarm clock buzzed at precisely five o'clock. Mary groped twice with her hand before she found the round metal frame in the darkness and pushed in the stop button. She climbed out of bed to light the kerosene lamp on the dresser. The flame flickered, casting wild shadows on the bedroom walls. She studied the forms, trying to wake up. There was a decided chill in the room which wasn't removed by the steady rise of warm air from the wood furnace in the basement. Had snow fallen over night?

Mary stepped over to the window and pushed back the drapes. The soft glow of a late moon made the ground glitter with a white sheen.

"Praise the Lord," she whispered. "An extra special—special day. A white Christmas!"

Quickly, Mary dressed and tiptoed downstairs. There was no use in waking Mam. She could handle the initial preparations for the day. Mam always wanted bread baked fresh for a family gathering on Christmas morning, a tradition which had been in place since Mary could remember. She picked the largest bowl from the counter, taking care not to bang the sides of anything else. The silence of the kitchen surrounded her as Mary measured the flour. She added the other ingredients along with the milk. Soft footsteps came from the bedroom, as she began to stir.

Mam's accusing face appeared. "You should have woken me. I didn't set the alarm so I wouldn't wake Dat."

Mary gave Mam a crooked smile. "You could have slept in. I can handle the bread making."

Mam ignored the comment to bustle about the kitchen,

while Mary transformed the contents of the bowl into a thick dough. She spread flour on the table and rolled the dough into a long thread. Mam stood ready with her knife to cut the 6-inch-long pieces. Lined up on the kitchen table in their individual pans, they were left to rise slowly.

Mary carefully tucked several loose hairs back under her *kapp* with her fingers. The faint memory of an Albert and a Joseph who were scheduled to arrive for breakfast flickered in her mind. There must be no flour on her face when her sisters appeared. They would raise a fit if they found her in an unpresentable state.

"I think I hear someone coming," Mam said, tilting her head to listen.

"I do hear buggy wheels in the driveway." Mary agreed.

"They're here." Mam's face glowed with happiness. "Let me get Dat up."

"Let him sleep. The poor man is tired from yesterday." Mary begged on Dat's behalf.

Mam didn't respond, rushing towards the bedroom. Moments later, there was a soft knock on the front door. Mary stayed in place. Whichever of her sisters had arrived, they would come in on their own. The knock was simply to announce their presence. They might have either Albert or Joseph in tow, eager to make introductions at the front door.

Mam's footsteps scurried back from the bedroom, and whispered voices rose from the front door. Esther had made her appearance. Her voice was easily recognizable, while Lois and Phoebe were difficult to tell apart at the whisper range.

"*Goot* morning." Esther's eldest daughter, Johanna, greeted Mary from the kitchen doorway.

"*Goot* morning," Mary replied. "How was the ride over?"

"I rode with Albert and Joseph behind Mam and Dat's buggy." The five-year-old said, beaming.

"I'm sure the time with your Dat's cousins was special." Mary agreed.

She grimaced after Johanna scurried away. Surely the two men wouldn't make nuisances out of themselves by coming into the kitchen while she worked. Depending on what Esther had told them, they might have the boldness.

"Sisters." Mary muttered under her breath.

"How are you doing this morning?" Esther appeared instead of the men, her cheerful voice filling the kitchen.

"What have you been telling Albert and Joseph about me?" Mary accused.

Esther smiled her sweetest. "So, Mam told you."

"Unlike my sisters who scheme behind my back."

Esther's smile didn't waver. "You need help, dear. Lots of help."

Mary glowered. "Where are these—"

"I couldn't leave them at the house alone. Not with the family gathering here. My—how perfect the loaves are this morning. I never could cut bread sizes like Mam does."

"You're avoiding the subject!"

"Albert and Joseph are here. I brought them for Christmas breakfast. You wouldn't want me to leave them starving at home, would you?"

"Of course not, but—"

"You're soiling your dress with dough crumbs." Esther scolded.

"What other plans have you made for me today, or rather for me and—"

"None at all." Esther appeared perfectly innocent.

"Answer me." Mary ordered.

"Actually ..." Esther let the sentence hang for a long moment. "You can forget about Albert or Joseph. On further consideration, we agree with you, since you didn't even notice them last night. Lois is bringing a family friend—a friend of Jefferey's."

"Now you have your husbands in the game?"

"This is not a game." Esther appeared quite serious. "We have to get our youngest sister married. Your single status is almost a scandal in the community."

"Why does the school board want me to teach again next year?"

91

"Which you should have turned down." Esther ignored the point. "You need to focus on finding the right man."

"How about letting me make the search, instead of throwing men at me."

"More like gentle suggestions." Esther lowered her voice. "You need help. At least we can see you do, if the school board can't. They would have you teaching your entire life."

"So much for the community scandal." Mary shot back.

Esther ignored the comeback. "Just take a look at Jefferey's friend. I haven't seen him, but Lois seems to think he'd be a perfect match."

Mary huffed and studied the pans of rising bread dough.

"They look *goot*." Esther beamed. "Just think. You could be baking bread for a husband."

Mary didn't respond. Any reaction would only push Esther to further extremes. The matter was decided already. She didn't want to think about anything today, but the Lord's birth and the angels singing. Certainly, not about finding a husband.

They worked in silence, slicing and frying the bacon in a large metal tub, while Mam entertained the grandchildren in the living room. Thirty minutes later, Mary carefully placed the fully risen dough in the oven and set the timer.

"The others are here." Esther announced, leaning over the kitchen window for a better look. "Four buggies at once. Just like my family, coordinating their arrival."

"What did you say the name of this friend was?" Mary asked. She might as well be pleasant about the matter on Christmas Day.

Esther beamed. "Mose, and do give him a chance. Lois thinks he's a nice man."

"I'm usually not impressed." Mary warned.

"Talk to him, at least." Esther begged.

"I'll have to, if he speaks with me." Mary grumbled. "Which he will, with the hints Lois has doubtlessly been busy dropping in his head."

"Mose is such a nice name." Esther cooed. "You know, short for Moses from the mountain, the meekness man on earth."

"If he's meek, he'll take my no for a no, and leave me alone. So there!" Mary lifted her chin high.

Esther's smile remained as people poured into the house. Mary could see her sister hadn't given up hope, and there were still Lois and Phoebe to deal with. Those two hadn't begun to apply the pressure.

She couldn't resist peeking into the living room, though, where the adults mingled, shaking each other's hands and catching up on family news.

Three young men stood by the front door. Two of them appeared ordinary enough. She wouldn't have looked at them twice under any other situation, which probably explained why she had missed seeing Albert and Joseph last night. The other one—well, he was blond and—. Mary pulled back her head quickly when Mose began to turn his head towards the kitchen. He seemed to know someone was looking at him. He didn't appear meek. Not from her brief glimpse of his face. His unshaven chin was chiseled into a square at the bottom, his nose prominent without being protruding. She hadn't caught a glimpse of his eyes, but they were probably blue and piercing. The kind of man who thought women should be impressed when he humbled himself to speak with them.

Her sisters would pick such a man! Well, he would have to find out otherwise. She had more important things on her mind than men who wanted her attention.

CHAPTER 4

An hour later, Mary found herself seated on the left side of one of the long tables set up in the dining room. Mose had been placed straight across from her. His eyes were indeed blue and piercing. He had sent smiles her way twice—bold smiles—and she had yet to return them. She couldn't exactly send him a frown or a glare. Not at the family table where someone would notice. In Mose's defense, he wasn't to blame for where either of them was sitting. Mary could see though, from the bold look on his face, Mose was prepared to take full advantage of his opportunity—even if the true culprit, or culprits, were her sisters. All three of them had bright smiles on their faces, looking the essence of innocence. Mam was old school and wouldn't have dared place their name tags across from each other.

"*Goot* morning." Dat greeted everyone from his place at the head of the table. "I must say how wunderbah this day seems to me. How happy I am everyone could attend, including our visitors Albert and Joseph, and this young man—?"

Mose raised his shaven, square chin to face Dat. "Mose Swartz, from Holmes County."

Dat smiled. "Ahhh—the land of swizz cheese and trail baloney."

Mose laughed along with the others. "And a few other things," he said.

"Indeed." Dat agreed. "What do you work at."

"I run a siding crew, traveling the state. Wherever the work goes, we go."

Mary was sure Mose gave her a quick glance, doubtlessly to make sure she noticed his well-traveled status, and upward mobility in the Amish world.

"Sounds like an interesting job," Dat said.

Mam nudged Dat with her elbow. "You can visit later. The food is getting cold."

Dat cleared his throat. "Yah, this is true. The food is prepared, spread out before us, delicious food as always, so let us pray."

Mose gave Mary another quick look before he bowed his head. There would be an attempt at conversation after the prayer, Mary was certain. The man was pleasant enough to look at. There was no question there. Maybe she could act a little impressed, and not lose the full enjoyment of the day because of her sister's constant meddling in her life.

"Lord, our gracious God, and the source of all blessing," Dat prayed. "Grant us the favor of your presence this morning in our humble gathering. We are so grateful for family, for the many gifts you give us, and most of all for the gift of your Son to grant of grace and pardon and the hope of eternal life. Bless this food. Bless Mam and my daughters for their hard work and diligent concern for the family. Be with us, give us the blessing of your spirit's guidance. May we part this afternoon being the richer for having known each other and the great grace of your Son, Jesus. Amen."

"Amen," Mose said, quite loudly. There were other murmurs of agreement, but Mose had made sure his voice stood out.

Mary kept her gaze fixed on the plates of food spread out on the table. Why did the man have to act so full of himself? Happy thoughts were usually filling her at this moment. Pancakes steamed under cloth coverings. The eggs were in a covered dish, with the bacon and sausage receiving the same treatment. Cottage cheese sat in open bowls, beside the sticks of golden butter. There was heated and unheated maple syrup. Mary forced herself to smile, as the pancakes were passed around, followed by the meat and eggs.

Mose soon leaned across the table to ask. "Do you have this gathering every year?"

"Somewhere," she said, sweetly enough, "either here or at one of my sister's places."

"What a great tradition. I'm impressed."

"You don't have family traditions?" Mary couldn't resist asking.

Mose appeared unfazed, helping himself to three pancakes. "We have plenty of them, but not for Christmas morning breakfast. We usually get together in the evening after supper. I'll have to take the idea home with me."

"You should." Mary lifted a pancake on to her place, not looking at Mose.

"How many men are on your siding crew?" Esther joined the conversation, clearly trying to help.

"Three of us," Mose answered. "Only takes three good men to side a home in a day."

"A day—" Esther trailed out the word. "What hard workers."

"We have been trained in the latest techniques." Mose made an obvious attempt at humility. "Lots of men have been doing this before us."

"Sounds very interesting," Esther continued. "Do you get into Cleveland and the other big cities?"

"We have been in the suburbs of Cleveland once, but mostly Akron and Canton."

"Have you gone boating or fishing on Lake Erie?" Esther asked, giving her husband Conrad a liberal helping of bacon before taking several pieces for herself.

"Thank you." Conrad gave his wife a surprised smile.

Mary wanted to give Esther a long glare. Wives should serve their husbands, she knew, but Esther didn't usually place food items directly on to Conrad's plate. Esther had done so for Mose's benefit. Mose was supposed to envision a future where he was served hand and foot by Esther's sister. Like Mose needed any encouragement. Unless she persuaded him otherwise, there would be a request for a date before

Mose left this afternoon. She had to calm down, though, and not blame Mose. From the signals he was receiving from her sisters, she was desperate for a husband.

"There is a group of us who go out once a year," Mose was saying. "Mostly young guys who can afford such a thing. The fishing is awesome with a decent guide who knows the waters."

"There must be plenty of income with such a high paying job." Esther egged him on.

"Are you trying to tell me something?" Conrad interrupted. He didn't look too happy.

Mary hid her smile. For once Esther was overplaying her hand with someone who could dial her back effectively.

"Maybe we could all three go together on a fishing trip sometime." Phoebe jumped to her sister's aid. "The expense wouldn't be too much split three ways with three couples. Think of the memories we could make."

"I guess we could think about this." Conrad allowed. "I didn't know you women wanted to go out on Lake Erie."

"I wasn't trying to make trouble." Mose appeared quite uncomfortable. "I mean, these trips aren't awfully expense. Otherwise I couldn't afford them."

"There you go." Esther's smile was pained. "I think we should entertain new ideas sometimes."

"Especially in the wintertime when the snow is on the ground." Mary deadpanned.

Everyone turned to look at her.

"I think a fishing trip on Lake Erie is exactly what my sisters need to spice up their lives," Mary continued. For once she had turned the tide to her sister's laps.

Conrad managed to grin. "I have to admit, I never thought of a fishing trip out on the lake, but who knows? What do you think Jeffery and John? Should we plan one?"

Neither of the two had been listening to the conversation and were quickly filled in on the details by Conrad. In the meantime, Mary took her sister's glares with glee. She knew neither of the three had liked to wade in the creek behind

Grandpa's house during their growing up years. Not like she did, at least. She couldn't imagine them enjoying boating or fishing on Lake Erie. No wonder the question had never come up with their husbands. Maybe this would teach them to stop meddling in her life?

Conrad had turned back to Mose. "Could you give us details on the guide outfits and perhaps the cost before you leave today. We might have to get serious about the idea next summer."

"Lake Erie has a lot of water." Esther glanced furtively at Conrad.

"Well, of course," he said. "Water as far at the eye can see, which is part of the fun."

"I don't know about so much water," Esther said. "I mean—"

"I understand what she means." Phoebe joined in. "Water right up to horizon—"

Mose shrugged. "We do go out a few miles, but you can usually still see the shoreline."

"Surely you girls aren't scared of the water?" Conrad was looking about skeptically. "Have you heard this before, boys?"

Jefferey and John both shook their heads. "Neither of them has said anything about a fear of water."

"Look what we've been missing," Conrad said, quite triumphantly. "With a little pinching of pennies, these three families will have their horizons greatly broadened."

Jeffery and John didn't appear quite on board yet, but the conversation had begun. Mary saw a vision in her mind of her three sisters in a small fishing boat, one like the twelve disciples were in during the night of the nearly disastrous storm, hanging on to the rails for dear life. What a shame she wouldn't be there to observe the scene. She didn't dare look at either of her sisters, less she burst out laughing right here at the Christmas breakfast table.

CHAPTER 5

Mary remained in her chair after breakfast had been eaten, the dishes pushed back from the edge of the table, listening to Dat read the Christmas story from Luke chapter two. He had taken the time to read the last part of chapter one where Zacharias had prophesied about the coming birth of the Christ child. "Blessed be the Lord God of Israel; for he hath visited and redeemed his people, and hath raised up an horn of salvation for us in the house of his servant David; As he spake by the mouth of his holy prophets, which have been since the world began. That we should be saved from our enemies, and from the hand of all that hate us."

How precious were those words. Dat didn't usually read them, but he had this morning. The whole day was special, even with Mose sitting across the table with his frequent glances fixed on her. There was something stirring inside of her, a hunger for new beginnings, for fresh horizons. Her sisters would say—for a husband, but they were wrong. All three appeared fully recovered from the conversation about a planned fishing trip to Lake Erie this summer. Her sisters would enjoy the venture—once they were out on the water. Who wouldn't? Maybe she needed an adventure. Not a fishing trip to the lake, but a new community perhaps. One where she could do what she did so well—teach school, without the constant oversight of her sisters. What a perfect blend of old and new. Who could guess where the road would lead? Perhaps even to a husband, but Mary doubted. If handsome Mose didn't impress her, who could?

Dat finished reading and closed the bible. "The Lord be praised," he said. "We have a Savior."

"Amen," Mose proclaimed again. A little quieter this time. He gave Mary a pleased smile, and her breath caught for a moment. His eyes were piercing and quite blue. She was imagining things though. Mose was a pleasant sight, but a man should also have her heart. She wanted a husband who could hold her tenderly, who would be brave and gallant at the same time. Mose was hardly the man.

Despite her thoughts, Mary returned Mose's smile, which was exactly the wrong move. Here she was encouraging him instead of discouraging him. Well—she would have to deal with the damage later. No one could fault her for smiling at a handsome man. Smiling wasn't the same as wanting to say the wedding vows with him.

Dat led out in another prayer, and everyone pushed back their chairs afterward. The men moved away from the dining room, while the woman began to work clearing the table. Mary had made two trips to the kitchen with stacks of dirty dishes when the sound of a man clearing his voice at her shoulder stopped her.

Mary turned to see Mose with a sheepish look on his face. "There are plenty of women working. Any chance I could—"

"Go!" A passing Esther ordered. "He's right. We're fine here."

Had Esther put him up to this? Hardly. Even Esther had her limits.

"How about a little walk outside?" Mose's sheepish look was gone. "The day has warmed up considerably."

She didn't want to, but on the other hand she was tired of saying no. This wasn't a request for a date. One might follow. Which was a bridge crossed in its own good time.

"Please?" Mose didn't quite look as if he was begging. "I'm leaving next week."

Mary finally shrugged. "Sure. I'll get my coat. Meet me out on the front porch."

Esther was whispering furiously to Lois and Phoebe when Mary walked into the kitchen.

"Just say yes." Phoebe gushed. "He's so handsome."

Mary ignored them to slip out into the washroom and pull on a light coat. Mose was waiting for her at the bottom of the steps with a pleased look on his face.

"Nice day," he said, "and a nice place you have here."

"Dat keeps it up."

"Shall we?" Mose motioned towards the road.

"We can walk back to the woods. The cows have cleared the path by now." Mary suggested. A passing buggy might see them on the road, and the rumors would spread. Mary finally has a boyfriend!

"Perfect." Mose motioned again. "Lead the way."

The man clearly believed he was in charge, but most Amish men did. Mary gave him a smile. She might as well be nice. In her heart she wasn't inconsiderate or unwilling to spend time with unmarried men. What usually followed was the problem.

"They tell me you teach school." Mose was right at her shoulder as they crossed the barn yard.

"Yep! You heard right."

"Love the job?"

"Who couldn't love school teaching?" Mary laughed.

"Spoken like a born teacher, but teaching is not for me."

"Did you ever think about teaching school?"

"Nah. Men usually don't, and there was the siding job. I started young, learning the trade."

"Sounds like plenty of adventures are involved." Mary glanced up at his chiseled chin. The man was even more handsome close up than from a distance.

"School teacher has its adventures, I'd guess." He grinned.

"Not quite like fishing on a lake, but we did put on a *goot* Christmas program last night. The children were awesome."

"You love children?" He glanced down at her.

"I do, and I love school teaching."

"Are you planning to teach again next year?"

"The school board has to make the request."

He looked skeptical. "If you're a *goot* teacher, I'm sure they have made their desires known."

"They have." Mary admitted.

"Have you accepted?"

"Not yet."

He looked very pleased. "Are you keeping your options open?"

"Depends what you mean," she said, not looking at him. She knew exactly what he meant. The man was bold, indeed.

"Your sister said you've put in your two terms."

"Who says I can't put in more?" Mary shot back.

He didn't miss a beat. "You must have other interests, or you would have agreed when the school board asked."

"There's a black-capped chickadee on the fence," Mary said, changing the subject. "We have quite a few of those around in the winter. Our woods must support them well. I've thought about putting out a bird feeder, but never got around to placing my thoughts into action."

"Are you a bird watcher?" Mose asked.

"I know my birds." Mary shrugged. "Not quite a bird watcher, though."

"Not enough of an interest to take you away from school teaching."

Mary pretended to miss the point. "I don't think so." Why couldn't the man enjoy a walk back a woodsy path on a snowy day without bringing up marriage.

"I know a few birds," he said, "but I'm not a bird watcher, either."

"There should be some white-breasted nuthatches at the woods edge."

"We'll have to keep out a sharp eye," he said. "I do find birds enjoyable."

Mary was careful to hide her sigh of relief. Maybe this walk would turn into a half pleasant one.

"What a surprise this snow was," he said.

"Yah, I know." Mary agreed. "The Lord has chosen to bless us."

"Have you ever visited Holmes County?" he asked.

Mary shook her head.

"I didn't think so." He made a point of gazing admiringly at her. "I can't see how I would have missed you."

"Look!" Mary pointed. "A flock of snow buntings. How perfect."

"They are beautiful birds." He didn't miss a beat. "Another of the Lord's blessings."

"We don't have a creek like Grandpa does," Mary continued.

"You like water?"

"I love water. A brook bubbling in the summer is a special thing. Even in wintertime—the water pushing out over the ice in places. The Lord God made everything."

"You talk like a schoolteacher." He grinned.

"Are you saying—?"

"Certainly not." Mose didn't hesitate. "I loved all my schoolteachers when I attended."

Mary marched on. She wasn't going to get away from the subject of marriage apparently, but the day and the walk could still be enjoyed. Behind her, Mose hurried to keep up.

CHAPTER 6

Dusk was falling outside the kitchen window by the time everyone had left for the day. Mary sat on the bench along the far wall, while Mam occupied a kitchen chair, a soft smile on her face. They were resting from the day activities. Esther, Lois, and Phoebe had made sure the house was spotless before the last buggy rolled out of the driveway. Mary wasn't tired—not really, more like restless. She had enjoyed the day, even the short walk with Mose, but something was missing.

"I see you went for a walk with the man I hadn't seen before," Mam said, her voice hopeful.

"Yes." Mary didn't feel like volunteering information, but Mam had right to now. "He's nice enough. He likes birds."

Mam's disappointment clearly showed.

"Maybe I'm a confirmed spinster?" Mary made a face.

"You're the best looking of my daughters." Mam protested. "There's no reason you shouldn't have a husband by now."

"Must we go over this again? Please Mam. Esther and Phoebe have been pestering me the entire day. I'm just not impressed—yet."

"The right one will come along," Mam said, but didn't look very convinced.

"He didn't ask for a date," Mary said, trying to justify herself a little.

"Is he staying over the weekend?"

"Yes. He did mention he was."

"He will ask," Mamm said. "You should accept. I was impressed with him, from what I could see."

"As were my three sisters, but I wasn't. They would marry me to any man who asked."

Mam's smile was thin. "I don't think we are in such desperate straits—yet."

"Thank you!"

"I'm worried though. I pray much, but I still worry. Word will get around soon about you always saying no, and the right man might never ask. Men can get to such a state. They give up."

Mary attempted a laugh, but Mam's words stung. "Maybe I need a fresh start. Move somewhere no knows anything about me. Where I don't have three sisters watching and criticizing my every step."

"Esther, Lois, and Phoebe love you. Don't even think such things." Mam warned.

Mary nodded, her mind racing. The very idea sent her blood racing. Another place where she could be her own person. Same person really, but a new person somehow, with a fresh start without the buzzing of her sister's voices in her head. Had the grace of Christmas Day planted the blessed desire in her heart.

"What are you thinking?" Mam sounded suspicious.

Mary felt her whole body tingling. "Don't other communities need schoolteachers?"

"Yes." Mam's alarm hadn't vanished. "What does this have to do with you? You have a job school teaching."

Mary ignored the point. "Where would I find this information? Find out without—" She could imagine exactly what Esther and Phoebe would say, and Lois hadn't even started to voice her opinion.

"Why would you want to know what other communities are looking for schoolteachers?"

"There must be a way." Mary was only half listening to Mam. "I guess I could ask Mose, but he would think—"

"You have me completely confused," Mam said.

"I think I know what I want."

Mam leaned forward with hope in her voice. "You will consider Mose when he asks for a date tomorrow?"

Before Mary could deny the question, Dat appeared in the kitchen doorway. "Relaxing, I see, after a long hard day."

Mam's face lit up with a smile. "Thanks for seeing everyone off. This day was a very blessed one."

"Blessed indeed." Dat pulled out a chair and sat down. "Your children have turned out very well."

Mam patted him on the arm. "I think they are also your children."

Dat turned towards Mary. "Did you enjoy the day?"

"I did. Immensely. Thanks for reading the extra Scripture this morning."

Dat nodded. "I thought the words appropriate, somehow."

"They were." Mary assured him. "I think the Lord may have just given me an inspiration."

"On Christmas Day? Finally, a decent man who has caught your attention."

Mary couldn't hide her smile. "Not quite."

"What did you think of Mose?" Mam interrupted.

"About what I thought of some of the others," Dat said. "I think Mary should make up her own mind, though."

"See, Dat isn't worried in the least." Mary justified herself.

"I guess he has a point." Mam agreed. "I wouldn't want you in an unhappy marriage."

"What was this inspiration?" Dat asked, looking very interested.

Mary plunged forward. "Where would I find out if other communities need schoolteachers?"

Dat raised his eyebrows. "You have a school teaching job."

"Exactly my point." Mam jumped in.

Dat ignored Mam to ask. "You wouldn't really, would you?"

"Don't you just think this might—"

Dat appeared pensive. "Maybe. None of my daughters have taught in other communities, but you have been here for two years."

Mary tried to control her excitement. "This would be the perfect answer."

"You don't really mean—" Mam's worried look was back.

"I'm sure Mary would make this a matter of prayer," Dat said. "I can't see her rushing into anything. I suppose Mose found this out today."

Mary ignored the reference to Mose. "Thank you. How can I know where these opportunities are?"

"The Budget," Dat said. "I'll keep an eye out for you. If I see an advertisement from some place decent, I'll let you know."

Mary gave him a big smile. "Oh, you're so wunderbah."

"Just taking care of my daughter." Dat smiled back.

"This will take lots of prayer." Mam muttered. "Lots and lots of, oh, I don't know—"

Mary patted Mam on the arm. "Not a word to any of my sisters. Not even a breath. Not until I'm pulling out of the driveway on the way to the bus station."

"There haven't been any ads yet." Dat stated the obvious.

"I know." Mary tried to keep her excitement under control.

"There's still a chance to give Mose a *goot* answer tomorrow," Mam said. "You might have another inspiration before then."

Which was highly unlikely, but this was Christmas Day. "Maybe you're right." Mary forced herself to say. "I'll keep my mind open."

"And I'll keep my eyes peeled for any ads," Dat said, standing to his feet. "What time is supper."

"You're hungry!" Mam exclaimed. "We've been eating all day."

"Get the man some food." Mary stuck up for Dat. "I think I'm hungry myself with these happy inspirations I'm having."

Dat grinned. "I'll be in the living room. No rush."

"Are you really serious?" Mam asked, once Dat left. "Moving somewhere strange and teaching school."

"I don't know." Mary hugged herself. "I'm just very excited now. I think the Lord is going to bless me greatly."

"With a husband," Mam said, hopeful again.

"There are other blessings in life other than a husband," Mary couldn't help from saying, "but if I do meet the right man, I will welcome him with an open heart."

"May the day come quickly," Mam said, already distracted. "We have to get supper ready for Dat."

"I'll help you." Mary busied herself at the counter, gathering the leftovers from the day's feasting. While she worked her mind was spinning, seeing endless possibilities, seeing happiness lying on the horizon. The Lord was going to bless. With a husband? She found the idea hard to imagine, but school teaching successfully in another wunderbah community. There, she had the faith to believe.

"What a blessed Christmas day." Mary breathed the prayer heavenward. "Thank you, dear Lord. Thank you so much."

EPILOGUE—

To discover how Mary's life continues, whether Mose will have success winning her affections, or if there is a new community on the horizon, read *The Amish School Teacher*. Available where books are sold.

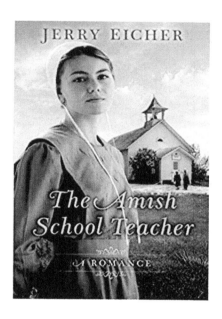

ABOUT THE AUTHOR

Jerry Eicher was born to Amish parents, and raised in an Amish settlement in Honduras, Central America. The family returned stateside in the late seventies, when Jerry was sixteen. He spent his youth with a beloved Amish youth group in Belle Center, Ohio, and was married in 1983 to Tina Schmucker, whose parents had moved to the community from Nappanee, Indiana.

Jerry and Tina left the Amish to join the Mennonites after the birth of their second son. He wrote his first work in the early twenties, a fictionalized version of his childhood in Central America. His second title was an Amish love story— *Sarah*. Since then Jerry has published over thirty fiction titles and sold nearly a million books.

A CHRISTMAS ROSE—

SEASONS OF HANNAH SERIES
WILLARD CARPENTER

PROLOGUE

TAKING FLIGHT

Sitting on the flight from Lehigh Valley International in the Lehigh Valley in Pennsylvania to Dothan, Alabama, I have the opportunity to start writing a Christmas story and an opportunity to follow up on James's and Hannah's life and what they had gone through.

I think of these contrasts again. Jacob and Isaac come to mind as they had met in a partially plowed field. Both had been caught up in the reality of the *Ordnung*, the Old Order laws within the church, contrasted with what they had discovered in Jesus Christ—grace, and salvation. The realization of salvation is forbidden within the *Ordnung* because to assume something of God's is considered proud and boastful. What had them in even greater trouble was sharing the good news of Christ and the *Englisch* bible. The Bishop had become upset with them. They had been shunned.

Hannah, daughter of Jacob, faced her own contrasts and contradictions. As she neared the end of her *rumspringa* or running-around-years, Hannah had fallen in love with James, an *Englischer* that her father, Jacob, didn't know anything about. To complicate matters, both her father and his friend Isaac had expected she would settle down with Isaac's son Abram.

Hannah and Abram had been friends since childhood. Amish women have expectations once baptized: become part of the community, marry, and obey their husbands.

Hannah had jumped the fence—left her family and her community. She herself was shunned. Hannah is now living with James's family—return you to their story.

I had been to Fort Rucker in the past visiting my youngest son, Mark. I had found it to be a peaceful place as to state of mind. The United States Army trains its pilots there, ergo outside the state of mind there is at any one time the sound of the dull beat of helicopter blades as they pass over head or in the distance.

Fort Rucker is in the woods. I had arranged thru James to stay on post, lake side at Lake Tholocco, just as Mark had arranged for his mother and I to stay there with his grandparents, my wife's mother and father for his graduation. I would be in the East Beach Cabins where I could enjoy the red sunsets on the lake.

I have plans to set up my laptop on the table within the screened back porch.

Perfect, five days of relative peace and tranquility. Even the rain would be welcome as I love the sound of patter as it hits the porch roof, sometimes softly other times violently. I will couple this with John Barry sound tracts on Pandora and I will be in that perfect place. A lot of writing is going to get done there. We are a half an hour out of Atlanta, Georgia. This was a quick flight, I will pick this back up on the ground.

I have found a southern restaurant within my terminal while I wait for the next flight. I had some buttered grits and hush puppies for a snack with a little sweet tea to wash down the savory delight. Now back on the next plane for the final leg of my journey into Dothan and a rental.

A short flight—the plane is half full and will make it easy to grab my carryon and make my way off the flight. While on the plane I make a quick call to Michele, my wife.

"On the ground in Dothan" I tell her.

"Be safe and have fun," she responds.

Just outside security at the small airport was baggage claim and the car rentals. Standing in front of the nearest car rental? Hannah, with a huge smile. "Hi, Wil ... surprise!"

"Yes, it is," I respond, returning the smile, "what are—"

I'm cut off with, "James sent me."

"James, sent you?"

"Ja, would you like to drive?" she asks, holding up the keys.

I had to ask, "How did you get here?"

Laughing, Hannah responds simply, "I drove, silly," giggling.

We walked and I thought, *Hannah drives, never thought I'd see that. We certainly are far away from horse and buggy.*

"You drive. It's been a few years since I've been down here—besides you know I've got to see this." Reaching their late model blue Hyundai Accent, I threw my luggage into the trunk and settled into the passenger seat as she had already started the car.

The drive becomes familiar as we make our way west to Enterprise. Hannah with her aviator glasses and long blond hair blowing in the wind keeps my attention as she begins to fill in the pieces since "jumping the fence." She is very comfortable, a natural, driving as she speaks and occasionally glancing over smiling.

Noticing the familiar shopping areas to my right, I ready my driver's license to get thru the all but very familiar Enterprise Gate. Military Police, a young woman no taller than five foot four in OCP (operational camouflage pattern) uniform with a badge and holstered 9 mm greets us with the traditional, "Welcome home, ma'am!"

Surprisingly, Hannah responds, "Above the best."

As I mutter the same words under my breath, the MP looking over at me, smiles and replies, "Good evening, sir, welcome back!"

Hannah, where have you come from? Where are you now? Except for the slight Pennsylvania Dutch accent, you are another officer's wife. "Hannah, pull up over there to the left—gas station."

"No," she responds.

I insist and up the hill she goes. "It's the least I can do!"

Hannah responds, "Okay, danke, thank you."

Upon entering the little cabin just for me, I am met by a potted evergreen sitting all by itself on the kitchen table. "What's this," I ask while pulling the plant over and taking in the essence of the ever late blooming flower.

"A story," replies Hannah, again with her captivating smile, and she continues, "It was a very special gift to James, it kept me company. Now this very special plant will keep you company. It's a Christmas rose."

CHAPTER I

LEMON'S BITTERNESS

When given lemons, they say, "Yes, make lemonade!" The greens and freshness of summer with its bright yellow roses and its welcoming fragrance along a walkway will shortly give way to the contrast of grays and crimson colors.

September has arrived in Honey Brook. With fall's bold colors around the corner, comes James's imminent departure for Fort Sam Houston in San Antonio, Texas. Sunday will be the first day. In all their excitement, neither Hannah nor James has had time to understand they will be separated.

James's family as a whole all left for church. Church has taken on a deeper and more personal significance. Without Hannah, this time would be difficult enough with their oldest, James, leaving.

It is a time of change. It is a bitter time. James, though he knows where he is going, doesn't know how his future will see itself through. The little nuances are missing. Only his faith in an all knowing God is for certain. Then again, sometimes that lingering doubt creeps in. The pastor, as he prayed for all who are in the military this day, prayed for James and his safety and for his family to have peace.

Brunch masked the otherwise somber church service at Living God Lutheran Church in Honey Brook, Pennsylvania. Everyone had turned cheerful, with Hannah laughs about what James wears to church—button-up, short sleeve shirt over shorts and sandals.

"What?" says James, while looking down at himself.

Hannah again looks over at him and smirks, "Ach!" she begins ...

James interrupts with, "Oh no, anything beginning with Ach is not good!" as the entirety of the table erupts in laughter.

"Was!" exclaims Hannah, now looking around the table.

Michael chimes in, "What? He's right, Ach is usually not good. You're in trouble, son." Grinning, he looks over at James. "Well, you know one of those warning signs going into a marriage."

Eileen, taking exception, begins, "Warning signs! Warning! What warning signs?" She laughs.

Michael, quickly quiets, looks over at James and whispers, "See, those."

James reaches over and pulls Hannah to himself, kisses her on the front of her Kapp-covered head. "God, I am certain, is okay with my wearing shorts. He knows my heart and soul, my thoughts."

"Ja," agrees Hannah as she stares into James's eyes, "but shorts and sandals?" Laughter erupts again.

"I love how you two look at each other," says Cecelia, as she continues, "I want that in my life someday."

Constance sitting next to her sister and directly across from Hannah says, "So do I." while she stares at Hannah, smiling.

"When is your flight again, James?" asks Michael.

"Saturday, Dad."

Hannah quickly becomes quiet and sniffles.

"Hannah, when James leaves, how about I take you to get your Learner's Permit?"

"Learner's Permit?" questions Hannah.

Constance quickly responds, "You can learn how to drive! Isn't that great?"

Hannah, perks up, "Can I?"

"Yes, let's do that," smiles Michael with finality.

The warmness of the first September day had come and gone quickly. In the quiet of the house from downstairs in the kitchen can be heard Michael's voice calling, "James."

"Yes, Dad?"

"Come on in here. Let's have a chat, son."

James enters the kitchen as his father pours coffee.

"A little decaf?" asks Michael.

"Yes, sure, Dad. Thanks, what's up?"

The single cup maker completes its pour, and Michael pulls out the cup placing it in front of James as he picks up the Italian sweet cream and begins pouring.

"Your mother and I would like for you to know it is okay that in those times when Hannah or you are in an emotional way or hurting, lonely, if you happen to fall asleep together, well it's ok ..."

"Dad, Hannah and I ... I promised her ... we can't ... we won't have sex," stammers James.

"I'm not talking about sex, James. Sleeping together isn't only about sex. Love is many things. It is also giving. Giving of one's self emotionally, spiritually, physically to reassure, physically to show warmth, physically to show security. Sleeping together is sharing many things besides sex. I'm not promoting sex. I'm promoting the time together in sharing, giving. You'll figure out the rest. Son, you won't be judged by us. We trust the two of you."

They looked at each other for some time, quiet, sharing the moment between father and son. James takes a final sip, stands and reaches out his hand, but his father says, "Come here," as they meet half way round the table and hug. "I love you, son."

"I love you too, Dad. Oh, Dad, thanks."

"You're welcome, son." Michael smiles. "I'm proud of the man you've become."

James, looking back, smiles too, "Thanks, Dad."

Returning upstairs, James hears a soft crying coming from Hannah's room. Two familiar voices from his childhood can be heard consoling her.

Hannah cries. She cries with Cecelia holding her and cradling her face with her hand as Constance holds her hand tightly within her own looking at her sister as if asking, *what can we do?*

"Hannah, everything will be okay," says Constance, reassuring with tone of her voice softened. "We love you and we will be here with you."

"Ach, everything is changing so quickly! Cecelia is leaving for college. Constance, you are back in school, and ... and ... James is ... leaving!" Quickly dissolving into uncontrolled tears, she wraps her arms around Cece as Constance stands.

"I'm getting a damp cloth." As she opens the door, she is met by James standing there with a solemn look in his eyes.

"Hi, Connie. Cee, I'll take it from here. Thanks, sis!" Stepping in, he looks down at Hannah, eyes full of tears, looking up at him.

The two loving sisters in their pj's, Cece with tears in her own eyes leave, closing the door softly.

"James!" Hannah bursts into tears again, simultaneously enveloping him within her arms. "James! Hold me! Please, don't let me go, please hold me."

Hannah reaches up for him as he sits and takes her into his arms, pulling her close, kissing away one, then another tear. Placing his lips on her through the sniffles, he kisses her softly, pulling away, whispers, "I love you, I'm here, shh ... I'm here."

A single whimper can be heard from Hannah as she begins to breath normally. James kicks off his shoes, pushing them off the bed. The clunking sound doesn't stir Hannah. Another kiss and Hannah quiets.

James repositions her in bed, and she whispers, "Don't leave."

"Okay," responds James, first sliding in behind her, cuddling, wrapping his right arm around her, burying his face into her hair. He takes in the familiar essence of lilac. Clasping his hand, she pulls his arm closer, pressing him against her softness. James, lost in feeling, thinks, *I understand, Dad, this is where I belong. I am so tired.* James hunches up and kisses his tomorrow on the cheek softly, one final time for the night, before settling in for a long night's rest.

They are awoken briefly after daybreak by Cece and Constance both saying goodbye as Cece leaves for college and Connie leaves for the morning. "Go back to sleep," says Connie as she pulls the door closed.

Hannah, smiling, closes her eyes and again pulls James's arm into herself, kissing his hand. James mumbles, "um-hm ..." drifting off unbothered. Both sleep off the bitterness of the season's lemons.

CHAPTER 2

LEMON'S SWEETNESS

From outside the window, within the still green trees, can be heard many birds chirping, which has awakened the Longacre family for the many years they have lived and grown here.

Today is no different as James and Hannah find themselves awakening to the chirping. Hannah opens her eyes. Sensing someone behind her, she slowly rolls over.

James, in T-shirt and shorts, comes into her peripheral vision as longing overcomes her. Reaching out with her left hand, she caresses his cheek. James leans forward and kisses her lips. "Good morning." He smiles, taking her hand and kissing her fingers.

Rolling completely over and onto James, Hannah smiles from atop and kisses James again, deeply. Her eyes inches from his, she stares and says, "You spent the night."

"Yes, I did. Are you okay with this?"

Nodding her head yes, she continues, "I needed you so badly. I have so many feelings that are all jumbled up. Sometimes, I need just to cry. Sometimes, I need to just be held. All the time, I need you to be there and understand. Just be there."

"I'm here," says James, reaching up to meet her lips, and again, softly. "I love you."

Passionately they begin to make out, and again tempered, they stop, and Hannah, in a panic, exclaims "Ach! What of your parents?" Rolling off and sitting straight up, she continues, "Your parents are going to be so angry ..."

"Hannah! Stop! No, they won't. Shh, they are fine. They both have spoken about this happening and are fine with it."

Hannah stares in disbelief and continues, "It, this sleeping together, is okay?"

"Yes, they understand. They aren't giving permission for us to have sex whenever we want. They do however understand that there will be nights like last night."

"We cannot have sex before marriage! Ne, but, I slept gut last night, ja."

"Good, then very good. So, did I. I like holding you."

"James, danke."

"You're welcome," smiles James. "Now I have to get a shower. We still have much to do."

Hannah reaches over and kisses James once more, agreeing, "Ja, so do I, go! I'm first!" as she grabs clothes and pushes past James towards the bathroom. Squealing with laughter, she rushes into the bathroom.

"Huh, wait ... my idea! Okay, I'll get my stuff, then!" He makes his way to his room, laughing, as he spots his mother at the bottom of the steps.

"You two up? Good! How is Hannah?"

"Good, Mom, she is good!"

Smiling, she says, "Breakfast is ready."

A moment later, they hear the shower, and Hannah's, "Ahh ..."

"Good morning, Mom. My mother's raisin bread—what are you making?" asks Hannah.

"Good morning, I am making French toast with sausage." Eileen looks up and over her shoulder. "Are you feeling better?"

"Ja, James held me," Hannah continues pacing. "I have so many feelings inside of me. James understands."

Eileen, sensing something, interjects, "Hannah, sit! You are making me nervous. I'm guessing you fell asleep in

James's arms. Many times, I have fallen asleep in Dad's arms, many times. I understand."

Looking up sheepishly, Hannah smiles. "Danke, thank you."

Smiling back, Eileen whispers, "you're welcome. Hannah, you are loved."

Hannah responds, "I know, I am so grateful for all of you. You have seen my mother again?" She looks at the raisin bread being sliced for French toast.

Eileen, with the last plate of Raisin Bread French Toast, looks out the door calling, "James!"

"I'm here, Mom," responds James, rounding the corner into the kitchen. Coming up behind Hannah he wraps her up and kisses her neck from behind. "Hey, you."

Eileen looks at James. "Good morning!"

Smiling, James responds, "Good morning, Mom!"

"Hannah, yes, I had seen your mom on Saturday. I was going to tell you, but we had all been so busy. She is doing very well, but she misses you. Ruth and Sarah were both there.

"Where are we going, James?" asks Hannah as she lowers herself into the car. She quiets, as James's mother comes out.

"Mom," says James opening the back door to the car.

"Thank you. You know where you are going, James?"

James smiles, "Uh-huh!"

"Where are we going?" Hannah asks again.

Climbing in, James leans over and kisses Hannah on the lips.

Unexpectedly, she looks cross-eyed and asks again in German, "Was es Das?"

James repeats what she asked in English, "What is this? You'll see! We're making some changes."

"Ok, James. We'll carry you on our insurance until you are back and married. Then you'll have to go out on your own, okay?"

"Yes, ma'am," answers James as he backs out of the driveway.

It was about an hour drive to Limerick. They passed the outlets on the right when the turn signal came on to exit. Hannah, quiet, just looked over at James, then back at Eileen, who just simply returned a smile.

"What are we doing here?" Hannah asks again as James pulls into the Hyundai dealer.

"Buying you a car!" responds James. "Should I say buying us a car."

"Buying a car?!" exclaims Hannah.

"Yes, nothing fancy, something easy. Mom and Dad gave us the down payment. You are going to take driving lessons. You'll have a little more independence. I think that covers it all. No! What color do you like? We are getting one of these leftover Accents."

Out of the car now, Hannah runs her hand over a red Accent. "Red?" asks James. Hannah just smiles and shakes her head no. Walking over in front of the cars, she stops in front of a navy-blue car with dust on it just as a salesman walks up.

"Lieutenant Longacre, isn't it?"

"Yes, it is, call me James, please," responds James, shaking hands with the salesman.

"James, thank you for your service! I'm Frank. This is?"

"I'm sorry, this is Hannah, my fiancée, and my mother, Eileen."

"James, I believe you have this handled. I'll be leaving you two. Hannah, have fun!" Eileen gets back in her car and leaves.

Early afternoon—the sun shines brightly on this Monday. Freshly washed, shiny navy-blue car purchased, the young couple sit in a popular chicken restaurant enjoying their sandwiches. "I don't want to hear about you being upset every day when I'm gone, Hannah. I need to be able to concentrate and study. I want to be a good leader. More importantly, I need for you to enjoy this part of your life."

"I will, James, I just had a bad night last night," responds Hannah.

"Do you like our car?" asks James with a smile.

"Ours?" Hannah looks in disbelief.

"Yep, the other half of this surprise is that Dad is taking off next Monday and taking you to get your driver's permit. He'll teach you."

"No ... I ... how ... really?"

Laughing, James responds, "Ja."

A playful kick is followed by Hannah's foot lingering on top of James's. She stares into his eyes. *How I love this man, how I want to have his bopplis.* Hannah smiles, whispers, "I love you, James Longacre." Looking down, she runs her lips across the top of the straw before drawing in the sweetness of her lemonade.

CHAPTER 3

EMPTY CLOSETS

September 8th, Hannah stands in James's room staring into a closet once bulging with summer and winter clothes from his civilian life and a stuffed duffel bag and storage boxes with his military items from his ROTC program. Now all but a couple of items are gone.

Ten weeks ... ten weeks ... how am I going to do this for ten weeks? But there is only but a single tear when James's mother walks in and stands next to Hannah.

"It will go quickly—there is much to do to keep you busy and this time will go quickly."

"Yes, we have much to do," said Connie, entering the room with Cece.

"Hi, sis, how are you?" Cece questions, placing a hand on Hannah's shoulder from behind.

"Dad is teaching me how to drive tomorrow," said Hannah, staring blankly ahead momentarily before turning around and smiling at everyone.

"Ladies," rings the familiar voice of Dad from down stairs. "Lunch in half an hour!"

"Ok, Hon! Girls, hurry now if you are changing out of church clothes!"

"I like still wearing my traditional clothes to church," said Hannah, pulling off her kapp and letting down her hair. "Now for my shorts!"

Her new sisters laugh, as Connie agreed, "Shorts sounds good."

Cece nods. "I'll see you both down stairs." She bounds for the steps, "Dad, need any help?"

Fort Sam Houston, Texas. Temperature is 99 degrees and dry at four p.m. Inside of IHG Army temporary lodging, James has completed settling in for the ten weeks he will be there. *Holiday Inn Express. I didn't realize that the army has regular hotels on post. What else is going to surprise me now? I'm starving. I missed church. Have to find out where the chapel is. I in-process tomorrow. I'm going to drop down to the grill for a bite to eat then call the family this evening.* The TV is turned on to a Baptist preacher giving a sermon. *I'm in the Bible belt. I'll watch this.* James collapses at the head of the bed, props a pillow behind him and fights sleep. *I just got here—it's exciting but lonely. I miss Hannah ... I miss my family. I'll finish this, then eat.*

Honey Brook, Pennsylvania. Temperature is 98 degrees and humid at four p.m. Inside of the Zook's home, Sarah, pensive, stands in front of her sister Hannah's closet space of pegs. One dress of hers, dark red with black apron remains. *Hannah, why did you leave? Where are you? What is so special about the Englisch world? I'm on my Rumspringa—I find nothing special there! Life here is so empty without you? Ach!*

A warm breeze blows through the open windows as her mother appears behind her, "Ja, I miss her also, Sarah. Kumme now, back downstairs, the meal is finished, and we are all having dessert."

"Ja, mamm! Daed gave a gut reading of Gott's word today."

"Ja, he did. Did you learn anything?"

"Ja, respect authority over me." Sarah smiles as she looks over at her mother, Mary.

"I will not remain on my rumspringa long, mamm. There is nothing there for me. Levi and I are becoming serious, and he is also not staying on rumspringa either."

"Gut! Vera gut!" Mary bursts out in relief.

Jacob, Isaac, and Isaac's son, Abram, stand in a corner of the room opened as in many years past for worship. Benches which were used for worship are now in front of tables for the meal. What has changed is that no longer are worship and hymns done in the old German. Instead, the day begins with separate prayer groups for healing, followed by Englisch praise hymns from colorful Englisch song books of worship. The stoic appearances are now replaced with smiles of salvation.

Only one person standing with Jacob and his friend Isaac remains stoic. Abram, who is not shy about his feelings, speaks to his father and his friend strongly, "Hannah belongs here! She has no right to leave! Ja, rumspringa is about that, but everyone knows we don't leave, we come back and do what we are supposed to do. She is supposed to be my wife! She must be brought to her senses and brought back here!"

"We understand how you feel, Abram, but she has made her choice and the Ordnung is clear about our responsibilities. She is shunned," exclaims Jacob.

"Ja," says Isaac agreeing with his lifelong friend, "better left alone and to Gott!"

"Gott wants her returned from the evil of this Englisch, ja!" Abram finishes his water, turns and leaves with, "Gott's will be done, ja."

With dessert finished and the last drink of water and lemonade swallowed, the men of this small growing church begin singing praises again. David King begins singing, "I'll fly away," quickly followed by Zeb King and his daughter playing violin. Then the families of the Lapps, Troyers, and Fishers join in. As the chorus begins, they file out of the house. As the house emptied, quiet reigned, and the sound of music echoed from the outside.

From inside the borough police department, narcotics detective Joseph Haines sits looking over surveillance photos this Sunday late afternoon.

"Hi, Chief!" he said as he is joined by his superior.

"What do you have, Joe?"

"Surveillance photos. The interesting one here is of a young Amish boy. I know him, Abram Yoder. I know his father."

"Isn't this our target selling drugs?" asks the chief.

"Yes, sir ... I don't know by these photos what the young Yoder boy was doing there."

"Who was on duty and took these?"

Joe quickly responds, "Lilly!"

"Lilly, wasn't she Amish? I hope we don't have the beginnings of that epidemic of Amish youth on their rumspringa into drugs again," responds the chief with concern on his face. Straightening, he finishes, "Well, she's in tomorrow. Leave those on my desk. I'll talk to her."

"Ok, chief. I'll be done in another hour processing faces and tags. I'll put them on your desk before I leave."

"Joe, thanks for calling me in." He turns and leaves.

The air is different on this day set aside for God. As the summer ends in two weeks, Hannah stands outside in the welcomed warmth, watching the sunset. She remembers that morning and the empty closet. She purses her lips while closing her eyes, whispers, "James, I feel your presence."

CHAPTER 4

A CRIMSON LEAF

"Hannah!" calls out Michael. "You ready?" Monday has arrived with the excitement of a drivers permit for Hannah.

She excitedly yells back downstairs, "Ready, Dad! Is this really happening? Am I really going to learn to drive?" The thoughts of the day before and her phone call with James is all but forgotten as she reaches into another day with open arms, welcoming it with wonder.

Abram, learning his father's trade as a carpenter, accompanies him on jobs building houses for the Englisch. They work for Zimmerman's Homes. Abram has become quite adept at walking across the peaks of roofs with balance and great agility. He smiles as he comes to the next roofing truss to be assembled. Settling in and with accuracy, he rapidly places nails into the white pine. His father looks up at him and smiles before resuming his work on the interior walls, assembling them on the floor then lifting them into place and nailing them down.

"Lilly," calls the chief, looking out the door of his office with pictures in his hand.

"Yes, chief!"

"What's your take on this Amish boy and this dealer?"

"It's nothing chief. I don't think so, anyhow. The dealer was already parked there when the Amish boy pulled up with his buggy—not able to get around because of traffic. He was approached by the dealer, and he waved him off! I would say he was pretty angry! This is nothing."

"Ok, good then. We don't need what we had going on in the past ..." begins the chief, but he's interrupted by the once Amish detective.

"I know, chief, my brother was involved in that. If it were that, I would have brought it to your attention right away. It's not that."

"Dad, what are we doing in this part of the parking lot? There is no one back here, and the store is all the way over there," questions Hannah, sitting upright in her seat and looking around.

Michael puts the car in park, looks over at her and simply says, "Time to get out!"

"Was!" she exclaims and again, "Was!" Looking over at her as he opens the door, he says, "You want to learn how to drive?"

"Now? Ach!

Laughing, he walks around the car and meets Hannah at her door, hands her the keys and says, "Your turn, young lady."

Hannah climbs in and, sitting behind the wheel, states, "I can't reach anything."

"First lesson," says Michael, smiling. "Reach down between your legs, feel that bar?"

Hannah listens attentively.

"Pull up on the bar and slide your seat forward."

With a smile on her lips, Hannah pulls the seat forward, then pushes it back and forward again. "There, I think I got it. Ja! Das ist gut!"

Her new dad repeats in English, "This is good. Then great! Now, let's set your mirrors. Can you see through them?"

"Ja!"

"Good! Pedals, those things on the floor. With your right foot feel for the right one."

The engine revs, and Hannah screams, "Ach!"

"It's ok, you revved the engine. Feel the one next to it, push on it. That's the important one. That stops the car."

Looking at him, Hannah smiles and nods her head okay.

"Are you ready?" asks Michael.

"Ready for what?" asks Hannah, nervously not wanting to hear the answer.

"To go!" Michael waves his hand forward, gesturing movement and laughing. "You have to do this. Here we go, put your foot on the brake. Look all around. Take your right hand and place it on the shift right here," motions Michael.

Hannah takes hold, squeezes the shift lock and pulls back to D as directed. The car lurches forward a little.

She looks around, and Michael says, "You're all clear. Take your foot off the brake and feel the car."

With a squeal from Hannah, the car begins to move forward as she looks around. "The car is going!" she exclaims.

"Yes, now very gently push down on the gas," instructs Michael.

Hannah easily pushes down on the gas, turns into the driving lane and soon is comfortable.

"Ok, time to humble you! You're going to take us home.

Hannah screams again loudly, "Ach, Was?"

"You're on the right path—just follow this around. I'll tell you what to do. You obey lights, signs, and laws while driving a horse and buggy right?"

"Ja," responds Hannah, now smiling again.

"Same thing. Onward."

Hannah finds herself on Horseshoe Pike making her way to her road. A turning signal, another left, and straight to the drive where she pulls in and stops with just a little lurch. Her huge sigh of relief is followed by a look at Michael.

"Good job! Put it in Park. See that button? Push it again."

The engine stops and Hannah claps to herself.

Michael and Hannah get out of the car, and Michael tells her tomorrow will be another lesson. Hannah smiles and nods her head okay.

The evening cools, dinner is over, and Hannah looks at Connie. "I miss Cece. I miss James. Would you like to take a walk?"

"Sure, where do you want to walk to?" Connie asks.

"How about to the diner for ice cream," responds Hannah, "I'll buy."

"Okay, Hannah, you're on!"

The two girls venture out into the early dusk, walking along the road and reaching a path into the woods paralleling the road. From a horse and buggy a distance away, an Amish young man watches quietly until the girls disappear from sight. A snap of the reins, and the horse continues on its way.

The sun has not set, and through the lush green of the wood's edge of maple trees, a large, undecayed yellow, orange, and red leaf came into both girl's view.

"It's beautiful. says Hannah.

Connie bends over, picking it up, and agrees, "Yes, it is beautiful. There is nothing like the beauty of a crimson leaf."

CHAPTER 5

LIFE'S RHYTHM

Thursday, October 31, 2019. Halloween has arrived and with it, the rhythm of Fall. The harvest is coming to an end. Jacob Zook's tobacco got a good price at market. Canning is well on its way, not only for Mary Zook, but also for Hannah, who is introducing her new family to the process of canning vegetables, fruits, and jams. Sarah Zook is taking on a more primary role in baking for her mother. Eileen regularly visits the Zook family farm roadside stand for baked goods.

Isaac Yoder and his son Abram are very busy with home building as they travel to many surrounding counties during this housing boom. Abram carries with him an angry affect, since Hannah moved away. He continues to disappear at times on Saturday and Sundays.

Both the Yoder and Zook family think Hannah will return and ask for forgiveness. Hannah remains shunned within all aspects of the Amish community. Though the bishop blames her father for the example he has made.

James connects with his family regularly via Skype. Hannah takes her James to her room where on her own laptop, she connects with her fiancée nightly before falling asleep. She got her computer while working towards her GED, which she completed two weeks ago.

Cece has settled into her new world as a business major at Penn State's central campus out in the country. Connie, in her junior year of high school, finds her extra time is spent working at the high school library. Her love for solitude and books has become routine. Together, they do the shopping in town and, oh yes, Hannah drives. She can be seen in town with her hair down, wearing a cami and designer jeans. When driving, she has her special aviator style sun glasses James bought for her after she got her driver's license. She also wears a bright smile.

In a quiet wood, where James and she used to meet, Hannah walks to find memories and solitude. The crimson leaves, a multitude, fall around her as she treks forward reflecting about the online classes she has begun. Her new goals—marriage, education, and later, babies, if God blesses her.

The sun breaks through the mix of yellow, orange, reds, and occasional greens. She enjoys the pale blue backdrop of the canopy overhead. *Gott is a wonderful painter. The beauty he creates cannot be matched by any of the artists I have studied. They all copy his work. We do have a remarkable creator. Danke, Lord Gott. Danke for this day and my life. Danke for the parents that brought me into this world. Danke for James's parents who have brought and accepted me into their family. Danke for my hardships and their lessons. Keep me seeing you, always. Know my love for you, Jesus.*

Hannah lowers her head in time to catch a glimpse of a familiar figure in the distance at the wood's edge. She hears the familiar clip clop of the horse's hooves in the distance as he disappears.

"Hannah, we don't know ... we think you don't do Halloween. We would like to ask if you want to hand out candy with us tonight. Because we live in a development, we have many children. We personally don't see any spiritual issues. We enjoy the children and their different costumes.

It's fun if you would like to join us. The church does an alternative for those who don't like the holiday," says Eileen while holding a plastic orange pumpkin with a funny face.

"I love the kinner! It sounds like fun, ja! What are we giving out? Little Deb ... bies. Ja, Wunderbar!" With the last word, the doorbell chimes its greeting in music, "Claire de Lune."

"Trick or Treat," echoes the sound of many children as they open the door.

Some of the children have plastic masks, some painted faces. There are princes and princesses, policemen, nurses and animals of all kinds. When the masks come off, smiles can be seen bright in the moon light.

Young children can be heard excitedly sharing what they are, and always they begin with, "I'm a ..."

Hannah replies, "You all look so nice! Ja, Wunderbar!"

With a laugh, one of the children mentions, "You talk funny!".

Hannah quickly chimes in, "Ja, I guess so, I'm Amish," pauses, then says it again while staring deep in thought, "I used to be."

A smile can be seen at the same time a tear is noticed by Eileen as she breaks the tension, "Yes, they are all really so beautiful! Hannah, I think this is for you. Enjoy the time."

As quickly as Hannah went away to another place, she returned with, "Ja, it is for me, I love the kinner!" Looking up at Eileen she smiles, "Thank you, Mom." The familiar clip clop can be heard from a short distance away. Hannah looks up to see the familiar gray over black buggy but not the driver.

"James! I miss you! Tell me about your day! We had Halloween tonight! I never had Halloween. It was so much fun, and the kinner, there were so many kinner. I want a lot of kinner!" Hannah could not be contained while on video.

Laughing, James tries to squeeze in a word edgewise as he begins, "Whoa! Wow! You had an exciting evening. First Halloween? Were there a lot of kids?"

"Ja! There was this one kinner with black hair dressed like a princess who noticed that I talked funny and I, for just a moment, missed home. Then your mom began talking to me, and I came back."

James said, "I have been having good days. Classes! Mostly classroom, as I had explained before. In a couple of weeks, we are going to the field. I won't be able to chat with you then."

"You won't?" Hannah asks urgently. "For weeks?"

James quickly corrects, "No, just for three days!"

"James, what makes you happy? I mean, what everyday things make you smile, make your day easier?"

"Hmmm," ponders James, and he continues, "I'm in Texas, and it brings to mind yellow roses, I love yellow roses. I love butterflies and birds. I find watching them is relaxing, and I don't have to ever go far to see a bird or butterfly. I like the smell of lavender, fresh mint, and fresh cut grass—maybe that's why I like mowing the lawn. I like the sound and smell of the sea."

Hannah responds quietly, "I've never seen the sea."

"We'll have to do something about that," answers James.

"Really?" Hannah smiles.

"Really."

"James, what do you like to eat?"

"Hmm, that's easy! Bacon, eggs in the form of an omelet or over easy. I also like Amish sticky buns and apple fritters. Then there are Hershey Kisses and Milky Ways that I really like. I like pepperoni pizza and beer. I like to read. I most like sleeping with you, your warmth, and the smell of your hair. Enough about me, what do you like?"

"I like four seasons. My favorite is spring because it represents renewal. I like the vivid colors of fall. I like the grays and whites of winter. I love Christ's birthday, Christmas. I like everything about Christmas. I least like summer because of the heat. I remember so many nights of not be able to sleep because of the heat.

"I like my mother's funny cake, AP cake, and apple dumplings with vanilla ice-cream. I love bacon also. I especially like the Christmas Rose. When I was a little girl, Christmas roses and the way they represent new life kept me from being lonely. There were times even though we were a big family, I would be lonely. My Christmas Rose would bloom at Christmas time.

"James, you always have a fresh scent that isn't too strong after you shave. I remember it when we spent the night together."

James was surprised. "My skin bracer!"

"Is that what it's called? I'll have to remember that," says Hannah. "I love you, lieb," says Hannah, feeling a little lonely.

"I love you also," says James, now saddened.

Time is slipping by, along with it planning for the wedding, which will be on the 30th of November. the Saturday after Thanksgiving. A small wedding is planned with fifty guests. Pastor Matt has come to know Hannah and James very well, and they both did the required premarital classes over the summer prior to James leaving.

They talked about their families, and Pastor Matt had dug in deep regarding family support and Hannah being shunned. They had both gone to the county clerk for Chester County and obtained their marriage license. The wedding was to be at one p.m. with the reception immediately following at Shady Maple Smorgasbord. As the seasons change, so go the lives of Hannah and James with its own established rhythm.

CHAPTER 6

BLESS US, OH LORD

November 15th, Friday, six a.m. Hannah is sleeping soundly when her door opens quietly. Without a sound, the essence of skin bracer wafts through the room, and Hannah dreams of James cuddling behind her. She dreams of James whispering in her ear, "Good morning, Hannah."

"Hmm ... James, I love you ... Hmm ..."

Hunching up on his left arm, James pulls Hannah's hair back and kisses the nape of her neck softly. Again Hannah dreams of James cuddling behind her and again softly responds, "Hmm ... James ... I miss you." She pulls James's arm into herself as she had done before, but unaware of his presence.

Cece and Constance softly laugh as Connie whispers, "She is completely and totally out of it."

Cece agrees, "Yep, maybe we should leave them alone."

Laughing a little louder, Connie shakes her head no and says, "No, I want to see this." With that, Hannah opens her eyes and sees her sisters smiling at her.

"Was?! What are you two up to?"

Connie laughs, shakes her head and simply says, "Oh nothing."

Cece agrees, "Yep, we aren't up to anything. "How about you, James? Up to anything?"

James quietly says, "Nope, not a thing."

Hannah jumps up and head butts James's mouth. She turns, screaming, "Ach! James! James? Oh my, I hurt you! Oh my, James!" Wrapping James into her arms tightly, Hannah leans back and kisses him deeply as James winces slightly.

"Now we can leave," says Connie, turning with her sister. James hugs Hannah tighter. "Lieb, you give the best hugs."

The phone call came during breakfast, "James, it's Pastor Matt! When do you get home?"

"Pastor Matt, hi! I just got home this morning."

"Are you with Hannah?"

"Yes, we're together. What's up?"

Pastor Matt says, "Well, maybe she should listen in."

James turns on the speaker phone, looks at Hannah and shrugs, "He wants you to listen in. Go ahead Pastor Matt."

"Hi, Hannah. Isn't Abram Yoder that young man who thought he was marrying you? I just got off the phone with him. He is pretty persistent! He is trying to find out where the wedding and reception are going to be. I told him I wasn't giving him any information, and if he was supposed to have it, you both would have given it to him. I just thought you should know."

"Thanks, Pastor Matt," says Hannah, with a look of concern on her face.

"Do you want to drive?" asks James.

"Really? Ja! I want to show you," says Hannah.

James opens the driver's side door for her, handing her the key fob as she sits. Hannah smiles, pushing the button as James settles into his seat after leaning over to Hannah and kissing her.

"You want to talk to me about Abram," says Hannah, with her eyes glued to the road.

"She's perceptive also," says James. "Yes, I'm concerned. Is he going to cause a problem?"

"I don't know," says Hannah seriously, glancing over at James. "Should I speak to him?"

"No, I don't like the idea of you being near him."

"Ja, I don't want to be near him either."

Pulling into the small grocery store in Honey Brook, Hannah parks, unaware of her surroundings. She and James exit the car, and as Hannah locks the car remotely, she is grabbed by the arm from behind and yanked around.

"Hannah, was ist das? You, driving a car! Wearing sunglasses! You should not be on your rumspringa any longer! Where are your clothes? Why do you continue to be with this Englischer?"

Hannah isn't able to get a word out. She tries to pull away but she is spun around, grabbed by the other arm and shaken violently.

James couldn't get to her soon enough. Hannah was tossed into James coming up from behind her. "Mind your own business, Englisch!" yells Abram, who turns and runs toward his horse and buggy.

The police are taking a report when Hannah begged James not to continue. "It's not our way, James."

"Whose way, Hannah? He assaulted you," emphasized James, visibly upset. The police officer agreed.

Officer Jane Nevils, following up on the assault, pulls up Isaac Yoder's driveway. As expected, she is met in the drive by Isaac and Jacob. "I'm here to speak with your son, Mr. Yoder. Can you get him for me?"

"Abram is not here. He left for his family in Michigan," says Isaac.

Jacob asks, "Is he in trouble?"

"Not yet, the girl he assaulted ..."

Officer Nevils is cut off by Jacob raising his voice, "Is Amish! She should not be with that Englisch! This is my dochder. This is between my dochder and Isaac's sohn! We will handle this!"

"Sir, I am handling this! As I was saying, the girl did not want to pursue charges. Her fiancée, however, does. I caution you, do not interfere with my investigation or I will be forced to arrest you, either one or both of you!"

Isaac continues, "I would think that we all want to make sure that Hannah is safe, Ja?"

"Yes, to start with, you can assure me he is not in town."

"Ja, this is true, he left last night and arrived today."

The officer, getting assurances, leaves and meets James and Hannah at the police station. Hannah is relieved, James is cautiously optimistic.

The leaves, having turned a variety of festive colors by this Thanksgiving Day, have now taken flight. The cool air carries the crimson colors in a ballet of swirls until they reach whatever perch lies beneath.

The house activities and conversations whirl around the upcoming wedding in two days. The excitement, palpable, inhabits the entire family. Hannah, having heard from the police officer what her father had said, decides to speak with him one more time. She hopes to speak with her mother and visit her brothers and sisters tomorrow, Friday.

"Bless us, oh Lord, and these thy gifts which we are about to receive from thy plentiful bounty, Amen," prayed the entire family in unison.

"Well, Hannah, excited?" asks Michael, looking at her, grinning broadly.

"Ja," says Hannah sheepishly as she looks down at the table smiling. "I am grateful for you this holiday, for all of what this family has done for me out of love. I am grateful that, because of you, I am able to feel this excitement. I am grateful for this man who loves me. I am grateful for new sisters. My life has, as it should like the seasons, changed. I am now entering the late spring of my life, with its newness. Danke." Hannah, as always, smiles except this time with a single thankful tear of happiness.

Cece says, "We are so very thankful for you, Hannah."

"Well, I or we are excited because we know your secrets. We know what Hannah is planning, and we know what James is planning," says Michael, finishing what he began.

At that moment, James and Hannah look at each other. "Was?" asks Hannah and "What?" asks James, both breaking out in laughter. "It's a surprise," says James.

"Great surprises," says Eileen.

Looking down at the turkey before them, Michael stands and begins, "Bless us, oh Lord,"

CHAPTER 7

As the Wind Blows

The blue sedan kicked up the now dry leaves of varying bright colors left unraked, uncollected. Browns and grays now line the drive to her father's shop on a property which had seen generations of her family turn the soil. Tobacco had always been sown, harvested, processed, and transported.

A little further down the drive, the car moves slowly with a soft whir. The leaves pick up and in a circular motion turn, the car blowing the leaves forward to aft on the right side, aft to forward on the left side. As a clock turns, so turn the dried bright colors.

Stopping the car, Hannah lowers the window. The welcoming coolness carries a yellow remnant of the lowly maple from amongst the vast oaks into the car. Pausing, the leaf appears to defy gravity.

Hannah and James have come to the place of her birth to bring closure to any open wounds left. "We will visit with and speak with each of my parents together then," says Hannah looking seriously and a bit scared at James.

"Yes, Hannah, it will be ok. It can only get better."

"Ja, it can only get better."

"Hannah!" screams Sarah.

"Mamm, Sarah's home," yells Joseph from the porch.

"Well, I guess we are starting with my mamm," smiles Hannah at James.

Hannah rises up from the driver's side of the car. James follows. Her long blond hair falls over her sweater to the waist of her jeans. She raises the sunglasses to the top of her head. Nine-year-old Ruth, with her hair pulled up, is the first one in her sister's arms. Looking behind she scowls at James. James notices. *Uh-oh, what have they been telling the others?*

Climbing the steps, she enters the back door to her mother exclaiming, "My dochder has returned, Danke, Gott!" Then she spots James ... quiet.

"Are you with boppli, dochder?" asks her mother

"Ne, Ne! Ich bin nicht!" responds Hannah shocked, "Ne!"

"You are not?" Mary repeats in a question.

"Ne, No! How can you think that of me?" Hannah questions, shocked.

"You are amongst the Englisch! Who knows what you are up to?" replies Mary.

"Mamm, you and Daed have taught me well. I have taken my lessons into my heart. James respects me, cares for me, and loves me. We are here to apologize for everything you have been through."

Mary and Hannah both cry and her mother takes her up in her arms. "Meine, dochder," weeps Mary.

"Mamm, ich liebe dich."

"I love you also, Dochder."

"Mamm, we understand that everyone must have gone and continue to go through a lot. We apologize for all that you have gone through. We will be married tomorrow. We want you and Daed to come, please," pleads Hannah.

"Let us all go and speak to your daed," gestures Mary pointing to the door. "We must all begin to heal, Ja."

Across the short span of the drive, crunching across the top of the same dried leaves, James takes in the essence of fall in what feels like a lifetime walk. The smell of leather and polish welcome their arrival into the shop.

As they enter, a distant clip clop can be heard, in the distant. A customer is making their way up the drive.

"Are you here to return and confess for your forgiveness, Dochder?"

"Hello, Daed. I am not here to return, but to acknowledge the pain that you and mamm have gone through and to apologize for any pain that you may have gone through because of our decisions."

"You are shunned, nothing has changed," says Jacob turning his back again.

"Jacob, we are not done," says Mary, again getting Jacob's attention.

Without saying a word, he turns towards her.

"Tomorrow is the day of their wedding. I would like to go and take the children with me. I want to see my dochder marry."

"Nein! Nein! She is shunned, I forbid it! You go, and you will be shunned!"

Turning towards her daughter, Mary says, "I will see you tomorrow. I will need transportation." Mary looks at her daughter and ignores Jacob.

"Ja, mamm! Danke!" Hannah excitedly turn towards James, who smiles.

"Jacob!" The customer who has now entered the leather shop yells for him.

"Go now, I have work to do," says Jacob, stoic and not looking at anyone.

"Kumme, dochder! Hannah, I have something for you." As they turn towards the house, another stiff breeze picks up more of the ground laden colors lifting them to their backs as Hannah's brothers and sisters watch from the house. "Kumme Kinner, we have a wedding tomorrow to get ready for, Ja."

"James, I am looking forward to seeing your mamm," smiles Mary, now looking at James with hope in her eyes.

"Yes, ma'am. I am certain she will be happy to see you also," says James reaching forward past the family. Grasping the door, he opens and holds it for the family.

"Mamm, the meidung?" asks Hannah.

Mary passionate, responds, "These are my kinner also, your daed he also needs to eat, I tire of this confusion without compassion. Now! I have been saving this for you! James, stay here."

Alone in Hannah's room, Mary pulls a plain, but beautiful, sky-blue dress with a pure white apron off the peg.

"Mamm ... my wedding dress?"

"Ja, it is for you. Would you like to wear it tomorrow?"

"Ja, danke."

"Then try it on."

As Hannah pulls off her sweater, her mother notices another change in culture. "Hannah, you become more like the Englisch."

"Was, Mamm?"

"You are shaving?"

"Ja, Cece, James's sister had taught me."

"Das ist Dumm, Ja?" questions Mary.

"Ne, Mamm, it is not silly. Anders, different."

Mother and daughter look at each other and laugh.

"We must hide this so James doesn't see it. Mamm, I like to dress plain when I go to church. May I have my other two dresses and aprons?"

"Ja, take them now," instructs Mary.

Everyone walks to the car. James opens the door to the driver side, lets Hannah in, as her family stare at Hannah starting the car.

Mary startles, "Hannah! You drive? You shave, and you drive?"

Hannah laughs, "Ja!"

Making their way down the drive, Hannah and James look at each other quietly and smile. The drive to the diner is not long, and they soon pull up into the parking lot. "Who are all these men, James?"

"One is my best man, two others are groomsmen, the other three make up an honor guard," answers James now looking at the young men and woman grouped near one of the vehicles.

"Gentlemen!" yells James as he leaves his car.

"Longacre! How ya doing?" They all step up to the couple as they leave the car behind them.

"Hannah, this is Stacy, Dawn, William, Mark, Kyle, and Joseph."

William and Mark step forward, "Ma'am, may I present my girlfriend, Lisa," says William.

"Ma'am, this is my fiancée, Caroline," says Mark.

"Everyone hungry?" asks James.

"I am!" say the guys in unison, while the woman laugh. While the men congregate, all the woman, including the two officers, Stacy and Dawn, come together with Hannah. excitedly speaking with her.

Following lunch, James explains where the church is located. "We will meet at five p.m.," says James. "Then, we will meet back here after rehearsal for the rehearsal dinner. Right now, we have a meeting with our pastor."

"James, I need for you to wait out here, I would like to meet with Pastor Matt alone," says Hannah, kissing James quickly as Pastor Matt waits in the door way.

"Ready? Okay, come on in and have a seat," says Pastor Matt, gesturing to the seat inside the door.

"So, what's this about?" asks the pastor as he shuts the door.

"The vows we had gone over," begins Hannah, "there is something missing."

Looking concerned, the Pastor sits in the chair next to Hannah's rubbing his chin. "I'm confused, you both wanted a traditional wedding with traditional wedding vows."

"They aren't," protests Hannah.

"What's missing?" Pastor Matt sits back, crossing his legs, looking perplexed.

"I grew up Amish, I grew up where it was expected once married to obey my husband. There was order, yes. Often times, the husband does not love the wife as Christ loves the church. Everyone played their role within the Ordnung or the laws of the church. I now have a man who loves me as Christ loves the church, and I freely choose to obey him in keeping order. It is my gift to him. It is a symbol of my trust in him that he will do the right thing as long as Gott gives us life," explains Hannah, determined.

Pastor Matt looking attentively at Hannah, quickly answers, "Never have I heard of such a beautiful and trusting act. Well, I have a sermon to revise for tomorrow! I will have to rewrite it, some."

Hannah smiling, asks again, "You will put the word obey back into the vows?"

"Yes. Yes, I will."

"We are done here, James," smiles Hannah as she shows up in the hallway with the pastor.

"Well, we will see you both tonight for rehearsal."

Leaving the church, the wind continues at their backs, picking up the dry leaves of color. Hannah looks around at God's wonder, *As the wind blows ...*

CHAPTER 8

A NEW LIFE

Hannah, having picked up her mother and siblings, is at her new home in her room. With her is her mother, Mary; James's mother, Eileen; her sister Sarah; and James's sisters, Cecelia and Connie, who is Sarah's age. A celebratory atmosphere exists as Hannah prepares.

Cecelia, pulling Hannah and her sister Sarah aside, confronts an issue. "Hannah, I am honored to be your maid-of-honor, but your sister is here now. I think it is important for her to now stand in.

Hannah smiles at Cece and turns. "Sarah, you are my schweschder, will you stand with me?" asks Hannah, facing her sister.

"Ja," says Sarah, typically quiet, now crying.

"Mom, I need to speak to Dad," says Hannah, turning to Eileen.

"Okay," she responds, opening the door and calling downstairs, "Michael, you are needed up here!"

When he shows up at the door, Hannah with a tear asks, "Dad, will you walk me up the aisle?"

"It would be my honor," replies Michael. "After all it is your wedding, and we will do whatever makes it special for you. You are beautiful in that traditional blue dress. The limo is here for you ladies." Michael smiles and hugs Hannah, kissing her on her head. "Hannah, we will ride in together."

"Okay," she says.

At the church, James is with William, his best man, in Pastor Matt's office. They stand in their dress blue uniforms with white shirts, bow ties, and sabers at their left side hung with saber chains from their ceremonial belts.

Stacy and Dawn sit in the center at the back across from each other dressed similarly, sabers resting in the pew next to them.

Mark and Kyle are outside when the limo pulls up. The driver opens the door and as the two mothers exit, the young officers offer their arms. "Ma'am," says Mark, offering his arm to Mary, who looks surprised. Kyle offers his arm to Eileen, repeating the gesture.

"Trumpet Voluntary" from the organ, joined by trumpets playing at the back of the sanctuary begins the processional. Everyone stands as Michael escorts Hannah slowly up the aisle.

Hannah looks behind her, hoping for a brief second her father will show up ... but no one is there. She frowns only briefly then resumes smiling. As they arrive at the front of the church, Michael kisses Hannah's forehead and shakes his son's hand.

"Please be seated," begins Pastor Matt. "On behalf of Hannah and James, welcome. I begin with First Corinthians. Or should I say, normally I would start with First Corinthians until I met with Hannah yesterday. We spoke about her wedding vows, how I left out the word obey," says the pastor as he continues, "Today in our society, it is politically correct to leave out as unnecessary the vow of obedience of a woman to a man. Hannah came to me and told me she wanted me to put obedience in place in order for her to show honor to her husband, who loves her as Christ loves the church. To show her husband how she trusts him with the vow."

"I now turn to you, James. In doing so, Hannah has placed in you the greatest of trust—that of love. Love is not a feeling but an action to which we are called. You, within the context of your marriage, are also called. You, James, are called to act out of love, to do, to sacrifice. You are called as Christ to selflessly give. In doing so, your rewards will be great. What a gift to you, James! You must have, in your courtship, proven yourself worthy for her to offer you what is normally considered outdated. What is expected within her own culture is now not expected to be given so freely. Pay this forward, James. As I ask you to repeat after me, you both should keep in mind what you are saying I will to. Take it into your being, take it seriously. Now your vows—repeat after me and respond with, 'I will.' James do you ..."

The honor guard standing perpendicular to the limo await the new couple outside of the church. At the end of the line nearest the car in the command position stands William, right hand on his saber. Across from him Stacy, then Mark and Dawn, followed by Kyle and Joseph.

James and Hannah, upon exiting, stand before the honor guard when the command is given, "One step forward, march," In unison, one step is taken forward.

William, in one crisp motion, draws his saber and, placing his hand at his side, sets the blade against his right shoulder. The command, "Draw," is given and the guard withdraws their sabers one foot from their sheaths, followed by, "sabers!" All the sabers are now as William's are displayed. The command, "parade ... rest!" is heard, and the sabers are crisply pointed simultaneously at the sidewalk in front of them.

With everyone standing and surrounding the honor guard, a bagpipe begins to play "Highland Cathedral." The order comes very quickly as the couple, Hannah on the right, stands before the two columns. "Present arms! Arch sabers! The glistening of the blades goes quickly and again crisply to the shoulder then crosses up into an arch for the couple to cross through.

As they walk through, William and Stacy ceremoniously, slowly, lower their sabers, stopping the couple to allow for a kiss. Following their kiss, William and Stacy raise their sabers back into the arch allowing James and Hannah to pass on. As Hannah passes through, William playfully swats her back side saying, "Welcome to the Army, ma'am!"

Hannah gives out a surprised, "Ooh!" and laughs, "I have much to learn!"

"Ladies and Gentlemen, it is my honor and privilege to introduce to you for the first time, Lieutenant and Mrs. James Longacre," hails the DJ. "Now for our first song," he says as a country/western song comes on. James smiling, takes Hannah in his strong arms, and the two begin to dance slowly.

Following the tradition of a military wedding, James's saber is used for the first cut of flower-shaped-fondant covered vanilla cake. James's wedding gift is a Christmas Rose made from crystal which adorns the top of the cake.

"Was ist das?" exclaims Hannah, surprised.

"This is my wedding gift to you! It's a Christmas Rose! When we are done with the cake cutting, there is a heavy crystal base that it locks into. There is also a glass globe to cover it. We can then bring it out on Christmas if you like," says James.

"This is so beautiful. Danke, James. I will let you know what I would like to do," Hannah says as she runs her fingers over the fine intricacies of the art work.

The reception ends with a last dance to the song, "Time to Say Goodbye." The dance floor starts crowded, but soon Hannah and James are left alone, pressed together with

Hannah's head resting on James shoulder, as she whispers, "I love you."

In another surprise, with passports in hand and lots of time, James and Hannah return home to get dressed and make their flight to Florida. Suitcases now loaded into the limo, Hannah asks, "where are we going?"

James smiles and whispers, "It's a surprise," as Hannah's mother and siblings listen from nearby in the living room.

"There is much I don't understand in your new world, Hannah. Just know that we love you—so does your father," says Mary, with the younger children now huddled around her.

"I love you, Hannah," says Sarah, continuing. "I enjoyed myself today. I understand why you left. He is a gut man."

Mary, turning to Michael and Eileen, looks down in thought. "Danke for accepting our daughter the way that we couldn't. We have much to learn."

Michael reaches out his hand and says, "It is our pleasure. She has been a blessing to all of us. You are welcome here anytime. Perhaps, you could visit on our Christmas, the 25th of December. Anyhow, blessings to you and your family."

"Ach!! We are taking a plane," expresses Hannah, surprised.

"Yes, we are," beams James.

"Where are we going?"

"Well, it's a surprise! I can tell you that we are flying to Florida.

"Florida! We are going to Florida! Das ist wunderbar!"

"It is, but that isn't what is wonderful," says James, holding back on his secret.

"Hannah and James arrive at the upscale hotel near bedtime. Honeymoon night kept Hannah thinking they had arrived to spend their Englisch honeymoon in Miami, Florida. They slept in the next day, Sunday, choosing to get up at the last minute before the hotel stopped serving breakfast.

"I'm going to unpack," says Hannah reaching for their single large luggage.

James stops her with, "Why?"

Hannah pausing asks, "Why? Because we have all these nice drawers to put our stuff in!"

"We aren't staying here!" James begins to laugh!

"Was?" questions Hannah.

"It's a surprise," explains James, continuing to laugh. With a backpack in hand, wearing shorts and sandals, they proceed downstairs.

"Everyone going to Dock A, please board the white van.

"Where are we going?" Hannah asks.

James responds, "I am taking you to see the ocean."

"We are going to the beach?"

"No, you'll see." James smiles, continuing with the charade.

The van arriving at the port pulls up to the cruise terminal.

"Surprise! Welcome to your hotel on the water for the next week!"

Hannah, standing, just stares, speechless.

"Say something, Hannah."

Hannah just smiles. "We are going on this?"

"Ja," kids James.

"I do not know what to say. I wanted to see the sea. I never would have dreamed this. Ne, never." Hugging James, Hannah whispers, "I know what I want to do with my Christmas Rose. I want to keep it out all the time as a reminder of our new life!"

CHAPTER 9

A New Adventure

December 9th, Monday. Four weeks until I have to report to Rucker. So much to do! I now have to move my family to Enterprise, Alabama. Set up a household. I have to get started today!

The time on the ship, though wonderful, proved to be very short. Hannah and James laugh about late nights and late mornings. They did not abstain from drinking, choosing to sample the free mimosa offered on the cruise at breakfast and various rum drinks in samplings on the different Islands.

They visited St. Thomas and spent the day on the beach at Magens Bay. Then to St. Croix, where they took the Island tour. But the most fun, and what they found most interesting was their trip to Belize, where they disembarked in Belize City and ventured into the town by foot. A familiar sight was to be seen. Horse-drawn carts with plain-dressed families. The woman wore white straw hats with colorful bands. The men wore white straw cowboy hats.

Hannah, curious, asked and found out that they were Amish from Pennsylvania. The carts were black, open carts with a top to keep the rain off. She talked with a young couple her age and also newly married as she could tell by the beard the man had just started growing. They conversed in Pennsylvania Deutsch.

Back in Pennsylvania, sitting at the dinner table, Hannah at his side, James broaches the subject of the big move. "We are going have to leave in the next day or two," says James, regarding the truth at hand.

Eileen, looking at a reaction from Hannah repeats, "In the next day or two?"

"Ja," says Hannah excitedly, "a new adventure begins!"

The family smiles.

"It's going to be very busy, and we have to drive down. We'll take two days. Shop for furniture. The Army is allowing travel, time, and hotel expenses," sums up James, looking at his father.

"Then we have Christmas coming up," adds Connie.

"Christmas," says Hannah, staring into the distance—into the past.

December 11th, Wednesday. The little blue car is loaded back seat to trunk with Hannah and James's clothes. Hannah, now taking a turn, helps to drive south through the gray of the usual green Shenandoah Valley. They pass through the fogginess of the mountains of Eastern Tennessee and into Northern Alabama. "Lieb," begins James. "You like the shore? We are only two hours away from Panama City, Florida, and white beaches. Even in the winter, it's nice there, I understand."

"Ja, gut!" Hannah responds enthusiastically.

Having decided to drive straight through, they arrive in the darkness of a typical rainy Alabama night. Tired and drained, they sleep through the night, waking to a full breakfast spent discussing the day on post.

"First thing we are going to do is register you at the gate, and go on post to Human Resources to get your ID card made up."

"ID card?" Hannah questions.

"Well, you are an officer's wife now, and what the Army considers a dependent, entitled to certain benefits. Your ID will allow you on post, through any of the gates, and will be your link to everything from shopping to medical care."

"There is so much to do, James, and so much to remember. Can we get it all done?"

"We will get it all done," responds James, pulling the hot coffee up to his mouth and taking a sip. "We pick up the keys to our apartment after lunch. Then we can have some fun shopping for furniture," he finishes, setting the cup down.

"We are actually shopping for our own furniture, James. Can I tell you what I like?"

"Hannah, this is our home. I will be looking to you to help make decisions. Well, let's get going." James smiles, standing in his OCP (operational camouflage pattern) uniform and pulling on his black beret.

"Welcome home, sir!" says the MP at the gate.

"Above the best," responds James.

The MP having noticed Hannah, stoops down greeting her, "Good morning, ma'am."

Leaning over, Hannah greets the young soldier, "Gut morning!" She stares in amazement at the soldier greeting her.

The gate raises as they pass through and past the AAFES (Army and Airforce exchange service) gasoline station on the left. "We'll fill up here," says James as they pull up the hill and to the pumps.

"This is the same as any other gas station, James. Except, there are many men and woman who are in uniform," notices Hannah as they enter and leave the small convenience store.

As in any town, there were any number of churches, banks, stores, fire departments, police, and fast food restaurants. "There are woman and children here, James!" she says excitedly as they pass a well-known coffee house.

"Look!" She now points to Military police pulled in behind someone.

"They're getting a speeding ticket," says James, shaking his head. "Remember, the traffic laws are strict on post. You speed, I'll hear about it, besides getting a ticket and having to go to the Provost Marshals office—"

Hannah interrupts, "I'm not driving."

"I'm sorry. I didn't want to scare you. You'll be okay. You'll want to drive. You'll be dropping me off those mornings. I forgot. I'll be away for two weeks in the beginning. I'll be away at SERE."

"SERE?" Hannah questions.

"Survival, Evasion, Resistance, and Escape training. I have to pass SERE in order to move on to flight training. They want to make sure I am fully trained to resist the enemy, if I'm captured." James, trying his best not to, is scaring Hannah, who now is staring at him.

"You are scaring me, James," she says.

"Seriously, nothing to be afraid of. You will make friends. It will be hard because of school. I will have, as I had said, a lot of studying."

"Hannah, Hannah." Attempting to get her attention, James walks slowly next to her and puts his arm around her. "Heh."

Hannah, smiles and looks up from staring at her picture on her ID card and holding it up. "I have my own ID card," she says as excited as a child with a special gift on Christmas.

"Yes, you do," agrees James, grinning. "Apartment keys, next!"

The apartment manager, opens the door quickly and clears out of the way. James lifts a giggling Hannah up and through the door of the living room, as she yells, "James! Was ist das?"

"This is our first home, and we are just married. It's tradition!"

Giggling some more she adds, "Das ist gut!"

"Is it now, this is good," as he spins her around.

"Ach! Okay, James, put me down. I am excited to see our new home."

"How can we afford this apartment?" Hannah asks, looking around, worried.

"The Army pays a housing allowance for whatever area we may be living in. The rent actually is a little less than the allowance, and we have a little extra left over to cover the electric and trash removal." James says with assurance.

"The Army takes care of everything."

"A lot of it," says James, looking around.

As they walk through the two-bedroom apartment with a dining area, they begin to figure out what they need for furniture.

"Ach, we need everything, James!"

"That's what's fun!" James says optimistically and adds, "We have a list of things we got for our wedding—when we are settled in here my parents will bring it down."

Hannah begins to write 'dining table and chairs, bedroom set, living room set, stools for island.

"TV. TV, Hannah."

'TV' she writes. "TV. Why TV? questions Hannah.

Staring, James responds, "For those few times I can just relax and watch nothing or the news."

Smiling mischievously, Hannah says, "I can fill in that time!"

"Oh yeah?"

"Ja! I am certain! Back to the list." She looks up. "TV. What do you want to do with the extra room?"

"How about a sleeper sofa or futon for guests to sleep on? Then we can use it to sit on other times. I'll need a desk to study at also."

"Ja, das ist gut." Hannah, while studying her list, nods her head yes.

December 16th, Monday. The furniture arrives, and the sheets go on the bed. "We now have a place to sleep, James."

"Time to move out of the hotel," adds James.

"I can't wait, we can start by unloading the car next," says Hannah, looking around the room until she locks onto James's eyes and finishes with a smile, "We begin a new adventure."

CHAPTER 10

A CHRISTMAS ROSE

December 18th, Wednesday. *One week until Christmas in this new and different place. I would like to see a small tree in front of the patio door. I want to speak to James.* "James, let's shop for a tree today. Also, I need the car for shopping."

"Okay, they are selling trees outside of Enterprise gate. How about we start there?"

"Gut!" Hannah says.

The small tree goes up in front of the patio door with just enough room to pass by it. "I will miss the snow," says Hannah, sadly, as she comes through the door from the outside.

"How about we plan a trip to Pennsylvania, lieb," suggests James.

"Really! Ja, I would like to go back to visit," says Hannah, suddenly putting her hand over her mouth.

"You okay?" asks James.

"Ja," reassures Hannah, swallowing hard and struggling to finish her sentence, "something I ate."

"Don't look, James! This area you cannot go to," says Hannah, eyes wide open.

"Okay, and you cannot go into my drawers, my top drawer in particular," says James. The both laugh at each other, playfully.

"I have an idea," says James, continuing. "How about we spread the Christmas holiday out? We can spend and celebrate our Christmas here through Sunday after church. Monday, we drive up to Pennsylvania and spend Christmas at my parents. We can visit your family for Christmas also," beams James.

"Really! Really James?"

"Yes! Do you like the idea?"

"Ja!" Hannah responds spontaneously!

"Then it's done!" James says, coming up and wrapping Hannah with in his arms from behind.

December 22nd, Sunday, six a.m. Christmas morning for Hannah and James. A large puffy bag lies besides the little four-foot scraggly tree. Hannah comes out in her light-weight pajamas and grins. James comes out rubbing his eyes wearing shorts and a T-shirt, looks around and spots a small slender box, lodged gently within the green tree branches. Then he spots another branch holding a card.

"Hannah, you go first, please," pleads James. "Our first Christmas—I hope you like it." James and Hannah cuddle on the sofa and look at each other.

"I am sure I will," says Hannah, turning and kissing James. "Good morning. I love you, husband."

Hannah pulls the large bag over to her.

"Wait, I forgot something," say James, pointing at the card under and behind the tree. "That one first!"

Hannah reaches around and under the tree. "Ach, your hiding is gut! I would have missed this!" Hannah says, fanning herself with the envelope.

Pulling out the envelope, she opens it to find a Christmas card and a gift card and three bus tickets. "Was ist das, lieb?"

"It is three bus tickets for you and my sisters to go dress shopping in New York City. The three of you are going to make a day of it. Buy a nice dress for yourself. We have a military ball coming up."

"I have never been to the city before. Your sisters can help me. This will be fun. Danke, James. What is a military ball?" Hannah questions looking over.

"It is a party for the students and spouses.

Walking over she kisses him longingly.

"Now the bag!" James points.

Returning to her seat next to James, she takes the tissue paper out and pulls out a queen-sized, Amish-made quilt. Hannah begins to cry, "It is a wedding ring quilt!"

"It's queen-sized to fit our bed," explains James, excitedly.

"It is beautiful," says Hannah, pulling the hand stitched fabric against her and burying her face. Pulling it away, she spreads the corner out on her lap.

"James, had you noticed the border? James, look! The entire border is made of Christmas Roses! Look!" she points pulling the fabric up. "Pink, five petal roses," says Hannah, now studying the entirety of the quilt pulling it around and smoothing it. "There is always one way you can tell an Amish quilt. If you can find it," says Hannah stopping at a corner and smiling as she holds it up. "Here it is!"

"What is it, Hannah?" James asks inquisitively.

"Only Gott is perfect," begins Hannah, eyes wide. "As perfect as you would think every Amish quilt is, an imperfection is sewn in, so it is not perfect. Here it is. See this ... Every pink rose has five petals except this one."

"Four," responds James noticing.

"Ja," she says as she pulls it up to her face one more time. "James, I love it. I want to put it on our bed right away, but first my gift."

"Open the card first," instructs Hannah, pointing at the green card.

James opens the envelope to a plain Christmas card with a handwritten poem.

She explains, "It is translated from an old 15th century German poem."

175

Es ist ein Ros' Entsprungen
(It is a Rose Sprung)
A Rose has sprung from a tender root,
From Jesus, as those of old have sung,
And it bore a flower,
In the middle of a cold winter,
When half spent was the night.
Isaiah foretold it, the Rose I have in mind;
Is Mary the pure, the little flower has brought us.
From God's eternal wisdom, she bore a child,
And remained pure.
The Flower, so small, whose sweet fragrance fills the air,
Dispels with glorious splendor the darkness everywhere;
True man and truer God, helps us out of all sorrows,
Saves from sin and death.
Oh Jesus, until we leave this misery,
Let your help guide us into joy,
In Your Father's Kingdom, where we eternally praise You.
Oh God, allow us this.
Author Unknown (public domain)

"I don't understand," says James smiling in wonder.

"James, out on the patio in the red color bag. Bring it in," says Hannah.

James, coming from the outside smiles and says, "It's a Christmas Rose!"

"Ja," agrees Hannah, continuing the mystery.

She tells a story, "A child, having found the Christ Child, felt bad she did not have a gift. As she walked away crying, an angel noticed and brushed away snow to present an evergreen which gave off a wonderful essence from the special rose as this was a gift for the Christ child. It is a gift of new life that I give you, James. Open the last little package."

James opens the small package and pulls out a plastic wand with (+) at the end.

As he stared, she continues, "My gifts to you, this Christmas, James, are a Christmas Rose and a baby."

After a long drive, Hannah and James wake up nestled in Hannah's bed against the cold. Christmas Eve morning brings the scents of frying bacon and freshly baked cookies.

The two, entwined face to face, move slowly. Resisting the tempting smells wafting from downstairs, they share the last of kisses and nuzzles. Hannah, kissing the front of James's neck one more time, caresses the side of his face.

James, running his hands through Hannah's hair, settles at the back of her neck, caressing and drawing her back into himself. Tenderly he kisses, first a wisp of tear at the corner of her eye, then her lips—moving to the nape of her neck.

"Hannah, I love you," he says.

"I love you also," says Hannah, pulling James's hands to her chest, looking down and kissing them. They both pull themselves together.

"Hungry," James says.

Laughing aloud, Hannah teases, "You are always hungry!"

"Ja!" James teases back.

"Good to have you two home," says Michael.

"Danke, thank you," glows Hannah as she replies.

Eileen, grinning, says, "There's something different about you two."

"Church this evening is at seven p.m. How about one gift tonight as we have in the past?" Michael suggests.

"Sounds good," says Cece.

Connie chimes in. "Yes, sounds great, Dad! Hi, sis!" Walking over, she hugs Hannah. "You okay? Something going on with you?" Connie continues the query.

"Ne, everything is gut!"

Christmas eve the doorbell rings, and unbeknownst to Hannah and James, a van door opens. "Hannah, James! Come on in here," calls Michael. As Hannah and James enter the hallway from the kitchen, the rest of the family join them.

"Dad, who's at the door?" James asks first.

"That single Christmas present for the night? Well, it has arrived," responds Michael, with the family smiling as though they know something.

"Hannah and James, Merry Christmas," says Eileen.

Cecelia and Connie, both with tears and smiles, whisper, "Merry Christmas."

The door opens, and Ruthie, followed by Benjamin, Joseph and Sarah come in the door and charge to embrace their sister.

"Hannah! Hannah!" scream Ruthie and Benjamin.

"Merry Christmas, Dochder," says a solemn Jacob.

"Daed, Mamm!" What are you doing here?" Crying, she embraces her mother, then her father.

"Merry Christmas, Hannah," says Mary, also with tears.

"This is the best Christmas," says Sarah.

"Ja, it is!" says Hannah picking up Ruthie and hugging her.

"Why don't we all crowd into the family room," invites Michael.

"Floor! In front of the fireplace," yells Constance, grabbing Sarah by the hand, "Come on!"

"Was!" she exclaims!

"You'll see," laughs Hannah. Hannah and James sit in front of the Christmas tree. All the children follow to sit in front of the tree.

"Hannah and I would like to offer our gifts to you all," begins James. "It is sort of a regift," says Hannah handing her mamm and mom an envelope and her dad and daed a small slender box. "First, open the envelope and read the poem."

"The title is in Deutsch," says Mary.

"It is about the Christmas Rose" says Eileen as she

finished reading the poem. "What's this about?" she asks.

Also confused, Mary asks, "Was ist das, dochder?"

"Dad, open the box," directs Hannah again. "Daed, I ... we are so happy you are here," she says to include her own father.

Hannah, repeating what she had told James, reiterates, "As the Christmas rose was a gift for the Christ child, it is a gift of new life that we give you all. Open the last little package, Dad.

Opening the small package, he pulls out the same plastic wand with (+).

"Oh my!" says Michael.

Eileen screams, "You're pregnant!"

"You are with boppli?" cries Mary.

Jacob, speechless initially, speaks quietly, "Das ist wunderbar, Grossdaddi."

"Ja, Daed. I love you," says Hannah, finishing with, "Our gift to you, our parents, this Christmas, is a baby and a Christmas Rose

Off to the side. Connie whispers, "I knew something was up."

EPILOGUE

Life's Fullest Circle

Flying back home, I reflect on my early March visit with Hannah and James. What I had not shared with you is that Hannah is just finishing her first trimester of pregnancy. She has a little bit of a baby bump. She also is now doing what I have noticed others doing many times—holding her belly. She is radiant as she carries. I never tire of seeing a woman with child. Blessings!

Hannah is due August 27th of this year. They plan to repeat their second Christmas in the same manner. First, they'll have their own small Christmas, then they'll go home to the beauty of the grays and whites of Pennsylvania. This coming year, the Longacre family will spend Christmas with Hannah's family.

James survived SERE and is in flight school. I got to watch with Hannah from the control tower as he practiced auto-rotations. It brought back nerve-racking memories as I watched him cut his engines and glide forward until the last moment when he would pull back on the stick, landing safely. Once done, he left the small orange and white helicopter while his partner took over and climbed in next to the instructor pilot.

Hannah continues to wear her traditional dress, apron, and kapp to church. It is just what she does. My first Sunday in Dothan, I attended church with them. We prayed before meals. Meals are quiet times together interrupted only by soft conversation and the familiar clicking of Hannah's plate with her fork as she finishes eating.

Eileen and Mary continue to see each other regularly every other weekend, and Eileen picks up Hannah and James's favorite pastries and mails them in a care package.

Jacob, tolerant and much more compassionate, has had coffee with Michael a couple of times.

Hannah is very comfortable with her life as the wife of an Army officer. We had lunch several times and talked about this story. Before leaving, I took them out to dinner. I treated them to a nearby Brazilian steak house that I remembered. We had a fine evening as I enjoyed their company one last time.

As I leave you, I wish you all a Christ-centered Merry Christmas, Frehlicher Grischtdaag. Blessings to you and your family and remember, a Christmas Rose.

For Coral ...

ABOUT THE AUTHOR

To know **Wil Carpenter,** one would probably not think of him as an author. He is a husband, a father, a Christian, a veteran, a business owner, and a servant. He has led a life of bold and diverse experiences that immediately capture one's attention.

Getting to know him more deeply, I've learned that Willard has an unexpected artistic and creative side—something that might be considered uncommon, given his life's works.

Wil's greatest inner strength is his expression and creativity. His life's works give a credit to his writing that few other fiction authors possess. This generates a vivid degree of realism above and beyond other works of fiction.

Upon reading Wil's first book, *Prodigal*, which was first published at about the same time as the first edition of the *Boyertown Bulletin*, I was immediately struck by the quality of the story line, and immediately expressed my desire for him to join the *Boyertown Bulletin*'s staff.

Since that time, he has been integral to our publication, frequently covering some of the most difficult topics in our modern society.

—Eric J. Eidle, President and Editor, *The Boyertown Bulletin*

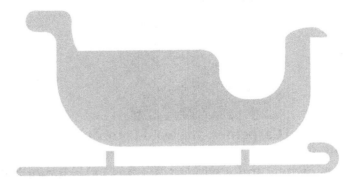

HOLIDAY HARNESS SHOP

Thomas Nye

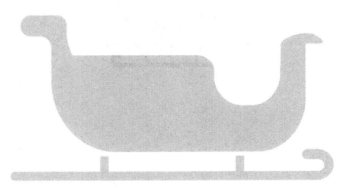

CHAPTER 1

A GOOD SALE

An icy blast flung open the door. Sleigh bells attached to the wooden door of the Holiday Harness Shop jumped and jingled at full volume. Harnesses hanging along one wall danced in the breeze and swayed on their hooks. Titus put a hand to his aching back as he dropped the project he was working on and started for the door, eager to keep the heat in.

Over the years, Titus's hair and chin beard had grown white. His eyes were still sparkling blue, highlighted by smile wrinkles at their corners. A few extra pounds had accumulated around his waist making a simple job more cumbersome. Before he could get across the room, a snowy figure emerged through the curtain of falling snow and shoved the door against the wind until it slammed shut. The personage shook off the white outer layer onto the welcome mat, and Titus chuckled as he recognized the snow-covered woman as his wife of fifty-two years.

Verna took off her headscarf revealing gray hair tied into a bun. She shook the scarf. Snowflakes jumped off the black material and floated around them. "Winter gets worse every year," she said with a shudder and tied the black scarf back on.

"At our age, we shouldn't be out and about in bad weather." He gave his wife a half smile. Titus still enjoyed teasing Verna as much as when they were newlyweds. He knew she came out to see if he made a "good sale" with his last customer. She always did.

Verna headed toward the wood-burning stove. Her thin frame weighed about the same as on their wedding day, only at this stage of life, her shoulders hunched forward. She used the counter and workbench as a handrail. Titus noticed her knuckles were swollen, and blueish veins crisscrossed her wrinkled hands as she warmed them near the stove. A red glow gleamed on crackling firewood as it produced a sweet, smoky scent, mingling with the aroma of harness leather.

"Did that Englisher buy something?" she asked.

"He wanted a horse collar."

"What would an Englisher want with a horse collar?"

Titus chuckled and shrugged. Verna's eyes, faded to a cloudy gray over the years, still had the power to give an intimidating look. He smiled at her insistence for an explanation and said, "Some Englishers have horses."

He retrieved the leather strap he had tossed aside when the door popped open and resumed his work. He used a leather punch to make a row of holes. Her eyes continued to bore a hole in him as she waited for a full disclosure of the business transaction. "This Englisher wanted to make a wall hanging for his aging dad. So—I sold him one of those old collars I bought at the fall horse auction."

"Did you make a good sale?"

"Good enough," Titus said.

Verna turned to brush the last of the snow off her crochet shawl—a shawl too thin to be worn out in a snowstorm. However, she always said, "It's enough to get me from the house to the harness shop in any weather. And besides, it's difficult to put on my heavy winter cape without your help." She eyed her husband. "You bought those horse collars for twenty dollars each and told me you could double your money on them."

Titus groaned and nodded.

"So—did you?"

"It's Christmastime," Titus said, and set down his work. He looked Verna in the eyes. "Did you see what a banged-up truck that young man was driving? Obviously, he didn't have extra cash. Why would I overcharge him?"

"Titus—we don't have extra cash either!"

He picked up his leather and fidgeted with it.

Verna stepped closer and kept her balance by holding onto his workbench. "We have to send in our hospital bill. It's due before the end of the year. Christmas is coming and with it comes extra expenses."

"It's the holidays—the hospital will be understanding if our payment is late."

She shook her head. "Big hospitals don't care about holidays. Besides—they were so good to you when you had heart troubles, we don't want to let them down."

"What other expenses come with Christmas?" he asked.

"Christmas gifts, and so many other things. For example, I need to buy extra flour if I'm going to bake goodies for the Christmas baskets we give out. You need to charge a little more for your labor."

Titus nodded.

She stared at him until he looked up. "We are not living in the 1900s—people can afford more these days. Will you please try to make better sales?"

"I'll try," Titus said, and smiled until she softened her glare.

The corners of her mouth played at a smile. "If you don't do better—I'll have to start coming out when customers are in the shop. I'll do the bargaining myself."

Titus chuckled. "I'll do better. I don't want you scaring off the few customers I have."

Verna picked up the leather strap Titus had punched holes in. "Is this part of the harness you're making for Lavern Chupp?"

"Yes."

"You need to work a little faster. The women at the quilting were talking about that new harness shop in Bridgeport. The Millers have four sons working in their harness shop, and people are taking their orders there. The Millers can get a new harness made in under a week."

Titus took the leather strap from Verna's wrinkled hands. "This is a double harness I'm making for Lavern Chupp. So,

189

it'll take at least twice as long to make. My customers would rather I did the work right. That's why they come to me."

Verna shook her head and adjusted her scarf. "You could fill more orders if you weren't so particular. And don't embarrass our granddaughter by taking too long with this project. Lucy is interested in Lavern Chupp's son, Harvey."

"How do you know that?"

"I have eyes—don't I?"

Titus shrugged. "I have eyes too, but I wouldn't know anything about Lucy being interested in Harvey."

"Take my word for it. Your eyes are about as good as your bargaining." She held the doorknob for a moment, hesitating before she said, "We need to help Lucy with the boys. She is self-conscious about her lisp."

Titus chuckled. "I like the way she talks."

Verna let out a girlish giggle. "I think it's cute myself."

He stood up to rearrange the harness he held. "What should I get you for Christmas?"

"I'd be happy if you'd take more of a lead in our home," she said with a sigh.

"What do you mean by that?"

"At your age I shouldn't have to keep after you about things." Her smile let him know she said her words affectionately. "And you ought to notice more about what's going on with our grandchildren without me having to tell you." With that, Verna turned the doorknob and let in a cold blast of winter wind. She leaned her already slumped shoulders forward pressing into the blast and pulled the door shut behind her.

CHAPTER 2

BUCKLES AND SNAPS

Titus's harness shop was not an "in town" type of business. The cinder-block building, originally built as a butchering kitchen, stood about twenty steps from the main farmhouse on the Yoder farm. It consisted of one long room with old fashioned windows on three sides. Old fashioned, because they, like French doors, had window grids of lead resulting in dozens of small windows. During winter months, each window became a display for Jack Frost's artwork. An island workbench filled the center of the space. Horse collars and rolls of uncut leather hung above the island. Those objects added a pleasant leathery scent. More workbenches lined the two side walls, each with leather-work tools meticulously organized into stations for varying types of projects. At the head of the island stood Titus's heavy-duty treadle sewing machine.

Just inside the front door, a counter jutted out with a cash register at least as old as Titus. Above the counter hung an ox yoke. Titus had bought the wooden yoke at a sale as a gift for his wife. He carved *My Yoke is Easy* on the crossbar with a wood-burning tool.

Verna suggested, "Why don't you put that in your shop." Possibly she did not want it in the house. Maybe she thought the yoke should be somewhere where more people could enjoy it.

A large display of snaps and buckles covered the back wall. The wood-burning stove, though hidden in a back corner, made its presence felt by radiating heat and a smoky aroma throughout. Harnesses new and old hung just inside the front door. They were draped over dangling hooks made specifically for such a display. However, the nylon strings tied to the hooks on the ceiling allowed the harnesses to dance and jiggle whenever customers—or family—came inside.

Titus and Verna had raised crops, hogs, horses, and children on the farm for the past fifty years. After their youngest daughter's wedding, Titus announced at a family meeting, "I'm going to retire from farming and set up a harness shop in the old butchering house."

His children all let out a sigh of relief. They had been agreeing with their mother for years that Titus should retire. Mahlon, their third oldest son, and his wife had a large family. They were living in the cramped quarters of a small house a few miles away. It was decided Titus and Verna would move into an apartment-sized wing of their farmhouse, and Mahlon's family would occupy the main living quarters and take over managing the farm. The land alone could have been sold for a million dollars at auction, but the thought of selling a family farm for any price was completely out of the question. Titus and Verna accepted the privilege of staying in the "grandpa house" apartment as their only reimbursement for the land. Mahlon sold his inferior farm and divided the profit among his siblings as their inheritance payment for the family farm. Everyone seemed satisfied with the arrangement and life went on.

When the bells jingled on the Holiday Harness Shop door again, Lavern Chupp's son, Harvey, accompanied the incoming icy blast of wind.

"Good morning, Harvey."

"Hello, Titus. My dad sent me over to check on our harness. Our big team has lots of work to do even though it's winter. You can see them out this window. Look at how bad our old harness is getting. We have part of it tied on with baling twine and other parts are held together with duct tape."

Titus stood to look out through a frosty window. Swirls of ice created delicate designs on the glass. Two massive draft horses stood at the hitching rack just beyond the window— one black and one sorrel. The horses appeared oblivious to blustery winds passing over their backs and ruffling their dark coats which were as thick as a grizzly bear's shag. Drab harness leather crisscrossed over their sides, pieced together with duct tape and twine, just as Harvey had said. Titus turned toward his customer. Harvey's dark hair stuck out from under his black stocking hat. His cheeks were rosy from being out in the cold. His face held the honest expression of a young man who knew what it meant to work hard.

"I've got your project on my table now." Titus lifted a strap with freshly punched holes as if to prove it.

"How long do you think it will take to finish?" Harvey asked politely.

"End of the week—maybe. Isn't Friday Christmas Eve?"

Harvey smiled as he answered, "Yes." He stood watching Titus as he polished the strip of black leather. "Our horses sure will look smart wearing a new set of harness."

Titus fixed the buckle in place and stopped to look out the window. Harvey looked over his elder's shoulder to see what the old man saw as Titus drew out a memory for them to examine together. "When I was about your age, I asked Verna if I could give her a ride home from a young folks' gathering." Titus stopped his story to chuckle. "Well—I didn't ask her. Her sister told me Verna wanted me to give her a ride home. So, I said, 'Okay.' Her sister asked, 'Okay what?' I said, 'Tell her I'll plan to give her a ride home.'"

Harvey laughed but caught himself with a gulp so Titus wouldn't be offended.

Titus continued, "I had a long-legged bay horse with a jug head. That's what we called horses with heads too heavy for their bodies. Anyway—I figured my horse would look a lot more impressive with a new bridle. I helped a neighbor make hay in one hundred-degree heat for three days to make enough extra money to buy a new bridle. When I put the bridle on Jug Head, it only made his head look bigger than ever."

Harvey cocked his head and held his laughter until Titus chuckled. After they shared a hearty laugh, Harvey asked, "What'd you do?"

The older man ran his hands over the new harness. "I put the new bridle on him anyway. I fretted and stewed about it, but after I married Verna, I asked her what she thought about my jug-headed horse. She didn't notice or remember his head. She only remembered worrying about her homemade shawl. She thought it looked too small on her. Funny thing—I didn't remember that."

Winds howling outside filled the awkward silence between them. Harvey opened his mouth to say something as sleigh bells jingled on the door. A cold breeze and Titus's granddaughter, Lucy, came into the shop. Her black hair, tied up in a bun, hid under her snow-covered blue headscarf. Tiny wisps of hair and dainty curls, not hidden by her head covering, framed her fair face. Her bright-blue eyes were significantly highlighted by the blueness of her scarf. Lucy's and Harvey's eyes met for an instant, and both teenagers blushed. Lucy cleared her voice before speaking in a near whisper, "Grandma thed you needed my help in the thop?"

Titus smiled at Lucy's cute lisp, and started to shake his head to say he did not need her help before he remembered Verna's words about Lucy being interested in Harvey. "Oh— yeah—I need someone to empty out this box of new buckles and snaps. They should be hung in order of size on those hooks." He pointed to the wall with a massive display of buckles and snaps.

With a box set precariously on an edge of one workbench, Lucy began sorting through the snaps. She started the tedious job of matching snap sizes with those already on the wall. Titus noticed something unusual about his granddaughter. *Is she wearing shoes instead of chore boots? Why is she in her Sunday cape instead of her everyday one?* Titus tried to remember the last time Lucy had come into his shop with her best shoes and Sunday cape.

Harvey scratched his head through his stocking hat, and his voice cracked when he said, "Maybe I should get going?"

Lucy glanced at her grandpa, her eyes showing disappointment. Titus spoke up, "Harvey—could you help me with your new harness for a bit? I need someone to hold the driving lines while I measure them."

"I'd be happy to help. Especially to get my harness done sooner." Harvey's face reddened as he took the end of the driving lines and backed toward Lucy. "I didn't mean you aren't getting them done soon enough ... I mean I was just saying..." In his effort to explain himself and stretch out the driving lines, he backed into Lucy's box of snaps and buckles and sent them sprawling across the shop floor with a splash of steel on concrete. "Oh, Lucy. I'm so sorry!" Harvey fell to his knees gathering snaps and buckles.

"Don't feel thorry ... ith not your fault. I thould have thet them on the counter better." She maneuvered gracefully past Harvey and gathered some snaps that had slipped under a workbench.

Titus reeled in his driving-line leathers. "Maybe you should help Lucy sort out those snaps and buckles for now. We can measure these driving lines later." The older man resumed his job punching holes in harness straps. Harvey and Lucy both decided to take off their heavy winter wraps. Lucy hung them on harness hooks. She wore a crisp-blue Amish dress, with a matching headscarf, and had eyes that matched both. Harvey's green shirt stretched tight between his broad shoulders. Suspenders drew the shirt in at his waistline accenting his muscular build.

"These thnaps need to be bethide those there," Lucy said. She placed them daintily into Harvey's work-worn hands.

Titus turned away from the teens to conceal his grin. He enjoyed the sound of Lucy's cute lisping and Harvey's extra polite replies. The sleigh bells attached to the front door jingled again. Three little Amish children tromped inside. Lucy's seven-year-old sister Janice was followed by her five-year-old twin brothers Abner and Silas, who came in laughing.

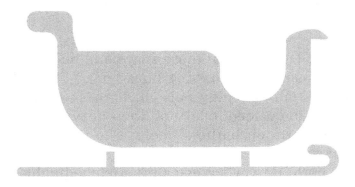

CHAPTER 3

Manure Pile Hill

Although Janice was small for her age, her brown eyes were full size and almost as dramatic as her personality. Her blond hair always protruded out from under her black bonnet like tufts of straw even though her mother tied it into a tight bun every morning. During winter months, Janice wore two thick Amish dresses and a pair of wool stockings to hold in what little body heat her small body could produce. She announced with a huge grin, "We've been sledding down the hill beyond the barn."

"Clothe the door," Lucy instructed. The twins worked together against the wind until the howl quieted, and the door slammed shut.

Janice repeated her earlier statement of joy, "We've been sledding on the hill beyond the barn."

"That hill ith a manure pile," Lucy said, "You'd better wipe your booths off if you've been thleading on that hill."

The little children, all three, stomped and wiped their boots profusely on the welcome mat. Janice announced, "Our boots only had snow on them. The manure is completely covered—the snow is so deep."

Lucy herded her little siblings away from the narrow isle where she and Harvey were sorting buckles and snaps. "What do you children want in here anyway?"

Janice, always the spokesperson for the little children, explained, "We came in to warm up by the fire. Mom won't let us come into the house unless we take our coats and boots off."

The twins removed their mittens and stocking hats, placing them strategically near the woodstove. Their bowl-cut hair rose and stood up from their heads by the power of static electricity. Grandpa Titus chuckled at the sight. Silas eyed Harvey, as if surprised to see him helping Lucy sort the snaps and buckles. "Harvey—are you going home soon?"

Lucy scowled at her brother. "Why?"

Janice explained, "We were wondering if he could pull us up the big hill on the road with his horses. Then we could sled back home."

Taking his coat off the harness hook, Harvey said, "Sure, I can. I should be heading home now anyway."

The little boys scrambled to get their hats back on. Abner brought his mittens to Titus. "Grandpa? Can you help us put our gloves back on?"

Grandpa Titus set down his harness leather again and helped the twins pull on their mittens. Lucy helped Janice with hers. Harvey buttoned up his own coat. "When should I stop in to check on my harness?"

"Come by and check with me in two days," Titus said.

Lucy stood by the window and gazed through the frosty designs to watch Harvey leave. Grandpa Titus joined her at the window, and they watched Harvey tie a rope on the back of his bobsled. Janice climbed onto the bobsled behind the seat and Harvey set her sled on board. The twins held to the rope, each bracing themselves to hold on tight as their sleds followed the team uphill. Snow continued falling around them. Harvey's huge horses arched their necks and trotted away, leaving the lane and onto Holiday road.

"Will you have Lavern Chupp's harneth done in two dayths?" Lucy's brow furrowed as she asked.

"Maybe not. Hopefully, I'll have it done by Friday, but it won't hurt for Harvey to stop in a few more times—will it?

The red ribbon of Lucy's lips curved into a smile. "Thankths, Grandpa."

Harvey and his team were almost hidden by falling snow as they reached the top of the hill. Harvey helped Janice off the bobsled and onto her coaster. He took the time to get the twin's sleds turned around. Harvey watched from the top of the hill and Grandpa and Lucy watched from the window as the three children zoomed downhill and tumbled into the steep ditch at the end of the lane.

Titus chuckled. "I wish our ditch at the end of the lane wasn't so steep. One of these times, someone is gonna take that corner too short and end up stuck down there." He paused for a moment and added, "Lord, please bless all who enter this lane. May those who come in feel welcome and those who leave be blessed."

Lucy nodded and headed back to her job of sorting out buckles and snaps.

After a few minutes, Titus said, "You don't have to finish that project today. You might want to work on it again in a few days."

Lucy gave her grandpa another warm smile and gathered her cape off the hook. She opened the door to leave as three little snow-covered children tromped back inside to stand by the wood-burning stove again.

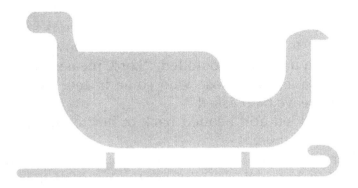

CHAPTER 4

HUSBAND AND NEIGHBOR

On Tuesday, the sun rose over a fresh layer of snowdrifts. Without wind chasing the snowflakes into ever-changing dunes, the sunlight melted the surface ever-so-slightly. Frigid temperatures refroze the droplets creating a crusty shell. Titus's boots made a crunching sound as they broke through on his short trek to the Holiday Harness Shop.

The wood-burning stove lost heat overnight. Its cast-iron body was a black ice cube until Titus scratched a single matchstick ablaze. A few crumpled newspaper sheets burst into bright, red flames. Those flames licked the frayed edges of splintered chunks of oak. Within minutes, the stove's iron door became too hot to touch. Titus warmed his hands over the heat. He drew in the smoky scent with a smile and latched the door shut and took off his coat. His hands went to his pockets for warmth while he examined Lavern Chupp's harness. The harness-maker made mental notes about how he should move forward on his project.

Crunching sounds beyond the window caught Titus's attention. He peered through the frosty squares of glass and watched his son and grandchildren head toward the barn for morning chores. Mahlon carried a lantern. Golden light radiated around the small troop, and their shadows danced in elongated images perfectly matching the children's movements. Titus stood and smiled at the sight. "Thank you, Lord, for blessing me with grandchildren. Help me to be a good example for them."

Titus made good progress on Lavern Chupp's harness through the morning. Just before noon, a stranger entered the shop. A red car with black stripes could be seen near the hitching post. The stranger examined rows of harness hanging on the wall by the door. The unfamiliar man wore a vest over a black-and-white-checked flannel shirt. It seemed barely enough to keep a person warm in such weather. His jeans were tattered, and his feet looked cold in thin canvas shoes. None of his clothes affected Titus's opinion of him, nor did the man's scar which ran through one eyebrow and into his cheek below a dark eye. *Scars can come from some misfortunate accident.* However, a dragon tattoo ran up out of his unbuttoned shirt, with claws reaching toward his whisker-bristled chin. *Tattoos are premeditated.*

The man pointed up at a row of silver bits. "What are those?" He did not let his eyes meet Titus's. They shifted to-and-fro around the shop even while Titus answered his question.

"Those are bits. As the Bible says, 'Behold, we put bits in the horses' mouths, that they may obey us; and we turn about their whole body' (James 3:3).

The stranger laughed through his teeth with a hissing sound. He turned to face Titus and opened his mouth to speak. A jingle came from the bells above the door and interrupted him. An Amish neighbor, named J. John, strode in carrying a bridle, laid it on the counter and the bit landed with a clunk. "Good morning, Titus. I wonder if you could take a few minutes to fix Maggie's bridle. Her throat latch broke, and it looks like it needs a new buckle."

Titus glanced at the bundle of leather searching for what could be wrong with it. The bells sounded again. Titus looked up to see the black-and-white-plaid shirt leaving through the front door.

J. John watched the man leave and slam the door of his red car. The stranger revved the engine and headed out the snowy lane and onto Holiday Road. "What did that guy want?"

"I'm not sure." Titus ran his fingers through his beard. "He didn't seem to know anything about horses."

Both men shook their heads as the red car fishtailed on the hill leading toward town. J. John groaned and said, "That's why I wouldn't want a shop like this—you never know who will walk in." He rattled his bridle and drew Titus's attention to the matter at hand. "Maggie rubbed her bridle against a hitching rack and tore the throat latch."

Everyone knew J. John's driving mare. Maggie, though small, could pull a buggy over hills and through valleys as efficiently as any horse. "It's almost noon, J. John. Would you mind if I work on it after lunch?"

"I guess that will be soon enough."

"I'll send one of my grandchildren to bring it over after I finish with it."

J. John stopped to look at Titus's current project. "Who are you making this work harness for?"

"Lavern Chupp. His main team has been in the same harness for years. I've patched it up countless times, and now it's hanging together with duct tape and twine."

J. John laughed, his long reddish-brown beard jiggling. "That Lavern Chupp pinches pennies until Abe Lincoln squeals. I'm surprised he broke down and ordered a new harness."

Titus chuckled to be polite. "I think Lavern Chupp wanted to give me business. He could've gone to the Miller's new harness shop in Bridgeport. They make harness faster and cheaper than me." A moment of silence stood between the men. Titus feared his neighbor took his words as a jab because they both knew J. John had his last harness made at the Miller's new shop. Yet, when he needed repairs, it was convenient to stop by the Holiday Harness Shop. To ease things over, Titus added, "And I wouldn't blame him if he did."

"Send a bill over with the bridle," J. John said. "I'll send cash for the repairs with whoever brings it. I'm not like some people. It'll be a wonder if Lavern Chupp pays you for this harness before next Christmas."

Titus picked up J. John's bridle and examined it. "I'll get right on this after lunch."

J. John opened the door to leave, and Titus's wife came in. Verna greeted J. John and said, "Tell your wife I have a quilt in. We'll have a quilting next Wednesday if she wants to come over."

"I'm sure she'll want to," J. John said. "She's been feeling cooped up with all this bad weather lately."

Verna held the door open and called as J. John walked away. "Tell her to bring her daughters and anyone else she wants to bring!"

Verna had a basket of food with her. She often brought lunch to the shop to save Titus time. He suspected her main goal had to do with keeping her easily distracted husband on task. If he went inside, he sometimes picked up the newspaper and did not get it put back down for an hour. She set her basket on the island workbench. "Did the man in the red car buy something?"

"No. I'm not sure what he wanted. He looked around for a moment and left as soon as J. John stepped inside."

"That's odd," Verna stated. "Did J. John have a repair project for you?"

Titus moved two stools near the worktable and pushed J. John's bridle aside. He motioned toward it. "Yes—this bridle."

They sat side-by-side and bowed their heads in silent prayer. When they looked up, Verna said, "It sure is handy to get your repairs done at the neighbors even if you buy your new harness elsewhere." She set egg sandwiches on the plates between them and shook a few chips from a large bag.

After a large bite of egg sandwich and a few chips, Titus replied, "He is good about paying right away."

Verna nodded while crunching on a chip. "You'd better start reminding Lavern Chupp you expect to be paid for his harness when you finish it." She took a few gulps of water. "Have you said anything to him or Harvey about it yet?"

"They know they'll have to pay me."

She set down her glass with a clunk. "You didn't say anything, did you? They might think we have plenty of money. You'd better let them know we have bills due before the year's end. We can't carry them like a bank."

"I'll hint at it."

Verna's eyes widened. "I don't think Lavern Chupp is good at taking hints. You'd better say something to Harvey. He can remind his dad."

Titus finished his sandwich and ran his fingers through his beard. "Do I have any crumbs on my face?" His wife reached over and plucked something from his chin. She kept her eyebrows raised to let her husband know she was waiting for a promise about mentioning money to Harvey. "I'll say something about the bill."

Verna bowed her head and Titus joined her in an after-meal silent prayer. Titus prayed within his heart, *Lord—help me to be a good husband and a good neighbor. It seems impossible to do both at the same time.* They raised their heads and shared a glance.

Verna said, "Amen."

And Titus smiled. "Amen."

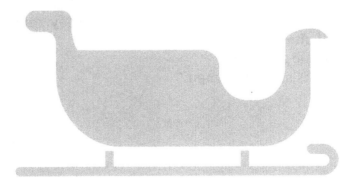

CHAPTER 5

NAMES AND SNOWBALLS

Shortly after lunch, Titus completed repairs on J. John's bridle. A jingle of the doorbells proceeded little seven-year-old Janice. "Grandpa? Can you fix this strap on my ice skates?"

He took the steel blades from her small hands and examined them. They were almost as old as Titus. Skates made in those days were double-bladed steel plates which could be strapped onto any boot or shoe. Janice pointed to a weak spot in the leather. "Can that be patched up?"

Grandpa ran the old leather through aged fingers. "I think it's time to replace this leather strap. We might as well do both skates while we're at it." He unthreaded the old leathers and used those to measure out a new set. He sat in a folding chair and set his spectacles on his nose to help thread the new leathers. Janice leaned against her grandpa's shoulder and watched his leathery hands repair her skates. "Did you used to ice skate when you were a little boy?"

"Of course, I did. I probably used these very same skates you're using. Only they were new then."

Janice's eyes grew wide, "I didn't know people got new things back in the old days."

"We didn't very often. One Christmas, my brothers and I got new ice skates." Titus finished fastening the leathers. "Now—let's see if they fit on your boots."

Janice climbed onto her grandpa's knee while he attached the strap-on skates to her boots. "There—how's that?"

She climbed down and leaned over to peer at her feet. She hoisted up the thick hems of her two dresses to examine her boots and skates. "Thank you, Grandpa."

"You can do me a favor in return," he said. "Will you go to J. John's place and take his horse bridle?"

Janice's large brown eyes grew pouty, her lower lip protruded, and her shoulders sagged.

"What's the matter?"

"J. John's redheaded boys are mean to us."

Grandpa let his forehead wrinkles gather in a bunch. "What do they do?"

"They throw snowballs at us. They tease Lucy about her lisp by calling her Luthy."

Grandpa's mouth hung open for a moment. "They probably don't realize how much that hurts."

"The snowballs?" Janice asked.

Titus smiled at his granddaughter. He handed her J. John's bridle and attached a note with the price of repairs. "Snowballs hurt for a moment—teasing a person about something like a lisp can cause pain for a lifetime."

Janice nodded and clattered toward the door, her skates clunking on the cement floor. She paused before heading out. "Someone told me God gave Lucy a lisp to keep her humble because she is so beautiful. Grandpa, do you think that's true?"

Titus ran his fingers through his beard in thought and let the corners of his mouth turn down. "God created each person unique. But just so you know—humbleness doesn't come from having a weakness or a lisp." He stepped near Janice and put his hands on her coat shoulders. "Just because we are embarrassed of something about ourselves doesn't equal humbleness. It actually can be a form of pride. Some people think they are humble because they don't like something about themselves. My nose is too big, I'm too skinny, I'm overweight. If a person is humble, they are content with how God made them. Pride is not only feeling pleased with a feature of oneself. It can also be focusing too much on what you don't like about yourself."

Grandpa and Janice shared a moment of silence while looking into each other's eyes. Janice nodded. "But how do we stop having pride?"

"When we realize we are focusing on ourselves—we should repent. That brings humbleness."

"Do I have to take the bridle to J. John's?"

"You can skate the creek under the bridge to his house. His boys won't see you coming. When you get to his house—climb the bank to their back door. The big boys will be out by the barn, and they won't even know you came by."

Janice's grin took over her face. "Thanks, Grandpa."

"Thank you, Janice. I'll pray the boys don't see you." He patted on her black bonnet. "And remember—saying mean things hurts more than snowballs. Even little girls can hurt people if they are careless."

Titus made good progress on his harness project during the following hour. That is, until the sleigh-bells over the door almost jumped off their hook as Janice blasted through the door laughing. Her skates clattered wildly as she ran around the center island of the workbench and hid behind her grandpa.

Titus turned to see Janice's face. "What's happening?"

She clung to her grandpa and continued giggling. "J. John's boys are after me!"

Titus peered through the icy swirls on the harness shop windows. J. John's teenage boys tromped toward the barn, snowballs in hand, obviously searching for Janice. "I see them out there, but I don't think they'll come inside. What did you do?"

Janice kept her grandpa between herself and the door as she explained in the high-pitched voice of an excited little girl. "I skated to J. John's under the bridge—just as you said. When I got close, I could see those redheaded boys were out by the barn hitching a horse to their buggy. I knocked on the back door and gave the bridle to their mom. She said I should take it out to the boys. I told her I was afraid of them, and she wanted to know why."

"Did you tell her about how mean they've been?"

"I just said—they might throw snowballs at me." Janice opened her oversized-brown-eyes wide. "Their mother said,

'They wouldn't throw snowballs at a little girl.' And I told her, "They already have!"

"What did she say?"

Janice stepped on her grandpa's chair to look out the window before answering. "Their mother called the big boys over and said, 'Tell Janice you are sorry for throwing snowballs at her.' They said, 'Sorry.' But I could tell it made them mad. They pretended to go back to work, but they followed me when I skated up the creek." Janice teetered on the chair. "There's F ... F ... red now!" She almost fell off. Grandpa caught her and helped her down.

"Who's out there?"

"F ... F ... Fred."

He looked into her pretty brown eyes surprised to hear her stammer in fear. "Do you want me to go talk to them?"

"No, Grandpa, that'll just make it worse."

CHAPTER 6

Problems to Solve

Wednesday morning, the sleigh bells over the door of the Holiday Harness Shop rang bright and early. Titus looked up from his work. Lucy breezed through the doorway with a smile. With great care, she set down a sack which reeked of cinnamon rolls. Her blue eyes looked bluer than ever because of her royal-blue scarf. Her black hair was highlighted by her jet-black cape. Her cheeks flushed pink with the chill of winter air. "Morning, Grandpa!"

"Hello to you, Lucy!"

She crowded close to her grandpa and watched his hands as he pushed harness leather under the foot of his heavy-duty sewing machine. He thumped a treadle with his foot, powering the machine with a clickity clack. He finished a line of stiches and held it up to assess his work in the light. "Does that look straight?"

"It lookths good to me," Lucy said with a smile. "Ith this Harvey's harneth?"

"Yes, it is. I expect him to come by sometime today to check on my progress. Maybe this would be a good day for you to sort out buckles and snaps again?"

Lucy nodded and her cheeks flushed rosy red again. "Grandpa, I have a little problem."

"What could that be?"

"Our young folks' group plans to go Christmas caroling thith Friday evening. They put me in charge of the event, and everyone ith meeting here on our farm."

Grandpa set down his work. "Well, what's the trouble?"

"I need to find thomeone with a team of horthes to pull the hay rack." Her cheeks continued to flush as she talked. "I wanna ask Harvey, but I'm too shy."

Titus pulled on his beard in thought. "I might be able to help you. I could ask him but ..."

"But what?"

"If he's gonna drive his team—he'll want to use this new harness." He met eyes with Lucy. "I'm not sure I can have it done by Friday."

"Ith there anything I can do to help?"

Titus opened his mouth to answer her question, but the jingling of sleigh bells over the door interrupted him. Harvey Chupp's large frame came through the doorway. Lucy hurried over to her snaps and buckles project as if she had been working on it all morning.

Harvey stepped close to Titus and looked over his shoulder at the harness. "It's coming together isn't it?"

"Good morning, Harvey. Yes, we're making progress."

Titus noticed Lucy glancing around the horse collars in a clear effort to see if Harvey noticed her. She dropped a buckle and giggled after it clattered on the floor.

Harvey looked over and his cheeks flushed. "Oh. Hi, Lucy. I didn't see you were in here."

"I'm helping my grandpa a little tho he can keep working on your harneth.

"I could help Lucy if that'd help you," Harvey said.

Titus turned away to conceal his grin. "Sure, Harvey, that would be nice."

Harvey hung his coat on a harness hook and joined Lucy at the back of the shop. Titus pushed himself to work faster on the harness. He kept his treadle pumping with a steady whirring sound while the teenagers chatted in hushed tones. After a good stretch of work, Titus had to stop to load his bobbin with thread. Without the sound of the treadle going, Titus could hear Lucy's cute lisping as she chatted with Harvey.

"Are you planning to come thith Friday for caroling?"

Harvey nodded. "What time is everyone coming over?"

"Well—people are going to thtart coming after they finish their chores. We'll have thinnamon rolls and hot cocoa before we leave. Grandpa ith going to have a barrel fire going out in our driveway, tho everyone can warm their handths."

"That sounds great! I love cinnamon rolls."

"Oh good! I brought a few out thith morning for Grandpa and me. Would you like one now?" Lucy scramble to put down her buckles and snaps before he could answer. She maneuvered around Harvey and pulled a pan of cinnamon rolls from her paper sack. Coincidentally, there happened to be a few extra paper plates and forks in her bag. She carved a big one out for her grandpa and set it on his workbench. A moment later, she had two more on plates and poured three glasses of creamy whole milk straight out of the milk-house tank.

"Here, Harvey, have a chair. You can have the thenter roll."

Grandpa smiled, because everyone knew center rolls were the best part of any pan of rolls. He stopped his work long enough to join the young people. Lucy's rolls were soft and flaky with cinnamon and frosting combined deliciously and baked to perfection.

While Harvey devoured his roll, Lucy casually mentioned, "Now, I need to find thomeone with a big team of horthes to pull our hayrack full of carolers."

Harvey took a long gulp of milk while Lucy watched. He set down his glass. "I wonder if J. John's boy Fred could bring over his team of Belgians. I could ask him if you want me to?" Lucy's face went pale, and she gave her grandpa a wide-eyed plea for help.

Titus pulled his hanky from his pocket and wiped his mouth and beard. "Maybe I could finish your new harness by Friday. If I can get it done, you could come by and we could fit it for your team. Would you be able to drive the wagon?"

"I guess I could," Harvey said, less than enthusiastically.

Titus let his brow furrow. "Don't you trust your team with a load of people?"

"I trust them all right—as much as any team around. I guess I just thought Fred would really be happy to do it. He lives right close by and J. John's big team of Belgians would look nice on a hay rack."

Lucy stood up with a sober face and cleaned up the empty paper plates and tossed them into the wood stove and let the door bang shut. She wiped her hands on her apron and set about sorting her snaps and buckles. Harvey looked at Titus as if confused by Lucy's sudden change of demeanor.

Titus winked at Harvey. "I'd really think it would be fun if we could try out your new harness with the Christmas caroling crowd. Please—let's use your team."

Harvey coughed and shrugged. "I'd really enjoy doing it if you want me to?"

Titus smiled and nodded. Lucy let out a breath she must have been holding. Her cute smile returned to her pretty face. "Thankths for being willing."

Harvey's face flushed. His voice cracked as he said, "You sure make great cinnamon rolls."

Lucy's eyes sparkled bright-blue and she blushed. Titus stood and announced, "I need to run up to the house for a moment. Lucy, will you watch the shop while I'm gone?"

Verna met Titus at the door of their small house. "What do you need?"

"I came in to get some cash for my register. I happened to notice I'm out of fives and tens."

His wife eyed him suspiciously, "Is Harvey out there with Lucy?"

"Yes, they're fine in there for a moment. It is a public place."

"I'm not asking for that reason. I was wondering if you mentioned the money to Harvey?"

Titus rummaged through his cash box. He drew out the bills he needed. "I didn't want to say anything in front of Lucy, but I'll look for a chance."

"Good idea."

Titus bumped into Harvey as he headed around the corner of his shop. Harvey mumbled, "Lucy told me she could finish the snap and buckle project easy enough by herself."

Titus wrinkled his brow. "Okay." He opened the shop

door, and his wife's instructions came to mind. He followed the young man toward his horses. "By the way, Harvey. Could you mention to your dad that the Holiday Harness Shop policy is to pay at least half when you pick up an order?"

"I'll make sure to tell him." Harvey's shoulders slumped as he drove away.

Tension filled the air after the sleigh bells stopped jingling. Lucy's face took on a stiff expression. Her lips were pinched shut—her eyebrows slanted sharply toward the bridge of her pretty nose. Snaps and buckles were clunking against each other and the wall as she sorted them. Finally, to break the awkward silence, Titus said, "I'm glad Harvey volunteered to bring his team for the caroling."

"I don't even want him to."

"Would you rather have Fred drive his team."

Lucy sniveled. "No, Grandpa."

Titus got busy with his harness project. After listening to Lucy's sniffles for a short time, he offered, "Maybe you'd rather work on those snaps another time?"

Lucy said, "Thankths." And headed out.

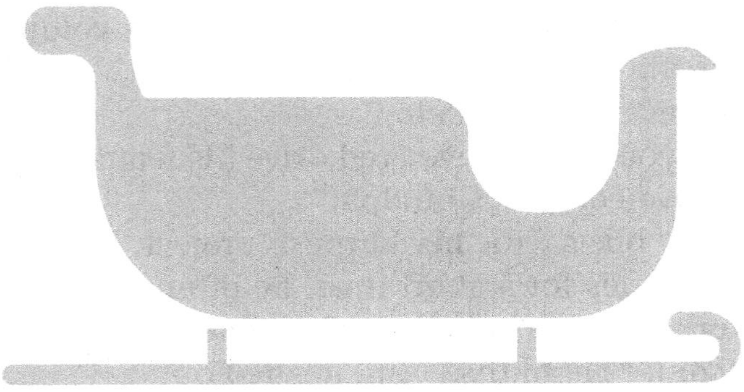

CHAPTER 7

Big Eyes

Verna found an excuse to jingle the doorbells within a short time. "I came out to see what you want to eat this evening."

Titus glanced at her. "What are my options?"

She looked at the ceiling as though she could see a menu written up there. Titus smiled to himself, knowing she was not there to find out what he wanted for supper—she obviously had not even thought of it. She put a hand to her mouth. "I could open a jar of canned ham, or we could have grilled cheese and tomato soup."

"I'm hungry for grilled cheese," Titus said to end the ruse. He knew why she came out to visit his shop.

She nonchalantly glanced at the harness project. "What happened with Lucy?"

"About what?" he said to tease her.

Verna let out an exasperated sigh. "Wasn't Lucy out here when Harvey came to check on the harness?"

Titus let his hands stay busy putting holes in a strap with his leather punch. He let out an "Oh" to feign surprise. "Yes. Lucy wanted me to set it up for Harvey to drive the carolers with his team on Christmas Eve. I found a way to bring it up, and Harvey agreed to do it."

"Then why did I see her stomp into the house in a huff?"

Titus laid the leather on his worktable and looked his wife in the eyes. "I can't even guess. They were as happy as two canaries in a cage when I came inside and talked to you. When I got back out here, he was leaving, and she was upset."

"Well—why didn't you ask her what happened?"

Her piercing eyes made him doubt himself, and he averted his gaze back to his leather project. "I didn't know how to ask about something like that."

Verna's hands went to her hips in disgust. She paced the floor for a moment and said, "A grandpa should know how to get to the bottom of things." She continued pacing for a few moments before adding, "Now I'll have to find an excuse to go to the big house and get it sorted out."

Titus fidgeted with his project to keep from meeting his wife's eyes. "I don't think Lucy feels like talking about it right now."

"That's the problem with you," she moaned. "You try to give people space when what they really need is someone to pry things out of them and get everything solved. Now I have to do it."

"I did bring up the money to Harvey," Titus said, hoping to improve his standing with his wife.

"At least you did something right." She let the door shut with a sharp jangle of bells when she left.

Shortly after Verna left, Janice and the twins came into the shop. They all stomped snow from their boots while the doorbells jingled. Grandpa Titus tried to keep his focus on the harness project instead of his cute grandchildren, determined to finish the job before the Christmas Eve caroling party. He listened to his grandchildren jabbering about snowmen and sledding. He overheard Janice telling her little brothers, "I don't blame Lucy for not wanting to take a ride with mean redhead F... F ... red."

The boys nodded in agreement. They changed the subject by saying, "We're warmed up now. Let's go sledding again!"

Grandpa Titus got up from his work. "Boys—go ahead and go outside. I want to talk to Janice by herself."

The twins fell into a discussion about which hill they should sled down next and hurried out. Janice's eyes grew wide in surprise, obviously nervous about Grandpa wanting to talk to her alone. He took her little hand and drew her over to a chair and sat her down. He pulled up another chair and eased himself into it. He studied her large brown eyes. "What is our neighbor boy's name?"

"Who? Fred?"

Grandpa Titus continued holding her gaze until she let her eyes fall to her lap. "That day he chased you back to my shop I heard you say, 'F ... F ... red,' and I thought you were stammering because you were afraid."

"I was," she said, and met eyes with her grandpa for a split second.

He reached down and lifted her chin with a finger till they met eyes again. "Why did I hear you call him F ... F ... red a few minutes ago when you were talking to your brothers?"

Her brown eyes shifted to one side even though Grandpa Titus held her face up with a finger under her chin. "He is mean to us and he calls Lucy, Luthy. So, I call him that."

Grandpa Titus took his finger away, and Janice glanced at him briefly before bowing her head again. They sat in silence for a few moments. He gave her time to think about it before he spoke. "We all know Fred stammers from time-to-time and that he has red hair."

She nodded.

"Do you think it might hurt his feelings when you call him that?"

A big tear rolled down her little cheek and dropped on her hands folded upon her lap. "Yes."

Grandpa Titus let out a sigh. "I think you should ask God to forgive you."

"Dear God, I'm sorry I teased Fred about his stammer and his hair. Please forgive me."

A few more tears dropped on her little hands. Grandpa Titus found himself surprised she prayed out loud at that very moment. He intended for her to think about it and hoped she would take care of it privately and soon. This was more than he hoped for, and he realized a few tears were leaving his own eyes. She seemed surprised when she looked up and saw his tears. He stood up and drew out a hanky and handed it to her. She wiped her eyes and blew her little nose. She handed it back, and he took his turn.

"Can I go out and play now?" she asked.

"Sure." As she headed for the door, he asked, "Did you say something about Lucy not wanting to take a ride from Fred?"

She nodded. "Harvey told Lucy that Fred wants to give her a ride home from the next young folks Singing. That made her so mad because she wants Harvey to give her a ride home."

"I see." Grandpa Titus smiled at Janice and said, "Go have fun with your brothers."

Titus set about his harness making at a faster pace than ever. He knew he wanted to finish before Christmas to get the money Verna needed and to encourage Harvey to drive his horses at the Christmas Eve caroling party.

The bells clanged solemnly. Verna shuffled in and sat on a stool near the cash register. She exhaled for a spell and sighed. "I can't get anything out of Lucy. She doesn't want to talk to me about it." Thumping sounds from a treadle sewing machine filled the small shop. A few more moans came from Verna. "I guess there's nothing we can do to help her if she won't tell us what's wrong."

Titus mumbled, "It sounds like she's upset because Harvey told her Fred wants to give her a ride home from the next Singing."

"What? Where did you hear that?"

"Janice told me."

Verna let out a cackling giggle. "Can you beat that? Our seven-year-old granddaughter got to the bottom of things before her grandpa could." On her way out the door she asked, "Why would Harvey help Fred date Lucy? It's plain-as-day that Harvey likes her."

With a tug on his beard, Titus mused, "I guess because Harvey is just that nice. His friend asked him to do a favor and he did it."

"We need to help her solve this," Verna said. "Lucy prefers Harvey and so do I."

CHAPTER 8

TWO CHRISTMASES

Thursday morning Titus awoke worrying about getting the Chupp harness finished. He concluded he might as well go get to work. Heading through the darkness, he used a flashlight to watch for icy spots. He made wonderful progress on his harness project without interruptions. At the first hint of light, he noticed the children headed out for morning chores.

Verna jingled the door bells around breakfast time. "Aren't you going to come in for eggs and bacon?"

"Now that I've promised Harvey I'd have this harness done by tomorrow afternoon, I'd better keep at it."

She looked over his shoulder while he laid out the leather straps, assembling them into the shape they needed to take. "Can you do it?"

Titus let out a moan as he stood. "Maybe. This harness needs to be buckled together like I've already done with that other one." He pointed to a mass of leather and shiny buckles dangling from a hook near the window.

"If that's all you have to do it should be no problem."

He groaned. "Besides piecing this together, I still need to make two belly bands and a set of driving lines."

Verna headed for the door. "You keep at it. I'll bring out a breakfast." She pulled open the door and added, "If you can finish by tomorrow, we can get the money in the bank before they close for Christmas. We have to get a check in the mail in time to reach the hospital before the end of the month."

Within a half hour, Verna popped back inside with a plate of food. "I put your egg, bacon and toast together into a sandwich. That way it will be easier to eat."

"And a little faster," Titus said with a wink. He took a bite and the combination amazed him. Savory bacon, fluffy scrambled eggs perfectly salted with cheese melted on top. "Why don't you make it like this more often?"

She giggled with a familiar sound. A realization came to him she had always used the same giggle whenever he complemented anything about her for the past fifty years. *I love that sound. I should complement her more often.*

"Look out there," she said. "Our grandchildren are building a snowman."

Titus continued devouring his sandwich while he and his wife watched Janice and the twins setting the middle section of a snowman on the larger ball of a base. He washed everything down with a hot cup of coffee which burned deliciously going down and warmed his belly. "Thanks for another amazing breakfast," he said as he headed back to work, hoping to hear her giggle again. She did not disappoint him but let out her usual warm cackle.

Verna stood watching the children building their snowman while Titus groaned and strained to slide buckles into place along the leather straps. He enjoyed listening to his wife's giggles and cackles while she watched the snowman take shape. He wanted to join her at the window, but he knew he should keep at the project. With a final laughing sigh, she stated, "Well—that snowman will be in the perfect place to greet all of the carolers when they arrive tomorrow evening."

He did not stop working even to comment. She headed for the door. "Good job keeping at your work," she said. "I'll bring out a lunch, so you don't have to come inside." The door jingled shut before he got out the word, "Thanks."

Grandpa Titus heard his grandchildren's voices getting closer. The doorbells jingled as they clamored inside with the stomping of boots and chirps of joyful words about their accomplishment. "We made a snowman," Janice announced.

He wanted to get up and look out the window, but he kept working. "Grandma and I saw you were building one."

The twins pulled off their mittens and warmed their hands by the fire, joyfully jabbering about their snowman. Janice stepped closer to her grandpa and looked at his harness project. "Is this one for Harvey?"

"Yes. I'm trying to get it finished before tomorrow so Harvey can put it on his team and take the carolers for Christmas Eve caroling."

She turned her head to one side as she looked at the harness. "Why are there two Christmases?"

Grandpa Titus stopped working at looked at Janice. "Do you mean December 25'h and then Old Christmas on January 6th?"

"Yeah—why do us Amish people have a different Christmas than everyone else?"

Titus tried to think of a short way to explain something complicated. "Years ago, someone in another religion changed the calendar. Our ancestors didn't think it was a good idea. We kept on celebrating the Old Christmas and let the world do what they chose." He checked her eyes to see if that was enough of an answer. "We kind of join the others on December 25th, but our real Christmas is January 6th."

She responded with an, "Oh." After a moment of silence where Grandpa Titus could see the wheels of thought turning in her large brown eyes, she asked, "Grandpa—do you have anything we can use for eyes and a mouth on our snowman?"

The twins overheard Janice's question and chimed in with excited agreement. "Yes—Grandpa—Mom didn't have anything in the kitchen but a carrot for his nose."

Grandpa Titus glanced around his shop. "Sleigh bells might work." He took down an old strap with harness bells on it. "Do these bells look about right."

"Yes!" All three children agreed by nodding excitedly.

A few snips later, bells were separated from leather and children headed out the door with hands full of shiny balls about the size of charcoal briquettes. Harness-making suffered its next interruption when Titus heard a car roar into the snowy lane. He hurried to the window to be sure his grandchildren were all safely out of the way. The red car with black stripes fishtailed between the house and barn, sliding to a stop where horses were usually tied. Titus murmured to himself, "What could that man want here?"

CHAPTER 9

MORE CUSTOMERS

The doorbells clanged with a dull thud. Titus smiled politely as the man with back-and-white checked shirt under a vest entered. "What can I help you with today?"

"Nothing," he answered flatly. "Just lookin' around."

Titus nodded. "Let me know if I can answer any questions." He resumed his harness making with occasional glances at the stranger. The outsider examined each wall as if doing an inventory or searching for a gift idea. He stopped at the ox yoke which hung over the cash register. "What's this?"

"That is a yoke for oxen. In the old days, farmers would hitch two steers together with a yoke. People don't use cattle as draft animals much nowadays. I like it because it reminds me of years-gone-by."

"How much?" he growled.

Titus touched the wood affectionately. "It's not for sale. I bought it as a gift for my wife."

The unhappy man pointed to the words, *My Yoke is Easy*. "What does that mean?"

"I'm glad you asked," Titus said. He tried to ignore the dragon tattoo which reached up out of the man's shirt collar and wrapped around his neck. "That is a quote from the Bible. Jesus said, 'Come unto me, all ye that labour and are heavy laden, and I will give you rest. Take my yoke upon you, and learn of me; for I am meek and lowly in heart: and ye shall find rest unto your souls. For my yoke is easy, and my burden is light.'"

"Sounds like gibberish to me," he scoffed, and walked away from the counter as though wanting to end their conversation.

Titus resumed his harness work for a moment. He decided to add another comment in a less intimidating way, by not meeting eyes while speaking. "I take it to mean, that if we let him, Jesus will come alongside and help us shoulder our load. That is what a yoke is—a way for two to work together to pull the same load."

Awkward silence filled the room when the stranger continued looking around as though nothing had been said. He stopped by the counter again, his eyes shifting but never meeting Titus's. "I hear Amish people don't defend themselves. Is that true?"

Titus looked up. For the first time, their eyes met, which sent a cold rush through Titus's veins. He tried to calm himself before answering. "We believe God will defend us." Those words appeared to surprise the stranger as much as they did Titus. He had not planned out his answer—it just came to him.

Mervin Miller burst through the door at that moment. The sleigh bells bounced off their hook and landed on the floor of the Holiday Harness Shop. "Good morning, Titus!" Mervin filled up the doorway as much or more than Harvey. He stood at least as tall but maybe fifty pounds heavier. His husky face wore a jolly expression. The only expression he seemed to own. He stooped, picked up the sleigh bells, and returned them to their hook on the door.

The stranger bumped Mervin as he rushed past him and out the door. Mervin said, "Excuse me," as if he had been the cause of the collision. As Titus considered Mervin's happy attitude, he also tried to remember his age. *If I remember right, he was born the same year as Lucy.* "Well—it is a good morning. What brings Mervin Miller down Holiday Road?"

Mervin looked out through the window at the red car fishtailing out of the lane. "I hope I didn't chase that guy off?"

"No worries—I feel better now that he's gone. What can I help you with?"

"My dad thinks I came here to have you fix this horse collar." He set a massive oval collar on the worktable. The adjustment buckle dangled where it had become unattached. "This is the only collar we have large enough to fit Jim."

"That Jim is about the biggest Belgian I've ever seen," Titus said. He eyed Mervin, "So did you or didn't you come here to have me fix the collar?"

Mervin laughed so hard his belly shook. "I did come to have you fix our horse collar. The adjustment buckle is broken. But my dad thinks that's the only reason I came to see you. The real reason I'm here is my mom wants you to make a new leather billfold as a Christmas gift for my dad."

Titus took the heavy leather collar up in his hands to examine it. While he looked it over, he asked, "Does your mother want to give your dad his gift on December 25th or on Old Christmas?"

"This weekend," he said enthusiastically. "That way my dad can take it on our trip. We are going to visit relatives south of here for Old Christmas."

Titus tugged on his beard in thought. "This may be a problem," he considered out loud. "I'm trying to get a new team harness made for Lavern Chupp by Christmas Eve. My schedule might be too full."

"Do you mean Harvey's dad?"

"Yes."

Mervin's eyes scanned the pile of half-finished harness laying on the counter. "Is that harness a Christmas gift?"

"No—it's just that Harvey is going to hall the carolers with his big team. His harness is so worn out it's almost dangerous."

Lucy came through the door with a gentle jingle of bells. "Hello, Mervin. Are you coming to join the caroling on Christmas Eve?"

Mervin's jolly face flushed rosy. "I sure hope to." He shuffled his feet as Lucy circled the worktable to stand by the wood-burning stove, and his gaze followed her. "Your grandpa just mentioned he's trying to get this big harness project done before Friday so Harvey can use it on his team."

Lucy rubbed her hands together by the stove. "I don't think Harvey wanths to drive the wagon."

"I've got an idea," Mervin shouted with such enthusiasm he dropped his horse collar. It rolled against the row of harnesses and they all jingled. As he retrieved his runaway collar he announced, "If Titus fixes this collar," he held it high with a grin, "he wouldn't have to finish Harvey's harness by Christmas Eve. I'd be happy to bring my team!"

Lucy rushed close and exclaimed, "Would you do that?"

Mervin backed away as if a little blue-eyed female proved as intimidating as a bull. He swallowed hard and lost his grin, but his cheeks continued to flush rosy-red. "I'd be happy to," he muttered.

Grandpa Titus interrupted the moment by clearing his throat. "I'm not sure we can change our plans. I've already promised Harvey to have his project done." Titus did not feel free to mention that part of the issue was money. He hoped to make his wife happy by finishing the project before the weekend and gathering the much-needed funds. Having Harvey drive the carolers fit perfectly with that plan.

Mervin turned away from Lucy and regained his composure. "I'm sure Harvey won't mind. I could check with him on my way home. I'll go right by Lavern's farm."

After a moment of thought and gazing out through the small windows, Titus said, "It's starting to snow again. You don't need to go tell Harvey. He'll stop by here tomorrow morning, and I'll say something about it then." He rubbed the window with his shirt sleeve to get a better view. "Look out there—Fred Miller is helping my grandchildren make a snowman."

Mervin laughed and his large frame shook. "I'll have to go tease my redheaded buddy about making snowmen with little children."

"Don't be too hard on him," Titus exclaimed. "I'm happy to see he is getting along with Janice. Those two haven't been friends before."

Mervin headed out, and Lucy called after him, "I'll thee you tomorrow!" She remained by her grandpa and they watched in disbelief as Fred, normally a bully, laughed and visited with Janice and the twins as they built a massive snowman next to an already existing snowman. Lucy used her sleeve to wipe her breath off the window as if her eyes were playing tricks on her. "That'th odd. I wonder what'th got into Fred?"

Grandpa Titus chose not to mention his conversation with Janice and her prayer, even though he assumed it played a big part in what they were witnessing. Verna stepped through the doorway and caught Titus gawking out the window with Lucy. "You'll never finish that harness on time if you stand there watching everything that happens in our lane."

He hurried back to his harness project and got to work. Lucy stepped through the doorway, heading back to the house. No doubt she wanted to avoid hearing her grandmother scold her grandpa. Verna began a barrage of questions, "What did that man with a red car want? Did Mervin come to buy something? Are you letting your grandchildren keep you from finishing your project on time?"

He kept his focus on the harness until she said, "Well?"

He chose to answer the question that would please her most. "Mervin wants me to fix his horse collar and make a new billfold for his dad."

"Did you tell him first come—first served? You need to finish that big harness project before you start on those little side jobs. We need the money from the Chupp harness before Christmas."

Titus let out a grunt, hoping it would be enough of an answer. He whispered, "Don't talk so loud—Mervin is still out in the drive helping Fred make a snowman for Janice and the twins."

"I'm surprised to see that, she said, and flopped a sack on the counter. "I brought out a sandwich for your lunch. Maybe you can eat it when someone interrupts your work again."

He muttered, "Okay," and kept his hands moving. "Lucy asked Mervin to drive the caroler wagon with his team. Mervin needs this big collar fixed before tomorrow if he's gonna do it."

"I thought Harvey was going to drive the carolers?"

Titus set his work down for a moment to let out a sigh. "Lucy is frustrated with Harvey because he tried to help his buddy Fred get a date with her. When Mervin was here, she asked him to drive the carolers instead of Harvey."

Verna rose to her tiptoes to look outside. "I suppose those boys keep coming around here because of our Lucy." She faced her husband and shook a finger. "You'd better not stop working on Harvey's harness to fix Mervin's horse collar. We need that harness money." She picked up the collar and looked at the broken buckle strap. "This project won't pay that well. Besides—we don't want Lucy to end up with Mervin."

Titus looked out the window to be sure Mervin and Fred could not overhear them. "Don't worry, Grandma. I'll finish the harness first. Lucy is a smart girl. She can figure out the boy situation without our help."

"Guiding our grandchildren in the right direction is our job," Verna said and headed out. The door clomped shut and the bells shook sharply.

Harness making went along fine until Titus heard a commotion out in the lane. He wanted to look out of a window to see what was happening, but he forced himself to ignore a few shouts from the children mingled with Mervin's booming laughter and Fred's stammering voice. Fred sounded upset, which brought out an overwhelming urge in Titus to stand up and look.

CHAPTER 10

TWO SNOWMEN

Janice and the twins came running through the door and burst into tears. The bells trembled on their hook while the children stood by the fire wiping their eyes and sniffling. Grandpa picked up his sandwich and stopped to bow his head before eating or tackling the matter at hand. *Lord, please bless this food. And please give me wisdom with my grandchildren.* "What could have you children so upset?"

With dramatic brown eyes opened wide, Janice explained, "Fred came by as happy as could be." She interrupted her own story to wipe tears from her cheeks with snowy mittens. "Fred said, 'I'll help you build a huge snowman for the carolers to see tomorrow night if you don't tell anyone that I helped.'" She sniveled briefly and continued, "We weren't gonna tell anyone. Then Mervin came out and teased him. Fred told him, 'You're just jealous because I'm driving Lucy and the carolers with my team tomorrow.' Mervin laughed and said, 'No, you're not. Lucy just asked me to drive.'"

Grandpa Titus took out his hanky and dabbed at Janice's cheeks. "Why are you and the twins so upset."

Janice's voice rose an octave as she forced out words through her tears, "Mervin teased Fred saying that everyone will see his snowman tomorrow night. Fred's face got all red and he knocked down the snowman he helped us make. Then Mervin and Fred both left." She burst out crying, which sparked another bout of tears from the little boys.

Grandpa Titus let them all cry for a moment before attempting to encourage them. "I can see your other snowman is still standing."

"Fred's snowman was bigger and better than ours," Abner blurted out.

All the sobs were interrupted by a loud rattling coming up the road. They all looked through the windows and saw Harvey driving his big team into the lane with a hayrack rolling thunderously behind them. Janice and the twins dried their tears and headed outside with an obvious effort to hide their red eyes from Harvey.

Harvey seemed sheepish when he came inside. The sleigh bells barely moved and clanked gently against the door when he crept inside. "What happened with Janice and the twins?"

Titus tried to avoid explaining everything by saying, "Their snowman fell down."

"I can still see it out there."

"There were two," Titus answered. Anxious to leave that topic behind, he announced, "I'm getting closer on your harness project."

The young man's face beamed as he examined a set of new harness with sparkling silver buckles. A moment later his countenance fell. "Actually, my dad hoped you wouldn't finish this project until after the new year. We've had a lot of bills come due lately, and he won't get another check until January."

Titus spoke without thinking, "When you kept stopping in to check on the harness, I thought you were urging me on."

Harvey let his eyes fall to the floor. "I will be happy for the harness when it's done. I come by often because I just enjoy stopping by your shop."

The older man immediately knew what the younger man meant: *He enjoyed stopping in to see Lucy.* "Harvey, tell your dad he can pay later if needs be."

"I wouldn't feel right using the harness tomorrow if we haven't paid you anything yet." His gaze fell to the floor. "I went ahead and told Fred he should bring his team over tomorrow. I brought our big hayrack so he can hitch to that for the carolers."

"Fred won't be driving the carolers tomorrow."

Harvey's gaze rose to meet Titus's. "What ... why?"

Scratching his balding head, Titus tried to sort out how to answer. "I'd really like to see this new harness on your team on Christmas Eve. Fred already knows he's not going to drive the carolers."

"Can you finish our harness on time?"

"I think so." Titus nodded with a smile. "If we can we use your old driving lines tomorrow. Lord willing, I'll finish your driving lines before the first of the year." He laid a hand on Harvey's shoulder. "Come over tomorrow afternoon, and we'll fit this harness on your team. I believe Lucy wants you to drive the carolers."

"That'd be great!" Harvey's face beamed. He headed out with a merry jingle of bells on the door.

A short time later, Titus noticed Harvey's horses were still at the hitching rack. He glanced out the lane as Harvey and the twins rolled a huge snowball into place beside the little snowman. The next time Titus looked up, Harvey and Janice hoisted a head onto a newer, bigger snowman while the twins cheered.

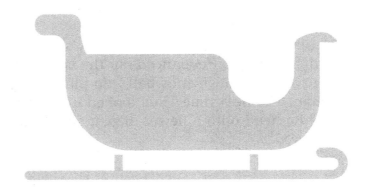

CHAPTER 11

Mismatched Team

Christmas Eve morning, Titus headed to his harness shop while the stars were still twinkling in inky blackness. His footsteps crunched loud enough to echo off the wall of the buggy shed. He used an LED headlamp to shine into his dark shop until he struck a match and lit his gas lantern. Another match flared as he lit his wood-burning stove. The glowing lantern and crackling fire created a warm and pleasant feeling inside the walls of Titus's shop. He hummed "Away in a Manger" as he began the final stages of making a team harness. It seemed impossible to finish before the carolers all would arrive. He still had two belly bands to make.

"Dear Lord, please help me finish this project on time. I don't want to let down Harvey and Lucy."

He finished up yesterday's project of completing the tugs, the set of double-thick straps horses pull a load with, and attached them to a set of shiny new hames. The pleasant aroma of new harness and freshly painted hames lulled Titus into a relaxed mode. He suddenly remembered his time-crunch and began humming "God Rest Ye Merry Gentlemen" with the hope a faster rhythm would speed up his work.

The afternoon came too soon. Harvey's big team came into the lane under light falling snow. They made a pretty sight as they trotted past two snowmen who welcomed all visitors on Christmas Eve. Sleigh bells jingled brightly with Harvey's happy entrance. The young man's cheeks were rosy by reason of a cold drive behind a team of horses. There seemed to be an extra sparkle in his eyes as he greeted Titus. "Merry Christmas," he said with a joyful expression.

"Merry Christmas to you, Harvey. I'm just finishing up your belly bands."

Harvey took off his leather gloves and laid them on the counter. "Look what I brought." He drew out his billfold and out of that, four stiff, new, one-hundred-dollar bills.

"Harvey—I don't want to be a hardship for your dad."

The young man's face stayed confident. "It's not a problem." He leaned close to Titus as if someone might overhear his words. "I took this money out of my savings. When my dad sends money for the harness, you can return that to me."

"You don't have to do this, Harvey."

"I want to. My dad and mom have had some hard times financially ever since my sister had an accident a few years ago. I'd be happy to pay for the harness myself, but Dad wouldn't let me. This is the least I can do."

Titus smiled at the young man. "Why don't you go take your old harness off your big team while I finish up in here. We can fit the new harness on them together."

By the time Harvey unharnessed his team, Titus had finished the bellybands and tucked the four one-hundred-dollar bills into his cash drawer. He put on his heavy coat and broadbrimmed hat. They each carried a harness outside to try on the massive horses. Titus waited while Harvey draped his harness on one horse. "I think I'll let you put this on this black horse, I can't reach up that high anymore."

Harvey chuckled and took the harness by the hames. Titus began adjusting snaps and buckles on the sorrel horse. "This is a dandy team, but I'm curious about why you drive a black Percheron with a sorrel Belgian. I know your dad has more of each."

"These are my two favorite horses. At first glance, they don't match, but they work perfectly together." Harvey moved around the huge horses with confidence and a clear sense of heathy pride in them—not of showing off, but of valuing the creatures deeply. "Some people tease me about driving unmatched horses. I don't mind. They are tempered so differently from each other, but that is what makes them a perfect team. If one has a weakness, the other is strong in that area."

"Such as what?" Titus asked with sincere curiosity.

"Well—this black horse, Cello is his name, is nervous around big vehicles on the road. Brick, the sorrel, doesn't mind traffic at all. That seems to help Cello. If he were hitched with another traffic-shy horse, he'd get worse. Brick helps him face his fears."

The two men finished snapping everything in place. Harvey gathered his old driving lines and threaded them through to the horses' bits. "This looks great. And I'll have a chance to drive them and see that the harness is fitted right before the carolers climb aboard."

"See you back here in a few hours," Titus said, and watched the young man drive away with his beautiful horses in their new outfits.

He stepped back inside and noticed Harvey left without his gloves. He chuckled and said to himself, "That young man is so pleased with his new harness and about driving Lucy's carolers he won't notice cold fingers until he gets home."

The door jingled lightly as Lucy stepped inside meekly. "Did Harvey come pick up his harneth?"

"Yes—and he forgot his gloves. Make sure and get them to him tonight."

Her face flushed. "Too bad he can't drive the carolerths tonight."

"He is going to drive the carolers," Grandpa Titus announced cheerfully.

Lucy's mouth dropped, "No heths not. I athked Mervin to drive the wagon and you were thupposed to tell Harvey."

Titus winked at his granddaughter. "I haven't had time to fix Mervin's collar yet. He can't drive his team without that. I'm going to make his dad's Christmas billfold next and the collar won't be finished until after Christmas. Mervin already told me they don't have another collar big enough for his horse. I'll take the blame when he comes this afternoon to pick up the billfold."

She eyed her grandpa suspiciously. "Wouldn't it have been eathier to finish the collar before Harvey's work harneth?"

He shrugged and winked. "Maybe that is true. Would you mind watching the shop while I run in and tell Grandma my good news about finishing my project. I'm also gonna find your dad in the barn and ask him to stop by and take my cash to the bank when he heads to town this afternoon."

"Hurry back before Mervin cometh," she said, her face beaming. "I don't wanna be the one to tell him about the collar."

CHAPTER 12

GOOD AND EVIL

A red car with black racing stripes sat near the hitching rack when Titus left the house and headed to the harness shop. He picked up his pace, remembering the strange man which visited the shop a few days ago. *I don't want that strange man in there alone with Lucy.*

In his rush, Titus felt his foot slide on ice and slip out from under him. He thought for a moment he could catch his balance. His center of gravity crossed over the point of no return and as he reached for the ground to break his fall, he could see Lucy through the window. She must have been standing on a chair. The form of her blue dress reached up toward the ceiling. The strange man stood behind her so close it made Titus shudder.

After he landed in a heap, Titus tried to see what was happening in the shop, but a snowdrift blocked his view. Movement in the driveway caught his eye. Harvey's huge horses trotted into the lane again, and the young man jumped off his cart and rushed over. "What happened, Titus?" he asked as he took a firm grip under Titus's arm.

"Don't worry about me! Get into the shop. There's a strange man in there with Lucy!"

Harvey finished hoisting Titus to his feet before rushing toward the Holiday Harness Shop. Following as fast as his aching hip would allow, he watched Harvey charge through the doorway of the shop. An instant later, the strange man came bursting out through the door. He ran to his car. Titus could only watch as the red car fishtailed and did a donut in the drive. It roared toward the road, but slid sideways and disappeared into the deep ditch by the mailbox.

Titus pushed his shop door open. "Is everything okay in here?"

Lucy sat on a stool behind the counter in tears as Harvey patted her back. She covered her face and moaned, "I'm thorry, Grandpa, but that man made me open the cash regither." She sobbed for a moment and forced out words with a high pathetic sound, "He took all your money."

"Don't worry about money—are you okay?"

She nodded while wiping tears away with her fingers. Harvey pointed at the cash register which stood open and empty. "Was all that money I just gave you still in there?"

Titus pushed the drawer shut. "Let's not worry about that now. We have a bigger problem. That man is stuck in the ditch by our mailbox."

Harvey opened the door and Lucy joined him looking out toward the ditch. "What should we do?"

Titus pulled a log-chain out from under his workbench. "Harvey, will you take your team down there and pull him out?"

"If you want me to?"

Lucy trembling fingers touched her grandpa's arm. "I could run down the back way by the creek and call the copths from the phone booth by J. John's house. Maybe the police could get your money back and put that guy in jail."

Titus ran his fingers through his beard in thought. "I don't think we'll call the police on Christmas Eve." He placed a hand on Harvey's shoulder. "If you'll help him get out of our ditch, I'll take fifty-dollars off what your dad owes on the harness."

Harvey marched out to his team of horses. Titus and his granddaughter watched from the doorway as Harvey drove his team to the end of the lane and backed them near the ditch. Only the front end of the red car could be seen from where they stood. Harvey had a short conversation with the man before connecting the chain. His horses leaned forward and brought the red car partway out. Lucy shook her head. "Maybe the Lord won't let him get away with it. Thould I run down and call the copths?"

"I think that man has already learned the Lord didn't let him get away with it. Harvey's horses are good and stout, they'll get him out yet."

They watched Harvey reach under the car and unhook the chain. He attached it again further back. He stood beside his horses and their massive frames dwarfed the tall young man. He spoke to his team briefly and took up his driving lines. Both horses crouched and arched their thick necks. One horse slipped a little and then regained his footing. All at once, the red car came sliding up over the ditch bank. Harvey turned his horses into the driveway dragging the little car behind them. Lucy and Titus retreated into the shop and watched through the little windows.

"Why were you up on a chair?" Grandpa Titus asked in a whisper.

"After he took the money, he told me to climb on a chair and get a bit for him. I think he wath trying to keep me from getting out and telling thomeone he robbed uths."

"Did he take a bit?"

"No. When Harvey's horthes pulled into the lane, he ran out."

The man stepped out of his car and watched Harvey unhook the chain. They had a short conversation and a handshake before the red car backed out and sped away. Harvey came in and headed to the woodburning stove to warm his hands. Titus and Lucy followed.

Lucy spoke first, "What did he thay?"

"He told me that my horses are amazing."

"Ith that all?"

Harvey shook his head. "No. He asked me why we didn't call the police. I told him that Titus said we weren't going to call the police on Christmas Eve." Harvey pulled his gloves out of his pocket. "He gave me my gloves back and said he stole them from the old man. He asked me if I'd give them to you." Harvey held up his gloves. "I didn't tell him they were my gloves."

"Of all the nerve," Lucy said. "He kept the money and gave back the gloveths."

Titus scratched his head. "I guess that was a start. We can pray the Lord will bring him to repentance. What made you come back earlier, Harvey?"

"It must have been the Lord. I realized I left my gloves at your shop and decided to come get them." Harvey stepped toward the door. "I guess it was my money that he stole."

"No," Titus stated emphatically. "The money came from my cash drawer."

Harvey squeezed the gloves in his hand. "Please don't take fifty dollars off our bill. It didn't take much to pull his car out."

Titus shook his head. "No. The Bible says to give to those who steal from you. I told you I'd pay for him, and I mean to do it."

"Grandma won't be happy about that," Lucy said.

"She'll forgive me," Titus answered.

Harvey turned to Lucy. "I'll come by in about an hour with my team to drive the carolers." He stepped out and the doorbells jingled behind him.

Lucy considered her grandpa's expression for a moment and smiled. "You wanted Harvey to drive me tonight, didn't you?"

"I wanted Harvey to try out his new harness. I didn't know he'd have a car to pull out first."

She pressed her lips together and squinted her eyes as if doubting his motives.

"And he's the kind of boy I trust around my Lucy."

Lucy opened her mouth to say something and the sleigh-bells jingled on the door. Harvey burst back inside. "I went to put on my gloves and look what I found." He held out four crisp, one-hundred dollar bills.

CHAPTER 13

MISPLACED OR HIDDEN

"My only remaining project before Christmas is a billfold," Titus announced to himself merrily. He took a template from the shelf below the cash register and examined it closely. He drew his own billfold out, turning the soft leather over in his hands to refresh his memory. After selecting a flawless piece of black leather, he carefully traced around the template with a pencil. Pencil lead left a faint line which would later disappear. Humming "Away in a Manger," he made the cuts and set himself about folding edges under, using paperclips to hold everything in place for stitching.

He sang a few of the lines from "God Rest Ye Merry Gentlemen" and hummed sections as he pumped the treadle of his sewing machine. The billfold project came together nicely. Titus began to worry he might finish it soon enough to have time to mend Mervin's horse collar issue before he stopped by. He slowed his hands by humming "Away in a Manger" again. Every few minutes, he glanced out through the window, searching for a sign of Mervin. Every buggy or horse-drawn cart which came over the hill caught his attention. None were Mervin's.

Before he knew it, Titus sat holding a handsome new billfold in his hands. He looked it over closely, almost hoping to find a mistake that needed to be fixed. Nothing. He took his time getting up and shuffled over to place the new billfold on the counter. After a long, slow breath he said to himself, "Okay. It's time to start working on Mervin's collar." As Titus lumbered over to where he left the collar leaning in a corner, he mumbled, "What am I going to say to Mervin about driving the carolers if I have his collar fixed?" The collar was not there.

"I must have moved it near the wood stove." He chuckled at himself for being absent minded. "I sure am getting old and forgetful." A sinking feeling swelled in his heart when the corner near his stove also failed to produce a horse collar. He scratched his beard just under one ear while his eyes searched the small confines of the Holiday Harness Shop. He completed a full circle and started a second round. He sat down feeling somewhat dizzy. The sleigh bells clanged at full volume and jumped off the door. Titus jumped along with them.

"Merry Christmas, Titus!" Mervin's voice rang out, almost echoing in the cinderblock building. He bent down and gathered the bells and put them back on their hook.

Titus caught his breath, took a gulp of much need oxygen, and muttered, "Merry Christmas to you."

"Did you get my collar fixed?"

Still unwilling to admit he lost a large horse collar in a tiny shop within two days, he changed the subject, hoping it would reappear. "Here is the billfold your mother ordered for your dad." He handed it to Mervin. While the young man admired it, Titus continued scanning around on every counter.

"This billfold is great," Mervin's voice boomed even more exuberantly than usual. "I'd better get my horse collar and head home if I'm gonna get my big team harnessed and back here for caroling!"

Titus let out a long breath. "I'm sorry, Mervin, I didn't get a chance to fix your collar."

The smile remained on Mervin's face. "Where is it? Maybe you could make a temporary fix for tonight, and I could bring it back after Christmas."

"That's the thing, Mervin. I seem to have misplaced it." Titus continued his search under counters and behind tools. "I went ahead and asked Harvey to bring his team to drive the carolers." He checked Mervin's face to see how much damage his words did.

Mervin lost his big grin. His eyes narrowed. He spoke through clenched teeth, "I'll bet Fred snuck over here and hid it. He's mad at me because he wanted to drive Lucy ... I mean the carolers tonight."

Titus shrugged, almost hoping it was true, rather than admitting he lost it. A thought crossed his mind, *Maybe Lucy hid it*? He turned to Mervin. "I would let you use one of these new collars, but I don't happen to have a twenty-five-inch collar on hand. That horse of yours is bigger than most."

Mervin regained his regular smile. "I'm gonna guess the collar will show up tomorrow." He chuckled and added, "I'm so happy you asked Harvey to drive the carolers instead of Fred. Serves him right." He headed toward the door. "I'm gonna go get cleaned up for tonight."

After torching a bonfire ablaze in the burn barrel just outside the shop, Titus brushed off the wooden tabletops and workbenches of the Holiday Harness Shop. He meticulously swept under every table and bench and even under his treadle sewing machine. He looked around the tiny room and smiled. All his projects were caught up, and he could relax through the holidays.

He popped open the woodburning stove and tossed in a few more logs even though he normally let it grow cold this time of day. His shop seemed like a friend. The little building had become the center of his world and a place where he, though aging, could interact with family, friends, neighbors, and even strangers. It seemed only right to add extra logs on Christmas Eve. Titus knew he would sleep better in his warm bed knowing the belly of his little shop would be toasty warm.

He sat on a stool near the fire and hummed his favorite Christmas hymn, "Silent Night." The sleigh bells jingled on the door, but Titus remained seated. He sat with his arms folded and watched to see who would be joining him. He smiled as Verna's familiar face came into view. "Why are you sitting out here alone?"

"I don't feel alone," he said.

"You should come inside before the carolers get here."

He pulled up a stool beside his. "Come sit here with me. It will be fun to watch all the young people arrive and warm themselves by the burn barrel."

Verna eyed him sideways but took a seat beside her husband. "Did Harvey bring all the money for his harness?"

"Most of it." Titus did not bother to tell her the money had come out of Harvey's savings. Nor did he mention the money had been stolen and then returned. Instead he gave her only good news, "Our son, Mahlon, took the money to the bank. We can send our hospital payment, and it will be there before the first of the year."

CHAPTER 14

CHRISTMAS CAROLERS

Titus and Verna gazed out through ice-swirled windows as buggies and horse-drawn carts came into the lane. Each visitor passed by two snowmen who greeted them with sleigh-bell smiles. A crowd of young people began gathering just outside the windows, warming themselves near the burn barrel. Harvey's huge, mismatched, yet perfectly in sync horses came trotting into the drive with bells jingling on their new harness. "What a beautiful sight," Verna said.

"What?"

She dabbed at the corner of her eye. "Everything. The horses, snowmen, young people, snowflakes falling, frost on the windows. Everything."

The sleigh bells on the shop jingled brightly. Lucy opened the door wide revealing a crowd of teenagers all gathered with smiles looking at the couple seated side-by-side. Lucy said to her grandparents. "What Christmas carol would you like to hear thung?"

Grandma Verna answered for them both, "We'd love to hear 'Silent Night'."

Janice and the twins slipped past the carolers and came inside. They leaned against their grandparents, wide-eyed and eager to share the moment.

The Christmas caroler's voices sounded angelic. Deep bass notes came from the back row. Harvey, Fred, and Mervin stood together peacefully among the group of young men. Lucy stood in front of Harvey, shoulder to shoulder with a group of teenaged girls. They took up the higher pitched parts blending sweetly with the boys. Grandpa and Grandma focused on Lucy. Her voice sounded as pretty as her blue eyes looked. Snowflakes fell around them. Each flake glistening by flickering lantern light as if came to rest on a hat or bonnet.

Silent night, holy night! All is calm, all is bright
'round yon virgin mother and child! Holy infant, so
tender and mild,
Sleep in heavenly peace, sleep in heavenly peace.

The young people repeated the first verse in German and it brought tears to the older couple's eyes.

Stille Nacht! Heilige Nacht!
Alles schlaft, einsam wacht
Nur das traute hoch heilige Paar.
"Holderr Knabe im lockigen Harar,
Schlaf in himmlischer Ruh'
Schlaf in himmlischer Ruh'!"

The perfect moment came to an end. Lucy announced, "Everyone get thituated on the hayrack. I'm gonna bring out a pot of hot cocoa."

Janice and the twins followed the crowd outside, obviously longing to be part of the event. Lucy stepped inside as the carolers headed to the wagon. "Grandma, could you refill thith pot after we leave? If you thet it on the wood thove in here, we can have more hot cocoa when we come back."

"I'd be happy to," Grandma Verna said, while dabbing a tear from the corner of one eye.

Grandpa Titus could not resist asking, "Lucy, you didn't put Mervin's horse collar somewhere did you?"

"No, why?"

"I guess I misplaced it. Mervin came to get it, and I couldn't find it anywhere."

Grandma Verna let out a giggle. "I hung it up with the new ones so the shop wouldn't look messy."

The carolers cheerful banter could be heard as Lucy stepped outside. Titus and Verna watched through frosted windows as the teens all climbed aboard the wagon and began singing again. Verna surprised Titus by asking, "Why does Harvey drive a mismatched team?"

"I agree they appear mismatched at first glance, but if you watch them work together, you will see that they complement each other perfectly— just like you and me."

"What do you mean?"

Titus smiled at his wife. "You told me you wanted me to be a better leader for our family. It occurred to me over these past few days—we are a team. Your strengths fill in where I'm weak. We lead this family as a team."

Verna nudged him with her elbow. "I like that."

His mouth dropped. "You didn't put Mervin's horse collar up with the new ones on purpose, did you?"

She smiled coyly.

Titus pointed to the ox yoke. "I'm so thankful to the Lord for making my yoke easy. Being yoked together with you in marriage over all these years has made my work seem easy."

Verna gave a girlish giggle even while another tear formed in the corner of her eye. "Maybe we should bring that ox yoke into our kitchen and put it on the wall behind our table."

"I'd like that," Titus said.

Grandpa and Grandma listened as bells jingled faintly on Harvey's horses. Harvey and Lucy sat side-by-side on a hay bale behind his big team, silhouetted against a snowy background. The sound of sleigh bells mingled with the singing while the horses trotted out of the lane. The beautiful melodies faded as the horses pulled their load of carolers through a curtain of falling snow. They trotted onto Holiday Road, over the hill, and out of sight.

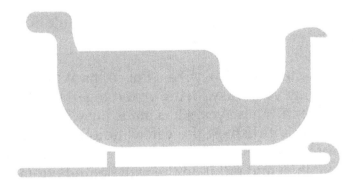

ABOUT THE AUTHOR

Thomas Nye writes novels about Amish life, with a touch of romance, and a foundation of faith in Christ. He and his wife, Shari, live on her family farm where they raised five children. They have seven grandchildren and a team of draft horses. Thomas walks a mail route for the US Postal Service. It keeps him close to nature and affords many quiet hours in which to dream up novels. "Over three decades of friendships with Amish neighbors has revealed a simple wisdom that inspires my writing." To find out more about Thomas Nye and his books, visit: amishhorses.blogspot.com

THE LIGHT AT ST. SILVAN'S

MURRAY PURA

PART ONE (APRIL TO DECEMBER)

CHAPTER 1

LEAVING AND BECOMING

Not that she did not wish to have friends--she loved to be around people. Not that she wanted to keep all her thoughts to herself--sharing her feelings with others, and listening to others share theirs with her, was an important part of her days and weeks. No, but just to be alone, by the sea, in the light, was a time to discover who she was, to know her soul in all its depth and intricacy and mystery. By the sea was a place to dream, to pray, to worship, perhaps even to dance where no one was watching except the gulls that swooped across a sky of blue or gray or gold. Here was a place only God knew, and here was where she came to know God.

> A strange admission, Sara King thought to herself. After all, she had been raised Amish, baptized Amish, married Amish. She was an Amish woman. Sometimes she felt she was more Amish than she was American.

Where ocean met sky did not seem real. There was so much of everything--air, wind, water, space--it was as if all of heaven was over her head and in front of her eyes. Trying to take it in, she felt she had to become a new person because what she used to be could not hope to contain the half of what rushed over her senses. She reached out with her hands to hold it but it slipped through her fingers and into her heart, all of it. She became the sea. She became the air and the sky, became the long stretch of shore and all its sand and rocks. When a wave broke into a spray of light, it was her.

It had never been easy. No matter what the tourists thought about the Amish––theirs was not life under a lilac bloom. Amish life was not the way so many of those who wrote Amish stories said it was––one long romance with God, and with farming, horses, and the land under beautiful sunny skies. One long romance with your man. The life could be so wonderful, yes. But that way of life could be hard. Hard as hidden boulders striking a plow.

"I am being born," she whispered. But there was no pain. Not for her, not for her mother and not for anyone else. There was only the release, the freedom, a delight that carried a child's innocence and a young girl's wonder at seeing beauty for the first time.

There had been one son. Sara was unable to conceive after that. Doctors were no help. Her husband blamed her. Why did he marry her? Why could she not give them a family like the Millers or Bylers or Hostetlers? When the boy had been killed in a farming accident at eight, her husband could not forgive God. Nor could he forgive himself. He could never forgive himself. Many tried to help. She could not deny that. So many in the Amish church tried to help them in their dark and terrible grief. But he took his life with rope in the barn. While she was in the house preparing their lunch. It was a cloudless April day. She thought of it as a perfect day, though her heart remained dark with the loss of her boy the month before. Perhaps the best day since the accident. She looked out the kitchen window at the farmyard while she peeled carrots. The barn was green and huge and silent, and her husband did not respond when she opened the window and called him to the table.

The light cut through mist and darkness and warned sailors about the rocks at St. Silvan's. It also guided them to port and to safety, no matter what sort of problems they were dealing with in their ships, or what sort of storms they were attempting to weather. She often wished, as she stood on the upper deck of the lighthouse and watched its beam stretch over the waters, that the light could do the same for her. At such times she began to pray, and the prayer was nothing like church prayers at all. They came up from deep within her and were often as wild and rugged as the Atlantic itself. But they were her words, and they were from her heart, and somehow, she was aware God knew that and loved her for them. That love burned through any night that had descended on her and any storm or cloud that shrouded her soul.

Sara King never thought of herself as someone who might run. But her husband's suicide, falling so hard upon her son's death, after a marriage of bitter words from a man who could not accept her or love her as she was, caused everything to collapse. A year after the loss of her son and her husband, she left. She gave the farm to the bishop in a legal document he would not receive until after she was gone. Friends who had helped her work the farm that lonely year would take care of things while she was away. She told them it was only for a few days. She had taken the train and the bus and finally an Uber. Then several ferries including one that only sailed on Fridays until July and August when it made the trip once a day. Her bid on an old abandoned lightkeepers' cottage on St. Silvan's had been accepted. A realtor met her on the mainland in Gloucester. They did the paperwork and Sara was handed the keys.

"It's fine for summer," the realtor told her. "Of course, it's winterized too. Keepers lived there year-round. But it will need a bit of TLC."

"Thank you," Sara responded. "I'll take care of that."

"Oh, are you handy?"

"I am, yes."

"Are you a carpenter?"

"I am a farmer. One who didn't stay in the kitchen or laundry room."

"Will your family be joining you on St. Silvan's?"

"No, they will not."

Sara had boarded the first train dressed Amish but changed into jeans and a blue chamois shirt in a restroom in the car, tying her sand-colored hair back with a blue bandana. She took her battered navy backpack onto the ferries along with a sky-blue mountain bike she bought in Gloucester. A man on the first ferry told her everything matched her eyes. She surprised herself by her reply. "My eyes aren't yellow like my hair."

The smell of the sea overpowered her and broke through all her fear and doubt about what she was doing. The tar of the wharves, the gray planks, the roll of the ferries, the spray, the gulls, all were part of a magic kingdom that promised far more than what she had left behind. Yet she sang an Amish hymn to herself as the ferry approached the wharf at St. Silvan's. And said a prayer in High German out loud when she unlocked the door to her cottage and stepped inside after a ten-minute bike ride. Peace. An overwhelming sense of peace.

"Lived in but lived in well," she said, after one long glance.

She knew keepers and their families had lived in the cottage since 1705 and that the house had been improved upon a dozen times to add plumbing and wiring and new roofs. But because most of it was stone, it had withstood the test of time and storm without sinking. Furniture from the 1700s and 1800s had been removed to a museum in Gloucester. The description of the property had said most of what remained was from the 1930s and '40s though the large oak desk was from 1912. She sat in one of the solid wooden chairs. There had been one room, then two, then three. When the light was automated in the 1970s, the government had turned the house into a writers' retreat—the only stipulations being occupants could stay no longer than three years, they had to write about the sea, and they had to have published something beforehand, however small or light.

After forty-five years, the government wanted the old cottage off their hands and listed it with the Gloucester realtor she had purchased it through. Since the light-keeper's house was a heritage property, all sorts of do's and don'ts were involved, which was enough to scare off any number of potential buyers. On top of that, no more than two people be in residence. There had to be a family connection to the sea through fishing or the Coast Guard or the Navy. There had to be a writer of fiction, preferably sea fiction, somewhere in the lineage. The successful buyer had to agree to write a weekly blog about the island that was upbeat and positive. Finally, they had to learn enough about the lighthouse that they could step in for a tourist guide if the need arose. Sara had no idea how many others met all the eccentric terms, but she did, and she was accepted.

The cottage could have been expensive and should have been more than she could afford. But a nest egg had been saved for her by an aunt who wasn't Amish. Sara had been certain she would never use it. When she did, the guilt almost paralyzed her the moment she made the bank transfer at the realtor's office. But the nest egg was little enough, truly. She would do good with it. And she was no longer Amish.

"Look at you." Sara got up from the chair, went over and stared at her face in the mirror in the cottage's bathroom. "Such blue eyes and dark eyebrows. Blonde hair and black eyebrows—how is that possible? Not that you were ever vain about it. But still."

She read her German Bible for half an hour that first afternoon. Prayed. Then went outside the red wooden door that had a weather-stained brass knocker of an anchor she admired a moment. The museum had not removed it despite fear of theft or vandalism. Something to do with a legend about good luck and God's blessing. She touched it, unsure. She walked around the stone cottage with its flower gardens and bright red window baskets. There was a sign on the cottage that named it Round Turn and Two Half Hitches. After that, she followed the worn flagstone path to the lighthouse which was two hundred yards away—locked. Only the crew who came and went and maintained the automated light had the key.

That didn't matter. There was a metal ladder, well-riveted from what she could see, that ran up one side of the lighthouse to the lantern deck. Signs warned people off and threatened prosecution. But since the end of the ladder was at least twenty feet off the ground, it would take an athlete to jump and grasp the bottom rung. Or there would need to be something or someone for a person to stand on. That night, she made a running jump and caught the end of the ladder on her second try. She hadn't expected to miss her first try. Jumping games like this had been common in the barns of the Amish when she was young. And she was still young. Only twenty-eight. She scaled the lighthouse and stood on the lantern deck while the powerful electric light blazed over her shoulder and out across the dark ocean.

"There be coastline here," she murmured. "There be rocks. There be dragons."

She stayed a long time watching the blackness. Now and then the lights of a vessel moved past from north to south or south to north. It was a warm April night without much of a breeze. Still, as midnight came and went, she hugged her jeans jacket closer to her body. Time for bed.

She missed the lowing of cattle and swirling fireflies and the clip-clop of Morgans pulling buggies home for the night. Though at one in the morning, everything would be as quiet there as it was on St Silvan's. Except she could hear the waves. Ocean swells thumping into the rocks. Just before a sleep of deep greens and blues, like the song she shouldn't have heard as a teen put it. The sound of water lapping against a sandy beach made its way through the dark and the noise of the surf pounding the rocks offshore.

Who are you now, Sara King? What is your name? Tell us. Tell the seven seas.

CHAPTER 2

SARA NOT SARA

I wasn't able to stop myself from rising early any more than I could stop the sun from doing it.

I made myself coffee from the beans and hand-grinder I had brought with me. My navy backpack had more tools than clothing. I'd left all my dresses and shoes behind, including the ones on the train. Jeans and shirts and hiking boots were good enough. After a quick shower that was colder than I liked, I went outside to water the flowers and window baskets with the hose. I saw there had been a vegetable patch once, maybe for strawberries too, and thought about purchasing seed packets in the village. A white pickup was parked by the lighthouse, so I decided to go down and take a look. There was no one around but the door to the light was open.

I waited, biting into an apple I'd brought along from a fruit basket. Someone had been kind enough to stock a few items in the fridge and cupboards too. I suspected the realtor. Surprisingly, she had bought items I could make use of-- corn meal, oatmeal, whole milk and butter from a local dairy, apples, pears, carrots with their tops still on, and some decent flour. I had to remember to thank her. I was halfway through my apple, a green one, before a young man and a young woman in bright blue overalls came down the inside staircase and emerged into the morning. Both of them seemed a little taken aback. I responded to that with one of my best smiles.

"Hello," I said. "I'm Lyyndenna Patrick."

The woman, about twenty, looking to me like a college student hired on for the summer just as English neighbors did in Pennsylvania, finally smiled a bit. "Hey. We're just making sure the light is a hundred percent."

"All's well?"

"It is. Are you a tourist? I don't think they start doing island tours till after July 4th."

"No. I live here. At least, I live here now. I'm in the cottage."

She was a redhead with the freckles and jade eyes. The jade eyes widened considerably and took in all kinds of morning sunlight. "You bought it? You're Sara King? I thought she was an old widow." Then she went crimson. "I'm sorry. What a thoughtless thing to say."

I wasn't bothered by her comment. What stung was my boy Daniel's death. That was what hurt the most. Not so much the loss of Jacob, my husband, to be honest.

"No, it's all right," I told her. "I guess I look old to you."

She shook her head. "That's the thing. You absolutely don't. You look amazing. It's like you're a Harvard fourth year or something. You're totally young and pretty."

Now I was crimson. I knew I was. It felt like I could fry an egg on my forehead. "Thank you. You're too kind, really."

"It's the truth. I'm Kara Wingate."

"And you can call me Lyyndenna."

"I thought the woman buying the cottage was someone called Sara King."

"Yes. That's me. The old me, I guess. The old me from a million years ago and a million miles away. Please call me Lyyn. Or Denna. Or the whole name at once. But never Sara."

"So, you're not Sara."

"I am. I was. But now I'm Lyyndenna Patrick. Which isn't much of a stretch really. Patrick is a family name. Back to Revolutionary days."

"I like Lyyndenna."

"And I like Kara."

The young man with her, sporting a full-blown black beard, carefully trimmed, nodded his head at me. "Lyyndenna Patrick. Good name. I'm Tyler. Tyler Franklin. Welcome to St. Silvan's. You really need to come down to Breakers some evening. That's where everyone gets together. Even if you don't drink. That way you'll get to know the islanders before all the tourists show up."

"Hi, Tyler. So, how many tourists are going to show up?"

"Thousands. We have some pretty nice beaches here and some great hotels and restaurants. Even in the winter we get people from Boston and Cambridge and Salem. Of course, they'd need to stay a week because the ferry is only a Friday ferry then."

"And you both live here?"

They nodded.

"Except sometimes, I go to be with my parents on Scrimshaw," Kara added. "It's a small island just south of us in Massachusetts Bay. Maybe eighty people on it. Dad just comes and gets me in our boat."

"Spoiled," teased Tyler.

She stuck out her tongue. "Jealous."

"You get so many storms on Scrimshaw. And so many sharks."

"We get some of the nicest weather, and you know it."

I jumped in. "I read that about eight hundred live on St. Silvan's?"

Kara gave Tyler a fierce green-eyed look before turning to me. "That's about right. I'd say closer to a thousand now. Some take their own boats back and forth. In the winter, they'll work from offices in their homes if they can. What do you do, Lyyndenna?"

"Well. Right now, it's going to be writing."

"Really? Like with Harlequin or something like that?"

"Something like that."

"Wow. Good luck. What a perfect place to write, hey?"

Lyyndenna smiled. "I agree."

"There's another writer," Tyler spoke up. "Hawthorne. His place is a couple of miles from the cottage here. Old like yours but a bit fancier. It used to be owned by a sea captain in the 1800s. It's kind of an old, dark, rambling house."

Kara grinned, her eyes coming even more alive. "It's fascinating. And he's not the only one, right? Isn't there a group?"

"An artists' group. Yeah. Like I said, you really need to show up at Breakers, Lyyndenna. You passed it coming up from the wharf. It's made of all that cool driftwood and the planking from a tall ship. Old man o' war. It busted up at the lighthouse two hundred years ago. I forget who retrieved it for the tavern."

"Todd Smiths. Remember?"

"Oh, yeah. Todd."

I felt drained after they left. I hadn't expected to talk so much, so soon. Why had I been going nonstop? Why did I have to act like I was some NYC writer when all I was going to do was produce a weekly blog? Why did I even bring up my name change? Now it would be all over the island. The old widow Sara King is really the young widow Lyyndenna Patrick. God help me.

"Be quiet, Lyyndenna," I murmured. "You need to talk much, much less. This needs to be a quiet place. Prayer, mediation, your German Bible, gathering wild flowers and driftwood. Why talk at all?"

I made my way from the lighthouse along a path through tall sand dunes that were half grass and came to one of the beaches. White—like beaches I'd seen the one time we'd visited the Amish community in Sarasota, Florida. Once I got closer, I realized the white came from seashells the ocean swept against the southeastern shore. From my map of St. Silvan's, I remembered there was a beach called White Shell. This must be it. The beach spread for several hundred yards before it changed into a light-colored sand for a few hundred more. I bent down and put my hand to the shells. Some were crushed but most were only broken in half or badly chipped. They felt smooth against my palm. I tugged off my boots and socks and went barefoot. It felt fine, it felt good. I walked awhile, enjoying the sensation. Somewhere sometime, I'd heard a line from a poem—nor can feet feel, being shod. I'd been barefoot a lot as a girl. Time to go back there.

The day was not hot, the day was not cold. When I reached the sand, I paid more attention to several families flying kites with their children. The kites were all colors and all shapes. They swooped and spun and darted into the sun. I couldn't see the lines that held them to earth, so they appeared to be more independent than they were. I craved that independence. From my past. From the deaths of my husband and son. From the years of my husband's cutting words. From the manner in which my faith had been lived out under the Amish ordnungs.

Does God really care if I pin up my hair? Or wear a prayer Kapp? That my clothing has no buttons? That my dresses are long and dark? Does it matter to God whether the men have mustaches or not? That they have beards that must not be trimmed? Is it a matter of life or death that Martin Luther's Bible be used, that we only sing hymns in German, that Pennsylvania Dutch be the language we speak among ourselves? Does God say no cars or trucks? Does God say no airplanes? Does God say no electricity? Or do men say all of that? I don't mind leaving those rules behind. It is the friendships I miss. The faces that wrinkle with smiles. The honest laughter. The many kindnesses. Working together with the other women at a quilt, or at baking five hundred loaves of bread, or at preparing all the food for a wedding. I miss someone taking my hand and praying for me. Like the kites, I am free to roam. But only so far. They are tethered to their lines and to the hands that hold them. Just as I am tethered to the lines of my past and my faith and to the many hands that hold those. Lines that can be as taut as steel cable and hold just as firmly.

A kite broke free and sailed out over the ocean.

"Yet even the strongest line might not hold forever," I whispered.

A boy ran along the sand calling out to the green kite.

A bishop from another county had visited our church once.

His message had been unusual.

"Sometimes some of us leave the Amish path. It may only be for a while. It may be forever. It may be a mistake. It may be the Father's will. Despite what others may say or not say, you must answer to God for your decision, you alone. Listen to the advice of your church. Then pray and make up your own mind before the Lord. Only take this with you if you must go--simplicity. Ours is a simple life and a simple faith. Do not lose the simple ways. Or if you lost them before you left, go out there and find them again and bring them back to us."

I was not surprised the sea and its shoreline brought so much into my head. I had always longed for what the English called blue water, but rarely had I been able to go to it. The farm kept me landlocked. Had I stood by the ocean more than five times? How often had my Daniel seen it? Once, twice? So that it should stir the blood and free up my thoughts--I had expected that. I had wanted that. It's why I'd fled to St. Silvan's to begin with and not into the deserts of New Mexico or Arizona. Saltwater that stretched out far beyond what my eyes could penetrate. A sky that poured into the sea so there was no way of knowing where one began or the other stopped. I'd wanted infinity. That's why I went to the sea to discover what was unknown.

I was just thinking about using a gas stove for the first time that evening when the brass knocker sounded. It actually had a deep bell-like ring to it, making me think it might be hollow. I opened the red door, pushing my loose hair back from my face. It was Kara. Bubbling.

"Hey, I want to take you to Breakers, my treat," she said, everything about her a bright smile. "They have the best halibut and chips. I'll introduce you to everyone you need to meet."

I knew protest would be in vain, but I tried anyways. "Kara. That's so sweet of you. But honestly, I don't have anything to wear. And my hair's a mess. So, I'll say no--"

She cut me off with a laugh. "Oh, Denna, believe me, you are perfect just as you are. You couldn't be more perfect. You mustn't change a thing. It's Saturday night at Breakers on St. Silvan's, and you absolutely look the part."

CHAPTER 3

BREAKERS

I was in the sort of fix Grandpa King used to call a perpedoodle, making up his own Pennsylvania Dutch word. On the one hand, I just wanted to be left alone with the sea and sky and God. On the other, I did want to make some friends and I didn't want to wait till the island was overrun by tourists. So, I climbed into Kara's green-like-her-eyes Jeep Rubicon and went hurtling down the road to the village, Kara talking like she drove, fast and nonstop. I wasn't at all ready for the interior of Breakers. A dory hung from the ceiling, anchors and nets and harpoons from the walls, empty barrels and kegs were our seats and tables, ship's brass lanterns our lighting. I wasn't quite ready for the crew seated around the barrels Kara steered me towards either. Her friends and Tyler and his buddies, about ten altogether and none of them older than twenty-two. It wasn't just that I was a widow with a name change that was widely known. That I was Amish was apparently island news too, and all of them wanted to know about the farming, life without electricity, the Morgans, and the buggies and the commitment to nonviolence. I was surprised I did not mind sharing the Amish ways with them as I was still very upside-down about what I'd done. However, talking about why I'd left was another matter.

"So, I have just lost my son and my husband," I told them, sipping my Pepsi and picking at my halibut and chips. "Both were ... farming accidents. Both a year ago. In March and April. I needed to get away. That's all. No, no, don't think the Amish community was insensitive or unsupportive. I just couldn't be there anymore. I needed a completely different place. I'd always dreamed of the sea, of being by the sea. So here I am."

"But why St. Silvan's?" asked Tyler, one arm around his tall, dark-haired girlfriend.

"Because of the cottage. I saw the advertisement in our paper in Pennsylvania for the lightkeeper's house so I wrote the people in Boston."

"There were a lot of questions they put to you, weren't there?"

"Yes, there were."

"And you have a naval person in your family?"

"Yes. Coast Guard. An uncle. All the way back to the 1930s."

"What about the writer?" This from Kara.

"Serenity Grace Greenwood. Popular in her day but overshadowed by Louisa May Alcott. Who she met."

"Like Little Women Alcott?"

"The same."

"Wow. So, you write like them? Like Alcott and Greenwood?"

Right then and there, as I sprinkled more malt vinegar on my chips, I decided to give up the ship. "Oh, I need to explain about all that. I did write stories as a girl, and they were smiled upon. But when I wrote stories as a teen, writing was frowned upon. So, I gave it up."

"But—" from one of Kara's friends.

"I'll be writing a weekly blog. I'm supposed to be getting a new iPad for that from Boston. I pray that may lead to something more. Something like Alcott or Greenwood. I have no idea. It may have been bred right out of me by the ordnungs."

"What are those?" the friend asked me.

"Rules. Laws. Policies. How the Amish organize and govern themselves."

"Which doesn't include painting The Last Supper or writing books or playing the violin." said Kara.

"No. It doesn't."

"Is that another reason you left? So that you could try and be a writer like your relative?"

I shrugged. "Who can say what God has planned? If my son or husband were still alive, I wouldn't be here."

"Or what the universe has planned," Said Tyler.

"As you wish," I replied, popping a chip in my mouth.

"Hey." Kara sat up in her chair. "There's Hawthorne. And Sydney Ryder. And Scott Munro. They're in that artists' group I was telling you about, Denna. I invited them here to meet you. Come on. They're sitting down at another table."

"You mean another barrel."

"Hurry. Grab your plate and your Pepsi. I'll introduce you."

"I'm good where I am, Kara. I don't want to intrude on them."

"How can you be intruding on them when the reason they're at Breakers tonight is to see you?"

"I'm a blogger. An amateur blogger. Not even that."

"Wait till I tell them about Serenity Grace Greenwood and Louisa May Alcott."

"Kara, Kara, please don't."

I took the three writers in, and they were a quick blur of faces. Honestly, later on I couldn't recall the details, exactly how they looked, exactly how they dressed. I remember one of them saying I looked like an islander. Kara told me on the drive home that was because I was tanned, my hair was streaked, my denim shirt and blue jeans were faded, and I had the jeans rolled just above the ankles.

"I bought the shirt and jeans at a secondhand store," I told her. "All my English clothes are second hand. My tan? Well, it is a farmer's tan, what else? And the sun streaks my hair, not a hair salon."

"Well, Denna," Karla said as she drove, "I suppose it will embarrass you for me to say this. But it all comes together extremely well. You're truly a beautiful woman."

I lowered my head and felt the burning on my cheeks. "I'd rather you didn't say things like that, Kara."

"It's true."

"I ... I am not used to compliments of that sort. They make me uncomfortable."

"Surely men have--"

"No. It is not the Amish way."

"When you were dating--"

"We do not date. There is only the courting. All right, yes, yes, Jacob said sweet things to me in those days. But such words quickly dried up."

"Why?"

"You will have to ask him."

"I can't ask him."

"And I can't speak for him."

Sydney wanted to know about Serenity Greenwood. Apparently, her works were experiencing something of a resurgence. She had a new paperback of my ancestor's novel Three Shorelines and wanted me to sign it. They used SG Greenwood for her name. I knew the book, I knew all of Serenity's books, even though I wasn't supposed to. For the longest time, I wouldn't sign. But Sydney, a firecracker of a brunette, wore me down. I finally took the pen from her hand. To me, it was just a simple signature. To her, it was something fashioned in gold. She showed it around the table and Hawthorne and Munro praised the curves of the letters and the broad loops of the capitals.

If I had been honest with them and Kara, which I was not, I'd have told them when I was a teen, and thought the bishop might let me become a writer, I'd practiced my autograph over and over again. I'd been caught and scolded for this and told to develop a signature that was plain. I'd thought my author signature was plain. So, I'd created something that made mama and papa happy. Which also meant meant not using my pen name of Lyyndenna Patrick, Patrick being my mother's maiden name as she was a convert to the Amish faith.

That night, I went down to the beach in the April dark. The crests of the waves gleamed. I began pitching pebbles into the surf. I was wondering if I'd fled the Amish because I couldn't stay where my son and husband had died or because I'd been restricted from being a writer and a thinker. Hawthorne had said Greenwood was superior to Alcott but had never received the breaks or reviews she deserved. Munro had agreed and quoted a line from Greenwood's August: The light never got through. Not through the windows. Not through the doorways. Not through her gray eyes and into her mind. The years had smudged her and put a thick streak of charcoal over everything that had life. She did not know how to kindle another fire.

"Brilliant!" he'd exclaimed. "You can't imagine how I'm looking forward to your writing, Ms. Patrick."

"It's blogging, sir, only blogging," I'd protested.

"I'm sure you've written something."

"I haven't."

A lie. I had. Munro seemed to be able to pluck that information right out of my brain. I had started the book at thirteen, hidden it at fourteen, thought about destroying it at fifteen, then resumed writing it at sixteen. Every now and then I had snuck it out and worked on it, right through my twenties, my marriage and motherhood. I'd brought it with me.

Munro the Magi. Yet all I could recall of him that night was his New England accent and that he wore glasses. And that he looked like pictures I'd seen of Stephen King. Hawthorne? I couldn't recall Hawthorne at all. But the lighting had been dim and the ship's lantern flickering.

Except. His hands resting on the table. Large. Rugged. Brown with sun and weather. Fingertips stained. From pushing tobacco into the bowl of a pipe, I suspected. Exactly like Grandfather Patrick's hands. Just younger.

I found larger pebbles and threw them too. Then stones. I was fighting something but I did not know what. It was my young son, Daniel. How he would have loved to have been here throwing stones into the sea in the dark beside his mother. How he would have loved it. And my heart broke all over again.

CHAPTER 4

MOUNT SURIBACHI

May and June passed like the ocean passed by St. Silvan's—in a hurry. I fell into a routine of reading, and blogging, and watering flowers, and wandering beaches, and praying. On July 4th, the ferry began bringing hundreds of people to St Silvan's. It ran four times a day, and a second ferry began sailing a week later. There were seventeen beaches on the island, and half of them had hotels right on the shoreline, far enough back to keep them free of high tide and storm surge. The Independence Day fireworks were set off at the rocks a good distance from the lighthouse. The crowds were kept well back as yellow and orange and blue burst over the sea—all new to me because I'd never attended any July 4th celebrations. And though I'd seen the fireworks from far away, I'd never seen them explode in front of my face.

The tours began then too. Guides took people inside the lighthouse between ten and four, and they walked around the cottage too though the guide kept them about a hundred feet away. I didn't know what to do with that. I wasn't the person to stand outside and grin and wave to hundreds of tourists. So, I hid indoors or made my escape between mobs to the library in the village or down to the White Shell. There were hundreds of tourists on the beach too but at least I was anonymous there as I rolled my jeans up and waded in the sea.

I desperately wanted to swim, but I had no suit, and the ones I saw for sale in the village, I found immodest. Kara to the rescue. It seemed she and her girlfriends were always at my side. They wanted to teach me to drive. They wanted to find me summer dresses I could live with—long ones with lots and lots of color. They chose the ball caps and sandals and the simple island jewelry of wood and bamboo I could actually say yes to. I was Amish Not Amish and trying to find my way in my new life and my new world.

The suit they picked out was a one-piece Speedo, modest enough except it was far too snug. The girls complained and remonstrated with me but I was unmoved. I purchased one in black two sizes too large. It drooped a bit, and that was what I wanted.

"Oh, Denna," Kara moaned. "It's summer and you have a perfect figure."

"I want to go in the water," I snipped back, "not parade myself down a runway."

"Well, you definitely could parade yourself down a runway, Mrs. Patrick," said her friend Jazz.

"Lyyndenna, please. Or Denna. So, becoming a supermodel is not what God and I had in mind."

Kara put her hands on her hips. "I thought you weren't Amish anymore."

"I'm not. But there is still some Amish I want to keep in Lyyndenna Patrick."

"How much?"

"Enough yeast to make the dough rise properly."

"What?"

"Just let's go swimming. All of us. I'll pretend to be your mother, ha-ha. Take me to your favorite beach."

"Our mother?" snorted Jazz. "They'll believe one of us is your mother before they'll believe you're ours."

I had quite a time with the girls that summer. In truth, I did need swimming lessons as well as driving lessons. They took care of both. I suppose I could tell a thousand stories about learning to drive Kara's Jeep Rubicon. What a trusting soul she was. I almost went off the wharf twice and off cliffs into the sea more than I want to say. Though the time that made Kara and Jazz laugh the hardest (the cliff times were screams) was when I panicked and hauled back on the steering wheel like a pair of reins to make the jeep stop. It didn't work, and we bounced off the curb. The times we didn't go over the cliffs, Jazz said made her believe in an Amish God. The time I pulled back on the reins, she said made her believe in a God who enjoyed a good laugh.

The beach? Well, what can I say about swimming and the beach? I didn't mind drowning and tried it several times. It's not as if I hadn't swum in ponds and creeks and lakes. But ocean swells were something else. I had to use stronger strokes, and kick harder, and hold my breath longer as I learned the crawl and the butterfly from Issime. She was a champion swimmer at Boston University and waitressing at Breakers for July and August. She had me using weights at the village gym, the Shoals, to put muscle on my arms and back and shoulders. So, by Labor Day, I was swimming better than I had my entire life. I surprised myself.

I surprised myself by buying a new Speedo too. The droopy one drooped too much. The undertow kept pulling it off. Not that anyone ever saw my Speedo struggles underwater. I was quite the aquatic gymnast, ha-ha. The girls were there to clap when I tried on a suit that fit like it should. But I now had the problem of swimming in a Speedo that fit like it should.

I was reminded me of my girlfriend Lydia Zook who was always getting in trouble at sixteen for what the bishop called her "rock and roll dresses". It's just that she wore dresses that were slender and hugged her figure a bit. Which her mother never seemed to notice. Now I had a swimsuit the undertow couldn't touch but which made me look like Lydia in a rock and roll Speedo. My solution to the problem was to run out of the water at full tilt and dive into the biggest beach towel I'd been able to buy. Wrapped up in that, I looked like a pile of laundry. The girls harassed me about being a prude, but I didn't care. I had no desire to be St. Silvan's new center of attention. I just wanted to swim, lie on the sand, look for seashells and live a simple, unobstructed, unnoticed life. Amish Not Amish.

So, by the end of July, I had a license and had been blessed by a local on the island who wanted to sell me his Willys Jeep from 1945. He had kept it in beautiful condition since he'd acquired it in Arizona in 2010 and had fought a winning battle against our saltwater climate. He also offered to be my mechanic as long as I owned the Willys which I accepted. Mike was sixty-two and a Vietnam vet. He and his wife, Amy, became my dear friends. As did the jeep which he'd nicknamed Bachi because it had actually been on Iwo Jima during the battle in 1945. (Mount Suribachi was where the Marines had raised the flag in the iconic photograph everyone knew about including my "no war" Amish church.)

Not that I knew anything about that except for the famous photograph. Mike had to explain Iwo Jima to me. There were three bullet holes just by the spare tire at the back of the Willys. "Nambu machine gun," he'd told me. I'd nodded. Of course. A Nambu machine gun. "They have to stay." I nodded again. Where would I take them?

"And it has to keep its sand camo. Ok?" It did have a paint job that reminded me of the color of light brown sand. I nodded a third time. "And it has to remain stock." Mike had a lot of faith in me if he thought I could customize a motor vehicle and give it chrome wheels and bumpers.

"Definitely, it will." I'd begun to pick up on the girl talk.

It was a standard. Kara's Rubicon had been a standard too. Just an easier kind of standard. It took a while. I popped and stalled and backfired my way around the island before I finally got the hang of it, but I was determined not to disappoint Mike. Why had he sold me his vintage jeep which had only ten thousand miles on it? He liked my online blog which also got printed in the island weekly, Spindrift. I honestly don't know why anyone liked my blog. But he did. Especially the one about an Amish woman who'd only driven Morgan horses learning to drive a Jeep Rubicon off a cliff. So now Bachi and I were partners.

Mike wasn't the only one who liked the blog. I began getting all kinds of good feedback. So much so that papers in Boston picked it up. It was God. What else could it be? My editor at Spindrift was ecstatic and offered me a salary.

A salary! The whole blog idea had just been a requirement for being allowed to purchase the cottage. There hadn't been any income attached to the deal whatsoever. I'd been living off what was left of the nest egg, which I hoped I could stretch over two years before it was exhausted. Now Fwanya, from Namibia, was talking about five hundred dollars a week but he wanted two blogs, one on Monday as well as Friday.

"Of course, I said yes," I told Mike and Amy at Inked, a coffeehouse in the village. "But. It's happening so fast. I'm farther away than I wanted to be this soon."

"Farther away from what?" Amy asked.

"From where I came from. From the Amish. From my past."

"How long has it been?"

"Over three months."

"You've told us you still believe in God, isn't that so?"

"Yes, yes, nothing about that has changed. I'm just trying to find a different way to live and express my beliefs."

"Then perhaps things are moving along as they should, Lyyndenna. It's still about faith for you, isn't it?"

"Of course. Yes."

"Then keep going that way."

"I will. I have to. I just don't always know what to hold onto from my past and what to let go. And I don't understand why my blogs should matter to so many people."

Mike smiled at me. "It's not just that you wrote a blog about learning to drive that amused me. We both like the way you mix your Amish memories and beliefs with discovering the island and Massachusetts Bay. It's an intriguing blend."

"Thank you, but to me it's a confusing blend. It's so difficult to work through what I've walked away from and what I'm walking into. I'm sorry that struggle is so apparent in what I write."

"How could it not be when you're so open? It doesn't make you odd or unpleasant to read. Lyyndenna, we are all struggling in one way or another. The blog is popular because you are a good writer, and you are an honest to God human being."

I hoped I was being honest to God. I felt like Sara King less and less every day. Yet I didn't feel farther from God or farther from my own soul. Just farther from what I used to be. Even though much of that still lived in me.

I had pored over the book I'd been writing since I was a teen, sure I'd be asked to share something with the artists' group besides my blogs. Which everybody could read anyway. I'd found out they didn't meet from May to September, so I began picking away at my book in August. I made changes and added new parts to the story. I didn't use my iPad. Just pen and paper. It was all pen and paper. Three notebooks so far. I was surprised by how autobiographical the book was. I thought there must be something wrong about that. But my pen and my mind kept writing that way. In a biography of SG Greenwood, there was a quote from her that helped. "All good fiction is, in one fashion or another, a matter of autobiography, of telling your own story through fictitious personalities and fictitious events. That's what gives it its reality and its power."

So, I carried on, sometimes thinking I knew what I was doing with my life and my writing and sometimes not. I drove Bachi everywhere, I walked everywhere, I cycled everywhere on my blue mountain bike, I laughed with Kara and the girls (who began including older siblings and friends twenty-five to twenty-eight for my benefit). I wrote everywhere too, in my head and in the notebooks. I visited all seventeen beaches and swam at each one. I got into beachcombing. I prayed at the seaside, and I prayed in the moonlight, and I prayed watching the phosphorescence burn bright in the ocean. By September, I can't say I felt complete. I can't say I felt incomplete. I mourned my husband, but I cannot say I missed him. However, I mourned my son and wept over him every day.

In Amish romances, a man would have come into my story to save me. A knight in shining armor. I didn't want a knight in shining armor. I didn't want to be saved by a man. My life wasn't Amish fiction. I wanted to be saved by a God. One true, loving, kind-hearted God.

So, when Mark Hawthorne tried to be that Amish fiction savior, I wrote him out of the story. Or tried to.

CHAPTER 5

THE GOD GAME

The artists' group was not just a writers' group.

There were painters, and sculptors, and actors, and musicians, and dancers, and poets and essayists. There were all kinds of artists of different races and different faiths. It was bewildering. I'd go away from the weekly get togethers with my head in a spin. Yet I couldn't deny the meetings stimulated and inspired me too. They made me want to write and write in a way that was honest to God, not sugar-coated and glossed over and fuzzy-wuzzy. Not a rose garden without thorns. I'd never been able to talk about my secret book with anyone before, let alone as freely as this.

There were three basic rules. No politics, no religion (including the atheists who liked to say they weren't religious and then go on to tell everyone what they believed), no cruel feedback. Unless politics and religion were part of a character's story. I listened for the first two months and said very little. Finally, one Saturday morning before the end of October (we always went from nine to twelve and then had lunch together at Breakers), I had been asked to be prepared to share from my WIP (work in progress). About two dozen of us were seated in a circle in a large study room at the library.

I thought I'd be far more nervous than I was. I suppose if I'd had to read from my notebooks in June or July or even September, I'd have been stuttering. However, I was in a different state of mind altogether. I felt like I was dreaming my reading to them. I read for half an hour. I was calling the book Harvest that Saturday morning. I told them I might call it something else by Saturday night.

There was this one thought that ate into Becca. If God was a father, was he anything like her father? Gracious and patient and kind? Well, how could God be? God was spirit. In the Bible, he roared and thundered and slaughtered Israel's enemies and broke people's hearts. Jesus was a better idea. Her father and Jesus were more like one another. Jesus was the father figure she wanted in her head and her soul. He was the one that said to love all her enemies. The other said to kill them.

And there was the suffering. Her two children dead as stones. Where was the love of God when they gasped for life after a truck smashed into their buggy? Where was the God who intervened and saved? She could never voice these thoughts aloud. But she thought about them in the long fields and in the barn with the horses. She thought about them before she fell asleep. Becca wondered if she would ever stop going over them. She wished she would. She prayed she would. It felt as if all the person she was and could be had been locked in chains and could neither grow nor be free until she resolved the issue of God and where God's love was or wasn't. The rain, at least, still fell, and the sun, at least, still rose, and the land, thank God, still turned every shade of green.

"How old were you when you wrote this?" It was a man named Erikk, who made sculptures with metal. "Didn't you say you've been working on this since you were thirteen?"

"I have," I told him and the circle. "I was about twenty-one here. I'd been married for three years and a mother for two."

"There's some lovely prose when you talk about rainfall and sunshine," said Munro. "It's poetic, and it works well with the heavier thoughts."

284

"Thank you."

"Let's hear something from later on in the manuscript. Let's see how Becca and your style grow together. Does this theistic issue continue to dominate?"

"I suppose we'll see."

It did. It does. Jazz was, not surprisingly when you combined her beauty with her energy and athletic ability, a dancer and part of the group. She made sure she sat with me at lunch. She wanted to talk about the part I'd read where Becca thinks she might be falling in love and is afraid. We actually took it to the beach, went for a swim, and then I dived under my gigantic towel before I froze. The Atlantic was an ice bucket in late October. Nevertheless, I would go on to swim at least once a week every month of the year. That's how crazy the sea air made me.

Jazz took off at one point to meet up with some friends at Inked but I stayed on at Northwest. I lay on my back and stared up at an impossibly blue sky that beat like a heart. I liked Northwest because it faced towards Gloucester and the shoreline so it was sheltered from the wind. I'd dressed under the towel and felt warm as a waffle. Not toast. A waffle. My son Daniel's expression. No, remembering did not make me cry this time. I smiled at the sky and one high white cloud.

I breathed in a scent of vanilla and tobacco. There might have been a hint of cherry. I recognized pipe tobacco because of Grandfather Patrick's smoking habits. I sat up and looked around but the smoker wasn't obvious. They should have been because the beach was half empty. What breeze there was came out of the south, so I walked that way, off to the left if you were facing Gloucester and the mainland. I still didn't see anyone.

"Your writing actually reminds me more of Virginia Woolf. With a dash of Melville. You're a thinker. A philosopher. It's not just about a narrative with you."

The smoker was behind a large boulder covered in seaweed.

"Mr. Hawthorne," I said.

"What surprises me is there is no bitterness. Angst but no bitterness."

I came around the boulder. Dark hair and dark eyes. Skin still dark from his summer tan. Khaki shirt and pants. A pipe I knew was called a freehand, looking as if it had been carved from a tree trunk. He had just successfully blown a smoke ring.

"I'm not bitter," I replied.

"But like Becca you felt you had to move on."

"There were too many associations with the deaths of my son and husband."

"And?"

"I needed to write freely. I realize that now. Without censure or condemnation. It's how I am working everything through."

"About God and suffering?"

"The love of God, God's absence, death, faith, loss of faith, all of that and more."

"I'm thirty-eight now. Exactly ten years older than you. In my twenties, I was a minister. Even while I was giving messages and trying to help others, I had questions no one could help me with. Finally, I had to move on from that. At least until I had figured things out."

"What things?"

"Well, some of the same questions you have."

"And?"

"I wrote my first novel. Break Break Break. From Tennyson's sea poem. Do you know Tennyson?"

"No."

"Yet you've read lots of other books an Amish woman wouldn't normally have access to."

"I felt compelled to use the library in our town."

"Openly?"

"Quietly."

"Have you read my novel?"

"No, I'm sorry, I haven't."

"It was on the New York Times bestseller list for three months."

"Lots of books are on that list, sir. Many of them are poorly written. You get on that list for selling a lot. Not necessarily because you're good."

"You're blunt."

"One of my virtues."

"Good is a matter of opinion, Mrs. Patrick."

"I'm not Mrs. Patrick. Lyyndenna, please."

"And I'm not a sir. Not with only ten years between us."

I smiled. "Fair enough."

"So, you haven't read my book?"

"Mr. Hawthorne, I didn't know you existed till a few months ago."

"Hmm." He blew out a cloud of creamy white smoke. "Perhaps one day."

"Perhaps."

I sat down on the sand facing him.

"One thing that happened for me, Lyyndenna, was reading the Bible and realizing it said I could also learn about God from the things God had made. It's in Romans."

"I know. The first chapter."

"Then I read in Matthew where Jesus changed the Bible. You know. You have heard it said but I say?"

"Ja. Of course." Grrrr. I annoyed myself whenever I slipped into German or Pennsylvania Dutch. "You have heard it said, love your neighbor and hate your enemy but I say to you, love your enemy."

Hawthorne went on. "So, for me, that changed a great deal in my brain. And in my heart. That is a very sweeping statement. It changes the Bible. All those nasty verses about killing Israel's enemies with vengeance no longer apply. They are not right. They are not true. That is not who God is. Jesus altered the whole picture. He set things straight. God is not slaughter and bloodshed. God is love your enemy. God is pray for those who persecute you. God is don't resist the evil person. God is turn the other cheek. Do you agree?"

Right from the beginning, Mark Hawthorne could be so convincing. And interesting. And, unfortunately, attractive.

Him and his rugged, handsome face and his flashing eyes. Ugh. Flashing eyes. I'd already put him in a romance.

"I don't know," I responded. "That's a lot to change with just a few words."

"To me, it's simple. Jesus says that verse is wrong, and he changes it. The verse has universal application. You can't have God telling you to wipe out your enemies, even the infants, say that's God, then say love your enemies is God too. God is one or the other. I decided to go with the change Jesus instituted. God is love, not hate. Simple. Are you opposed to simple? Perhaps Lyyndenna Patrick prefers layered, complex, and complicated?"

He made me laugh and I didn't want to laugh. I didn't want to react to him in any positive way at all. I was totally frustrated with myself. "Simple is good if simple is true."

"You have left the Amish behind. Have you left Jesus behind?"

"No. And I haven't left the Amish behind either. Just parts."

"So, Jesus still matters to you?"

"Ja. Na sicher."

"What he says makes all the difference to you?"

"Ja. Yes. Of course."

"That is what he said. What will you do about it? Hmm?"

I didn't respond.

He got to his feet and knocked his pipe against his palm to remove the ashes, then slipped it into his pants pocket. "Would you like to walk the beach a bit, Lyyndenna?"

No, as a matter of fact, I would not. I am perfectly fine here on this island without you intruding. But, I liked his voice, and I liked listening to what he had to say. So off we went. Grrrr.

"Would you like to play a game?" he asked.

A game? "No, thank you."

"From that verse in the Bible. In Romans. We can know what God is like by looking at the things God has made."

"How does that become a game?"

"What does the sea make you think of? Quickly. Don't overthink it."

"Why ... power."

"God's power?"

"Nature's power, God's power, yes."

"What about the sky?"

"The sky? Heaven. Peace. When it's a blue sky."

"Wind?" he asked.

I thought as fast as I could. "Wind? A strong wind?"

"Yes. A strong wind."

"God is spirit."

"Fire."

"God is intense."

"A breeze."

"God is gentle."

"Sand."

"God is infinite. His ways are infinite and past counting."

He kept coming at me. "Sun."

I had no intention of losing the game. "God is warm.

"What else?" he prodded.

"God is light."

"What else?"

"God is clarity."

"Stars."

"God is light in darkness."

"What else?"

"God is beauty."

"That piece of driftwood there."

"Just a minute." I seized his arm without thinking and then swiftly drew back, horrified at what I'd done. "Uh ... it's your turn. Not mine. Driftwood yourself."

"God takes what is lost and turns it into something marvelous. God restores."

"Salt air," I put to him.

"God is bracing," he responded. "God is invigorating."

"Seashells."

"Eternity. God is eternal, and we are eternal with God. Death cannot change that."

"Seagulls."

He laughed. "God soars."

I wish he hadn't laughed. A peculiar tingling silvered through my body. No, no, no.

"Uh. Thank you very much, Mr. Hawthorne. I must get going. And ... and ... we probably shouldn't meet like this again."

"Why not? It was a chance encounter."

"Nevertheless, Saturday mornings are sufficient."

"But, Lyyndenna, we're having an amazing time."

"Yes, yes, we are. Too amazing. I'm not used to social interactions with men. It's awkward. It's uncomfortable."

"You're not uncomfortable."

"I don't even know you."

"Well, how else do we fix that except by chatting?"

"I don't want to chat. I don't want to fix it. I'm a widow. I just want to leave."

"But, Lyyndenna."

"I have to leave. God knows I have to leave."

And I fled.

I ran all the way back to where I'd parked my jeep.

I was breathing so hard I waited five minutes to start the engine.

What a mess.

CHAPTER 6

SOMETHING RICH AND STRANGE

I am not an unburdening person.

But I wound up unburdening myself to Kara.

I did not want anything to do with men romantically. Saturday morning and Breakers was enough. It was casual but professional. Whatever that meant. I did not want to be dated as the English dated. I for sure did not want to be courted the way we Amish courted.

"What do you want from men?" Kara asked me.

"Nothing!" I snapped. "I don't want anything from men. Except to leave me alone."

"Were things so bad with your late hubs?"

"What?"

"Your husband. Were things so bad?"

"No, no, they were fine. Oh, what a lie. He was very harsh with me. Very unkind. Thank God, I had Daniel at nineteen so I could pour my affection into him. And receive his in return."

"Don't you think the way your husband treated you has something to do with the way you're feeling about Mark now?"

"I don't feel anything for Mark."

"I mean the way you don't want to feel."

"I don't know. I definitely don't want another Jacob. And I definitely don't want another man. I don't want anyone."

"Well, I doubt he'll talk to you again except about writing. Not after you ran from him and left him standing there like a duh."

Hawthorne didn't talk to me. I'd had my hour and wouldn't have another till the new year. When I interacted with others in the group, he listened but never jumped in. He let others do that. He'd only speak up after I'd had my say about someone's art and water had passed under the bridge. At lunch, he sat with Sydney and Munro. And that's the way it went for three Saturdays. Hawthorne wasn't rude, and he didn't snub me. He just made sure he gave me my space. As Jazz put it.

It was what I wanted. I felt good. I blogged, prayed, walked the beaches, collected driftwood to place around the cottage, spoke to tourists now and then, drove Bachi to the cliffs to admire the view, sang hymns in German there where no one could see or hear me, weathered the storms as November ended with a howl, sat in on the Saturday meetings and enjoyed the talks given by landscape painters and photographers, worked on my novel. I knew eventually I'd have to get it typed into Word, but for now I was content to scribble away in my notebooks and leave the book like that. Sometimes the skies were navy and indigo, other times the color of steel anchors. I wrote on and prayed on regardless.

I have tried to understand what happened at the end of November. The very last day. I deliberately drove to Northwest, did what my friends called the Iceberg—jumping in the cold ocean—dressed under my towel and went exploring. I thought my wandering was aimless. Till I smelled the pipe tobacco.

You might think I'm making it up and knew exactly where I was going. I had no idea. The cliché applied to me--my head was in the clouds. The clouds were grey as mud and my head was stuck in them. The moment I took in the scent of tobacco, I started to go back. I thought that's what I wanted--to turn around and go back. Instead, I went towards the boulder and stepped in front of him.

"It's a bit like following the smell of cookie dough or baking bread," I told Hawthorne.

"This comes from a tobacconist in Boston. Pippin and Took is the shop. She calls the blend Sea Change."

"That's an odd name."

"It's from Shakespeare. 'Full fathom five thy father lies, of his bones are coral made, those are pearls that were his eyes, nothing of him that doth fade, but doth suffer a sea-change, into something rich and strange.'"

"So, the sea changes him into something rich and strange?"

"Or you. Or me. It can mean any big change, Lyyndenna. Like a caterpillar turning into a butterfly. Metamorphosis. Maybe the sea does it. Maybe a song. Maybe a book."

"Maybe God."

"Maybe God. But God usually uses something or someone."

I sat down on the sand and faced him like I had before. "I just want a friendship. Someone to talk with who understands what it means to write your life and feelings out in a book."

"Sydney or Munro could do that."

"No."

"Why Hawthorne?"

"I don't know."

"You don't need to worry about relationship or romance. I don't want a serious relationship ever again. And I don't believe in romance."

"Well, I feel the same way."

"Good. Then that's settled. The air is cleared. We can carry on with our sea change."

I smiled. I felt as light as air. "Into something rich and strange."

He fussed about a moment, relighting his freehand pipe. "Where are you with your epic?"

"My epic? Becca is working through her feelings about her Amish husband who was killed in a haying accident. It isn't feelings of love she's wrestling with. She feels guilty she is grateful he is not there to hurt her with his sharp tongue anymore."

"How sharp a tongue?"

"Carving knife sharp."

"Is she getting anywhere?"

"Not really. She is supposed to love her enemy. He acted like her enemy. She loved him when they were younger. Her love eroded over time as he became more and more strident with her. She doesn't know what she feels for him now that he's gone. When she was crying at his funeral, she was crying over what they'd lost, the years they'd lost, the kindness toward one another they'd lost. She doesn't know how to pray. The Bible is like a dead stick when she tries to read it."

"We should walk, Lyyndenna." Hawthorne kept smoking as we roamed the beach under a sky as gray as the sides of a warship. "What is it Becca wishes to achieve?"

"She? Or the author?"

"She."

"She would like to be reconciled to her husband. She would like to recover the love they lost for each other. Even in death, she wants this more than anything else."

"What about the children she lost?"

"She did not lose them. The love was always there. She is confident she will see them again, and the reunion will be beautiful. Although she cries over them, all her memories are wonderful. It isn't that way with her husband. There are good memories from their first few years together. But they are buried by the pain."

"Because they weren't able to have more children?"

"Yes."

"He blamed her?"

"Yes. Constantly."

"Can she forgive him?"

"She wants to. Very much."

"What does the island offer that your Amish do not?"

"I can write a book about my struggle. There is no shame in that."

He took his pipe out of his mouth and tapped it against his palm before slipping it into his pocket. "We have some potters in our group. Pottery can be made in two ways. Where each piece looks virtually the same depending on the theme—cups are identical, saucers, vases, pitchers. Or where pieces, even of the same theme, do not replicate one another—each cup is unique, each bowl, each vase. The first approach is manufacturing. The second is art--especially when the potter is not exactly sure what she will get when she removes each piece from the kiln."

"All right. You're going to tell me it's the same way with books."

"Yes. Fiction can be manufactured just like pottery. Books can look the same when it comes to the covers. They can sound the same when you open them up and begin to read. The characters can resemble the characters in other books. Plots can be the plots you've experienced a thousand times. Many people like this sort of repetition in their fiction. They like it in their religion, and they like it in their life. It makes them feel comfortable and secure and that there will be no unpleasant surprises. It may not be true to life, but they don't want true to life. Just peace and quiet. The books are manufactured to give them the same experience over and over again. Just like getting the same sort of cup, the same sort of painting, the same sort of clothes. I pass no judgment. It is what people choose, and we all benefit from manufacturing. But when it comes to fiction, and you are trying to be honest to God in what you write, and you are not exactly sure what your book will be like once you work through the process and remove it from the kiln, that is art. The book will be unique. It will not be like another, though it may share certain qualities. It will be one of a kind in every way including the cover and the ending. Art not only surprises the audience. It surprises its creator. It surprises the writer and painter and photographer. You don't know how things will end for Becca, do you?"

"No. And I don't know how things will end for me."

It began to snow.

He looked up. "Snow is better than rain sometimes."

"When it's gentle, yes."

CHAPTER 7

AMISH FICTION

I wanted it to be real. I wanted it to be real for Becca, and I wanted it to be real for me. I remembered standing by an open door at one of the library rooms in Pennsylvania and listening to a chat with two Amish romance authors—one a woman, the other a man. What struck me was how real the Amish characters in their books had become to the people in the audience. They acted as if the fictional lovers were real. I thought they were crazy, the way they went on. Why did she do that? Why didn't he say he loved her? How come she's so reluctant to get close to him or go to a hymn sing in his company? I could not take it seriously. The English and their butter churn fictions about Amish life and how we fall in love.

Now, I found out differently. Becca was real to me. She not only took on a life of her own as I wrote her story. She took on a mind of her own. She did things I didn't plan. She said things that weren't in the script in my head. Sometimes, I knew exactly what she was going to say. Other times, I had no idea what was going to come out of her mouth. I wanted to understand suffering and how to comprehend it in the light of God's love and mercy. She had other ideas. Becca wanted to find true love again.

She felt she'd had it once, for one or two years, before her husband began to speak harshly to her and avoid her. After waiting what she considered was a reasonable amount of time after his death (six months), she decided to pray about a second husband. The man who seemed kindest was not Amish. However, she was determined he would become Amish.

It started when she was running for her buggy in a sudden thunderstorm in town. The buggy was three long blocks away, and she knew she was going to get soaked. Then she slipped and fell, causing her to cry out as her hip slammed into the pavement. The bishop and his son were suddenly there, helping Becca to her feet and guiding her along the sidewalk to the buggy. Still, the rain was pelting down. Then it stopped. Only because a man was holding a large umbrella over the three of them. He held it over them until they had climbed into their buggy. Of course, he himself was drenched. The bishop shook his hand warmly. Becca did not look up but she memorized every detail of his face and smile regardless. She wondered if he would have come to her rescue if she had been by herself. She decided, yes, he would have held the umbrella over her head all the way to the buggy.

So, that was the man she began to pray about--handsome, polite, gallant. She asked God if she might see him again. Her request appeared to be granted. The next five times she went into town, she spotted him each time. Once, Becca was in the company of the bishop and his wife, and the bishop waved him over. He introduced his wife and Becca. This time she smiled and did not drop her eyes. Oh, he was beautiful. Such a pleasant spirit. Samuel. She thanked him for his rescue. As the four of them chatted, he mentioned he was a member of the Episcopalian church. Becca thought, Well, Lord, soon enough Samuel will convert, and then he will be a member of the Amish church. A moment later, the bishop invited him to attend their church picnic the following Saturday and he accepted.

ME: Oh, Becca, for heaven's sakes!

BECCA: Vas? What is the problem?

ME: Life is not that neat and tidy.

BECCA: Sometimes it is.

ME: I suppose you will make sure you are at the bishop's picnic table, ja?

BECCA: So? Why not? Wouldn't you?

ME: No, I would not be that forward.

BECCA: Forward? How is that forward? The bishop will invite me to sit with them, and I will accept. You are far worse than me.

ME: I am? I? How?

BECCA: Oh, my goodness, here is a boulder. Oh, my goodness, someone is sitting with his back against it gazing out to sea. Oh, my goodness, it's Mark Hawthorne, the kind and handsome writer. Who would have guessed?

ME: I had no idea who it was the first time.

BECCA: What about the second, third, and fourth time? Etc., etc.

ME: I can't believe I'm arguing with a fictitious character.

BECCA: I am not a fictitious character.

ME: Yes, you are. I made you up.

BECCA: You did not. I was already there. You just made use of me.

ME: I made use of you? To do what?

BECCA: To try and figure out your life. I'm you.

299

ME: You are not me. You are just an idea.

BECCA: I am very much you. I'm just way ahead of you. I know I want to get married again. I know who I want to get married to. I've given my future to God. I've given my past to God. I've given my pain and suffering and confusion to God.

ME: I'm there too.

BECCA: No, you are not, Sara or Lyyndenna or whatever your name is today. We're not even in the same county on all this.

ME: Hey. I decide what you say and do. I'm the writer.

BECCA: No, you don't. I'm the character and I tell your head what I'm supposed to say and do. You're just an innocent bystander.

ME: I'm involved.

BECCA: Your buggy is far, far behind mine and I'm pretty sure your Morgan has thrown a shoe.

It was insane. Who was writing my book *Harvest*? Me or my fictitious Becca? In a roundabout way, I brought it up with Hawthorne. He had a good laugh over that.

"Every writer talks or mutters or complains or pleads with their characters," he said. "Readers do the same thing. It's inescapable. Imagination can give the breath of life to anything and make it three dimensional."

"What if you have an argument with your character and lose the argument?"

"From the moment you wrote your first page as a thirteen year old girl, any plans you had for how your story was supposed to work went out the window. The same is true every time you sit down to create. The process and your mind and your fiction takes over. You race to keep up. Sometimes your plot is extraneous to what's really going on in the story and between the people who are in it."

"So, who's writing who?"

"You're just one of many authors, Lyyndenna, and not always the dominant one."

Well, all right, fine. In a second conversation, Becca pointed out that while I was still tumbling with pain and suffering and a good God, she had embraced that dark side of life. Jesus had legitimized it with his own suffering. So, had all the people in the Bible. And there weren't two Gods, one in the Old and one in the New. There was only the one. Jesus was the face of God in the whole Bible from Genesis to Revelation. You have heard it said but I say. He was the Living Word. He was it. His words finalized everything.

ME: So, you believe all Hawthorne's gobbledygook?

BECCA: I wouldn't call it gobbledygook. He's just trying to figure it all out. Most people are complacent and swallow whatever they're fed. Ja? So, my Bishop Mueller believes the same thing as your Hawthorne.

ME: He is not my Hawthorne.

BECCA: Jesus is the face of grace, the face of love, the face of the Father, the face of God.

ME: And he is not your Bishop Mueller. I invented him.

BECCA: (laughing) You don't invent anyone. You are just a writer. Not God Almighty. Bishop Mueller was given to you and me. You just wrote him down.

ME: Never mind. Is it true you have forgiven your dead husband?

BECCA: I have.

ME: So easy, hmm? So simple?

BECCA: The problem was not simple, but the solution was. What about you?

ME: I'll get there when I get there.

BECCA: I thought you liked simplicity?

ME: I do like simplicity. I like sincerity just as much.

BECCA: Oh, I'm sincere all right. I just decided I'd never get an apology from a dead man. But I might finally get some love from a live one.

ME: Really.

BECCA: Your buggy is stuck. Your wheel is in a rut. Maybe it's broken. All I know is, you're not going anywhere.

ME: Oh, what do you know? You're a work of fiction.

BECCA: If I'm a work of fiction, then so are you. I came out of your head.

ME: I thought you were already there, and I just made use of you.

BECCA: I was already there. But you're the one thinking up my story. Or trying to. You're still getting a lot of it wrong, and I have to correct you in your sleep. Or even when your eyes are wide open.

ME: Imagine it however you like. You are not my story anymore. Our stories are completely different.

BECCA: They aren't. I told you. I'm just well ahead of

you, that's all. I can forgive. I can accept suffering and the loss of my girls. You can't accept loss, and you can't forgive. Because of that, you can't see the love of God. It's hidden.

ME: I wish you would please stop talking. Just stop. I'm trying to write.

Becca had a wonderful picnic. Samuel was a charming guest, in the best sense of that word, making magic and drawing people out of their woes, making the whole table smile and relax. Becca had made up her mind she was going to chat with Samuel as long as possible. She sat across from him and kept him engaged for the better part of three hours. The next day Bishop Mueller dropped by to tell her Samuel had been to see him.

"He is interested in our faith," the bishop explained. "I promised to meet with him once a week and answer all his questions."

Her blue eyes sparked. "Why, that's wonderful. Isn't it?"

"Ja ja, sure, sure. It's wonderful if he's sincere."

"Why wouldn't he be sincere?"

"Because he likes you very much. And why not? You are sunlight, thanks be to God. But I mustn't judge. I mustn't jump to conclusions. He could be sincere about you and our faith both. You pray. I'll pray. We'll find out."

"Amen."

"Amen."

Becca was so excited she wanted to dance. But the Amish do not dance. Yet David had danced. And she'd decided Jesus would have danced at the wedding feast at Cana. So, in her kitchen, all alone, she danced after the bishop had brought her his good news. She danced until she dropped into a chair, exhausted and laughing.

"Praise God!" she sang out loud.

"Do we write the stories or do the stories write us?" Lyyndenna asked Hawthorne during a snowstorm walk the third day in December.

He managed to keep his pipe lit and puffed a few times. "You know how they say. Everybody has a story. Or as Anna Deavere Smith puts it, 'each person has a literature inside them.'"

"What does that mean?"

"It means you don't just have a story or write a story or have a story writing you. You are it. You're the story. All that you are. That's the book. That's the work of art."

CHAPTER 8

CAPPUCCINOS

Kara and Tyler and a work crew wrapped bulbs around the lighthouse. They had to keep them white so as not to confuse shipping. The mayor and council spared no expense. The tall column blazed like the star of Bethlehem once the sun was down. Kara said the mayor would like permission to light up the cottage as well. I told her to go ahead. Christmas lights were something I never had with the Amish. I was also asked to join a caroling group that dressed up as if it were 1890 on the island, and I said yes to that too. Caroling was something else I was never able to enjoy in Pennsylvania.

"So, what did you enjoy when you were Amish?" Hawthorne asked me over cappuccinos at Inked.

"Oh, well," I replied, "I guess I still am Amish in so many ways. I like the quiet way of doing things. I like the German. I know many find it a harsh language, but I don't. I like the plain and simple way of living a life. We go at a horse's walking pace so much of the time. I like the emphasis on prayer. I like the emphasis on kindness and forgiveness. There is so much centered around God's love. So much centered around Christ's compassion and giving his life so we could have a good life to live. And, you know, I adore the horses. Not just the Morgans that drive the buggies. I loved watching the Percheron plow the fields and bring in the hay or the harvest."

"Would you go back?"

"I've thought about it, of course. A part of me expects the bishop and elders to show up here one day and coax me to return to Pennsylvania. Would I be persuaded? Maybe yes, maybe no."

"So, then, explain to me what hold the island has on you."

"The island? I suppose, well, the ways are simple here too. It's easy to find quiet spots and solitude. Easy to pray and think. And I can drive a jeep here, beachcomb here, look out over the wide rolling sea. In Pennsylvania, it's waves of grass—here it's waves of blue water and whitecaps. I like the people. I like the food. I like my cottage and my privacy. Hmm, and it matters a lot to me that I am free to write."

He paused to sip from a ceramic mug with his name on it. "And your novel is going how?"

I had to roll my eyes. "Ha. Well, I thought it was about me finding my way. But my Becca is finding her own way without me. She has no plans to leave the Amish behind, she has forgiven her dead husband, she's met someone she likes, and the love of God dazzles her."

"Isn't her story your story?"

"Do I look like a work of Amish fiction?"

"Well, Lyyndenna, the best fiction is autobiographical."

"Who said that?"

"I did. And many others."

"Is it true? But I've been self-absorbed. Forgive me. How is work on your own novel going? Do you have a title?"

"Titles come and go, though they can help you focus on the main theme of the book. Today, it's *Gale*. Last week, it was *Storm Surge*. Tomorrow, it will probably be *High Tide*. I could also go with *Paean*."

"That's a big switch. Paean to what?"

"The lonely sea and sky."

"So, is that what the book's about?"

"It's about a person reaching out for a rediscovered life living by the sea."

"Hey. That's what I'm writing about."

"I thought Becca was on the farm in Pennsylvania."

"She is. Her author and creator is here by the ocean trying to make sense of everything."

Hawthorne smiled that good smile he had. "Then I guess we're on the same page."

"Well. I think others have been there before."

"In one sense. It's a familiar theme. But that doesn't mean each story will be the same. It can be manufactured. Or it can be unique."

I paused a moment. Then blundered ahead. "I hesitate to ask this but is there ... is there romance in your story?"

"Why do you hesitate to ask it?"

"Because you said you didn't like romance. And because ..."

"You don't want to go there with me."

"Something like that. I'm sorry."

"Nothing to be sorry about. We both agreed on friendship and not a seashell more. As a matter of fact, Lukas is content with waves and sand and bowls of clam chowder. His last book was a thriller about the Navy Seals, and he doesn't want to write thrillers anymore. Even though that genre has made him a pile of money."

"So, then ..."

"So, then, he wants to write stories about transitions and transformations. People going into tunnels and emerging into the light."

"Metamorphosis stories?" I asked.

He drained his cappuccino. "Sure. Chrysalis."

"And no romance? Ever?"

"So far nothing like that. Why? What does it matter?"

"It's just that for Becca, I see that romance is a big part of her healing. She wouldn't be so far ahead of me except for recovering God's love and recovering man's love."

"Does a man love her?"

"No. And she doesn't love him. But it's leaning that way."

"Does it bother you?"

"A little. My main character is far more content than I am."

"Just remember that romance doesn't have to be slick and cheesy. It can be honest and true. Just because publishers might use it to bait readers doesn't mean the real thing isn't out there."

"Out there like the sea wind?"

"Out there like the seagulls crying."

I tinkled my glass of water with a spoon. "I want to hear something from Paean."

That smile. "I don't have it with me, and there's nothing on my phone."

"I'm sure you have something memorized."

"Are you?"

"I am."

He plunged right in.

> It got to the point that any wave that touched the island touched him. Any breeze, any stiff wind, any gale. Every gull that perched, every ship that docked, every shell cast upon the sand. Whenever a big roller shook the black rocks, making them run with water like a beard, he felt the blow in his body. Soon he could not distinguish between the island and his own skin and body.

I honestly had nothing to say to except a pathetic "good work." It was more than good work. Hawthorne deserved accolades. I wanted to write like that. But how?

I decided to snub Becca and her romance and focus more on Christmas and the wild winter sea like Hawthorne was obviously doing with his novel. The village was festooned with all sorts of wreaths shaped like anchors, waves, gulls, and ships of every shape. The older section, which had buildings and streets from the 1700s, was literally dancing in holly with its bright red berries every time the wind gusted. Which also set silver bells tinkling and ringing that were hidden among the spiky green leaves.

The tall ship Paul Revere docked at our wharf for a week, its rigging flying the colorful signal flags the Navy relied on in times past, at night the same rigging streaming with Christmas lights of every color, some of them flashing and winking. Men and women in naval attire from the War of 1812 (a war even I knew New Englanders hadn't approved of and wouldn't participate in) formed up on the main deck every night, regardless of snow or cold or cutting winds, and belted out a mix of sea shanties and carols. I couldn't get enough of "Haul Away Joe" followed by "Joy to the World" and didn't miss a night. I bundled up in an old pea coat I'd found at Davy Jones with all its vintage clothing and marvelous antiques. The coat was two sizes too big, and I loved it that way.

I did my own caroling too as I'd promised I would. The outfit they gave me, replica of a winter coat, skirt, and bonnet from the 1860s, in forest green, wasn't too big or too small but, like the porridge I'd heard about as a child, just right. Of course, I was used to singing without musical accompaniment, so caroling outdoors with just our voices was pure joy for me. It not only took me back to Pennsylvania, it took me back into a great warmth of the heart. We did this three times a week for most of December, and it never got old. Good things never get old.

But, from time to time, I had to leave the carols and wreaths and tall ship and roast chestnut vendors behind because I needed to go to sea again. Outside of my iceberg dips, I hadn't sat and gazed at the blue waters for some time. Waters, to be honest, which were sometimes steel gray or a kind of chilly raw green. The sea wind nipped and bit and cold spray chilled my face, but I embraced it all.

I was never a tropical girl. Our one visit to Florida was long enough at two weeks. I liked the Pennsylvania snowfalls and the sleet of New England. I wanted to be able to wear boots and sweaters and heavy warm jackets. I was a North Country Woman. Like Kara and Jazz and Isieese and their friends.

There was one small beach which wasn't even listed with the other seventeen. It was only fifty yards long and sandless. I discovered it, you could say, by accident. I heard a long sharp rattling sound, like hundreds of marbles rolling over one another, and found a stretch of smooth stones, stones that fit nicely in my palm. Every time a wave came, it pushed the stones up. Every time a wave fell back, it drew the stones with it and created the smooth rattling sound. It wasn't irritating or unpleasant. It relaxed me. It soothed. As I had so many times on the island, I imagined Daniel beside me, and I knew how much he would like the round rolling stones carried back and forth by the sea.

It was only natural I should feel the sting. A mother doesn't expect to lose her son. Outgrow him. Outlive him. You should be towering over me at sixteen. Picking me up in your arms as if I were no heavier than a vase of roses. Making me laugh. Bringing home girlfriends I don't think are right for you. Giving me grandchildren that exhaust me with joy. Now it's a cold darkness.

But not for you. Not for Becca's two girls. You're in light. You're with a God of love. I have to trust something, and I trust that. I'll live and die with that.

Jacob. We had love once. We lost that love. You never lost God's. Everything I see in nature, in the sea, in the Bible tells me what is lost, God recovers. You too. Never in my Amish life have I believed that unbaptized infants go to a hell. It is not the Amish way to baptize infants or teach such a horror. Never have I believed that to take your own life is stronger than the mercy of God, the love of God, the strength of Jesus. You live. I should like to have been reconciled with you here. This is the best I can do. From here by the stones, I forgive you.

God. It's bitter for me some days. I'm not sure of myself. I'm lonely. I'm wind and rain and ice. I could not do this if you were not someone who knew pain. If you were above it all, my story would be impossible. Becca could not have mercy on her husband or be reconciled to the loss of her daughters. She could not love a man again. And if she can't, I can't. You are a man of sorrows and acquainted with grief. Isn't that how the English Bible puts it? That's my hope. That you have suffered like we have suffered. And know us. And carry us. That's my only hope.

The waves were still there when I fell asleep in my cottage, Round Turn and Two Half Hitches. The stones rolled up and rolled down and provided a rhythm for my dreams. When I woke up I felt different. I picked up my mobile which I was beginning to use more and more. I texted Hawthorne. It was five o'clock.

ME: Are you up?

HAWTHORNE: I've been writing since four. Good morning.

ME: Can we walk and talk?

HAWTHORNE: When? Where?

ME: Once the sun's up. At White Shell.

HAWTHORNE: Just like that?

ME: Yes.

HAWTHORNE: What's so important?

ME: I don't know.

HAWTHORNE: Can't it wait?

ME: No, it can't.

CHAPTER 9

I'M NOT HERE

Poor Hawthorne.

The sea wind reminded me of a hammer and anvil. It struck and sparked. A hard-blown spray coated our jeans and jackets and faces. Yet it seemed like I just had to talk to him by the open ocean in a cold gray dawn. Nothing else would do.

"Well, this is bracing," Hawthorne laughed. "You've really become an island gal, haven't you?"

I hadn't expected him to be that warm and forgiving about being dragged away from his cozy house and his writing. "I wanted to tell you in person."

"Tell me what?"

"I've made peace with the loss of my son. With my dead husband. With a God who has the face of a dead Jew. A Jew who isn't dead but knows what it means to bleed."

"That sounds like a lot."

"I guess it is a lot. Except, it's not complete."

"What do you mean?"

"I'm still angry about my life. Hurt. Disappointed with God. I feel like this island still isn't far enough away from my past. I need to get on a boat and go farther."

"Really?"

"Yes. Really. Maybe I need an island off the coast of Africa. Or off the coast of Vietnam. Or maybe I need another planet."

"So, you've accepted but haven't accepted?"

"I'm not sure how that works but yes. I'm content in my discontent. Or I'm discontent with my content."

"Now is the winter of our discontent made glorious summer."

"Who are you quoting now? I wish I did feel like glorious summer inside. I did for a while. I thought I'd resolved all this at Rattling Stones Beach. Honestly, I felt different inside. But I wake up, and I still don't understand the reason for putting people through suffering, especially suffering they had no part in causing. I don't understand why some women have experienced nothing like what I have, while others are exactly where I am––they feel like a sword has pierced their hearts. I don't like God's selective interventions––some are spared, some aren't, some are healed, others aren't, some are lifted out of darkness and many, too many, are left there. I hate to say it, but I feel like throwing a brick through God's front window."

Hawthorne could light his pipe under the most adverse conditions. He took his time doing just that, his back to the sea wind and to me. Then he blew white smoke that was immediately caught and carried away.

"You are a woman who not only values faith but clings to it. Yet faith does not mean you see everything and comprehend everything. It's very much a trust thing. You won't get all your answers here, Lyyndenna. You can't get all your answers here. You have to carry everything that's unresolved, believing there's more to it and that somehow the agony is a fit. That there's a purpose. That God isn't indifferent or malicious or void of love or powerless to make things right. Faith is about the invisible and the not yet and the incomprehensible. You know the prayer of the man with a desperately ill son in the Bible? 'I believe, help my unbelief?' It sounds like that's where you are. Not a bad place to be. Considering the outcome he enjoyed."

I was in a mood despite all his strong words. "I've never enjoyed that kind of outcome."

"No one can say what the outcome will be. It's the faith route, Lyyndenna. It's unseen."

For a flash of a moment, I thought he was going to put

his arm around me as a fierce gust rocked us both. To my surprise, he didn't. To my greater surprise, I realized I wished he had. Inwardly, I kind of cringed. Now what was happening in my head?

I begged off going for breakfast at Breakers and drove to the cottage. I was about to burn my since-I-was-thirteen manuscript in the wood stove in the front room. Then I decided to retain it as an historical artifact and locked the notebooks in a drawer of the 1912 desk I wrote at. The desk Sydney Ryder called The Titanic. Because that was the year the ocean liner sank.

I immediately began a new manuscript. Typing it on my iPad rather than scribbling with a pen. I wrote the title, *I'm Not Here*, and the first sentences--

> I'm not writing a novel. The novel is writing me. I have no narrative in mind. But a narrative is happening just the same. I am writing about what someone else is writing about me. I'm keeping track of the storyline. That's all I am doing. Running to catch up. I have no real idea of the plot or it's denouement. I'm just going to tell you about what I feel, what I think, what I pray, what I see and what I don't see. Scrapping *Harvest*. Becca has it all together anyway and doesn't need my meddling.

To begin again. *I'm Not Here*. Under the pen name of Lyyndenna Patrick.

> At dawn, she went to the sea and told a friend about her struggles with loss and suffering and God and realized, like a breaker crashing completely open on the rocks, she didn't want him as a friend anymore. She wanted something more. It was an overwhelming thought she was by no means ready to receive. She denied it. Said no to breakfast with him and raced home in her jeep, driving sloppily, skidding on icy patches despite the winter tires. Without removing her pea coat or brushing off

the snow, she sat down at her iPad and stared at the screen. Nothing came. She never had writer's block, but nothing came. Finally, she typed out two sentences. "It's not just the man. No woman is an island either, John Donne."

Which was the first thing I said to Kara after driving far too quickly to her condo in the village. "No woman is an island. I can't be that anymore. Don't ask me how I know about John Donne."

Kara stared. "What's going on? You look like you came in with the tide."

"I'll explain. But don't you—?"

"I have today and tomorrow off." Kara peeled off my pea coat, hung it, took my hand and tugged me onto a glassed-in balcony where it was warm as summer. "Sit. Exhale. I'll be back with coffees and some cinnamon rolls."

She had a perfect view of the harbor. The tall ship Paul Revere was at one side of the wharf, and people were standing in a long line ready to board and view it. Revere wouldn't weigh anchor for another two days. The wind was still up but not as raw, the sun was over the cloud bank, the bright signal flags snapped against the blue. I felt my body uncoiling. But I was still determined to say everything I felt I needed to say.

Kara shared the place with Jazz and Issime. Jazz was assistant manager at Breakers, and Issime was back from Boston U for Christmas break. Both were asleep.

These Compass Rose units were new and pricey. Kara's parents had bought her condo for her, and she shared it with her friends who chipped in for utilities. I liked Jazz and Issime, but I was glad they were still in their rooms and under the blankets.

Kara was in her Snoopy pajamas. She came with the coffee and rolls. Swept a tangle of red hair back from her forehead and plopped in a big, fat, comfy chair facing me.

"What's the drama?" she asked.

I wrapped my fingers tightly around the coffee mug she'd given me. I liked the heat. But I didn't say anything.

She swept her hair back again. "No woman is an island. So, is that what you feel like you've been?"

"Yes."

"You have a lot of friends now. Me and the gals. The artists' group. Don't you and Hawthorne have a good friendship?"

"No. Yes. But no. No."

"What?"

"He's been so good to talk to. He's such a good listener."

"Totally. He's the nicest guy."

"I have to let him go. But how do I avoid him when we're both living on a small island?"

Kara stopped sipping from her mug and put it down on a round coffee table. "I must have missed something. Why are we letting him go?"

"He's too nice."

"Too nice?"

I blew out a lungful of air I'd been holding in. Time to stop shaflooting around. A word my mother had made up. "I want him to hold me in his arms."

This information stopped Kara cold. I got the big eyes, green eyes stare. "You do?"

I nodded once and held my coffee close enough to my mouth to cover most of my face. "Very much. Too very much."

"Umm. I guess I'm having trouble seeing the problem here, Denna. A nice guy. A nice woman. God or fate or the universe brings them together to give them some happiness. And the issue is—?"

"I'm a widow."

"So? Widows find new relationships all the time."

"It's only been eighteen months."

"How long do you want it to be?"

"Two years. Three years."

"What? Who told you that? The Amish?"

"No. Amish widows may remarry sooner than that."

"The Bible?"

"No."

"So, who?"

"Me."

"So, Sara King is alive and well and punishing herself. Why?"

"I'm not punishing myself."

"Do Amish widows take three years to remarry?"

"Not if God brings a good man to them."

"So, hasn't God brought a good man to you?"

I closed my eyes. "What am I supposed to do? Approach him? Women don't do that."

"It's the 21st century, girl. A woman can do whatever she wants."

"It's too bold. It's awkward. It's uncomfortable. And I have no idea about dating. No Amish do."

Kara bit into a roll and chewed a moment. "Do you want him or not?"

"I ... I would like to see if we could draw closer, yes."

"So, talk to him about it."

"I can't. It's too ..."

"Weird?"

"All right. Ja. It's too weird."

"It's only weird in your head. He'll be perfectly fine talking about it."

"No, he won't. He said he didn't want anything to do with romance. Friendship was all he was interested in."

"Yes, well, I'm sure he said that because he knew that's where you were in your thinking, and he didn't want to scare you away. Any man would be a fool not to take you up on an offer to explore the possibility of a romantic relationship."

"It's not what he wants."

"Why don't you ask him if that's what he wants today? Now? This Christmas?"

"How do I do that? I can't do that. I have no idea how to say I want him to hold me in his arms."

"Mark, I really want you to hold me in your arms." Jazz had showed up. "It's easy. Only eleven words. You don't even need German or Pennsylvania Dutch."

I made a face. "Easy for beautiful you, Jazz."

"Ha. Which should make it even easier for far more beautiful you, Lyyndenna."

I shook my head. "It cannot happen. It simply cannot."

Kara raised those dark, dark eyebrows of hers at Jazz. "Better get Issime in on this. We're going to need all the help we can get."

CHAPTER 10

WE ARE AND WE ARE NOT

She spent the morning with the girls. It was all about dating and relationships and being real and being herself. In their words. She went away bewildered. And completely uncertain about the role she was supposed to play. Among the Amish it was easy to court and be courted. Everyone knew what they were supposed to do. Out beyond the Amish farms and communities? Everything was out the window. There was no one way of doing anything. Let alone courting. Or dating. Or relationships. Or romance.

Romance. Was that truly what she wanted? She realized she had to be the one to broach the subject with Hawthorne. She had, in Issime's words, dumped him at least twice, "... leaving the sad dude on the beach with his hands in his pockets, the wind in his face, and his heart in his boots. No way in the universe is the guy going to bring up a romantic relationship with you. I don't care how uncomfortable you are, Denna. If you really want something to happen with this guy you're going to have to do the heavy lifting."

She brooded about this. Decided she either had to spill all to Hawthorne or forget about him forever and find another island. Like Martha's Vineyard, ha-ha. It had three.

She bit her lip and texted him a week before Christmas.

SHE: Hawthorne?

HE: 'Lo!

SHE: Can we get together?

HE: I just saw you Saturday at the group.

SHE: Ok, yes, I know, I mean another kind of get-together.

HE: A beach get-together.

SHE: Yes. That.

HE: Which beach? What time?

SHE: Northwest? In half an hour?

HE: I'll be there.

She waited the whole half-hour and a bit longer. Almost didn't leave the cottage. Then hurled herself into Bachi and drove to the beach. Her fingertips felt as cold as snow and her heart as rigid as cast iron. She took her time walking to the boulder covered in seaweed. Hawthorne was actually sitting on it.

"Hey." My new way of talking I'd picked up from Kara and the crew.

Hawthorne turned around and smiled. He was wearing an old army jacket in OD, olive drab. The sight of women and men in jackets like his was not uncommon on the island.

"Hey," he responded.

"Are you warm enough in that?"

"I am. It's got sheepskin lining."

"Would you like to walk?"

We headed along the beach. It was cold and quiet and still. Not yet lunch. He started chatting about Christmas Eve so I knew I had to jump in or that's all we'd end up talking about.

"Hawthorne," I interrupted.

I think my tone was a bit strident. He stopped walking and looked at me. "What is it? What's the matter?"

All my careful plans about when I would say what, in a perfectly choreographed progression, flew away with the December wind. I had to give him the opportunity to say what he truly felt, and I didn't want to lose my nerve. I looked up at him, and I know very well I was looking at him differently than I ever had. Not that I thought about it at the moment.

"Is it difficult for you to spend time with me?" I asked.

Which was not what I intended to say. My brain and my tongue were clumsy. And now it was out there and up to him to deal with. I only regretted it sounded confrontational. But better that than nothing.

Hawthorne was perplexed. "Why ... what makes you say that? Have I given you cause to say that? I'm truly sorry if I have, Denna. You're a delight to be with."

"Truly?"

"Of course. Yes. Truly. What makes you think otherwise?"

"Nothing makes me think otherwise, Hawthorne. I just want to know if ... if you think well enough of me to take our friendship further."

"Further?"

This was getting more difficult instead of easier. Do I have to spell everything out? "You once told me you didn't want romance. Ever. With anyone. Do you still feel that way?"

I could see he was staggered. "Romance?"

Oh, Hawthorne! I am terrible at this. But so are you. Are you going to keep on repeating back to me everything I say? "Yes, romance, Hawthorne. Like in your novels. Like in your characters' lives. Is romance completely out for you? Do you ever, would you ever, do you think it would be something special ... if ..." I prayed and took the plunge. I might as well get it out and over with. He could call me crazy and we'd go back to our lives and iPads and loneliness. "If we had a romance of our own? A real genuine honest to God romance that was more than skin deep?"

Okay. Done.

I was still looking up at him as the wind picked up, and pieces of snow caught in our hair and melted against our faces.

So, I don't know what I expected, but I should have expected more from a writer because that's what I got.

"You have the bluest eyes." His voice had dropped almost to a whisper. But I heard him. "I've never given myself permission to really look at them until now. But you have the bluest eyes."

I liked the warm feeling his words gave me. Thank the Lord God he felt something for Lyyndenna Patrick. How much? Who knew? For that matter, how much did I feel for him? But no one other than my mother had ever drawn attention to the vivid color of my eyes. They simply were not plain. For years I had hated their brilliance and felt they made me mawkish and ugly. Now I was having a new sensation altogether. Hawthorne was gazing so deeply into my eyes I felt his look penetrated to the red marrow of my bones. There was an immediate rush of pure happiness that made me almost cry.

So long. It had been so long since I mattered to anyone. So long since a man I liked had liked me back. I sank my head upon his chest. I didn't even think about it. It was either that or sit down. I didn't consider it bold or presumptuous. It was simply the most natural thing to do. Jazz had said, "Go with simple and uncomplicated. Go with natural and uncontrived. But go." The great gift came seconds after I closed my eyes over his heart. His arms slowly and carefully wrapped themselves around me, as if I were fragile, as if I might say no. If he only knew.

His great kindness was in those arms. His friendship. It was the thing I wanted most. I placed a mittened hand on his coat and chest. I was in seventh heaven. I didn't say it out loud but I wanted to be held a little tighter. Just a little tighter. As if he were listening, bit by bit his arms put more strength around me like a band of copper. I snuggled. I burrowed. My cheeks shone with the quiet crying from my eyes. I felt safe. So safe. So wanted. I felt his lips gently press against my forehead. The wind struck and struck, but I didn't care. I didn't want to go anywhere. I understood nothing except that right now was the place I most needed to be.

It felt strange, strange, but the best kind of strange, a strange that did not paralyze, a strange that beckoned and enticed and exhilarated. If you thought I was going to pull back and run again, you had no idea of how his spirit drew me in and held me. His arms were wonderful but had little to do with my staying in his embrace. It was all that I felt far past his skin and muscles and bones. Far past his heart. The essence of who and what he was held me. The Amish would call that his soul.

At some point, we walked again. It snowed, it stopped, it snowed, it stopped. "Be a little presumptuous," Kara had advised, "but be presumptuous gently and a little secretly." My plans now were even simpler than they had been when I first showed up on the beach. I went with the flow of the tide. The tide within. I took his hand. I leaned my head against his shoulder. It made walking more awkward. I didn't care. It felt spiritual. It felt right.

I prayed to God he would not kiss me. I did not want that. It would break something. Everything was so fragile right now. We needed time to grow into something more. He must have felt the same way because the only kisses he ever gave me were on top of my blue knit beanie. I could feel those from far away, and I liked them very much. I suppose the biggest realization was that I liked him very much too. More than I thought I had. A seven, the way Issime put it, was actually an eight and hovering at nine.

"No, it's not a nine," I told her that evening at their condo in the Compass Rose building. "But definitely a solid eight."

Issime smiled. "Definite?"

"Definite."

"What's next?"

"Another long walk and then dinner at Bowline on a Bight."

"Ooooo," they all went at once.

"Fancy." Kara.

"Posh." Issime.

"He does like you," laughed Jazz. "All along he's had this secret crush he didn't dare talk about. Now he can cut loose ha-ha-ha."

"Ha-ha-ha yourself," I fired back. "I'm sure he's nowhere as interested in me as you think he is."

Which I didn't think was true and certainly hoped wasn't true but I'd learned to have the last word with that crew whenever possible.

Hawthorne understood I was still Amish enough not to enjoy posh. The truth was that Bowline on a Bight wasn't posh at all. It was old (I think 1745), brick, splendid with antiques, and the food was excellent. A little more than chowder and sourdough but, to be honest, the meal wasn't the highlight of the evening. It was a calm night, and Hawthorne drove us away from the village in his pickup so we could watch the Christmas stars glittering over a flat black sea. Then he took me to a church away and gone I didn't even know about, a simple white wooden church with a simple white steeple. It was locked, but he had a key.

"How did you get that?" I asked him.

"Well, the long story is my novel Walking on Water."

"I'd like to know right now. So, what's the synopsis?"

"I can do better than a synopsis. I can give you the two sentence blurb. Mark Hawthorne used to pastor here many moons ago. When I returned to be Joe Writer on St. Silvan's, they gave me a key, so I could pray here whenever I wanted."

"Now I want to read the novel."

"It's at the public library in Gloucester. You can have it sent here to ours and snag it."

"You were a pastor here. I'm amazed." I tried to read the sign in the dark. "What church is this?"

"St. Mark's."

"How appropriate."

"I thought so."

He guided me inside and flicked a light switch. Electricity

at the snap of a finger was still something I was getting used to. I rarely used it at the cottage. The church was small, lined with enough wooden pews for fifty or sixty, had a sturdy pulpit carved like a wave, and stained glass windows lit from beneath that were fragments of blue. I adored the blue. Which I knew he knew. I sat down by one of the windows. Closed my eyes. Let my mind drift. Deep greens and blues, just like that song again.

"You're not going to fall asleep on me, are you?" Hawthorne teased.

I smiled, leaving my eyes shut. "I'm mediating. Just waiting for the service to start."

"It started the moment you walked in the door."

"Then I'm waiting for the message."

"The message? I don't do that anymore."

Be bold when it suits, the girls had coaxed. Boldness was in my nature. I was able to admit that eight months after leaving the farm. But not when it came to men. About whom I knew nothing. Nevertheless. "You'll do it for me."

I couldn't believe I actually said that.

Truthfully, I thought my feigned self-confidence was going to fall flat on its face.

I could feel the heat in my cheeks.

Then he began to speak.

I can't describe the storm of emotions that set off in me.

He really was going to do it for me.

I wasn't used to that from anyone.

Let alone a man I'd come to admire.

Still, I did not open my eyes.

"This chapel was built for fishermen and whalers and their families in 1699," he said. "Of course, it's been repaired and refurbished over the years, but it's still substantially the same chapel set on the same foundation. There was a garrison here once too, but its barracks and brick buildings were destroyed during the course of the Revolution. It changed hands many times so far as denominations go—Methodist, Calvinist, Baptist, Episcopalian. Now it's considered interdenominational. Various members of the congregation, women or men, speak on Sunday evenings when they gather."

I didn't respond.

So, he picked up where he'd left off. "I suppose you want me to say something spiritual and not just recite a history of St. Mark's. So, then it's this--we're all rebuilt and restored and renewed over a lifetime. There's fire and theft and storm and destruction. But we're built on the foundation we had from the beginning. Our body and our soul. Foundations are improved upon and strengthened. But it's still us with different windows and roofs and doors. In one sense, we are always ourselves from day one. In another sense, we aren't because we are constantly in flux and constantly changing. We are old, and we are new. We're ourselves, and we're different selves. We're still us, and we're altered versions of us at the same time. We are, and we are not. God help us."

I was thinking of Daniel and Jacob. I was thinking of the Pennsylvania I left behind. I was thinking of how good life had been during my twenties, and I was thinking of how hard and painful it had been too.

God help us? Yes, sometimes God's presence and blessing were obvious. Other times God was nowhere to be seen, felt, or heard. What did it mean to live and love by faith? To never see the unseen but still trust it? To never hear the unheard but still hear it? Did it mean to walk through the valley of death over and over again but fear no evil regardless of a constant shadow or grief or threat? What if there was no healing, never any healing, what if Jesus did not come by? Was my foundation truly still there being restored and rebuilt? Or was I a wreck built on sand and sinking, sinking, sinking ...

My tears were streaming down my face. I could not help it. I kept swiping at my cheeks with my hands, but it did not help. I could not stop the pain and bewilderment and loss.

"Denna," came his soft troubled voice. "Lyyndenna."

"Don't talk," I told him as I sobbed and choked. "There's nothing to say. Just hold me, Mark. Just hold me. Please."

I wept into his arms and chest and could not be consoled.

CHAPTER 11

BEAUTIFUL

So, if my story were one of the Hallmark Christmas movies the girls got me to watch, my life would have been put in order and healed by God and romance on Christmas Eve. If it were one of the Amish fictions so many read and enjoy, the result would have been something along the same lines. I know because I've read the Amish love stories. Three of them.

Few Amish read such books. Few English who read such books become Amish. It is a pleasant entertainment to them and, I pray, a spiritual encouragement. I do not begrudge them their innocent pleasures. But real Amish life is both beautiful and difficult, light and shadow, sweet and sour. It is a different path and for some the best path. But no path on earth is free of stones and stubble any more than any bed of roses is free of thorns or every green forest, lovely as it may seem, is absent of poison oak. Yes, I know a number of the Amish romances are honest about that. God bless them.

Still, according to a typical Hallmark or romance storyline, Amish or not, Hawthorne and I should have kissed under the English mistletoe about the same time as everything dawned on me, and I understood exactly what God was doing and had been doing all along. Any bitterness or resentment would have been washed away. Or if not then, I would have been granted an extraordinary spiritual resolve to get me through and keep me going. I suppose if you wanted to stick to that script then Hawthorne was my miracle.

But he wasn't really. He was simply a good man who did not have all the answers or the keys to all the doors. He was my rock, for sure, as much as any human could be, but he wasn't God or the universe or the road through the valley of the shadow of death. We had to walk that together. Everyone has their own wounds and they seek their own healings. Including Mark Hawthorne. So that's what happened Christmas Eve and Christmas Day. That's what happened New Year's Eve and New Year's Day. Beginnings. Not endings and resolutions.

Besides. The whole week was a blizzard. In the books, the skies would have been crystal clear Christmas Eve. Or, if we did get snowed in, we'd finally be stuck together and kiss. Instead we met in the storm New Year's Eve and walked by a raging sea, tightly holding hands as the wind beat and battered us.

"Would you return to Pennsylvania?" Hawthorne asked me, holding his head close to mine, so I'd hear him despite the howl.

"I might." I was just being honest. I wasn't trying to hurt him.

"Would you take up the Amish ways again? Pin up your hair? Wear the long dresses?"

"I might."

"So ..."

"So, no, I can't tell you what will happen next year. And you can't tell me. But I'm also being honest if I tell you I might stay on this island with you for the rest of my life."

"You might?"

He looked so hopeful. Like a puppy. I laughed and patted his cheek. "You're too sweet for me. Ja, I might. Just as you might return to Pennsylvania and convert. So much is possible. But I confess. The crooked places in my head and heart need to be made straight and the rough places plain before I'm going anywhere. Whether that's a geographical location or a relationship."

"What about us then, Lyyndenna?"

"Us? This is us now. Life isn't a movie or a storybook, is it? Things don't come to completion in one reading or in two hours. We have a lot to talk about, don't we? It will take time. But please don't look so worried. I'm ready to take the time. And I want to be with you, Mark. Take a moment to look at what my eyes are saying. I want to be with you."

He stared past my frozen eyelashes and laughed. "They certainly are saying something nice to me."

"Good. I'm glad you're picking up on what Jazz would call my vibes, ha-ha. Are you picking up on anything else?"

A fierce blast tore my knit beanie from my head and sent it spinning off into the sleet and dark. I squealed as the storm grabbed a hold of my hair and played with it, streaming it behind me like the mane of a palomino mare. I could almost hear the wind laugh in a silly, happy, boyish way. I could certainly hear Mark Hawthorne's laugh. It was the same kind.

"Yes, I'm picking up on something else." He was smiling, trying to catch my hair for me while it ran and looped through his hands like a golden rope. "You're beautiful, Lyyndenna. The most beautiful woman I've ever seen. You're more beautiful than the ocean. You're more beautiful than a dream."

END PART ONE

ABOUT THE AUTHOR

Murray Pura has over twenty-four novels to his credit and, in addition, has published dozens of short stories, novellas, and poems along with numerous books of nonfiction. He has worked with Baker, Barbour, Zondervan, Harvest House, MillerWords, HarperCollins, Harlequin, Harper One, and Elk Lake Publishing. His fiction has won or been short listed for a number of literary prizes. Pura has lived in the UK, the Middle East, the USA and Canada. He now makes his home in the Rocky Mountains of Alberta.

A LIGHT IN THE WINDOW

PATRICK E. CRAIG

A NOTE FROM PATRICK E. CRAIG

The Amish have been in America since 1720, the year they first came to Pennsylvania. In 1740, they built the first identifiable Amish community at Northkill in what later became Berks County. For many years, the Amish lived out of the mainstream of public life, but in the last twenty-five years, there has been a growing interest in the Amish culture, popularized no doubt by the huge number of "Amish Romance" books that fill the shelves of bookstores across America. Unfortunately, most of these books have ignored the deeper issues of Amish life and focus on an over-romanticized cozy fiction approach to the Amish culture. As an author who writes about the Amish, I hope in my stories to dig down below the superficial and address the deeper issues, since the Amish, like all of us, can find themselves in desperate situations that only God can fix. This story is about one of those issues.

Since the Amish arrived, America has suffered through several major wars and there has always been a question that arises concerning the Amish during these conflicts—what will they do when asked to defend the country that allows them to be non-violent from forces that would overwhelm America by violence.

Some of my novels have dealt with this question as the major theme—*A Quilt For Jenna*, *Far On the Ringing Plains*, *The Amish Princess*—but it is a theme that underlies all of my Amish books. In *A Light In The Window*, I hope to take another look from a fresh perspective—through the eyes of a child who may not understand the deeper ramifications of war on the world around her, but certainly feels their effect on her family.

Patrick E. Craig

PROLOGUE

Whenever I see snow, I remember the miracle.

I remember the white flakes falling like tiny angels outside the window. I remember the flickering lamps, the wonder on my mama's face and my grandmother's whispered prayers of thanks. Yes, I remember the miracle.

I know we all have small miracles every day, because the hand of *Gott* guides each of us, and he is always doing wonderful things if only our eyes are open to see them. But this was a big miracle, and though I am old now and my failing memory hides many things from me, this miracle has never left me, shining through all the days of my life, like the Hanukkah Menorah that burned in our window in the winter of 1945, tended by a little girl who was hoping and praying her papa would come home for Christmas.

In those days, I lived in Colorado with my mama, Emily, my grandmother, Magda, and my papa, Gerd. We all came to America from Germany in 1940—to the beautiful San Luis Valley. My papa bought a ranch and raised Mustang horses. After we were there for a year, Papa, Mama, and my grandmother became citizens. Then the war came to America. Because my Papa was German, he knew he could help the American cause, so he enlisted. Mama said joining up was hard for him because he was raised in the Amish faith, and he always believed violence toward other men was wrong. But he also believed he needed to help defend America from the evil that was Hitler—an evil he had seen firsthand. He became an officer and left us to go with the army. The day he went away—oh, he was so handsome in his uniform, and my mama cried.

Now the war in Europe was over, but my Papa was not home, and we had not heard from him for several months. My mama was so anxious, and I remember hearing her cry at night when she thought I could not hear her.

Back in 1936, there were bad times in Germany. My Papa was an Amish man who owned a farm in the tiny village of Ixheim, right on the border with France. He lived there with my grandmother. That was before I was born. My mother was a Jewish girl who was being hunted by the Nazis. She was trying to escape to France, but she only got as far as my Papa's barn. When my Papa found her hiding there, he fell in love with her. He married her, but the Nazis found them and sent them to the Dachau concentration camp. On the way there, they met a Jewish man who helped them escape. He also helped them to discover their Messiah, Yeshua Hamaschiach, Jesus Christ, but that's another story. That is why we always had Christmas and Hanukkah at the same time in our house in Colorado. And that is where the miracle began.

When my papa and mama left Germany in 1936, my papa also left the Amish Church. The Nazis had convinced the Amish to turn in Jews and Communists to the Gestapo, and there were other things the church did my papa could not agree with. Papa sold his farm to his friend, and my parents and my grandmother escaped over the border to France. I was born there, in the village of Épernay, outside of Paris in 1937. Papa found work in the vineyards, and mama taught in a school for Jewish refugee children. My *Mütti*, that's what I called my grandmother, stayed at home and took care of me. Though I don't remember it, *Mütti* said we lived in a little cottage in the middle of a large vineyard where they grew grapes to make French Champagne. It was very long ago, but sometimes I see a picture in my mind of a rock wall with purple and yellow flowers spilling over it and my *Mütti* sitting in the sun in an old chair.

Then things got bad in France and the French Army moved to the border to keep the Germans from getting in. My papa was very smart, and he knew all the Jewish people in France were in danger if the Germans came, so with the money he got from selling his farm, he bought tickets to America. And so, when I was three years old, we came to Colorado and bought our ranch. Then my papa went away to the war. And that's where *this* story begins.

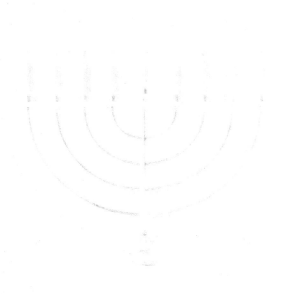

CHAPTER 1

SNOW—DECEMBER 1945

Adina Hirschberg looked out the window of the front room and watched as the heavy flakes floated down from a leaden sky. As far as she could see, the fields and pastures around their ranch were covered with a deep fall of white. It had been snowing for a week, a rare occurrence in the San Luis Valley. Now it was eight days until Christmas.

The sound of her *grossmütter*, Magda, entering the room made her turn her head. Magda held an armful of wood that she laid on the hearth before the roaring fireplace.

Adina ran to her grandmother. *"Mutti, Mutti!"*

Magda turned and embraced the girl. "What is it, my Dina?"

"When will Papa be home?"

Magda shook her head. She looked over the little girl's shoulder at the snow swirling outside. "We don't know, little one. He has not sent a letter in some time."

"Will he be home by Hanukkah? By Christmas?"

Magda smiled. In the Hirschberg house, Hanukkah and Christmas happened at the same time.

Emily Hirschberg came in from the kitchen. "We are getting low on flour and oil, Mother, and I'm worried you won't be able to make *stöllen*."

Adina's face puckered. "No *stöllen!*"

Magda smiled. "Don't worry little one. We will find some flour to make your favorite."

The little girl jumped and clapped her hands. "Oh, good!"

Emily took hold of her daughter's hand. "Run upstairs and see how the kittens are doing."

Adina ran off to play with the new kittens that their cat, Hansli, rather than face the cold in the barn, had birthed in an extra upstairs closet. Emily watched her go.

"I don't know, Magda. We have not been able to get to the store for a week. There is too much snow. Our truck can't get through it. Billy Roberts has not been by either. I'm afraid all of our neighbors are in the same predicament. Oh, I wish Gerd had not bought a ranch so far out of town." She burst into tears.

Magda took Emily in her arms. "What is it my girl? Gerd?"

Emily snuffled in the safety of Magda's shoulder and then finally raised her head. She pulled a hanky from her apron pocket and dabbed her eyes. "Yes, mother, I am so worried. I have not heard from Gerd since September, and his letters were so vague. He said even though the war was over, his duties were keeping him in Europe for some time. He said he would be coming home as soon as he could."

Emily held Magda tighter.

"Why did he have to go to the war, Magda? We were so happy."

Magda sighed and pulled her daughter-in-law closer. "It is exactly because you were so happy that he had to go. When we came to America we found a new home, good friends, and a country that accepted us just as we are. We found freedom, and that was what Gerd went to the war for. He felt that he should do something for the country that has given him so much even in the short time we have been here."

"But the Amish are against war."

Magda nodded. "Yes we are ... for the most part."

"What do you mean?"

Magda drew Emily to the couch in front of the fire, and they sat. "I have spoken with the other Amish who live in this valley, and they tell me that many of their men have faced the same dilemma Gerd went through. I think the Amish in America have struggled with this since they first stepped ashore in Philadelphia two hundred years ago."

Magda paused and looked out at the snow. "Gerd faced this when the Nazi Glauss tried to lay hands on you. Even though our Lord Jesus tells us if we are struck on the cheek, we should turn the other cheek, there comes a time when a man must choose to defend his family and those he loves. Many Amish men have watched their families murdered before their eyes, and I am thinking that did not please the Lord."

"*Mütti!*" Emily's eyes widened.

"When you watched your mother and father being taken away and your brother killed by the Nazis, what did you feel in your heart?"

Emily looked down. "I wanted to protect them, I wanted to save them. I would have killed the Germans if I had a gun."

"I don't think those feelings are from the devil, Emily. That is why, when we left the Amish church in Ixheim, I felt free for the first time. I know the Lord wants us to be kind and gentle, to turn the other cheek if we can, but I think he also expects us to defend those he has given us to protect. That is why Gerd went. He wanted to make sure that the country that had given his wife and child a future would continue to exist in the face of great evil. That is why I gave him my blessing."

Emily looked at Magda and then sank back against her. The old woman brushed Emily's hair back and kissed her forehead. "I understand your worry for Gerd, and I am worried too. But the Lord has directed our path since the day you came to us. I am so thankful you hid in our barn, Emily, for you are truly a daughter to me."

Adina heard them talking and paused at the top of the stairs. Their words troubled her.

What if Papa can't find his way home? Maybe he's lost in the snow.

She went into the room where the kittens were. The tiny soft balls of fur were snuggled up against their mama. Hansli looked up at Adina and then yawned a big cat yawn.

"How are your babies today, Hansli?" The cat answered with a soft purr. Adina counted the kittens and made sure they were all alive. When she was satisfied, she sat on the bed. It was cold in the upstairs room even though the heat from the fireplace could spread through the well-designed ranch house. Adina pulled a down comforter around her and thought about her father. She tried to remember what he looked like, but it was hard for she was only five years old on the day he left. She did remember one thing, though. Her father, a tall man wearing brown clothing, took her in his arms and held her close. His whispered words were still with her.

"Do not worry, Adina. The Lord Yeshua will be with me, and I have asked him to watch over you and your mother and *Mütti*. That is all we can do—put our lives into his hands and trust him. I will do my best to come home to you, I promise, but if I do not, always remember that I love you so much."

Her papa had been gone for three years now. Even though she sometimes had trouble remembering exactly what his face looked like she always remembered his words. Hansli climbed out of the box, leaving her now-sleeping kittens, and climbed up on the bed. Adina pulled the cat under the comforter so that only her head was sticking out. Hansli settled down and began to purr.

"What should we do, Hansli? Why hasn't Papa come home?" She bowed her head.

"Yeshua, where is my papa? We need him to come home. Mama needs him, and I do too. Won't you help us?"

She sat silently for a long time. Suddenly an idea came to the little girl. "Hansli! I know what to do! It's almost time to start lighting the Menorah for Hanukkah. We'll put it in the window instead of on the mantle. That way Papa can see it, and the light will guide him home."

Adina put Hansli on the bed and jumped up. The cat protested, but Adina was already out the door and clattering down the stairs.

"Mama! Mama! I know how to bring Papa home."

CHAPTER 2

DACHAU—APRIL 1945

Gerd Hirschberg sat in the passenger side of the Jeep with two more MIS officers in the back seat. It was April 29. He and several intelligence officers had been embedded with the 42nd Rainbow division and sent with them to liberate the Nazi concentration camp at Dachau. Behind them, a group of newspaper reporters and photographers followed in another jeep. Gerd's heart was pounding as they drove slowly toward the camp looming in front of them. He turned to one of the Intelligence officers behind him, Major Heym. The Major was a German refugee like himself. He and Gerd had gone through training at Camp Ritchie, the secret installation where American soldiers who spoke fluent German trained in interrogation and counterintelligence techniques before being sent to Europe.

"This is the camp where the Nazis sent my wife's father, Emilé Weissbach, in 1936."

Major Heym had a quizzical look. "I didn't think they were rounding up Jews so early."

Gerd shook his head. "Emilé was also a Communist, so he was one of the first to go. They took his wife with him and murdered his son Jürgen, my wife's brother."

Heym looked away. "I came from Munich. We saw what was happening, and I escaped with my wife and children in 1934. The rest of my family has disappeared. I hope that some of them fled as I did, but I am afraid they waited too long and the Nazis rounded them up and sent them to the camps."

As they drove up the road toward the main gate, the snow was still two feet deep in places, and it was cold, very cold.

There was a line of railroad cars on a siding by the road. US soldiers were opening the cars, and many were stumbling away and vomiting. Gerd could see piles of human bodies inside the cars.

"*Mein Gott!*" said Heym, slipping into German. "These soldiers did not understand what we would find here."

Gerd turned his head away, his mind refusing to believe what his eyes were seeing. Even though they were briefed the previous week about what the Allied forces were discovering in the concentration camps, Gerd could not assimilate the enormity of what he was seeing. Another Jeep drove down from the gate. A colonel on the passenger side spoke to them.

"Hirschberg, Heym! We need you at the gate for translating. General Linden is waiting."

They drove to the gate and clambered out. A young man in the uniform of the Waffen SS stood surrounded by Army personnel and some reporters. His face was pale and his hands trembled. General Linden nodded to Gerd. "Captain Hirschberg. Please ask this man his name and rank. Then ask where the camp commandant is."

Gerd spoke rapidly to the German. The officer answered. Gerd translated for the General. "His name is SS 2nd Lieutenant Heinrich Wicker. The camp commandant, Martin Weiss, who fled with most of the regular guards last night, left him in charge. Lieutenant Wicker is ready to surrender the camp."

Just then the the sound of tumult interrupted them. Gerd turned. Men, obviously prisoners, poured out of the barracks behind the barbed wire fence. They shouted in unison. American soldiers stood watching in dismay, many of them weeping at the sight of the horribly emaciated prisoners dragging themselves to the fence. Gerd saw several German soldiers being led away to a separate enclosure. They disappeared from sight and then shots rang out. Gerd turned to Major Heym. "What is happening, Major?"

Heym shook his head. "I think that any German soldier caught inside this camp will not leave it alive."

"But what about the Geneva Convention?"

Heym shrugged. "These Germans, these animals, have given up their rights under the Convention. I suggest you stop with the questions, Captain. We are in hell here and our men are furious. Whatever happens, these Germans have brought upon themselves."

Gerd looked back for the young man who had surrendered the camp. He had vanished along with the soldiers who had been with him . Heym shrugged. "As I said ..."

Shots rang out, and everyone ducked and ran. Gerd saw soldiers pointing at a guard tower. He saw flashes of light as whoever was in the tower fired their weapon out the window. The Americans surrounded the tower and unleashed a maelstrom of bullets into the tower. Two men pitched out of the window, and the firing stopped. Gerd watched as the Americans ran up and finished the Germans off with bursts of rifle fire.

Around the camp there were other outbursts of gunfire as some German soldiers fought to the finish rather than being shot by the Americans or torn to pieces by the prisoners. Gerd saw GIs rushing by, their faces contorted with rage and grief. Gerd shook his head.

Dear Lord! Who could even think that human beings could descend to such behavior? It is beyond belief.

That evening, Gerd sat with his commanding officer, Gen. Oscar Koch. Gerd had spent the rest of the day interrogating the few surviving German soldiers.

"What I understand from the interrogations, sir, is the Germans knew the Allies were coming and started shipping prisoners here from other camps so they would have time to exterminate them. The death train outside the camp was part of that. It arrived a week ago. When the Nazis realized they would not have time, they locked the doors and let them all die."

Koch shook his head. "Linden told me that when our boys saw what was going on here, there was a period of about half an hour when the GIs went crazy. They shot any German they saw or turned them over to the prisoners, and they were beaten to death. Awful."

Gerd looked at General Koch. "Sir, I would like to ask a favor—well, two favors."

"What's that Hirschberg?"

"First, this camp is where the Nazis sent my wife's parents in 1936. I would like permission to look at the records and speak with some Jews here to see if I can find out what happened to the Weissbachs."

"What's the second favor, Captain?"

"I would like permission to communicate with my wife and let her know where I am. She hasn't heard from me for several weeks."

Koch stood up. "The first request I will grant, Captain, since we need you to speak to as many prisoners as possible and get to the bottom of what happened here and in the other camps around Germany and Poland. I must deny the second request. This entire operation has gone top secret. We need to keep any information about it on a need to know basis. Many Nazis involved in this, like Weiss, are in hiding. They must not know what we are doing. So no communication from now on."

"But, sir, that may take months."

Koch went to the door and turned. "I'm well aware of that, but we have a lot of cleanup to do here, and you are an important but secret part of that. No letters or phone calls until further orders. Understood?"

Gerd stood and saluted. "Yes, Sir. Understood."

Koch turned and left the room. Gerd sank back down in his chair.

This is not good, Lord. Emily will be very worried.

CHAPTER 3

THE MENORAH

Adina ran down the stairs to her mother. "Mama, Mama! I know how to bring Papa home!"

Emily pulled the child up close. "How, Dina?"

"Tonight, we light the Hanukkah Menorah, right?"

Her mother looked down at Dina's eager face. "Yes, my darling girl, but ..."

"Don't you see, Mama? This year, instead of putting it on the mantle, we will put it in the window so Papa can see it and find his way home."

Emily looked away and tears formed in her eyes.

If only it were that simple ...

"Mama? I know it will work. The light in the window will be like a star to guide Papa home"

"Oh, to have the faith of a child again."

Emily turned to see Magda standing there with a smile. She turned back to Dina. "You are right, Dina. We will put the Menorah in the window. And each day, we will light a new lamp, and by Christmas, there should be enough light for Papa to see all the way from Germany."

That night, they gathered in the living room. The fire was bright and warm. Outside, the gray light of dusk was giving way to nightfall. Emily brought the beautiful Menorah from its place of honor in the hallway cabinet and placed it on the table they had moved in front of the large window. The golden lamp gleamed—its many cups and arms reflecting the light from the fire.

Emily said, "My grandfather made this *menorat—hanukkah*. He passed it down to my mother, and it is the only thing I have left to remember my father and mother by. When I was a little girl like you, Dina, we started celebrating Hanukkah on the tenth day of December. But that is because most Jewish homes have not yet seen the truth that their Messiah, Yeshua, has already come. Your papa and I know that Jews and Gentiles alike share the wonderful savior of the world. So we celebrate Hanukkah and Christmas together to remember the coming of the Light into this world."

Dina nodded. "So we are the only house in the world who does it this way, right?"

Magda laughed. "That may be true, Dina, but knowing Jesus, there may be many other Jews who have seen the truth. You just never know."

Emily pointed to a cup in the middle of the lampstand. It was higher than the other eight cups. There was a wax candle in the cup. "This is the *Shamash*, the servant candle. It is used to kindle the other cups. That is why we use a wax candle here, so in case the other lights go out, it is ready to serve them by relighting them. Each night, we will fill another cup with oil and we will keep the Menorah burning for an hour. By the end of the eighth day, all the cups will be lit."

"And the light will be so bright that Papa will see it, and it will guide him home."

Emily looked at Magda. "Yes, Dina, it will guide Papa home."

"Before we light the candle, tell me the story, Mama."

The three Hirschberg women sat together on the comfortable couch in front of the fire. Emily began. "Some twenty-one hundred years ago, the land of Israel came under the rule of the Syrian-Greek emperor Antiochus, who issued a series of decrees designed to force his pagan beliefs and rituals upon the Jewish people. He outlawed the study of Torah and observing its commands and defiled the Holy Temple in Jerusalem with Greek idols.

"A small, vastly outnumbered band of Jews waged battle against the mighty Greek armies and drove them out of the land. When they reclaimed the Holy Temple, they wished to light the Temple's menorah, only to discover the Greeks had ruined all the holy oil. All that remained was one jar of pure oil—enough to last one night—and it would take eight days to procure new, pure oil so they could keep the lamp lit day and night."

"But Yahweh gave them a miracle—the one-day supply of oil lasted eight days and nights. Ever since then, the Jews light the Hanukkah menorah on each of the eight nights of Hanukkah."

Adina turned to her grandmother. "Now the Christmas story, *Mütti!*"

Magda reached over to the table by the couch and took up the Bible lying there. She opened it. "Mary and Joseph knew the baby Mary carried in her womb was the Messiah of Israel and the entire world, for they had been told by angel messengers who came from God. Then the Emperor in Rome decreed everyone should go to their hometown to be counted in a new census so he could tax them. So Joseph took Mary to Bethlehem for the census, but *Gott* was in it, for many centuries before, the prophet Micah had foretold that the Messiah would be born in the town of David. So they came there ..."

"But they could not find a room in the inn, right *Mütti*."

Magda smiled. "No, Dina, they could not. So Joseph found a man who let them stay in his stable. Can you imagine that the God of the Universe chose the most humble of places to be born?"

"And then the angels came?"

Emily laughed. "Soon you will be old enough to tell the story, Dina, for you know it by heart already."

Magda opened the Bible and read. "And it came to pass in those days, that there went out a decree from Caesar Augustus that all the world should be taxed. And this taxing was first made when Cyrenius was governor of Syria. And all went to be taxed, every one into his own city. And Joseph also went up from Galilee, out of the city of Nazareth, into Judaea, unto the city of David, which is called Bethlehem; because he was of the house and lineage of David: To be taxed with Mary, his espoused wife, being great with child.

"And so it was that, while they were there, the days were accomplished that she should be delivered. And she brought forth her firstborn son, and wrapped him in swaddling clothes, and laid him in a manger; because there was no room for them in the inn.

"And there were in the same country shepherds abiding in the field, keeping watch over their flock by night. And, lo, the angel of the Lord came upon them, and the glory of the Lord shone round about them: and they were sore afraid. And the angel said unto them, "Fear not: for, behold, I bring you good tidings of great joy, which shall be to all people.

"For unto you is born this day in the city of David a Savior, which is Christ the Lord. And this shall be a sign unto you; Ye shall find the babe wrapped in swaddling clothes, lying in a manger. And suddenly there was with the angel a multitude of the heavenly host praising God, and saying, 'Glory to God in the highest, and on earth peace, good will toward men.'

"And it came to pass, as the angels were gone away from them into heaven, the shepherds said one to another, Let us now go even unto Bethlehem, and see this thing which is come to pass, which the Lord hath made known unto us. And they came with haste, and found Mary, and Joseph, and the babe lying in a manger. And when they had seen it, they made known abroad the saying which was told them concerning this child. And all they that heard it wondered at those things which were told them by the shepherds."

Emily put her arm around Dina. "When Yeshua grew up, he taught the things of God to the people of Israel. But many people who were not Jews believed also. That is because God sent Jesus to everyone to tell them they did not have to live in the darkness of sin anymore. He said, 'I am the light of the world: he that followeth me shall not walk in darkness, but shall have the light of life.'

"When your papa and I met, and I showed him the Menorah, he said *Gott* spoke to him and said 'I am the light.' Then when the Nazis found us and sent us away to the concentration camp ..."

"... That is when you met Joshua?"

"Yes, Dina, that is when we met Joshua, a Jew who knew his Messiah. He gave his life so your papa and I could escape from the Nazis. When we light the Menorah, I always remember him, for not only did he save our lives, he showed us the one who gives eternal live."

"*Yeshua Hamaschiach*?"

"Yes, Dina, Jesus the Messiah."

Dina sighed. "And then you escaped and went to France, and I was born." She snuggled into her mother's arms. "Oh, Mama, how I love the stories."

Emily looked up. Night had fallen. "Come, Dina, it is time to light the Menorah."

CHAPTER 4

THE MARCH—MAY 1945

The man pulled the ragged coat around him. It was spring, but he was cold, always cold. His feet moved on the road, feet that no longer seemed connected to his legs. Steady now, one foot in front of the other.

I must keep moving ... if I stop, I will die ...

They had marched for three days, and today, a heavy snow had been falling since before dawn. It chilled him to the bone. Still they marched, trudging along in the snow, their naked feet turning the white into a morass of mud and blood. They kept their eyes down, so they would not make eye contact with the guards and draw their attention.

One foot in front of the other ...

He watched those who could not keep up a steady marching pace pulled out of line and shot by the guards. Others, many of them friends, collapsed and died along the side of the road.

Keep moving or you will die ...

The man looked up. The clouds were breaking, and the steady snow turned to random flakes. He wanted to end it all, just stop, let the guards take him.

So after all these years of surviving, I am to die on a muddy road in the south of Germany. Ach zo! Then I will be with you, my beloved ...

But his feet would not stop. They moved as though they had a life of their own. He looked down at the hands that were showing out of the frayed cuffs of. Once they had been powerful hands, the hands of a man in his prime, now they were the hands of a scarecrow, the skin clinging to the bones and thin as parchment paper. A small smile played over his once handsome face.

Oh my dearest, if you could see me now ...

In the days before Nazis forced them out of the camp, rumors abounded that the Americans were only hours away. Many of the guards deserted, and a spirit of hope grew among the Jews. Still, conditions were horrific, and hundreds died every day. Typhus raged. Then, early in the morning of April 26, the Nazis put many prisoners on a train. After it left, the guards came to the barracks. The old man had been told to prepare to leave. The SS troops formed up a large group of prisoners, half Jews and half Russian POWs, and marched out of the camp.

The old man had fallen in beside his friend, Hirschel Grodzienski. "What's this all about, Hirschel?"

"They say Hitler is fleeing to Tyrol to keep up the war there. They need us to build a fortress for him to hide in."

Another man next to them scoffed. "That's another lie. The Nazis do not want to be caught with so many of us. Then the world will know what they have done. Did you not see the guards passing out food and clothing as we left? They are trying to smooth things over, to make the prisoners say how kind they were to us. The animals."

A third man whispered, "Kaltenbrunner will kill us all. Even in the death throes of the Third Reich, the Nazis will do their best to murder all the Jews."

And so they marched, rumors swirling up and down the line.

It was late at night in the former offices of the camp commandant. Gerd Hirschberg sat at a desk going over the lists of prisoners. He did not expect to find anything good about Emily's parents, but he looked anyway.

The record keepers divided the information in the records into five columns: family name or given name, place and date of birth, last place of residence, prisoner number and barracks, when they had arrived, and what had happened to them. Name followed name with "died" and the date in the last column. Gerd went through the files until he found the records from 1935 to 1936. Now he was going through them, name by name.

So many deaths ... This cannot be!

Gerd leafed through the records page by page until he came to March 1936. Then he saw the entry. There they were! Emilé and Rachel Weissbach from Munich. His eyes went to the last column. His heart sank. Rachel was dead—soon after they arrived, it appeared. He looked at Emilé's entry. The last column was empty! He checked again—there was no entry, it was blank.

This can only mean one thing. Emilé died within the last few days and the Germans did not have time to make an entry or ...

Gerd lifted the phone and called in his aide, Sergeant Rosko.

"Sir?"

"Sergeant, Have they dispersed the prisoners from the barracks yet?"

"No, sir. The transports to the hospitals have not arrived, so our men are making the survivors as comfortable as possible until they do."

"Good." He pointed to the map of the camp. "I want you to go to these barracks and find someone who has been in charge. Bring him to me."

"Yes, sir." Rosko turned and left.

In about half an hour, there was a knock on the door.

"Come." Gerd looked up.

Sergeant Rosko entered. He looked back. "Don't be afraid, come in. The captain only wants to ask you some questions."

Then a man shuffled through the door—or what was left of a man. Gerd shook his head in disbelief. The man before him was skin and bones, skeletal, but his eyes were alive.

Gerd motioned to the chair in front of his desk. "Sit, please," he said gently. The man complied.

"What is your name?"

The man lifted his head. "I am Yitzhak Perlman."

"Have you had some food? Blankets? Are you comfortable?"

"Yes, they fed us, Captain, but the food was too rich for my stomach. I threw up. The clean water was good, though."

Gerd turned to his sergeant. "Rosko, go down to the mess and have the cooks make some broth for these men. Something light that they can handle."

Rosko nodded and left.

Gerd looked at the man. "Mr. Perlman, was Emilé Weissbach in your barracks?"

Perlman nodded. "Until three days ago."

Gerd's heart sank. "He died?"

Perlman shook his head. "No, Captain. Before you got here, the Nazis rounded up several thousand prisoners and marched them out of camp. They went south. I think the Nazis were trying to get as many prisoners out of the camp as they could, so you would not see the enormous evil of what they have done here. I think they meant to kill us all, but you arrived too soon."

"And Emilé?"

"He was taken in the march. He was alive when last I saw him."

Alive! Emily's father is alive!"

Gerd picked up the phone. The operator answered him. "Yes, put me through to the general's office immediately!"

One foot in front of the other. If I stop I will die.

The snow had started again and then stopped, but he did not feel the cold anymore. He had fallen into a rhythm with his feet—

Step, step, left, right, move or die, move or die ...

The men moved in a long column down the road. They had not rested for hours. The road wound through the trees, rising toward the mountains, and the man could see the tops of majestic peaks lifting over the horizon. Soon they came into an area of heavy woods where the trees grew right down to the road, muffling the sound of the marching feet.

Hirschel marched next to him. "Tyrol, they are taking us to Tyrol."

He answered his friend. "Does Hitler think he can hide in the mountains? His kingdom is over. Why doesn't he just let us go?"

Hirschel shook his head. "He is a madman. Even as his mighty Third Reich crumbles around him, he sits in Berlin like a horrible spider, spinning his webs and pursuing his murderous schemes. I think he will not rest until every one of us is dead, or he is dead."

Hirschel began to speak in a low monotone.

May the Lord answer you on the day of distress; may the Name of the God of Jacob fortify you.

May He send your help from the Sanctuary, and support you from Zion.

May He remember all your offerings and always accept favorably your sacrifices.

May He grant you your heart's desire and fulfill your every counsel.

As his friend spoke, the man began to speak the words with him ...

We will rejoice in your deliverance and raise our banners in the name of our God; may the Lord fulfill all your wishes.

Now I know that the Lord has delivered His anointed one, answering him from His holy heavens with the mighty saving power of His right hand.

Some rely upon chariots and some upon horses, but we rely upon and invoke the Name of the Lord our God.

They bend and fall, but we rise and stand firm.

Lord, deliver us; may the King answer us on the day we call.

The tears in his eyes surprised him ...

CHAPTER 5

TO SEEK AND TO FIND

The jeep rolled slowly down the snowy road. Ahead of him, Gerd could see the tracks of feet, hundreds of feet. All along the way, they had seen the bodies of dead men. He had stopped to look at the identification number tattooed on each arm. He had memorized Emilé's—123356. None of the men he saw were Emily's father.

Yeshua, help me!

They pushed on up the mountainous road. Above them, a Stinson Sentinel purred through the sky, looking for the column of prisoners. The snow thinned, and the grey curtain of clouds lifted. The radio in the back seat crackled to life. Gerd looked around. The radioman listened and then turned to Gerd. "Sir, the advance scouts have entered a village called *Waakirchen*, about a mile ahead. They found many dead and dying in the snow and a lot of prisoners wandering around but no Germans. The guards seem to have run away." Gerd pulled over and signaled the two platoons behind him. A young lieutenant raced to the side of the Jeep. He was Japanese, a member of the 552nd Division.

"Sir!"

"Lieutenant, get your men up the road on the double. Be sharp. It looks like the Germans have abandoned the prisoners, but there may be some up there still willing to die for the Führer. And once you have secured the village, have some of your men collect any dead bodies. We need to identify them for the record."

"Yes, sir." The young man shouted orders, and the two platoons of Japanese troops left on the run. Gerd shook his head.

Only in the American army could a German captain command a group of Japanese GIs ...

They had come to a small village in the mountains. The guards let them rest in a large meadow. Then a German armored vehicle came roaring up. The man in the *Kübelwagon* shouted at the officer in charge. "*Die amerikanischen Truppen kommen!*"

The officer turned to his men. "*Töten Sie soviel Gefangene, wie Sie können!*"

Some guards began firing at the prisoners. Others threw down their guns and ran away.

Hirschel grabbed him. "Run, run for your life."

He ran toward the woods as fast as he could. Others were with him. He saw a man get shot, stumble, and fall. Then they were in the woods, racing through the trees ...

Gerd pulled into Waakirchen. In a large meadow outside of town, he found the 552nd boys rounding up the survivors. All around, there were mounds under the snow. He could see men lying on the ground, still moving. He called the lieutenant over. "Lieutenant, what's your name?

"Ichiro Imamura, sir."

"Well, Lt. Imamura, I want your men to check every body in this meadow. Some of these prisoners are still alive."

"Yes, sir." The Lieutenant went off to gather his men.

Sergeant Rosko approached with an old man in a ragged coat and striped pants. "Sir, this man wishes to speak to you."

The old man spoke in German. "*Guten tag,*"

Gerd replied. "*Guten, tag, wie gehen sie?*"

The old man smiled. "Ah, you speak German? *Gut.*"

They continued speaking in German. Gerd asked the man what he needed.

"When the Germans started firing, many ran into the woods, maybe a few hundred. They are probably hiding, afraid of the Germans."

Gerd shook the man's hand. "*Danke,* now go with the soldiers, they will help you. We have trucks coming to take you back to the hospitals. We will find the others."

The old man bobbed his head and then shuffled away. Gerd turned to his Sergeant. "Rosko, get me twenty or thirty men. Bring them to me."

In a few minutes, Rosko was back with the men. Gerd addressed them. "There are several hundred prisoners hiding in those woods. We need to bring them out. As you walk through the woods, I want you to shout this phrase. '*Wir sind amerikanische Soldaten! Haben Sie Angst nicht. Sie sind jetzt sicher.*' It means 'we are American soldiers, do not be afraid, you are safe now.'"

Gerd led the men into the woods. They spread out—each shouting the phrase Gerd had taught them. Soon men came out from behind trees and out from under logs and brush. Soon there was a large group. Gerd stepped in front of them. "Emilé, Emilé Weissbach?"

A man stepped forward. "I am Hirschel, Emilé's friend. he fell back there. I think they shot him."

Dear Jesus, not after all this ...

"Show me!"

The man led, and Gerd and Rosko followed. They came to a small swale where a brook ran through the trees. "Emilé, Emilé Weissbach, can you hear me?"

Nothing. Gerd shouted again. There! A voice!

"*Ich bin hier..*"

Gerd pushed through the brush. A man in a ragged coat was lying beneath a tree. Hirschel ran forward and knelt down beside him. "Emilé, Emilé, are you hurt? I thought they shot you."

The man opened his eyes. He smiled. "*Nein*, Hirschel. These old legs just gave out, and I fell."

Gerd came and knelt beside Hirschel. "Are you Emilé Weissbach from Munich?"

"Yes?" A question came into the man's eyes.

"Do you have a daughter named Emily?"

Amazement came over Emilé's face. "Yes, I had a daughter, but she is dead. She must be dead."

Gerd laughed out loud. "Thank you, *Yeshua*!"

The two Jews looked at him in wonder. Gerd put his hand on Emilé's shoulder. "No, Emilé, she is not dead. She is safe in America."

"America, but how, when ...?"

"She is my wife, Emilé, I saved her from the Nazis when she came to my barn after they took you away."

"Emily, alive?"

"Yes, Emile, we live in Colorado, and now I will take you home to her. *Kumm*."

Gerd put his arms under Emilé and lifted him. He was light as a feather. Gerd carried him through the woods and out into the meadow. There were jeeps and trucks waiting. Gerd laid Emilé on a stretcher. The soldiers lifted him into the back of a truck. Gerd climbed in after him. He turned to Rosko. "Sergeant, you work with Lieutenant Imamura and get the people on board and headed to the field hospitals. I'm going with my Papa."

Emilé looked up. "Papa?"

"Yes, Papa. You are coming to America with me. Emily is there. You will see her again."

Emilé's face twisted, and he wept.

And Gerd wept too.

CHAPTER 6

WHO HAS BELIEVED?

Gerd sat beside the bed of Emilé Weissbach in the field hospital and looked down at Emily's father. Though the face was haggard, worn, and pale, Gerd could see Emily there. Emilé had a drip solution of glucose attached to his arm. The curtain parted, and a doctor came in. "How's our patient doing?"

"He's sleeping, Doctor. What's the prognosis?"

"Well, apart from the fact that these despicable Nazis nearly starved him to death, he has a robust constitution, and I believe he will recover."

"Completely?"

"No, he will never be the man he once was, but with good care, he should be with you for quite a while."

"Yes, some of my *Mütti's Buttermilchsuppe* will be good for him." He smiled at the doctor. "Buttermilk soup with dumplings."

The doctor smiled back. "Sounds like just the ticket." He dropped the curtain and left.

Gerd turned back to Emilé. His eyes were open, and he was looking at Gerd. "So you found my little Emily in your barn?"

Gerd nodded. "Yes, she was hiding from the Nazis. She was across the street from your house when the Nazis came. She saw everything. After they left, she took what she could and came to Saarbrücken, hoping to cross the border into France. But the German army had marched into the Rhineland, and she could not cross."

"So you kept her and fell in love with her?"

"From the first moment I saw her." Gerd felt himself blushing, and he lowered his head. "You have a granddaughter, Papa. Her name is Adina. Your friend, Joshua Rosen, named her."

"A granddaughter?"

"Yes, Papa."

Emilé turned away. Gerd heard him sob. "What is it?"

"No one has called me Papa since I last saw Emily and ... since ..."

"Since the SS killed Jürgen?"

"Yes, Gerd, since they killed my son."

Gerd put his hand on Emilé's shoulder. "Emily told me he was trying to defend you when the Nazis shot him."

Emilé nodded. "Yes, he was a wonderful son, strong and honorable."

"Well, the Lord has sent me to defend you now, Papa. I will do everything I can to get permission to bring you home with me. I lost my father many years ago, and now, I will be your son and take care of you."

"You said Joshua Rosen named my granddaughter. Where ... how ...?"

"We met him when the Nazis were sending us to Dachau on a train. They captured us. They said they were taking us to the camp, but on the way, the SS came and killed everyone on the train. Joshua saved us. He gave his life for us. It was through him Emily and I discovered that we have the same messiah, *Yeshua Hamaschiach.*

"Who?"

"The one you know as Jesus the Christ. He was your Messiah and mine too."

"But he was a Christian."

"No, Emilé, he was a Jew, a direct descendent of David on both sides of his family. The Torah speaks of him quiet plainly."

"I have not read Torah for many years, but I do not remember that."

"Have you ever read Isaiah?"

"The prophet? Yes, of course."

"But you have not heard Isaiah 52:13 through 53:12?"

"I don't remember that."

"Because the Rabbis always skipped it."

"Why would they do that?"

"I'll show you."

Gerd reached into the pocket of his coat and pulled out a small Bible. He turned to Isaiah and read.

> Behold, my servant shall deal prudently, he shall be exalted and extolled, and be very high. As many were astonished at thee; his visage was so marred more than any man, and his form more than the sons of men: So shall he sprinkle many nations; the kings shall shut their mouths at him: for that which had not been told them shall they see; and that which they had not heard shall they consider.

> Who hath believed our report? And to whom is the arm of the LORD revealed? For he shall grow up before him as a tender plant, and as a root out of a dry ground: he hath no form nor comeliness; and when we shall see him, there is no beauty that we should desire him.

> He is despised and rejected of men; a man of sorrows, and acquainted with grief: and we hid as it were our faces from him; he was despised, and we esteemed him not. Surely he hath borne our griefs, and carried our sorrows: yet we did esteem him stricken, smitten of God, and afflicted. But he was wounded for our transgressions, he was bruised for our iniquities: the chastisement of our peace was upon him; and with his stripes we are healed.

> All we like sheep have gone astray; we have turned every one to his own way; and the LORD hath laid on him the iniquity of us all. He was oppressed,

and he was afflicted, yet he opened not his mouth: he is brought as a lamb to the slaughter, and as a sheep before her shearers is dumb, so he openeth not his mouth. He was taken from prison and from judgment: and who shall declare his generation? For he was cut off out of the land of the living: for the transgression of my people was he stricken.

Gerd stopped and looked at Emilé. He was staring back at Gerd.

"Go on," he whispered.

And he made his grave with the wicked, and with the rich in his death; because he had done no violence, neither was any deceit in his mouth. Yet it pleased the LORD to bruise him; he hath put him to grief: when thou shalt make his soul an offering for sin, he shall see his seed, he shall prolong his days, and the pleasure of the LORD shall prosper in his hand. He shall see of the travail of his soul, and shall be satisfied: by his knowledge shall my righteous servant justify many; for he shall bear their iniquities.

Therefore will I divide him a portion with the great, and he shall divide the spoil with the strong; because he hath poured out his soul unto death: and he was numbered with the transgressors; and he bare the sin of many, and made intercession for the transgressors.

"But this is the suffering servant. This is the one foretold of in many parts of the Torah. The one who will come to save Israel."

"Yes, Emilé, and he came. To die on Passover as the perfect lamb for the sins of mankind, to rise from the dead after three days and nights as foretold in the Scripture, to send his Holy Spirit, the one he promised to the fathers by Jeremiah and Ezekiel, fifty days after he rose, on the day of first fruits, fulfilling all the Law of Moses."

"Can it be true?"

"Emilé, listen. I was a simple Amish farmer with a large farm. I was to be the elder of my community and live out my days in Ixheim, Germany. Then Emily appeared in my barn. We fell in love, married, then the Nazis captured us and sent us to Dachau. We escaped with the help of your Jewish friend, Joshua, which in Hebrew is Yeshua, and we came to America. Emily, and my mother and I became Americans. When war broke out in Europe, I joined the Army because they needed men who could speak German. They sent me back to Germany."

Emilé looked puzzled.

"Who else would save me, give me a wonderful wife and then bring me back to Europe and send me to find you in the woods? Who would keep you alive all those years so he could bring you back to life? And like he did for me, he did all these things to show you how much he loves you."

Emilé's eyes had tears in them. "Tell me more," he whispered.

And so the father back from the dead and the son who saved him began to speak of the wonder of the cross, until Emilé fell asleep in the wee hours of the morning.

Then Gerd kissed him on the forehead and arose and went to his bed, confident once more of the surety of his faith and the love of God.

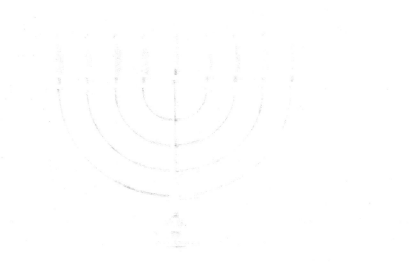

CHAPTER 7

THE DELAY—JULY 1945

Gerd Hirschberg sat in the waiting room of the operations center of MI in the new Army Occupation Headquarters at Frankfort am Main. The building he was in had been part of the I.G. Farben complex during the war. Gerd found it fitting the military occupation of Germany centered in the building that had manufactured Zyklon B gas, the chemical used to exterminate so many Jews in the death camps.

A young WAC lieutenant appeared in the doorway. "Colonel Heym will see you now, Captain."

So Heym is a Colonel now. Good for him.

Gerd entered the office. Colonel Heym was sitting behind the desk, but he rose when Gerd came in. Gerd snapped a salute, but Heym came around, shut the door and shook his hand. "Never mind the formalities, Gerd. We're both Ritchie Boys, and it's good to see you. Haven't seen you since Dachau. Sit down and please be at ease."

Gerd sank into a chair.

He seems overeager to please. I wonder what's up?

After a few banalities about the weather and how everything was going, Heym got to the point. "I've got your request for leave here on my desk. I'm afraid I can't grant it ..."

"But why?"

Heym held up his hand. "I can't grant it ... just yet. There is still some business to be finished I before I can send you home."

Gerd frowned. "But I need to get Emilé home to his daughter. Emily is not yet aware her father is alive, and I'm locked down. The brass won't let me send any messages home."

Colonel Heym picked up a folder off his desk. "And I'm afraid it's because of Mr. Weissbach that I can't send you home yet. Emilé Weissbach was on the front lines of the Communist movement, along with Werner Scholem and Joshua Rosen, during the 1930s. Now that we have defeated Germany, we have entered into a new struggle."

Gerd started to speak, but Heym held up a hand. "Our new struggle is with the Soviets."

"But they are our allies."

"Were our allies, Gerd. If we pull out of Europe, Russia will take over the whole shebang, and this continent will be one solid communist bloc from the Atlantic Ocean to Vladivostok. We have some German Communists who fled to Russia, but once they saw which way the wind was blowing, they slipped back into Germany before the Red Army and showed up on our doorstep."

"What's Emilé got to do with this?"

Heym cracked his knuckles, a habit Gerd found annoying, but he put up with it. "It seems Emilé knows these men, and I want him to be part of the interrogation, or at least be there to let the Commies know we are playing square with them."

Gerd shifted in his chair. "What do we need to find out?"

"As much about the Russian plans for Europe as possible. That's why I need you there. You are my best interpreter, and you have a way with the Germans that I don't have, since I'm Jewish and have a built-in hatred for Nazis."

Gerd grinned. "I'm not sure I am especially fond of them either."

"You know, Gerd, I am always amazed how you seem to have lost your German accent. You speak English like a native. How did that happen?"

"When we got to France in 1937, there was a little enclave of American expatriates living in our village, and we got to know them well. I already spoke some English, but my long conversations with them helped me. Then when we bought land in Colorado, I met a bunch of sure-as-shooting cowboys who showed me the ropes with my horse business. When you work with those old boys, you can't hang on to any 'furriner' stuff. So I lost the accent as quickly as I could." Gerd smiled. "But it's still there a little."

"So about your leave ..."

"All I want to know is when do I get to go home."

Heym stood up and went to the window. "I wonder how many barrels of Zyklon B the Germans made right here?"

"Colonel Heym, about my leave?"

Heym turned back to Gerd. "I'm authorized to make you a deal, Captain."

"A deal?"

"Look, Gerd, the American army is planning a big trial of the Nazis. It won't start until November. I need you here to do a lot of the prep work, and I need you to interrogate as many of the Germans, both communists and Nazis, as we can find. If you do that, not only will I give you leave, but I will expedite your honorable discharge from the Army, and you'll be home by Christmas."

"Christmas? But it's only July. I'm already due for discharge. The War is over, Colonel."

"Gerd, I know you should go home today, but I really need you."

"What about Emilé?"

"If you stay, I will promise Emilé will have his passport and visa and be free to go. If you don't, I can't guarantee anything."

Gerd stood up. "So you're blackmailing me, eh, Colonel?"

Colonel Heym shook his head. "Sit down, captain, have a smoke, relax please. Let me explain the situation." He came around the desk and offered Gerd a Camel.

Gerd took one, pulled out his Zippo and lit up. He took a drag and looked at his friend. "You know, Colonel, when I was Amish, I would never have smoked one of these." He took another drag. "I'm waiting, Colonel."

Heym lit a cigarette too and sat on the corner of his desk. "Emilé Weissbach was a big deal in the Communist party, pre-Hitler. Oh, he wasn't the spokesman or anything, but we know he was very close with Werner Scholem. Emilé Weissbach wrote a lot of the communist literature that got published under Sholem's byline in the Communist newsletter. Sholem got thrown in Dachau almost as soon as Hitler came to power. Weissbach went underground, but they got around to him, eventually."

"So?"

"We are still at war, Gerd, but not with the Germans."

"The Russians?"

"Yes. We allied with with Stalin to beat Hitler, but now we have to look at a new reality. The Russians are Communists. They want to make the entire world Communist. If America doesn't stand up to them, they will. Right now, the war with Germany is over. But the Japanese have not surrendered. What I tell you next is for your ears only and must never leave this room. Understood?"

Gerd nodded.

"We have a new secret weapon, a bomb of some sort. It's in the last stages of development, but the Joint Chiefs and President Truman are deciding whether to use it on Japan. They are certain it will terrify the Emperor into surrender. Once we deploy it, the Russians will do everything they can to get their hands on it. The Soviets captured the Nazi V2 rocket facility and took a lot of the German rocket scientists prisoner. Now they can make long-range rockets, and they will want to put this new weapon on top of them. That would make them the world power. Lucky for us, we got some V2 rocket boys too, like Wernher von Braun and some of his buddies. So we have to find out as much about the Russian Communist internal operations as possible."

Gerd took another drag. "And that's where Emilé and I come in?"

Heym nodded. "Because of Emilé's relationship to these men, the government is very suspicious of him. They'd like to hold on to him. If it weren't for you, MI would be holding Emilé. But if he cooperates and does America a good turn, and seeing what great service you have rendered, I'm fairly sure I can get him to America."

"Fairly sure, Colonel?"

"As sure as I can be in these times. But it all hinges on you staying."

Gerd rubbed his chin. "Okay, let me talk to Emilé. I'll let you know first thing in the morning."

"Okay, Gerd, but remember—the deal means you stay until November."

"Understood, Colonel." Gerd rose to go.

"Oh, and, Gerd ..."

Gerd turned at the door. "Sir?"

"You're still under lockdown as far as communication goes. You can write one letter to your wife, but you cannot tell her when you will be home, nor can you tell her any of the details of your work. It will go through Army censors so watch what you say, understood? And no phone calls. We do not want your whereabouts known."

Gerd nodded. "Understood, Colonel. Understood."

CHAPTER 8

A LIGHT IN THE DARKNESS—

MONDAY, DECEMBER 17, 1945

Adina stood waiting while her mama placed the Menorah on a small table in front of the window. Emily arranged it and then turned to Adina.

"Do you remember what comes first, Dina?"

"Yes, Mama. The blessing prayers to bless the Menorah."

"How many, Dina?"

Adina thought for a moment. "Two ... no three, because tonight is the first night."

Emily smiled. "Yes, Dina, three prayers. Before lighting the Menorah, we thank God for giving us this special mitzvah, and for the incredible Hanukkah miracles. I will say them."

She began. *"Baruch Atah Adonai Elohenu Memech haolam Asher kideshanu bemitzvotav vetzivanu lehadlik ner Chanukah.*

"Blessed are You, Lord our God, King of the universe who has sanctified us with His commandments, and commanded us to kindle the Hanukkah light."

Emily paused and then went on. *"Baruch Atah Adonai Elohenu Melech Haolam sheasa nisim laavotenu bayamim hahem bizman hazeh.*

"Blessed are You, Lord our God, King of the universe who performed miracles for our forefathers in those days, at this time."

Dina tugged her mama's skirt. "Can I say the third one, Mama?"

Emily nodded. "Do you remember it, darling?"

"Yes, Mama, you wrote it down for me, and I memorized it."

Magda smiled at her precocious granddaughter. "Such a smart girl."

Emily nodded to her daughter. "Go ahead, Dina."

Dina took a deep breath. *"Baruch Atah Adonai Elohenu Melech Haolam shehecheyanu vekiyimanu vehigianu lizman hazeh.*

"Blessed are You, Lord our God, King of the universe who has granted us life, sustained us, and, um ... oh yes... and enabled us to reach this occasion."

The two older women smiled at Dina. "Very good, Dina."

Emily took the candle that was standing in the cup in the middle of the Menorah. "Now we will light the *Shamash*."

She held the candle out, and Magda struck a match and lit it. She moved to the first cup on the right, which was filled with oil and had a wick floating in it. She lit the wick and then placed the *Shamash* candle back into its cup in the center. "We will leave the candles burning for one half an hour."

The light of the *Shamash* and the first candle flickered in the window, reflecting off the glass, a tiny light against the darkness outside. A gust of wind shook the glass as though the darkness wanted to reach in and snuff it out, but the candle and the lamp burned bravely, unbowed. Emily took Magda and Dina's hands in hers, and they stood silently watching the tiny flickering flames.

Dina spoke first. "Dear Jesus, please make this Menorah be a light that will guide my papa home."

Dina felt her grandmother's hand squeeze hers. "Yes, Lord, please bring Gerd home to us safely through the storm."

After Adina had gone to bed, Magda took Emily in the kitchen. "I was looking at the oil, and I don't think we have enough." She held up the bottle of olive oil. There was only a small amount in the bottom. "We have not been able to go to the store for a week. I thought we had more, but I looked everywhere and we do not."

Emily frowned. "But how will we light the Menorah for eight nights? There is only enough here for three days."

"I don't know, Emily, I don't know. Unless we can get out to the store, I don't know how we will keep it lit for eight days. And I might not have enough flour to make *Stöllen*. Oh, I hope it stops snowing."

Emily patted Magda's hand. "Let's wait until morning, and we will see what happens. I think we just need to trust the Lord."

Across the plains, huge dark clouds were massing as a cold front pushed into the San Luis valley. The wind picked up, and the snow fell, thicker and faster. A rare blizzard was moving through from the mountains.

TUESDAY, DECEMBER 18, 1945

In the morning, they looked out over a solid blanket of snow. At least three inches had fallen in the night, adding to the snow already on the ground. As Emily looked out the window, she saw an old Chevy truck making its way through the drifts on the road into their ranch. "Magda, Magda!"

Magda hurried into the room. "What is it, Emily?"

"It's Billy Roberts. He'll have news."

The truck pulled up in front of the house and Billy Roberts, a lanky man with a Stetson hat and a long handlebar mustache, climbed out. He trudged through the pristine snow to the front porch and knocked on the door. Emily flung it open. "Billy! Come in! Come in!"

"Morning, Emily, Magda!"

"Uncle Billy, Uncle Billy!"

Dina came rushing down the stairs and flung herself into the tall man's arms.

"Hey, hey, how's my little Buckaroo?"

"Just fine, Uncle Billy, just fine."

Billy turned to Magda. "Got any coffee for a poor old cowboy?"

Magda smiled and nodded and went off to the kitchen to fetch a cup.

Billy sat down at the dining room table. "Are you ladies all right? I tried to call, but the lines are down all over this part of the valley and Ma Bell can't get them fixed until after Christmas. I'd have come sooner, but I had to get the herd down into a closer pasture. I got them all down, including Gerd's, so we are good for the winter."

Emily gave Billy a hug. "Thank you, Billy, Gerd so appreciates that you've been watching the horses. And we do too."

"Well, no difference between taking care of a hundred and a hundred fifty. A lot of Gerd's mares are with foal, so come spring, your herd will increase."

Magda sat next to Billy. "Have you been into Alamosa?"

Billy pulled off his hat and laid it on the table. His long graying hair curled down around his collar. "Yeah, I went in for supplies, but the snow shut Highway 285 from Denver down and they have had no trucks in. They are expecting some just before Christmas."

"But that's a week away. I need flour and potatoes and ..."

"Oil," Magda said.

"Yes, oil."

"Cooking oil? I got some Crisco at the ranch."

"No, it has to be olive oil if I can get it."

Dina pointed to the Menorah in the window. "For the Hanukkah lamp."

Billy shook his head and took a swig of coffee. "I don't know, Emily. Fred at the market is pulling his hair out. Christmas is coming, and people are running short on everything. I have extra flour and potatoes at my place, and I can bring some eggs and a side of ham over. I got plenty of beef in the freezer." He grinned. "I even have a turkey I can bring if I can stay and help you eat it. We won't starve before Christmas."

Emily smiled back. "You know you can. I was going to call and invite you, but ... no phone."

Dina piped up. "We have enough oil for the Menorah, right, Mama?"

Emily hesitated and then looked at Magda. "I hope so, Dina, I hope so.

The Douglas DC-3 airliner droned on through the night. Captain Gerd Hirschberg sat in a seat next to the window, unable to sleep. Next to him, Emilé Weissbach snored. Gerd reached over and pulled the blanket up around the older man. The WAC flight attendant came down the aisle with some pillows. She saw that Gerd was awake and stopped. "Would you like a pillow, Captain?"

Gerd reached up and took one. "Thank you, Corporal. Maybe it will help me sleep."

The WAC corporal looked down at Emilé. "How's Mr. Weissbach doing? I don't see many civilians on military flights."

"He's fine. The Army took good care of Emilé after his liberation, and he's put on some weight. He earned his flight home by participating in some operations I'm not at liberty to speak about. I'm hoping to get him home by Christmas.

His daughter, my wife, has not seen him since 1936. How much longer is the flight?"

"We'll be landing at Gander in about four hours. After that, we'll connect you with a flight to get you down to Presque Isle Army Air Field in Maine."

"Thank you, Corporal. You've been very kind."

The young woman smiled and headed back to her seat in the back of the plane. Gerd looked out the window. It was pitch black, with clouds hiding the stars. As he stared out, the clouds thinned and the plane came out into the open. Gerd gasped. The moon was full and shone down on the ocean, lighting the tops waves with millions of sparkling lights. Behind the moon the vast panoply of stars were set like diamonds in the vault of heaven. Gerd shook his head in wonder.

Once I was a simple Amish farmer in a tiny village in Germany. My future was before me, unchangeable. I would always be an Amish farmer, always live in Ixheim, grow old and die in Ixheim. Then you brought me Emily and now I am in an airplane flying over the Atlantic Ocean, flying home to America.

A verse from Romans came to him. "O the depth of the riches both of the wisdom and knowledge of God! How unsearchable are his judgments, and his ways past finding out!"

And then a voice in his heart he had not heard for a long time.

I am the light, Gerd. I will guide you home

CHAPTER 9

In His Hands—Friday, December 21, 1945

Chicago's O'Hare Airport was crammed with holiday travelers and hundreds of servicemen. Gerd was speaking to a gum-chewing young lady who seemed more concerned about her makeup than getting him home on time.

"I'm sorry, sir, but we have delayed your flight to Denver. There is a big blizzard moving through, and they shut the airport." She looked at her schedules. "I'm sorry, nothing until Monday." Then she looked around and beckoned Gerd closer. "I'm not supposed to tell anyone because there are so many servicemen trying to get to Denver, but there are military flights going from here to the Army Airfield at Lincoln, Nebraska. If you go down those stairs and walk down the hallway, you'll come to the Army Air Force office. Maybe they can help you."

"Thank you, Miss." Gerd nodded to Emilé, and the two men headed for the stairs.

As they went down the stairs to the lower level, Emilé chuckled.

"What?" Gerd asked.

"I could have walked across Germany in the time we have spent to get across your America. I did not understand it was so big."

"Wait until you see the San Luis Valley, Emilé. The mountains go to the sky, and the land has no limits. The horses run wild, and the farmers grow wonderful crops."

They walked down the hall and went into the office of the Army Air Force. A young sergeant was sitting at the desk. He stood and saluted.

"At ease, Sergeant. The war's over and I'm on my last duty—getting home for Christmas. I need a flight to Lincoln if I can get one."

"I'm sorry, Captain, but we do not book flights here—it's for equipment transport and getting our pilots to their duty stations."

"You mean you don't have a bare bench for a European vet and his father-in-law?"

"Well, I'm not sure, but if you gave me your name and the phone number where you are staying I could see if I can find something ..."

Gerd grinned. "Right now, we're staying in the airport lobby. So all you have to do is call us to the courtesy phone."

"I'll see what I can do—names, please."

Captain Gerd Hirschberg and Emilé Weissbach.

The Sergeant looked up. "Did you say Weissbach?"

"Yes. Is something wrong?"

"No, I ... wait here a minute, Captain."

The sergeant got up and went through a door into an inner office. In a moment he returned with a major in tow. The sergeant pointed to Emilé.

The major came around the desk. "Is your last name Weissbach?"

"Yes," Emilé nodded.

"Well, this is a strange coincidence. I have never met another Weissbach before ... except for my family."

"Another?" Emilé said.

The major nodded. "Yes. My name is Edwin Weissbach."

Emilé stepped closer. "Are you Jewish?"

"Yes, I am."

"Where does your family come from?"

The major thought for a moment. "I believe from Munich. My grandfather came here right after World War I."

"And what was his name?"

"Awiezer Weissbach."

Gerd could see the astounded look on Emilé's face. "But this is not possible. My father had a cousin, Awiezer, who left Germany in 1922."

Now it was the major's turn to be amazed. "Yes! That's when grandfather came. So we are related? Distant cousins, it seems."

Gerd was smiling. *How do you do this, Lord?*

The major turned to Gerd. "Captain, what was your difficulty?"

Gerd shook his head in amazement. "We are trying to get to Denver, so we can get home to the San Luis Valley. This is Emilé Weissbach. He spent the last ten years in a Nazi prison camp. I am married to his daughter. We wanted to get home by Christmas. I was hoping to get at least as far as Lincoln and then go from there."

"Captain, have you men had breakfast?"

"No, sir."

Major Weissbach smiled. "Well, come with me. I'm buying. We have a couple of hours to kill, and I want to hear your story before you have to catch your plane."

"Our plane, Major?"

The major turned to the sergeant. "Get these two men seats on the C-47 that's headed for Lincoln at 11:00. And not the benches in the back. I want you to make sure they have backup crew seats."

The sergeant smiled. "Yes, sir. Right away, sir."

Major Weissbach turned to Emilé. "Come on, cousin. I want to hear everything." He nodded at Gerd. "You too, Captain. I'm very interested in how you met your wife and how in God's world you found Emilé."

"Yes, sir."

Because it is God's world, major ... it is God's world.

It was Friday evening, but the sun was still pale in the leaden sky. Dina, Magda and Emily stood before the Menorah. Emily picked up the bottle of oil.

"Shabbat starts at sundown today. It is forbidden to light a fire on Shabbat, so today we light the menorah before the Shabbat candles. We must leave the Menorah lit for one-half hour after sundown. That means we have to add extra oil to the five lamps we are lighting. I'm not sure ..."

Dina smiled up at her mother. "Go ahead, Mama. There will be enough oil."

"How do you know that, Dina?"

"An angel told me."

Magda and Emily looked at Dina in amazement. Magda took Dina by the hand. "An angel, my Dina?"

"Well, it was in a dream, I think. I knew you and Mama were worried about the oil, and I was trying to find some more. I even prayed for it. Then in my dream, a man came, and he told me not to worry, there would be enough oil. So I believed him. I think he was an angel."

Emily slowly shook her head and poured the oil into the cups. "One ... two ... three ... four ..." She looked up. "And five, Dina. Your angel was right. But ..." She held up the empty bottle.

"I think there will be more tomorrow, Mama."

Magda looked into Dina's eyes. "You know about the oil? How there is always enough each new morning?"

"No, *Mütti,* I did not know that. But in my dream, the angel was so real. He told me to have faith—that the Menorah light would lead Papa home. So I have faith."

Magda looked at Emily. "And Jesus said, 'Verily I say unto you, Except ye be converted, and become as little children, ye shall not enter into the kingdom of heaven,'" she whispered.

Emily came over and took Dina in her arms. "We shall have faith then too, my daughter. Lord help our unbelief."

She stood and light the Shamash with a match. "Tonight is the fifth night of Hanukkah. *Baruch Atah Adonai Elohenu Memech haolam Asher kideshanu bemitzvotav vetzivanu lehadlik ner Chanukah ...*"

CHAPTER 10

ALMOST CHRISTMAS—

SATURDAY, DECEMBER 22, 1945

Gerd and Emilé sat in a reception area in the Army Air Force Base at Lincoln, Nebraska, on Saturday evening. Christmas Eve was a day and a half away. Emilé put his hand over Gerd's. "It is fine, Gerd. We will get home at some point. You have tried very hard, but I think maybe our luck has run out."

They sat for several minutes. Finally, Emilé spoke again. "Why is Christmas so special to you? Is it the birth of this Jesus that you celebrate?"

Gerd nodded his head. "Yes, it is the time we welcome him into the world, but it's more than that, Emilé. In our house, we celebrate Christmas and Hanukkah together—a tradition we have. A unique one, I know."

"Christmas and Hanukkah together? That is interesting."

"It's because of the Menorah that Emily brought with her from Munich."

"The Menorah. Do you mean the golden lampstand that my wife Rachel's father made?"

"The same one, yes."

"She saved it from the house?"

Gerd stretched his back against the hard bench and nodded. "Emily was across the street when they took you away. She saw everything, including the murder of Jürgen. After the Nazis left, she went in the house through the back door and took what she needed—money, her passport, a few clothes. Then she got on a train and headed west. She had to get off because she heard that the Nazis were blocking the roads. Emily walked for two days through the woods. She brought the Menorah, because she knew it was precious, and she thought she might have to sell it to get to France."

Emilé nodded. "Emily was always resourceful. So you found her in your barn?"

"Yes, hiding under the hay mound. She was so beautiful and so brave. I loved her from the first moment I saw her."

Emilé looked away. "That is how I felt about her mother. When we met at a friend's wedding, I knew Rachel was for me. We married, but then I followed Werner Scholem. Rachel, well she knew that communism was bad, a lie. But I was young and impassioned, and the words of Marx and Lenin sounded so fair, so real—to each as they need and from each as they can give. Everything shared. No more bosses or rulers. But it was a trap. The people at the top only wanted power for themselves. They did not care about the masses. Rachel knew this, but she was a good wife. She let me proceed in my foolishness."

Gerd nodded. "But she kept her faith in God?"

"Yes, and she taught Emily and Jürgen. I did not like it, but I let her do it. Then when they killed my son and took us away, it broke something in Rachel. She got sick and died soon after we arrived at the camp. I saw her on her last night. Before she passed, she told me that communism would not save the world, only *Gott* could do that. I did not want to hear it, but it was her dying wish for me to give it up. After that, I struggled with many questions, but after I had been in the camp for a long time, I heard about what Stalin was doing in Russia— murdering so many who opposed him—then I saw that there was no difference between him and Hitler. They had different political views, but they were after the same thing—absolute power over the people. I think it was a joke that *Gott* played on me to steal the best part of my life, my son, my wife ..." Emilé began to cry softly.

"No, Emilé, *Gott* did not play a joke on you. There is someone else who wanted to bring misery and death to you."

Emilé sniffled and wiped his eyes on his sleeve. "Oh, you mean, *ha-Satan*, the Accuser?"

"That's the one. *Gott* has a better plan for you than Dachau. Your Jewish prophet Jeremiah said 'For I know the thoughts I think toward you, saith the LORD, thoughts of peace, and not of evil, to give you an expected end.'"

"Jeremiah said that?"

"Yes, he did."

Emilé sat thinking for a minute. "So you said you have a somewhat unique Christmas tradition because of the Menorah?"

Gerd slowly nodded. "When she first showed it to me, Emily set it on my kitchen table, and the sunlight came in the window and refracted off the beautiful gold lamps. I believe that for the first time in many years, the Lord himself spoke to me. He said, 'I am the light.' I thought Emily said it, but now I'm sure it was the Lord." He paused. "Then , we discovered that Jew and Gentile worship the same God, Jehovah, and eventually, that Jesus, the Messiah, came to both. The Menorah became a symbol to us of how God worked through the Jews to bring salvation to the rest of us."

Emilé nodded his head slowly.

Gerd went on. "Then the other night, when we were flying across the Atlantic, we flew out of the clouds, and the moonlight lit the sea like diamonds—like a path heading west across the ocean. And the Lord spoke to me again and reminded me. 'I am the light, Gerd,' he said, 'and I will guide you home.'"

Emilé nodded and smiled. "And so it seems he has been doing, but now we are stuck here and I do not think he has any more miracles for us ..."

"Excuse me?"

The two men looked up. Standing in front of them was a young man in a suit of brown warehouse clothes. There was a patch on his chest that said FFE Transport.

"Excuse me, are you the two men looking for a ride to Denver?"

391

Gerd looked at Emilé and nodded. "Yes, we are."

"My brother Frank told me about you. He works here, and I bring frozen beef here from our warehouse in Denver. I'm dead-heading back tonight, and I sure could use some company to help me stay awake. I got room in the front."

Emile laughed out loud. The young man looked puzzled. "What's funny?"

"*Hineni,* young man, *hineni.*"

The comment puzzled the young man.

"It's a Hebrew word. It means 'here I am.' Jewish people say it when God is about to test their faith."

Gerd spoke up. "We'll gladly accept your offer. We should get a thermos full of coffee and some dinner in us before we go. Then we'll have all night to tell you about faith—or the lack there of."

Both Gerd and Emilé burst out laughing.

The young man just shook his head. "Say, I'm not taking a couple of nut cases to Denver, am I?"

Gerd and Emilé laughed even harder. Gerd slapped him on the shoulder. "No, young man, no. We are perfectly sane, and I assure you, we can prove it."

They collected their things and followed the young man toward a dining area.

Gerd!

Gerd stopped and turned. Then he knew who it was. "*Hineni,* Lord, *hineni.*"

Shabbat had come to an end. The sun had gone down, and it was time to light the Menorah. Dina brought the bottle of oil to her mother. They all looked at it in wonder. The container was half-filled with oil.

Emily took the bottle. She poured the oil into the lamp cups. There was just enough for six cups. Emily prayed. "We thank you, oh King of the Universe, who maketh good things to spring forth from the earth."

She lit the Shamash. "Tonight is the sixth night of Hanukkah. *Baruch Atah Adonai Elohenu Melech Haolam sheasa nisim laavotenu bayamim hahem bizman hazeh ...*"

Later in the small hours of the night, something awakened Dina. A sound? She got out of bed and crept to the door. Slowly, she opened it. The sound was coming from downstairs—music, the wind? She went down the stairs clinging to the railing drawn by ... There! Under the pantry door, a light! She slipped up to the door and opened it a crack. A man! A man in the pantry, the same man she had seen before. He was dressed in white and very tall, but somehow, she was not afraid. The light bulb hanging from the ceiling was not on, but light filled the room. The man turned.

"Hello, Adina."

"He ... hello ... again." Dina drew closer. "Are you an angel?"

The man smiled. "I am a messenger, yes. Don't be afraid. Your prayers and your faith have brought me. He wants me to remind you he is the light. The light will bring your Papa home. And he is bringing a very special Christmas gift."

The man reached out and touched the jar of olive oil. More light filled the room. "This miracle happened once before, a long time ago in Israel. I was there too." The man smiled and touched Dina's face. "Go back to bed now, little one. Sweet dreams. Do not worry about your Papa. He is on his way."

When she awoke in the morning, Dina stretched beneath her covers. Hansli jumped up on the bed and bunted against her until Dina pulled her under to snuggle. "I had another wonderful dream last night, Hansli, such a wonderful dream."

CHAPTER 11

A LIGHT FOR CHRISTMAS—

MONDAY, DECEMBER 24, 1945

Gerd and Emilé sat in a small diner just down the street from the Hertz Drive-Ur-Self building in Denver, Colorado. They had arrived in the city very early Sunday morning after the nine-hour drive from Lincoln. The young FFE Transportation man, Bert Hayes, had proven to be good company, and the three had talked most of the night, bolstered by a thermos of very strong coffee and some sandwiches they got from a lunch counter at the Lincoln Army Air Force base. Bert had dropped them at the Brown Palace Hotel in downtown Denver, where they got a room and grabbed some sleep.

Nothing was open on Sunday, so they stayed around the hotel. Gerd took Emilé to a movie in the afternoon— *Back to Bataan,* with John Wayne. Before the movie started, the Movietone newsreel came on with a story about the Nuremburg trials. When the camera showed Ernst Kaltenbrunner, Hermann Göring, and the rest of the Nazi criminals sitting on the bench, Emilé stiffened in his seat. Gerd heard him whisper, "Kaltenbrunner ..."

Then the newsreel cut to a story about the liberation of the death camps, and when Emile´ saw the pictures of the prisoners, he wept quietly. Gerd put his arm around the older man's shoulder and comforted him. When they left the theater, Emilé did not speak. He was pale and withdrawn. That night before they went to bed, Emilé turned to Gerd. "Thank you," was all he said.

On Monday morning, the hotel clerk told them where to find Hertz. They took a cab to the rental office. The Hertz rental man had rented all his cars to Christmas travelers, but there was a return coming in at 2:30 that afternoon. So now they were waiting.

"Did you try to call Emily?"

Gerd nodded. "All the phone lines in the valley are still down."

"So Emily still does not know about me?"

"No, Emilé. I think this will be the best Christmas surprise ever."

Emilé stirred his coffee. Gerd noticed Emilé put three teaspoons of sugar in before he drank it. He glanced at his watch. "It's 2:15, Emilé. We should go down to the rental place."

"Ah yes, Gerd, just let me finish this sweet concoction I have blended. Sugar was the thing I think I missed the most at mealtime in the camp. If you could call those meals." He smiled.

"Well, I don't think you'll miss it from now on, Papa."

At the Hertz office their car had come in early, so within a few minutes, they signed the paperwork and were ready to go.

The man at the desk pulled out a map. "They shut down highway 285 through Buena Vista, so you have to go the long way around by Pueblo. It adds fifty miles to the trip, so you'll get there after dark. Come on out back. and we'll get you into your car."

He took them into the lot and showed them a nice 1942 Oldsmobile. They put their things in the back and headed toward home.

Emily stared out the window just before sundown on Christmas Eve. The snow covered everything and stretched away to the horizon. A pale sun tried to break through the gathering clouds.

I thought he would be home by Christmas. Lord, where is Gerd?

Billy had come in the morning with a fresh-cut tree in the back of his truck, and they had set it up and spent some time decorating. The tree stood in a corner of the front room, draped with garlands, tinsel, and large golden balls. At the very top stood a beautiful angel.

Magda was in the kitchen making *stöllen* for Christmas day. Billy had brought a large turkey with him, and it was hanging in the cold room waiting for morning.

Dina stood in front of the tree, looking up. She turned to her mother and pointed to the top of the tree. "That's my angel, Mama."

"Your angel, Dina?"

"Yes, the one I saw in the pantry. He was filling the oil bottle. At least I think he was ... it might have been a dream. But he was so real, and how else could the oil bottle get filled?"

"I don't know, Dina. I don't know."

Around five o'clock, they drove through Pueblo. Gerd stopped at a gas station and filled up the tank, and they grabbed some sandwiches at a local diner. The streets were gay with Christmas decorations and wonderful displays filled the storefront windows. People were out on the streets, and the mood was festive. Emilé looked around in amazement. "It will not be such a happy Christmas in Germany, I think."

At the gas station, the attendant, a gangly young man with a missing front tooth, checked their oil and water, cleaned the windows, and topped off the tank. "Which way you headed?"

"Alamosa. We're headed home for Christmas."

"You a vet?"

"Yes, my father-in-law and I just arrived from Europe."

"You fought against the Germans?"

Gerd smiled. "In my own way, son."

The young man put the cap back on the tank. "Gee, it must have been swell. I was too young to go. I was just going to sign up when the big show ended."

Emilé shook his head. "Not so swell, young man, not so swell."

"Well, take it easy. There's a big blow coming through down there, so drive safely."

Just before sundown, the four people gathered by the Menorah. The lights from the Christmas tree reflected off the wonderful golden lampstand. As she filled all eight cups, Magda told Billy about the oil that had not run out.

"Well, don't that beat all," he shook his head and smiled. "Christmas is a time for miracles, I guess."

Dina took his hand and held it. "And Hanukkah too, Uncle Billy, Hanukkah, too."

Billy looked down at Dina. "Yep. Hanukkah too, Buckaroo."

Emily lit the Shamash. "Today is the final night of Hanukkah. In our house, this is also the night before the day we celebrate the birth of Yeshua Hamashiach, Jesus Christ

398

the Messiah. On this night, the Jews stood in the temple and gazed in wonder at the lamps that remained lit for five more days than they expected. Not too long after that, all the angels in heaven celebrated the birth of the Son of God. So we too celebrate the Menorah that has remained lit five days longer than we expected, and we join all the angels in heaven as we say, 'Joy to the World, the Lord has come. He is the light of this world. Whoever follows him will not walk in darkness but have everlasting life ...'"

Dina bowed her head. "Dear Jesus, please bring my papa home to us safely." She looked up at Emily. Her mama was wiping the tears away from her eyes and nodding. "Yes, Lord, please ... *Baruch Atah Adonai Elohenu Memech haolam Asher kideshanu bemitzvotav vetzivanu lehadlik ner Chanukah ...*"

The Oldsmobile chugged through the darkness. The wind had whipped up, and snow was blowing across the road, making it very difficult to see. Gerd and Emilé had passed through Alamosa and were on the last twenty mile stretch to the ranch. Gerd was driving slowly.

"It is very hard to see the road, Gerd?" Emilé asked.

"Yes, Papa, very hard."

Just then something came at them out of the darkness—a large black shape. "A cow!" Gerd shouted and jerked the wheel. The car spun slowly to the right and powered off the edge of the road into the ditch. They came up against the bank with a shock, and then the engine died.

Gerd reached for Emilé, who had fallen against the passenger door. "Emilé, Emilé, are you all right?"

Emile sat up slowly, rubbing his head. He smiled, but his face was pale in the light from the headlamps. "Yes, Gerd. Aside from the fright and a minor bump on the head, I am still alive."

Gerd got out of the car. The headlights angled out over the fields and the wind caught at his coat. He walked around the car and then got back in. He tried to start the car, but it just made a grinding sound and then quit. Gerd shook his head. "I'm afraid we are stuck here."

The Menorah had been burning for a half hour after sundown. It was time to extinguish the candles. Emily sighed and reached over to snuff out the first wick.

"Wait, Mama!" Dina clutched at Emily's arm. "Don't put them out yet!"

"But Dina, the oil is almost gone."

"Don't put them out yet, Mama. The light is bringing Papa home."

Emily looked down at her daughter's eager face. Then she looked over at Magda. Magda shrugged. "What can it hurt, Emily? Let them burn until the oil runs out."

And so the light from the Menorah candles kept burning in the window.

CHAPTER 12

THE HOMECOMING

The inside of the car was growing bitterly cold. Emilé spoke in the darkness. "Can't we walk to the ranch, Gerd?"

"If I could see the way, if it was daylight, yes. But the snow has covered everything. I would not know which way to go. I'm sorry, Emilé. To have come so far and now this ..."

Just then, Emilé put his hand on Gerd's arm. "What is that sound?"

Gerd listened. At first he heard nothing and then, faintly, tinkling in the darkness ... "Bells? It sounds like jingling bells, Emilé. What in the world ..." They both stared out the window.

Out of the darkness, a large black shape loomed up. A horse! And then behind the animal appeared a sleigh with the figure of a man sitting wrapped in a heavy blanket. A white bushy beard poked out above the collar of his coat. Sleigh bells covered the harness and they jingled softly in the wind.

Emilé rubbed his eyes. "The cold has addled my brain. I'm seeing *Weihnachtsmann*."

Gerd shouted. "No Emilé, it's not Father Christmas. It's Jakob Shrock!" He turned to Emilé. "It is one of my Amish neighbors. He is driving his sleigh. Thank you, Lord!!"

Gerd jumped out of the car. "Jakob! Jakob Shrock! It's me."

The old man in the sleigh pulled the reins, and the horse stopped next to the car. "Who is it? Do you need help?"

Gerd shouted against the wind. "It's me, Jakob! Gerd Hirschberg. We are stuck in the ditch."

The old man stared down at Gerd. "Gerd! Gerd Hirschberg, you are home at last. *Kumm!* Get in the sleigh. I will take you to your house."

"But the snow, Jakob, how will you see?"

Jakob laughed. "I don't need to see. Freyla will take us home. Her dinner is in my barn. The road to my barn runs right past your gate. Get in! Get in before you freeze to death."

Gerd helped Emilé out of the car and they clambered into the back of the sleigh. Jakob shook the reins, and they set off into the darkness.

Two hours after sundown and the Menorah continued to burn, its bright steady light reaching out into the storm.

The wind howled around them, but Gerd and Emilé were warm under a huge robe in the back of the sleigh. "It's a buffalo robe, Emilé. It's from a bison. They used to roam this country by the millions."

Jakob turned and shouted back. "We are close, but I can't see anything. Freyla will just keep going unless I can find the gate."

And then, like a searchlight, a brilliant light flashed across the road ahead of them.

Jakob shouted. "There! I see your house. There is a light! I see it."

Gerd and Emilé stared at the light. It flooded the snow with glory, and Gerd could see the window of his house down the long driveway. In the window he could see something golden.

"The Menorah, Emilé! They have lit the Menorah for Hanukkah, and it is guiding us home."

Jakob laughed and chucked the reins. Freyla turned into the road to the house and they headed toward the light.

Dina heard them first. "Bells, Mama, I hear bells, sleigh bells!"

Magda, Emily, and Billy turned toward the window. Yes! Bells.

Dina ran to the door. There were heavy steps on the porch and a knock. Dina pulled the door open. Standing there was an old man with a white beard—their Amish neighbor, Jakob.

Emily went to the door. "Jakob Shrock, what are you doing out in this weather?"

Jakob laughed. "I was coming back to my house, and I found someone on the road. I have brought them home."

He stepped aside and there was Gerd, smiling and covered with snow.

"Papa!" Dina cried. She flew to Gerd, who picked her up and held her close. Emily and Magda just stared at him. Then Emily shrieked. "Gerd! Gerd!"

Gerd put down Dina and opened his arms. Emily came into them. "Gerd, you are home, you are home." She began to cry as she clung to him. Dina gripped his legs. Magda came and Gerd put one arm around her. "Hello, *Mütti*, I am home."

The four of them stayed that way for a long time. Then Emily noticed someone was standing behind Gerd. She wiped her eyes. "Who have you brought with you, Gerd?" She brushed more tears from her eyes.

"Hello, Emily." Emilé smiled.

Emily took a step closer. "Who are you?" Then she opened her eye wide. "Oh *mein Gott!*" She closed and then opened her mouth. "But, but ... you are dead!"

"No, daughter, I am very much alive, thanks to Gerd ... and your Jesus."

"Papa?" She took a step closer and touched Emilé's face. "Papa, is it you?" Then Emily was in his arms and clinging to Emilé and sobbing, and Emilé was weeping. And everyone was weeping and then laughing and the joy of Christmas filled the house.

Then the last of the oil ran out and the Menorah candles went out, one by one.

And so that is the story of the Christmas miracle. So long ago, but I remember it so clearly. *Grossdáddi* Emilé came back from the dead to live with us for the rest of his life. My papa was back from the war, and my mama and my *Mütti* were happy again. My papa raised Mustang horses, and one day, I had a little brother, Jürgen, and our house was always full of light and laughter. Every year, we lit the Menorah in the window. And we never forgot how the Light of the World brought my papa home.

Adina Hirschberg Thompson

ABOUT THE AUTHOR

Amazon bestselling author **Patrick E. Craig** is a lifelong writer and musician who left a successful music career to become a pastor in 1986. In 2007 he retired to concentrate on writing and publishing fiction books. In 2013, Harvest House Publishers published his first Amish series, Apple Creek Dreams. His latest Amish series, *The Amish Heiress, The Amish Princess,* and *The Mennonite Queen,* as well as the reprinted Apple Creek Dreams are published by Patrick's imprint, P&J Publishing.

In 2017, Harlequin Publishing purchased *The Amish Heiress* for their Walmart Amish series and released it in April 2019. He also recently signed a contract with Elk Lake Publishing to produce his middle grade/YA mystery series, The Adventures of Punkin and Boo. His latest release is *Far On The Ringing Plains,* a literary fiction work with Murray Pura, who also collaborated on *The Amish Menorah and Other Stories.* Patrick and his wife, Judy, live in Idaho. They have two daughters and five grandchildren. Patrick is represented by the Steve Laube Agency. His website is www.patrickecraig. com

Made in the USA
Monee, IL
01 November 2020